The Xmas Factor

Annie Sanders

An Orion paperback

First published in Great Britain in 2006
by Orion Books
This paperback edition published in 2017
by Orion Books,
Carmelite House, 50 Victoria Embankment
London, EC4Y ODZ

An Hachette UK company

1 3 5 7 9 10 8 6 4 2

A CIP catalogue record for this book
is available from the British Library.

ISBN 978 1 4091 7267 3

Typeset by Deltatype Ltd, Birkenhead, Merseyside

Printed in Great Britain by Clays Ltd, St Ives plc

www.orionbooks.co.uk

To the Spirit of Christmas.
Every last glass of it.

Prologue

'There is nothing more magical than the glow of candlelight in the rosy cheeks of small children as they gather round the tree ...'

Oh bollocks. How can candlelight glow in cheeks? Holly pressed delete, pulled her cardigan further around her goose-bumped arms and tried again.

'Who cannot fail to be entranced by the fragrance of pine needles and the light that sparkles...?' Holly faltered, sighed deeply, and drummed her fingers on her desk. Nope. Swivelling in her chair, she ran her fingers down the spines of a small pile of CDs on the shelf behind her, selected one from near the bottom and slipped it into the machine. Popping another mini mince pie into her mouth, she closed her eyes and let the agonisingly sweet sound that came through the headphones wash over her until she felt herself begin to glow with warmth and tingle with excitement.

Once in Royal David's city... warbled the chorister and, opening her eyes and flexing her fingers with determined resolve, she began to tap the keyboard.

'As the warm scent of cinnamon and pine needles fills the air this month, get ready for the joyous season with berry-red accessories, sparkling decorations...' Oh, I like it, I like it. Holly began to type faster, '...and exquisite...exquisite?' She paused.

What on earth could she think of that would be exquisite? She closed her eyes again.

... and his shelter was a stable ...

'... *exquisitely* wrapped presents under the tree. Here are the top-ten tips to see you to your best Christmas ever.'

'Ah ha!' Pulling out a flattened cardboard party hat from the bottom drawer of her desk, she squeezed it in an attempt to return it to somewhere near its original shape and plopped it onto her dark curly hair, pulling the elastic down under her chin. The muse had finally landed.

Half an hour later she was still over a hundred words short. What had she missed? She'd managed a ludicrously excessive list of ideas for things to do with ribbon from VV Rouleaux, several novel ideas for tasteful Christmas lights, and even a round-up of the best shop-bought mince pies. She glanced at her watch. Crikey, she'd have to crack on. What else would make Christmas delicious and perfect?

'Hi, you look cute. How's it going?' Denise from the art department stuck her head around the partition. 'Aren't you on your way yet?'

Holly moaned. 'God, I know, but I haven't finished this yet and it was due this morning. Come on, Den. I need ideas. Christmas? Picture perfect?'

The young woman in the doorway leant again the partition and ran her finger over her lips in thought. 'Oh, I don't know. You're the word woman. Novelty knickers? Actually I'd rather go as far away as possible. You know, some lovely cottage somewhere in the country. Log fires? Chestnuts roasting? All that crap.'

Holly looked at her carefully, a thought beginning to take shape in her mind. 'I do believe you've done it! Just a couple more calls to make and I'm off!'

Denise shrugged and turned to go. 'Glad to have helped. Have fun and see you afterwards.'

Holly absently waved to her as she continued to type, florid prose pouring from her fingertips, hyperbole increasing with every hackneyed adjective. She knew that the cottage she was describing for 'that perfect Christmas' – a rather neglected little place tucked away behind the church in the village where she had grown up – wasn't quite as idyllic as she was suggesting, but frankly she'd run out of time. A quick search on Google for a chocolate-box cottage picture to go with the text, then ten minutes later she clicked on 'save', made a mental note for when she got back to tell her stepmother to turn down anyone trying to book the place, stood up, and gently eased off the hat from her head, pleased to be shot of the elastic chin strap, which was beginning to dig in and hurt.

Her feature on 'Your Best Christmas Ever' was going to be a triumph. Switching off her desk fan with theatrical finality, she picked up her bag, grabbed her sunglasses, and headed out of the glass doors at reception into the blistering August heat.

Chapter 1

September

It's never too early to start planning for Christmas. If you prepare your 'to-do' lists well in advance, and take them with you everywhere you go, you'll beat the rush and leave the competition standing!

'Sorry, sorry. So sorry.' Sweating slightly, Beth stepped from the heat of the September sunshine into the gloom of the village hall. The rest of the committee was already there, of course, on stacking chairs ranged round the splintery trestle table, papers fanned efficiently in front of them. The wooden floor felt slightly gritty under her sandals (probably due to badminton on Wednesday nights) as she made her way over to take the only chair left vacant.

'Well, you're here, that's the main thing.' Irene smiled briskly, formidable in her chairwomanship, with only a hint of disapproval. 'And just in time for coffee.'

Right on cue, a clinking, over-laden tray nudged cautiously around the swing door from the kitchen, followed by the tiny, tweed-clad figure of Mrs Godfrey. Beth forced herself not to watch the old lady wobble slowly towards them, her snowy hair, as always, so tightly permed that it looked as if she had a cauliflower strapped to her head.

Just three months ago, at Beth's very first VEG (Village Entertainments Group) meeting, she had instinctively leapt up to offer the minute octogenarian a helping hand – not a mistake she would make again. Not after the ticking off she'd received. It didn't seem to matter that half the coffee ended up in the saucers, or that the heavy-duty crockery, with its distinctive blue rim, was dwindling faster than dew on the village common on a midsummer morning. Mrs Godfrey had apparently been making teas and coffees for the committee since the late 1950s, and was not going to relinquish her role any time soon, thank you very much. She regarded Beth now with sulky suspicion – although according to Jacob that was the way she behaved towards anyone who had moved into Milton St David in the last forty years.

Once the tray was safely deposited on the table, Beth wrenched her full attention back to matters arising. The agenda was always more of a starting point than anything to be too strictly adhered to and this time, item three – the mooted Safari Supper – had provided a springboard for a debate about the merits of various TV chefs.

Beth knocked back the tepid brew from her half-empty cup, and glanced round the table. To her right, the Ancients – stalwart, creaky widows, for the most part, who inhabited some of the prettiest and most significant houses in the village. Immaculately coiffed at all times, they dressed in serviceable tweed winter and summer alike but, despite appearances, were the real powerhouses in the community, and because they had lived there for years, could provide precedents for almost every decision the committee ever came to – and inclined to revisionism that would make Stalin blush.

To Beth's left, the incoming professional mummies – she'd dubbed them the Village Fates – a terrifying and highly competitive bunch. Glossily groomed and expensively highlighted, this lot had abandoned careers 'outside the home' and were now channelling all their considerable ability and energy into their domestic lives, their pretentiously named children and, their real goal, making the little village of Milton St David desirable and chic, in an interior-decorating-magazine kind of way.

Not for the first time, Beth found herself positioned between the two factions, and leant back in her chair to make the most of it. Like Switzerland, she remained resolutely neutral. Neither side seemed to want to claim her and, so far, being the new girl on the block she had only been entrusted with washing-up and selling raffle tickets, despite Jacob's gentle urging that she 'get stuck in' to village life. Although she was of an age with the Fates, the fact that she had a 'proper job' with a doctorate to boot, no children and no desire to listen to them drone on and on about nanny misery and the pros and cons of three-wheel buggies meant she had nothing in common with them. She was so busy preparing for the imminent arrival of a new year's influx of students in college that time for 'a quick tennis four and a bite of lunch' was mercifully out of the question. Her marriage seven months ago to Jacob, moreover, meant that they bracketed her with the older set along with him. Didn't they know sixty was the new forty?

The Fate that had befallen Beth today was Tamara Sinclair – all leggy and alluringly tousled. She turned to Beth, sniffing, looking rather like an Afghan hound. 'Mmmm. Nice perfume. Very spicy.'

Beth felt herself flush. Rumbled! The aroma from the morning's cookery orgy must be clinging to her clothes. 'Er, yes,' she improvised, 'that's it. Jo Malone. I absolutely adore it, don't you? It's the nutmeg and ginger fragrance.' Tamara had a definite look of respect, and Beth turned away smiling. And a dash of suet thrown in, she laughed to herself.

'Order!' Irene tapped her cup with a spoon and looked down at the sheet in front of her with ill-concealed disdain. 'Well, that's the, er, Safari Supper taken care of. We've never done anything like it before, of course, but it might just work. We'll see, shall we? If we put a little mention in the newsletter,

3

perhaps you can write that, Alison, to explain exactly what's involved? Personally, I think it's better to stay with the tried and tested. Our whist drives are always very popular.'

The Fates sat back, exchanging amused glances but triumphant that their idea had been accepted, albeit slightly railroaded by the Ancients. Irene cleared her throat and plunged on. 'And now what about the Mistletoe Meet? I think it should be resurrected after four years' absence. How about you?'

Silence.

Irene gazed round the room but all eyes were averted. Beth looked around. Now this was interesting. Normally the Ancients and the Fates were jockeying for position to seize control of functions.

'It used to be such fun and it would be good to have something to bring the village together at Christmas again. Who's willing to take the plunge?' Her eyes swept the group, who studiously avoided them. 'Beth, perhaps you'd like to take on the mantle this year?' There were some suppressed gasps around the room from the Ancients, but Irene's voice was warm and coaxing. 'It would be just the thing for you. Help you get to know people. And you'd have plenty of assistants. Wouldn't she, everyone?' Vehement nods and smiles all round. 'So I'll put you down for that, then. I'll just run through the details with you later. I think we've got the lists from previous years. I'll look them out so you can get cracking.'

Hang on – this was beginning to sound serious. What the hell were they talking about? 'Sorry, what are we talking about here? I mean, mistletoe – it's got to be something at Christmas, right?'

Irene used a tone of voice that she probably reserved for the feeble-minded. 'It's a village tradition, dear, which has slightly fallen by the wayside. But perhaps Jacob wouldn't mention it under the circumstances. It's on Christmas Eve. It's always on

Christmas Eve. Has been for the last hundred and forty-odd years. I know it sounds like a hunting thing – gosh, awfully non-PC these days – but the reason it's called that is lost in the past. It's just a lovely party and a chance for everyone to get together. One of our proudest village traditions and it's always a wonderful occasion – isn't it, ladies?'

This was sounding a bit too much like coercion, and it wasn't as if Beth didn't have enough to do. Christmas was, without doubt, a hectic time of year at work. The entire History of Art department would be frantically marking, interviewing and advising and she would barely have time to get Jacob a present let alone organise anything like a party. 'Well, perhaps I could lend a hand. But I don't know *really*. It's a terribly busy time for me at the university ...'

Irene smiled pityingly. 'It's a busy time of year for all of us, dear, and you working wives must find it hard to fit everything in, but we thought it might help you settle in to the village.'

Beth faltered. God what a fuss they were making. Honestly, organising a Christmas party couldn't be rocket science, could it? Drinks, a few sausage rolls, party hats. It couldn't be harder than a do for her college tutees. It might even be fun – and wouldn't Jacob be incredulous? He'd teased her unmercifully about the bottle of warm Chardonnay and bowl of peanuts she'd thrown together for their friends when they'd announced their engagement, saying clearly her talents lay in Renaissance art and she'd better not give up her day job. What *would* he make of this? Oh go on, it would be a laugh. She was aware of every eye on her. 'Mmm, maybe.'

'Oh, but everyone would help – wouldn't you, ladies?'

Vigorous, even frantic nodding again.

'Oh all right them. If I must.'

She was vaguely aware of a warm feeling sweeping through the room.

'Right, well that's that decided.' Irene crossed something off her list. 'I'll pop by later on today with the details, Beth. Thank you very much. I'm sure you'll make a fine job of it.'

Beth looked sceptical. 'Well, I wouldn't bet on it …'

But the committee were off nattering again, although this time they seemed to be in perfect accord: 'You can never start too early for Christmas,' Mrs Godfrey muttered darkly, and the Ancients and Fates together nodded their heads sagely in agreement. Beth lapsed into silence the better to overhear the new stereo of conversations on the subject of the festivities. '… goose fat's the only thing …', '… thought we'd try guinea fowl for a change …', '… sprouts are no good any more, with no frost in December …'. Goody. Tips. Beth covertly made a couple of scribbled notes on her pad.

'Now, about Burns Night …'

The rest of the meeting passed in a blur for Beth. So much for Jacob's assertion that she'd have to be patient and wait for people to get used to her after they married. It looked as if she'd be Madame Chair by next week. She glanced at her watch – he said he'd be home early that afternoon. Maybe they could take the dogs out together before getting back to her desk and her symposium notes – that way she wouldn't have to handle them herself – and she could tell him all about it. As the meeting came to a close, Beth, keen to get away, was buttonholed by Stephanie Jackman, eager to bore on about her little Inigo (and her tribulations with finding just the right nursery for him). Extricating herself and hoping she'd made the right noises, Beth made for the door, not before bestowing on Mrs Godfrey her most genuine smile – and was curiously touched when the old lady squeezed her arm in such a warm way. She strode out of the hall and, safely out of earshot, murmured, 'Milton St David – I've arrived!'

As she walked up the drive, five brisk minutes later, Beth's steps slowed. Jacob's car wasn't there and she could hear the dogs barking and hurling themselves at the kitchen door from here. Oh God! She'd have to take them out – there was no putting it off. If she waited until Jacob arrived, they'd probably have eaten her alive. When they heard her put her key in the door, they would go completely crazy and that would be it. Maybe she could hide for a few minutes in the garden. Beth tiptoed along the path that ran by the side of the house, crouching as she passed the kitchen window, so they wouldn't see her. She was almost there when her mobile rang and the dogs went into a redoubled frenzy at the noise.

'Hello?'

'Bloody hell, Beth. I thought hunting was illegal – sounds as if you're in the middle of a pack of blood hounds.'

'Oh don't, Sal!' Beth made her way down the garden, blocking her free ear in an effort to hear over the howling. 'It's the demon doggies – just the usual two, but they make like a crowd. I managed to escape earlier, although I had to bribe them with doggy chocs to get them in from the garden – Jacob doesn't understand why they're getting so fat – and I ended up late for my meeting and all covered in dog hair.'

'I thought that was compulsory attire in Mingbury St Bollocks,' said Sal sarcastically. 'Anyway, what meeting? Term hasn't started yet, has it?'

'Er, no. It was a sort of a "village get things done" kind of meeting.' Beth could almost hear Sally's eyes light up and pulled a face in anticipation of her next question.

'What, you mean a pressure group or a political thing?'

Sitting down heavily on the wooden swing under the apple tree Jacob had made years ago for his daughter, Beth had a nasty feeling her old friend wasn't going to let this go, and she tried to change the subject. 'Nothing really, just a local thing. So what are you up to?' she hastened. 'How are rehearsals? Is that Camden High Street I hear in the background?'

A peal of gloating laughter from the other end of the phone. 'You've done it, haven't you? You've gone and joined the WI.

Well, your old gentleman will be pleased. They'll teach you to make Victoria sponge and apple pie. You'll be a proper wifey before you know it...'

'You're just jealous! It was actually a meeting about local issues,' Beth exaggerated, suddenly embarrassed about letting down the townie sisterhood. ' A kind of action group with a bit of welfare on the side, you know, rural bus services and so on. Anyway, there's this traditional village do on Christmas Eve, and it's been going on for hundreds of years – bit of a get-together for the locals – and I volunteered to organise it this year. And what are you doing for Christmas, my hard-bitten urban-decayed old mate, while we rosy-cheeked bumpkins are frolicking at the Mistletoe Meet? Want to join us for a bit of country Christmas? All feet up in front of the fire and chilling? It'll be a blast.'

For once Sally sounded impressed, for a while at least. 'Ooh, that sounds rather nice actually. Rather picturesque and whole-some. I'd be there like a shot, but sadly I'm doing panto in Bolton and when I'm not I'll be snuggling up with my bloke. I can just see you as Lady Bountiful, handing out alms to the peasants while your doting, doddery old hubby looks on proudly—'

'Oh bog off! You just wish it was you.' Beth laughed. 'He'll be home soon to ravish me – again – I expect. With age comes experience, so I can't waste my time talking to you. I'll have to go and wrestle with the hounds of hell before I slip into my négligé. Wish me luck!'

The sound of baying was almost deafening when Beth swung open the front door and picked up the fresh wave of Christmas catalogues, all still addressed to her predecessor. She paused only to drop them and her bag in the hallway beneath Jacob's hanging jackets in various shades of mottled green and brown. The fragrance of the ginger and nutmeg that Tamara had noticed at the meeting permeated the air. She hadn't had

8

time to clear away her cooking properly before going out, but she'd have to now, before Jacob came home. How to tackle it?

She sidled towards the kitchen. 'Good boys,' she could hear the quaver in her voice, and picked up the leads. 'Walkies.' She flattened herself against the wall and reached out to flick open the door. This must be how the SAS feel on a raid. Flash and Jig-Jag stormed past, a torrent of black fur and wildly thrashing tails, and she hurled herself into the kitchen and slammed the door behind her before they had time to realise she'd trapped them in the hall. At least they were out of the way for a bit.

In the larder, covered in clingfilm, sat three large ceramic bowls, her morning's work, each containing a subtly different mix of Christmas mincemeat. Compare and contrast. One contained unblanched almonds and fresh orange zest. Another glacé cherries in with the dried fruit. The third was, as far as Beth could surmise, more adventurous with chopped walnuts and finely minced dates. In fact, since she'd started collecting mincemeat recipes she'd realised that, really, you could go on for ever. But Beth, acutely aware she was a virgin to this Christmas-planning thing, had decided to approach the challenge of the festivities in a way she could understand: as if it was an academic thesis, and she was determined to go on experimenting until she found the very best.

Even by the standards of any of the published guides to running a successful Christmas, Beth realised she was starting a bit early. But the Christmas cards were in the supermarkets already and, for someone who'd always stayed with friends since her mother died, a mere fifteen weeks to C-Day didn't feel like a very long time. She ladled the mixes into the jars she'd sterilised, slapped little paper discs on top, folded more clingfilm over the top of each, then stashed them in a corner and arranged packets of cereal as camouflage. She wasn't sure she wanted Jacob's teasing about her over-zealousness when he

9

found them. There – she'd sample them baked into pies in a week or so. Once she'd got the hang of pastry.

In the hallway, the dogs were whining with renewed urgency. Urgh! Suppose they needed a wee! Beth opened a window in the kitchen to let the spicy air out and sidled back into the hallway, where the dogs surged back at her, breathing wet canine approval and anticipation all over her linen skirt.

After a few tentative gestures, she managed to slip their leads on and grabbed the keys before they had a chance to haul her out of the front door. Damn! She'd forgotten the whistle again – although she never remembered which sequence of peeps meant what. Her shoulder yanking in its socket, she tried to keep up with them, belatedly realising she hadn't changed her shoes either. These lovely little beaded sandals were not the thing for racing through the long meadow grass down by the river.

Down the lane past the old church the dogs dragged her. The meadow, which ran alongside the pretty little river, was about the only place in the village that Beth could let them roam free and burn off their energy. Now, once she was out of sight of any houses, she gave up even pretending she was in charge of the dogs. But already there, thigh deep in the long sweet grass, was the last person Beth wanted to see in her present predicament. Jenny Williams looked in her element, *her* six dogs racing off obediently to retrieve the tennis balls and dummies she threw for them in long, elegant, accurate arcs. Any infraction on the part of her dogs earnt an instant slap or an alarming growl. It was perfectly clear who was top dog here. Flash and Jig-Jag gave voice as soon as they saw their pals and Jenny glanced round – too late for Beth to make an escape.

Jenny was very much of Jacob's vintage. That would have been fine, except that it also meant that she had been a contemporary of Becca's. And Jacob's first wife still cast a long shadow in these parts. Quite an achievement for someone who had been dead and buried in the churchyard for the last four years.

A brief, not unfriendly nod from Jenny, then back to her dogs – first things first. Beth's lack of control loomed even larger by comparison. To let her two off the lead or not? Would they ever come back? Could she face the humiliation if they didn't?

Jenny was characteristically direct. 'Well, are you going to let them off or aren't you?'

Beth decided to come clean. Although she barely knew Jenny, she was predisposed to like her, formidable though she was, for two reasons. The first: because she was the only woman in the village as tall as Beth. The second: because she was the only person in the whole village never to have called her Becca, either by mistake or by design. 'Yes, I think so, but I forgot my whistle. I'm not sure if I dare risk it.'

Jenny tutted. 'Wouldn't make much difference if you had it. You have to know what you're doing, y'know.'

Ouch! 'Is it that obvious?'

A sideways glance. Was that the hint of a smile on Jenny's fine aristocratic face? 'Yes, perfectly. But the dogs have to know too. And those two are thoroughly spoilt and ill-disciplined. They need some good basic training. You too probably.'

Yes, it definitely was a smile. Beth was encouraged. 'Do you think we could ever learn?'

Jenny whistled her dogs in and gathered up her clobber, then coolly assessed Beth. 'Certainly. Provided you don't mind putting in some hours.'

Silence. Did she dare to ask? 'Well, would you ...?'

'Of course I would. I'd be delighted, in fact. But you'll have to fit in with me.'

Beth was nodding fervently. Jenny went on. 'Right. You could start by wearing some jeans and a pair of waterproof shoes or boots. And wear a jacket with pockets. I'll be free tomorrow. A bit earlier, please.' She passed through the gate ahead of the dogs, surging round her long legs then opened the boot of her muddy Volvo, which was a signal for the dogs to sit quietly and wait for their names to be called before they leapt neatly in, one by one. 'Bring your whistle next time too.'

With a casual wave, Jenny pulled away, leaving Beth quietly delighted and getting horribly tangled up in the leads while the dogs sniffed happily around. To her delight, Jacob's car was parked outside when the dogs dragged her home. They hastened in through the front door to see him.

He must have arrived soon after she'd left because he'd had time to make a cup of tea for himself, but as usual he'd forgotten to take it upstairs and it was stone cold already, abandoned by a stack of papers on the kitchen table. There was a bunch of flowers beside them. He hadn't put them in water so she quickly dumped them in the sink and turned on the cold tap. She scrutinised – lilies. At least she hadn't had to train him out of chrysanths and pinks – that had all been taken care of under the previous regime. The dogs rushed upstairs while she made him another cup and she could hear his delighted voice as he greeted them and asked them, in turn, about their day. At the top of the stairs, she paused in the gloom and watched through the door of his study, delaying the pleasure of the moment when he would spot her and come striding out. He was crouching by the door, his hair dishevelled and his glasses swinging on a cord round his neck as he fondled Jig-Jag's silky black ears. The collar of his striped shirt was awry, and Beth felt a wave of almost protective tenderness sweep over her.

'Fresh tea, darling?'

He glanced up happily, eyes creasing at the corners, then sprang to his feet and covered the corridor in just a few long-legged paces. 'Sweetheart!' He took the steaming mug from her hands and placed it on the small table then folded her into his arms and held her close. Beth allowed herself to be engulfed – there weren't many men who could make her feel protected but, tall as she was, Jacob still topped her by half a head. She'd been able to bring her high heels out of storage once he'd appeared on the scene – not that she'd had much use for them since moving out to Milton after their marriage only seven months ago now. Milton didn't do high heels. It was all Tods and Le Chameau.

Whatever had distracted Jacob from his tea was completely put aside now, his attention solely on her with the intensity that had so fascinated her from the start, and he urged her downstairs so they could exchange news. Sitting down at the table, he pulled her onto his lap and nibbled at her neck just where it was most sensitive and expected her to concentrate as he reported, between kisses, the latest from his department, Modern History, where the faculty was also bracing itself for the new intake of students. She looked at his long sinewy hands, still tanned from their delayed honeymoon in Italy, as he stroked her thigh. She could feel herself becoming aroused. Thank goodness she had already exercised the dogs.

Half an hour later she was lying in his arms on the bed, their bodies bathed in the afternoon sunshine, satiated and relaxed. 'Now come on,' he urged, stroking the side of her breast with his hand, 'I want to know about your day.'

She rolled towards him and hooked one of her legs over his. 'Panning out quite well so far thanks.'

He laughed and patted her bottom. 'Now what's the latest from the trenches of the VEG? Were rock buns thrown? Have the young upstarts overthrown the oligarchy?'

It was so typical of Jacob to remember that she had a meeting that day. She fixed him with a teasing look, keen to impart her news from the front. 'I have made progress! My onslaught on the established hierarchy of Milton continues unopposed. And today I definitely got the vote of confidence when Irene almost begged me to take on the Mistletoe Meet. How about that, Jay? She said it would be a good way of getting to—'

But Jacob was not reacting as he should. Beth had been anticipating gasps of admiration but, instead, he pulled away from her, a frown creasing his forehead. 'Is everything all right, darling?' she said, unsure of what was going on here. 'You look a bit gobsmacked.'

'Er, no, no.' He shook his head, though the frown hadn't quite disappeared. 'I'm sure you'll do it beautifully. It's just – well, I wouldn't have thought it was quite your thing, a party for the village worthies. It's an awful lot of bother at a busy time of year. I'm sure Irene would understand if you changed your mind.'

Beth felt affronted. Was this a slight on her organisational skills? She was about to retort, but paused for a moment and bit her tongue. He'd have to eat his words when he realised her skill with pineapple chunks on cocktail sticks. She pretended to reflect on his suggestion, then – ever so delicately – changed the subject.

The rest of the day was spent poring over her notes for the new term's lectures. She was already making inroads into *Uccello and the Birth of Perspective* but she'd need to get to the library to check something out. Jacob came out of his study at about six and after pouring himself and her a glass of Merlot, took the phone into the sitting room to make his weekly fatherly calls to Noel and Holly.

Beth discreetly left him to it and started preparing the roast chicken. Becoming a stepmother of adults meant she didn't have to get too involved, but secretly she had to confess that the way in which Jacob spoke to Holly drove her mad. The girl was petulant and spoilt at the best of times, but listening to her father's efforts to placate her as she milked the Daddy's-girl act was enough to turn Beth's stomach.

Over supper he filled her in on their news – Noel was in love, and Holly in debt, despite her 'marvellous new job on a top magazine' – and later she joined him in bed where he was reading, glasses perched on the end of his high-bridged nose. 'Oh, I forgot to tell you,' she said as she tucked her feet under his legs to warm them, 'Jenny Williams invited me out to exercise the dogs with her tomorrow. With any luck she can show me what to do with that flaming whistle.'

Jacob closed his book and reached out to pull her close so she could nestle in against his square shoulder. 'Jenny! I haven't seen her for ages. She's one of a kind, she really is. An amazing woman. I didn't realise you knew her so well.'

'I don't really.' Beth played with the edge of the navy cotton quilt cover. 'I see her out with the dogs of course, just to say hello to. But she's so nice and straightforward. What you see is what you get. And she clearly knows what she's doing ...' She chatted on about the dogs' recalcitrant behaviour for a while. 'Oh they were embarrassing!' She paused. Dare she ask? 'Did, er, did Jenny get on well with Becca?'

There was silence, interrupted only by Jacob's gentle breathing as he slept. Beth smiled. Perhaps it was better he hadn't heard her ask.

Next morning, after Jacob had left for the faculty, Beth was ready for action. In jeans, walking boots and an old T-shirt, and the whistle hanging round her neck, she was just about to attach the dogs' leads when the phone rang. The barking was interrupted only by excited whining and she strained to hear what the caller wanted.

'Hello? Sorry, you're calling about what?... The cottage? Oh really? To rent? How odd. I didn't think it was in a fit state.' She hadn't the time to argue the point now. 'Oh, OK then. Hang on, I'll get a pen.' She rooted around on the hall stand. 'I'll have to contact the owner and she's away a lot of the time. When did you want it? Christmas? Well, yes, you can never get started too early, can you? I'll just take your details and someone will get back to you ... And you are?'

Chapter 2

Same day and only 100 shopping days to go

Don't feel tied by tradition! A change of venue at
Christmas time can be refreshing for everyone.

'Carol. C-A-R-O-L. Could you ask the owner to call me?' Carol
gave out her number. 'That would be great. I'll look forward to
getting the booking form.' Keen now to finish the conversation
with the nice-sounding woman at the other end of the phone,
Carol started to sift through the papers in front of her, happy
that she had completed at least one of her assigned tasks for
the day. She needed to get on. She was already late getting to
her desk this morning and the hordes would be descending any
minute. She hadn't even had time to fire up her emails.

'Great. I'll wait to hear from you. Bye.' Result. That was
Christmas ticked off in her head.

As she put down the phone, she could see her assistant's
pixyish face peeking in through the glass panel in her office
door. No chance of picking your nose or adjusting your thong
with that peephole there, as anyone who passed seemed to make
it their business to peer in. Carol had flirted briefly with the
idea of covering it up with a little sample of Osborne & Little
fabric that a PR had sent in – very tasteful of course – and
which was now piled up on the sofa in the corner with lots
of other equally tasteful little samples. But that might make it
look as though she was doing something covert behind it, and
she couldn't be seen to be doing that – not when, only weeks
before, having taken the editor's job to steer this particularly

adrift ship back on course, she'd had a welcome meeting with the staff on the theme of the open-door policy.

'Drop in any time – your input and ideas are invaluable,' she'd heard herself chirp merrily to a sea of distinctly judgemental faces in front of her. 'We must all pull together. It's not my magazine, it's *ours*.'

Though now, as she indicated for Jemima to come in, and began to cast an eye over the pile of post, she couldn't escape the feeling that it was *entirely* her ship. She was admiral, captain and first mate too, so low was morale around the office and so pitiful the lack of inspiration. In the two months since she'd been hauled in at very short notice (OK, charmed away) from the very safe and successful *Style* magazine, she'd already had six staff hand in their resignation. It wasn't surprising as the number of pages continued to decrease in direct relation to the drop in circulation, and, as Jemima stood now in front of her desk, Carol prayed once again that she wasn't going to do the same. This cool, gamine girl with unfeasibly narrow hips, and dressed today in a floral fifties-style skirt and tight black cardigan, was not only super-efficient for one so young but also frighteningly bright. And she would no doubt be hungry to work on some glossier, sexier and infinitely more successful title.

'You look pretty, Jemima,' Carol said encouragingly. 'Anything urgent before the meeting?'

'L'Oreal want to know if you can make the conditioner launch.'

'Can you persuade Beatrice to do that one? I reckon I could do conditioners as my specialist subject on *Mastermind*.' She smiled weakly to be met with a blank appraisal through dark, narrow Prada specs. 'Anything else?'

'I've pencilled in the focus meeting for the fifteenth here on the fourteenth floor, and booked the room provisionally, you've the DIY Homes Christmas press event at twelve and Ian has requested a meeting with you at five.' She snapped shut her book.

Bugger, thought Carol. Bugger because she'd forgotten the press launch. Double bugger because a meeting with Ian would mean she wouldn't get away early and triple bugger, it would inevitably mean having to account for her performance so far, when she really had very little to say.

She sighed. 'Tell everyone to give me ten minutes, then we'll start the staff meeting.' She turned to her computer to download her messages, dismissing Jemima with her back. The girl's superior manner was beginning to bug her.

Oh crikey. Would she have time to get her head around everything before five? Ian Cameron had a reputation for being the toughest of the company's publishing directors: utterly ruthless ambition and determination veiled in an utterly charming, public-school demeanour and expensive double-breasted suit. Amazing what you could disguise if you said it in that plummy, apologetic way posh men have, thought Carol as she watched the emails cascade onto her screen. When he'd called her into his office on the sixteenth floor back in July, he'd delivered the charm in spadefuls, telling her how she really was the only woman for the job, and how sorry he was that he'd had to pull her away from the amazing work she was doing on *Style*, but that *Woman's Monthly* needed her skills and she was really the *only* safe pair of hands.

Of course, Carol had found out as soon as anyone had that *Woman's Monthly*'s previous editor had been fired unceremoniously one Friday lunchtime only a few weeks earlier. Bad news seemed to travel through the air con in this tower block. She also knew that *Woman's Monthly* had been for a good while the lame duck in the group compared to the golden goose that was *Style*. Well, it was a wonder really that any magazine could survive with a name that sounded like a coy euphemism for periods, but in its heyday, before the onset of up-market lifestyle magazines *for women over thirty and proud of it*, it had had a loyal and large following of well-heeled women seeking sensible advice about fashion, home improvements and recipes, with the odd feature thrown in. And not a multiple orgasm in sight. The majority of readers took it on subscription – not an impulse buy – but, reflected Carol, how times have changed. Only days before she'd left *Style*, she'd spent two hours trying to secure a notoriously difficult but achingly beautiful actress to grace the front cover of the November issue because she'd heard *Vogue* had scooped a Hollywood darling. Reader loyalty? Oh life had been so much simpler then.

Ten minutes to the second it seemed there was a light tap on the door and Jemima Pixie-face stuck her head around it again.

'Ready?'

'As I'll ever be. Bring it on!'

Behind Jemima, notepad clenched to her infinitesimal breasts, followed the motley staff of *Women's Monthly*. First was Melanie, breezing through the door with the air of someone who has tolerated, survived and seen off many occupants of the editor's chair. Fashion editor supreme, it seemed she had held her position like a sinecure since Mrs Beeton had had a recipe column. A familiar face at press events and launches, she surrounded herself with the coterie of her fashion department like a royal entourage, hogging young and enthusiastic assistants to herself until they had the courage to disentangle themselves from her didactic grasp.

God, thought Carol, watching Melanie seat herself centre stage in front of her desk, arranging her wide-cut and impeccable linen trousers, she must be the only fashion editor in London who doesn't wear jeans. There's no hope of progress with her around. But what choice did Carol have? She wasn't going to attract the fashion editor of *Tatler* with sod-all page budget and a readership that would be causing a parish magazine to lose sleep.

The others trickled in behind Melanie; editors and sub-editors, assistants and work-experience girls – an array of younger faces all in strappy tops and jeans in the warmth of the September morning. They took up their positions around the office, some perched on tables, others leaning up against the crammed bookshelf, confident perhaps that the meeting wouldn't take long. Carol busied herself with her emails for a second as they settled, aware that they were watching her, and tried to look businesslike as she tapped out an enthusiastic reply to her old mate, Kate, who'd asked her to meet her for a drink after work next week. That, she reckoned, would be something to look forward to. She pasted on her brightest smile and turned to her audience.

'Hi, everyone, hope you've all had a restful weekend and are feeling full of enthusiasm.' Their expressions said nothing. 'Couple of things first—' The door opened suddenly and in slipped one of the sub-editors, a waif-like girl with shoulder-length curly hair caught up in a clip and such an air of 'sod you' attitude in her stubborn chin that Carol didn't know whether to be cowed or amused by her audacity. She tried to scour her memory for the girl's name – Holly. That was it. Yes, she remembered now it was some Christmassy name like hers (God bless her mother). Carol watched her settle herself against the wall by the door and continue chewing her gum without a murmur of apology for her lateness.

They all looked back at Carol expectantly.

'Right, now we are all here, a couple of things first. I thought the last issue looked great,' she looked down at the paper in front of her to cover her lie, 'and it's really standing out on the news-stands – especially with the free hairbrush. I'm sure it will sell like hot cakes. Hope you all agree. ' She didn't wait for assent or otherwise, and moved swiftly on.

'So, the Christmas and New Year issues.' She felt brisk and in control now, glad she'd worn the pale blue linen suit.

It was a strategic choice that always paid off when she had to look scarier than she felt. 'How're things coming along? Beauty?' She homed in on the expectant face of Beatrice, new to the job of beauty editor in a meteoric rise to the top that had nothing to do with the fact that no one else wanted the job.

'Er …' Beatrice looked down at her pad. 'We've got some lovely shots for the "Your Party Eyes" feature. I think they've turned out very well…considering.' She cast a sidelong look at Melanie, who picked an imaginary thread from her trousers and smoothed them down.

'Quite.' Carol had heard from Jemima that there had been a contretemps between the two of them at the photoshoot and she felt quite sympathetic towards the plump beauty editor. 'It made much more sense to combine the two shoots. Great way of keeping down costs. What have you got lined up for the Jan issue?'

'Your Party Lips?' Beatrice's face was hopeful. Melanie's mocking.

'Mmmm. That should be great and perhaps we can do something else too? Let's talk later. Moving on. Emma – features. How's the celebrity interview shaping up?' And on it went, a tour around each department head and each up-date less and less inspiring. The 'My Struggle with Depression' interview with an erstwhile soap star was hardly going to have the punters fighting over the latest issue, now was it? And 'Top Ten Best Artificial Trees' made Carol want to suppress a sob of despair. She turned hopefully to the food editor, a much older woman than all the rest with fair hair cut into a sensible bob and a face creased from years of smoking. Felicity Long was a veteran of the magazine business and Carol was hopeful that she would come up with something a little more exciting.

'I thought we'd do low-calorie canapés in minutes,' Felicity explained in her gravelly voice, pushing her half-moons up her nose. 'You know how fattening party nibbles can be – plus Your Ten Day Countdown. The readers always love that one – we do it every year. You know, when to peel the sprouts or stuff the bird, with perhaps a panel of time-saving tips. Do you think they'll like that?' She smiled her very open, innocent smile, as if all this was new to her. But even Carol's mother had a Felicity Long cookbook from the 1970s. This woman had probably been stuffing turkeys and giving foolproof tips on perfect mince-pie pastry since Jesus's first birthday party.

Carol sighed. Nothing original at all. Perhaps there was nothing new to say about Christmas anyway. 'And you, Holly? How's Your Best Christmas Ever feature going? I liked your first draft.'

The girl who'd come in late looked up from her fingernails on which she'd been doodling with her pen. 'Uh? Oh sorry. Yeah. Well, I've got some pictures in and Brigitta,' indicating the art director in case Carol wasn't sure, 'says we can do the rest with graphics.'

Carol didn't doubt it. Their German art director, resplendent in bicycle shorts, floral smocked top and pigtails, was so in love with her graphics that the actual text in most features seemed to disappear altogether, squeezed out by what she called 'en-novatif unt exciting design'.

'We'll see how it looks, shall we?' she said cautiously then turned back to the room in general, taking in the slumped shoulders, the fidgeting and the distant expressions. Time to move on in.

'I'd like to make a few changes.' She could feel a stirring as people shifted anxiously. She waded on. 'Something's missing and,' she held up her hand, 'don't get me wrong, I know I said the last issue looked fine, but we really have a bit of a mountain to climb here.' She watched as some of them cast their eyes down to the floor, or whispered to each other, raising their eyebrows. 'I really think we could beef things up a bit.

Georgie,' she turned to the managing editor, 'found anything we can put on the cover as a freebie?'

Georgie looked flustered. 'Well, I'm holding out for a teabag.' There were suppressed snorts from around her.

'A teabag?' Carol enquired slowly.

'Well yes. Green tea. Very restorative for the morning after the night before. I thought that might be great for Christmastime. You know ...'

'Mmm.' Carol rubbed her temples, wishing she'd brought in a bottle of mineral water. 'I think we need something a little more irresistible.'

'A bauble?' Holly's voice came out quietly into the silence.

'Sorry?'

'You know, a decoration.' She glanced around the room, poutingly but suddenly a bit unsure now she was in the limelight. 'There are some really pretty ones – angels and stuff – and they're dead cheap to buy I expect.'

'Holly, great idea,' Carol enthused. At last! Some inspiration. 'Georgie, can you look into that? Something tasteful but a bit modern and fun? Now, sex.'

The snorts from around the room were louder this time. 'We don't really cover that sort of thing,' said Emma, the features editor, nervously. 'We generally cover more practical stuff – homes, things to make, practical hints and tips.'

'Exactly.' Carol slammed her hand down on the desk. 'That's what people need hints and tips on. Emma, let's do something in the New Year issue about making your man happy this Christmas. The magazine comes out early December so that will be perfect timing. Can you call in some how-to sex guides? See if we can get an expert to give us some pearls of wisdom.' She watched the girl making notes frantically on her pad. 'And what about some sex toys?'

This time she had the whole room's rapt attention. Even Melanie had forgotten to purse her mouth. 'Yep – this will be the article to leave out for your man to see. Let's call it *What's Going To Ring His Bells This Christmas*? You know the kind of stuff: knickers to get him going. The best vibrators you'll want in your stocking – our three top choices. And we'd better test them – I'll be wanting volunteers! Get to it!' A few moments later and the meeting disbanded, everyone chatting animatedly to each other as they left the room. Carol turned back to her emails, a small smile on her face.

Jemima stuck her head around the door. 'Your mum's on the line again. Shall I put her through?'

Carol grimaced and nodded. 'Hi, Mum. Everything OK?'

'Now why shouldn't it be?' Despite living in Croydon all her adult life, Mary Macgorrigan still hadn't shaken off County Donegal. 'That wee son of yours was a bit snuffly about going in this mornin', but I promised him we'd bake shortbread when he got home. And that nice chappy rang again about delivering the tumble drier. I told him four thirty was pointless cos I'd be taking Tim to violin then so he's going to work a bit later and come when we've got home.'

'I bet you charmed the pants off him, Mum!' Carol scanned a page proof that Sheena, chief sub-editor, had slipped under her nose.

'Now less of that sort of dirt, my girl!'

'Sheena, that pull-out quote.' Carol put her hand over the receiver. ' I thought we'd settled on the other one? Sorry, Mum, what's dirty?'

'I can hear you're busy, dear. I'll leave you to it. Only I'm meeting Adele this evening for our little get-together. What time will you be getting in, love?'

'Hang on, Sheena. Oh God, Mum, I've got a meeting I forgot all about. It's with the big cheese. Top gorgonzola.' She could hear the sigh down the line. 'I'm sure it won't take long. Would you mind awfully just holding on until I get back? You can take Adele to supper at that new gastropub – my treat?'

'Now, if it's not one thing it's another. You'll have to check your diary a bit more often, won't you? Just don't be too late.' There was a pause. 'And come back safely.'

*

Holly pretended to yawn and leant back in her swivel chair to check that the coast was clear. Open-plan offices may be ideal for generating team spirit – she shuddered at the thought – but they were a sod when you wanted to conduct a little private business. At least Sheena was out somewhere or other. God only knew where. The prissy chief sub had, of course, explained exactly where in tiresome detail before lunch, but Holly had done her usual thing, just nodding occasionally with her head on one side, while thinking about something else completely. Frowning slightly was a good technique too, and tapping a pencil against the teeth really worked. But not all at once. You had to kind of alternate them, or it looked like you were taking the piss.

Anyway, the old bag wasn't there. Melanie was looking at layouts, bending over so far there was a flash of her whole-some knickers over the waistband of her trousers. Holly's little face twisted as though she was sucking a lemon. It was so disappointing having to work with these has-beens whose idea of cutting-edge fashion was Country Casuals linen. For God's sake, even Carol sometimes appeared in the office in those awful dreary linen sleeveless dresses. Holly had had such hopes of her too, coming from that fashion bible, *Style*. Why did old women like Melanie insist on exposing their bodies anyway? Couldn't they see their elbows were sooo disgusting – all wrinkly and grey. Holly stretched her arms above her head and admired her own flawless skin. Once she was over thirty, she'd never wear stuff like that. She'd only wear Comme or maybe Shirin Guild – kind of anti-fashion stuff – or maybe some really nice vintage Missoni, and her arms would never go all bingo wings. Why did women let that happen? She shook her head sadly.

Another quick check. The coast was pretty clear, so she lifted the phone and tapped in the number with a pewter-coloured nail. Two o'clock. He'd almost certainly be there and alone, and she listened to the phone ring, once, twice, three times. Click. The familiar low voice. He sounded preoccupied and she felt a jolt of protectiveness mingled with the anticipation of hearing the pleasure in his voice once he knew it was her.

'Hi! It's me. You busy?'

'Never too busy to talk to you. I was just thinking about you this morning.'

'Really?' She fiddled with the new piercing in her ear, smiling into the receiver. 'What were you thinking? Good stuff or bad?'

'What do you think? I was thinking I miss you. You haven't been up for ages.'

'Weeell, it's tricky. I mean I'm working really hard, like all the time. And after work, there's loads of launches and receptions to go to. I'm hardly ever in, even at weekends. You know what it's like on a magazine as exclusive as *Style*!'

'Well, I don't actually but I'm sure I can't compete with your glamorous lifestyle, darling.'

Holly sighed dramatically. 'Yes it's exhausting but couldn't we meet up when you come down to London? We could do lunch. *I'll* take *you* to lunch. How grown up would that be?'

He laughed. 'You'd hate it if *I* said that.'

'Yeah, but it's me so it's all right. It's ironic when I say it. Oh go on. It's ages since we've seen each other – just you and me.'

Silence. Had she gone too far? Was he going to go all self-righteous on her? She could hear papers rustling. His diary? A couple of emails trickled onto her screen. Wouldn't it be great

26

if she had one of those handheld thingies? She could get them anywhere. He cleared his throat.

'Here's an idea. And just consider it for a moment. Don't just react.'

She rolled her eyes. She knew what was coming. 'Yeah? What?'

'Well, I'm coming up for a meeting next month. I can make some time in the morning and perhaps we can have an early lunch. The only thing is, do you think you could manage a weekend up here before too long? It would mean so much to me. To us. Perhaps we could go shopping when I come down, eh? Buy you a nice warm coat or something. What do you say, Berry?'

She paused just long enough. 'But I don't need a coat. And I'm so busy. I'm looking at my diary right now.' She flicked noisily through a magazine, holding the receiver close to the fluttering pages. 'It's going to be tough. I'll have to cancel something...'

'Well, not a coat then. Something, you choose. Whatever you need. See if you can manage it.'

Result. Time to reel him in. 'Okaaaay. But it's really tricky. I'll have to keep checking in with the office. You know, I have to be available twenty-four, seven. Have you even got broadband up there yet?'

'Oh yes, and Wi-Fi or We Free, or whatever it is. We are lurching into the twenty-first century, you know. You're welcome to hog my computer for the whole weekend.'

Holly scowled. 'It's more the journey. It's so boring on the train. If I had a palm top or something like that, I wouldn't even have to touch your antiquated machine. They're really cool, you can ...' She was gearing herself up to explain exactly what she was talking about, but he laughed knowingly.

'Yes, yes. I am familiar with the technology. I've been brought up to speed. And would you stop texting me if you had one? Can't abide all that l-8-r stuff. That'll be the death of the English language, you mark my words.'

That was more like it. A lovable old fogey to the core. 'Oh yes. I promise. No more texts. Real, proper emails, all with flawless spelling and punctuation.' Shit! Carol was approaching across the office.

'I doubt that very much. But we'll have a look when I come down, shall we? And darling? Do make some time for a visit. I'm counting on you.'

'Yes, yes,' she sat up very straight and made a show of writing something down. 'Well, thanks for calling. It's very good to speak to you. I'll sort that out then, straight away.'

'Er, OK. Love you, Berry.'

Carol had paused at the flat plan on the wall. Holly covered the receiver and blew a kiss. 'Love you too, Daddy.'

*

It really was very endearing the way her mother always made sure she'd got home safely, thought Carol as, two hours later, she pulled down the cab window even further to allow in as much air as possible. At forty-one she was rather beyond needing the nurse-maiding, but she knew it was well meant.

'Stifling, innit?' shouted the cabbie over his shoulder as he pulled up at the traffic lights.

Carol murmured in assent then quickly pulled out her organiser from her bag so he wasn't encouraged to talk further. She had little enough head space as it was without having to contend with his opinions on the congestion charge or London in this heatwave. Slipping a stray Minstrel that she'd found at the bottom of her bag into her mouth – she'd missed lunch and even though this tasted of perfume, it was better than nothing – she turned to the back and the blank pages. Cover mount, she wrote, not too fragile? Back-page feature? Lingerie shoot?? Tapas menu – could Felicity cope? Tim, school shoes. SATS (when are they?), Tampax, make hair appt, back-door key – get another cut.

By the time she reached Kensington, she'd filled the page and taken three phone calls on her mobile. Crammed into the lift up to the exclusive roof garden where the press event was to take place, she squared her shoulders and did her well-practised mental scan. What event was this? How big were they in advertising terms? What was the name of the head honcho? And by the time the lift doors opened to spew out the sweating contents, Carol had plastered on her smile and strapped on the mental uniform.

Under normal circumstances the innumerable press invitations to events would be handed out around the office. At *Style*, of course, she'd been able to handpick the glossiest and smartest events to attend – Louis Vuitton, Prada, Estée Lauder – but her blasé days were over. Carol my love, she admonished herself as she stepped out into the fray, today DIY Homes is going to have to be your DKNY.

For a moment Carol thought she must have died on the way up in the lift and this was the pearly gates. The scene that awaited her was like a celestial version of B&Q. Covering the floor of the roof garden was three inches of fake snow, and from it sprouted tall trees, also in sparkling white, each one adorned with glass and silver baubles. Giant Perspex stars hung from mock-Victorian lanterns, and frosted green and white Christmas trees seemed to sway to the sound of George Michael and 'Last Christmas' emanating from several strategically placed loud speakers.

'Mulled wine?' squeaked a voice from about her waistline. She looked down to see a tiny Oriental woman dressed from head to foot in a fluffy white elf costume, her face puce in the heat. Carol was so taken aback by this vision that, without thinking, she picked up a glass and took a slug. The warm taste of cinnamon and oranges spread over her tongue, completely at odds with the sunshine bearing down on her through this Forest of Narnia.

'Canapé?' came a camp voice beside her, and she turned to see what looked like the builder from the Village People, only dipped in bleach. His jeans were white and tucked into white Caterpillar boots. Around his six-pack waist was a white tool belt complete with white hammer and chisel. On his head a white hard-hat and his face and muscled body were sprayed with silver paint. He smiled sweetly at her as she took a Thai prawn from his silver tray, trying hard not to stare and, turning smartly on his metal toe caps, he flounced off, tray held high.

'Bloody hell, I thought I'd seen it all!' Carol turned to the sound of a familiar deep voice behind her. 'But I don't think he'd be interested in *my* sort of underpinning.'

'Dotty!' Carol gave the woman beside her a warm kiss – making sure she made contact on each cheek. God forbid she'd stoop so low as to 'mwah mwah'. It was eons since she'd seen her old mate; they'd known each other since they'd been staff writers years ago on a weekly woman's title. They'd drink after work together and, when they could afford it, stay later than they should eating lamb chops and spring onion mash for lunch at Joe Allen's in Exeter Street. But whilst Carol had conquered the Himalayas of the up-market magazine world, Dorothy had always stayed firmly in the foothills. 'How lovely to see you! No, sweetie, I think the erections he's interested in are altogether elsewhere. What brings you here?'

'Oh you know.' Dorothy lit a cigarette, blowing the smoke out of the side of her mouth away from Carol's face. 'Still churning out home improvement copy and marvelling at the miracles you can achieve with a staple gun and some MDF.' She grabbed another glass of mulled wine from a passing elf. 'But what about you, my girl? Any man managed to seduce five minutes out of your over-stuffed schedule or are you still the Sister Chastity of the publishing world?'

Carol laughed. 'Fat chance. The nearest I get to sex is ten minutes of some late night Channel 4 soft porn before I go to sleep in my winceyette.'

Dot looked through narrowed eyes. 'And I gather you've...er, made an interesting career move recently.'

'Oh yesss! *WM*. All very exciting. Big challenge, you know.' Carol smiled brightly but could see the scepticism in her friend's face. 'No, really. Tremendous fun. Lots of potential there.'

'Mmmm right.' Dot inhaled deeply. 'The money must have been good.'

'Why?' Carol pretended to be wide-eyed.

'Two reasons. One: *WM* is ailing and everyone knows it. And two, this isn't exactly your stomping ground, is it? It would take something quite extraordinary for you to attend a press do where the goody bag didn't include a Hermès scarf!'

'*DIY Homes* is a big advertiser. Important people.'

'Yeah, they're big movers all right, but only in the lowly world of home improvements. It must be a bit of a comedown for you, Ms Moschino.'

Refusing to be beaten, Carol lowered her voice. 'Mark my words, people will get tired of the celebrity-obsessed rags and start wanting something more interesting to read than face-lift speculation about C-list celebs.'

Dorothy didn't look convinced. 'Well, their appetite isn't showing any signs of diminishing from where I'm standing. But if you think you're right, then stick to your worthy articles.' She looked hard at Carol. 'Sure you weren't just flattered by that bloody Ian Cameron and his line in smooth talk? You know he's turned on by success.' And she wiggled her eyebrows suggestively.

Carol wrinkled her nose in disgust. 'What an awful thought. Ian Cameron in a state of sweaty arousal.' She laughed but Dorothy was looking at her with a very serious expression.

'He's also a bastard about failure.' She leant in towards

Carol. 'Sweetie. Word from an old hackette who's mopped up the tears of many who've shinned further up the greasy pole than I've ever dared. I've seen more women brought to their knees by Cameron than I care to remember. And not in a Bill Clinton way.'

Carol felt a vague feeling of disquiet. 'Oh? Have you been hearing rumours about *WM*?'

Dorothy lightened up suddenly, as if she'd gone too far, and waved airily. 'Oh just gossip and a couple of bits of nonsense.' She patted Carol's arm. 'Don't listen to me. It'll be fine, you'll see, especially once you've worked your magic on it.' Then she steered off the subject by regaling Carol with the latest on her notorious and prolific love life and, after ten minutes of hilarious up-dating – much of which concerned Dot's brief affair with a lawyer she'd met over the internet who liked to be whipped – Carol did a quick sweep over the 'new for Christmas' displays, schmoozed with the right people, dumped her glass with one of the Albino builders and made her excuses.

Back at her desk, she found the pile of phone messages Jemima had left for her and her screen was splattered with unread emails. She spent the rest of the afternoon fielding and returning some of the more urgent ones, had a quick consultation with Brigitta about the November cover, trying tactfully to suggest that a model in a woolly hat was a bit clichéd, then noticed with pleasure that the freelance writer, Lisa Fairley, had returned her call. She dialled her number.

As she waited for Lisa to pick up, she glanced at the latest issue of *Style*, which Jemima had placed rather too strategically on her desk. The cover lines shouted out at her: 'Delicious Winter Fashion for Your Aspen Skiing', 'Escape to the Maldives', 'Your Top Ten Private Jets'... All the feature ideas Carol had had before she left. How galling. She simply had to inject the same excitement into *WM*. Putting down the phone – the woman clearly wasn't in – she grabbed a scrap of paper, and began to scribble.

'Carol?' Jemima stuck her head round the door a while later. 'It's time for the meeting with Ian. He's just called down to say he has to be at the Saatchi Gallery at six, so can you get there now?'

Sighing and keeping her scribbled piece of paper with her, she rode up the lift to the sixteenth floor, head still buzzing, and added to her list as she waited for Ian to come off the phone. Sleeves of his immaculate cotton shirt rolled up in the warmth of the evening, tie – undoubtedly Thomas Pink – slightly loosened at the neck, he was absently running his hands through his thick wavy hair and rubbing the back of his neck, laughing loudly and unconvincingly every now and then at something the person on the other end was saying. With his double cuffs, cufflinks and expensive Penhaligon fragrance, there was something vaguely Officers' Mess about him, and his charm, unique to the well-bred and privately-educated, made him one of the most sought-after single men in London.

'Sweetie.' He urged her in to his office with an expansive wave of his hand and, getting up from his chair, gave her a kiss on the cheek, tightened his tie and shrugged on his suit jacket.

'Bloody private view with the P of W so I'll be brief. How's it looking?'

Carol grabbed the moment. Engaging as he may be, Ian Cameron had an attention span that would shame a child. As she outlined her plans, those laid out so hastily on her scrap of paper, she watched him gather up his bits and pieces, and check messages on his computer. Was he listening?

'Mmmm,' he mused and she realised he hadn't even asked her to sit down.

'It all sounds very exciting.' He clicked his pen and tucked it into his inside pocket. 'Thing is, Carol my darling, I've had a call from DIY Homes. They've been looking at their marketing spend apparently. Well, when they say that you know there's trouble.' Carol could feel anxiety rising in her stomach. 'Their regular double-page-spread booking, inside front cover?'

Carol's mouth went dry.

'They've pulled out.'

Carol couldn't think of anything to say.

'I don't need to tell you what that means in terms of revenue.' Ian paused for effect. '*WM* has always been a solid title. We need to get that back, Carol.' And he marched out of the room.

Chapter 3

October

Only 75 shopping days to go

Christmas is a time to renew old friendships and
exchange news, particularly with those far away.
Go on, pick up the phone and make contact at this
special time of year. Show you care.

Beth thumbed through the yellowing leaves of the address book. Leather-bound, it looked as though it had probably been a wedding present. The numerous crossings out, inkings over, scribbled notes in the margins in Becca's firm, loopy script seemed to Beth to contain the history of Jacob's first marriage in agonisingly incomprehensible detail. A bit like the Rosetta Stone. Beth couldn't stop herself feeling that, if only she could crack the code, it would all come clear and she could stop bloody obsessing about a past she hadn't even been part of. I mean, how the hell could you feel threatened by a woman who was dead? Yet it felt oddly furtive, running her fingers down the indented edges of the pages, as though she were a spy on a secret mission, even though Jacob had told her to check it in the book for herself. To make sure the number he'd given her was the right one.

S ... S. She flipped the page over with her fingernail. Steaggles. Probably a relatively new entry, this holiday villa in Portugal. One of the last Becca was ever to make, before her short illness had started to tug the reins of the household from her hands, gradually at first, then with terrifying speed according to Jacob – or so Beth had pieced together from the snippets Jacob had revealed about that hideous time. Beth hadn't wanted to upset him more so hadn't asked questions.

She flicked over another couple of pages. There it was – Steaggles, Diana and Alan. She scrutinised the address. No hint of what was to come in the determined slope of the letters. Proper fountain pen, rather than the succession of gel pens and biros that Beth was constantly using and losing.

She'd have kept the pen in its box, no doubt, that formidable first wife of Jacob's, on her neat rather over-ornate antique desk in the sitting room. Beth avoided it, as she avoided most of Becca's stuff (or what she assumed to be Becca's), almost everything in the house in fact. In the eight months since her marriage to Jacob, she simply lived her life round it, swerving occasionally when it took her by surprise, and just pretending it wasn't there. She carefully copied the number onto a notebook in her bag then firmly closed the address book and returned it to the drawer in the hall stand. Out of sight ...

In the sunny kitchen, with a generous slug of Kenyan coffee in one of her mugs – one of the few things she'd brought with her from her flat in Oxford – she compared the number with the one Jacob had given her. Yes, he *had* got it right. So why was there never any bloody answer? Beth picked up the phone again and checked her watch. With the time difference, surely she'd catch them now, probably having breakfast on the vine-shaded veranda, eating yoghurt and fresh walnuts. The phone rang, distant and foreign. But this time, instead of ringing unanswered, allowing Beth the luxury of imagining Becca's oldest friend and her husband in sandalled splendour, growing leathery and languid in the year-round sun of ex-pat heaven, it was picked up abruptly, taking her by surprise.

'Hello? Steaggles residence?' Even in three words and over

a crackly line the voice managed to convey that it was far too early for any reasonable person to be calling. Tough.

'Oh, yes, hello. Is that Diana?'

'Yeees? Hello? Who is this?'

'Hello, I wonder if you can help me,' Oh for goodness' sake, Beth. *You're* doing *her* a favour. 'It's Jacob Layham's wife. We met briefly at the Winters' cocktail party in the summer. Do you remember?'

'Who? Jacob's wife? Is this some kind of joke?'

'Beth, it's Beth. I'm calling about your house.'

'Who? Oh *Beth*.' Beth could hear a clatter as the receiver was covered, presumably by a be-ringed hand, as Diana alerted whoever else was there to her identity via a muffled conversation. 'Yes, that's what I said, the *new* one...' The hand was withdrawn. 'Hello, Beth, what a lovely surprise. Yes, of course I remember meeting you. And in such an unusual dress. Now, how's Jacob?'

'Fine fine. Well, I won't keep you. It's just that I've had a booking for Stable Cottage over Christmas. I've got all the details here, so I can either give them to you now or email them if you like.'

'You've had what? But we haven't let it out in ages. You must be mistaken.'

Beth could feel her irritation mounting. 'No. I had a phone call from a woman in London who wants to book your cottage over Christmas, just for four days actually, but she said she was willing to pay for the whole week and she wants to know where to send the deposit. Hello? Can you hear me?'

The line fractured into a symphony of static. When it cleared, she could just make out the discontented voice as though through a swarm of angry bees.

'... very peculiar. I don't know where this person has got my number from ...'

'Not your number,' Beth retorted, '*my* number. She called

me almost a month ago, and I've been trying to get in touch with you ever since.'

'. . . have to tell them yourself . . . easier for you being there . . .'

'If you didn't want to let the cottage, perhaps you could have let me or Jacob know. I managed to dig out one of those photocopied leaflets you did – there was only one left actually, but there was no booking form or anything.' Beth raised her voice through the deafening interference. 'Can you sort it out with her and perhaps you could arrange for our number not to be made available again? I'll give you her details and you can get in touch with her yourself.' Beth carefully dictated the name and phone number of the woman who had tried to book the cottage. What a shame. That Carol woman was going to be disappointed that she couldn't have it for Christmas – and when she'd planned so far ahead too. Still it was probably a good thing. When Beth had last walked down that way with the dogs, she'd peered through the hedge and decided the place looked distinctly run down. Well, it wasn't her problem. Diana could tell Carol it wasn't for rent. Meanwhile Diana was trying to cut in.

'. . . much easier if you could contact her. After all, you've spoken to her already . . .'

'I really think you should do it if you don't mind.' Beth was polite but firm. 'Have you got that number? Do you want me to repeat it?' Faintly, from behind the swarm of bees, Beth could hear plaintive bleating. Diana was trying charm. 'Couldn't you . . .? Won't you just . . .?' But Beth kept up her steadfast deflection, talking constantly in an effort to make herself heard over the appalling line and the distant swell of emotional blackmail. 'Right, so that's agreed. I'm handing this over to you completely now. I'm busy with work and the blessed Mistletoe Meet. I'm not going to have any further—'

Just at that moment, the bees fell silent. The line was clear enough to hear a single cicada chirp, but Diana was still shouting to make herself heard. 'You? Taking on the Meet? And Jacob agreed? Well, you amaze me. I thought he'd have had enough with Becca doing it year after year – but you must know all about that. Oh, those were the days. She used to do it virtually single-handed, you know. It's a lot for one person to manage ...'

Thankfully, the buzzing started up once again. Not even bothering to say goodbye, Beth dropped the phone back into the cradle. She swallowed hard. 'Becca doing it year after year.' So that explained the gasps in the village hall when the idea was mooted that Beth resurrect the Meet tradition. That was why Jacob was so unenthusiastic. Here she was trying to create a perfect Christmas that would be Jacob's and her first together; a perfect Christmas that would show his family that Jacob had made the right choice in marrying her. And she'd walked into an ambush. She had better see what she was up against now.

She found the folder for the Meet, delivered by Irene and ignored by her, under a bag of courgettes. It was ancient and worryingly thick. Beth started to flick through the careful hand-written records. The earliest entries were from the 1950s, rather workaday, faded almost beyond legibility and listing recipes that had the tang of rationing about them. There were guest lists, raffle prizes, lists of suppliers, recipes and more. Sausage rolls, mince pies, baked potatoes. Innocent days, before Elizabeth David was beatified, when a glacé cherry on top of a half grapefruit was positively racy. So far so good.

The sixties were better documented, but dips were omnipresent, and everything else seemed to have been served on cocktail sticks. Prawn cocktail (with a handy recipe for dressing made of salad cream and ketchup), fondue and Black Forest gâteaux made occasional forays – oh the sophistication! Beth smiled indulgently, and flicked onwards through the seventies. As that decade wore on, she could detect a swing towards vegetarianism, and the menus started to exhibit high-fibre, League of Nations tendencies, with shepherdess pie, chilli non carne, cassoulet, grated salads *en masse* and carrot cake. She shook her head in amusement – you could have too much of a good thing.

Terrines seemed to have been big in the early eighties, along with pasta dishes and French onion soup. Mmmm. Just right for a winter party, along with some decent baguettes or garlic bread. That might be nice, with people cuddled up close at scrubbed trestle tables. Easy to keep warm too. Beth made a mental note to revive that combination. Perfectly manageable, with a little help from the redoubtable members of the VEG.

But as Beth moved closer to the present, the number of pages for each year's Meet increased markedly. With a sinking heart, she recognised the arrival of the imperious hand from the address book. Nineteen eighty-four – how incredibly ironic! Well, never mind CND, the miners' strike and Live Aid. The mid-1980s in Milton St David reverberated with another epoch-making event: Becca Layham had seized the Mistletoe Meet by the scruff of the neck and made it her very own.

The endearingly amateurish notes of the past were replaced by clear plastic wallets containing itemised bills, lists, samples from printers, detailed hand-written comments, laminated menus, even photographs. With mounting horror, Beth stared at the evidence. Year on year, the Meet became ever more extravagant and the ticket price ever higher. Marquees. Helium balloons. Dinner jackets. Venetian masks, for heaven's sake. A jazz band. A palm court orchestra. Jugglers. Fire eaters. Beth sank weakly into a chair.

And the food! Lobster. Fresh oysters. Foie gras ravioli. And clearly themed: a Chinese banquet; a Russian Imperial ball with ice sculptures, Samovars and blinis. Becca catalogued exquisite platters of canapés. Plate art in the most rigorous traditions of Nouvelle Cuisine.

Beth forced herself to look at the photographs. There was

Becca. It had obviously become a bit of a tradition to have a picture of her every year with a glass of champagne in one hand, Jacob at her side, about to pull out the winning raffle ticket. Blonde, sleek, supremely self-confident and always dressed in something clingy and sparkly, she looked quietly triumphant as the village worthies buzzed round her. Beth stared at her image with guilty loathing. And Jacob – her Jacob, who so hated getting dressed up for parties, who was so attached to his mud-coloured cords and tweed jackets. What was he doing there in his starched shirt, looking resplendent and gorgeous and proud of his glamorous first wife? It was like looking at a complete stranger. Beth felt sick.

After the year of Becca's death, the records tailed off. It was as though the Meet had died with its chatelaine. And now it was all down to Beth.

'Oh bloody hell!' she moaned. 'Oh bloody, bloody hell.'

Jig-Jag and Flash lifted their heads at the sound of her voice. They had been dozing in their corner in a patch of autumn sunshine, but now untangled their many limbs and pulled themselves up to shake sleepily and noisily. 'Hello, boys,' Beth sighed. 'I'd forgotten about you. Shall we ... well, shall we?'

Even before she said the W-word they started spinning round in circles. What was it with dogs? Beth rose to her feet and said, 'Sit up!' with exactly Jenny's imperious inflection. No effect. She raised her hand in a kind of halt sign over their heads, as Jenny had shown her. 'Sit up!'

Miraculously, incredibly, they both settled their bottoms on the floor, shoving each other slightly as they jockeyed for position, tails wagging like metronomes and expectant doggy grins on their almost identical faces. 'Blimey!' she exclaimed, then remembered herself and rubbed each glossy head enthusiastically. 'Good boys.' She glanced at the clock. She wasn't due to meet Jenny for another twenty minutes, but perhaps she'd go early this time. Get started and maybe do some 'sit and stay'.

She was having some success when Jenny screeched to a halt in the lane that led down to the field, and she sensed the older woman watching as she ordered Flash to sit, then walked away backwards. When she clapped her hands and he came running, she felt absurdly triumphant – until he veered away and zoomed towards Jenny's Volvo with its furry cargo, Jig-Jag hot on his heels. She stamped her foot in frustration and started towards Jenny, who, much to her surprise, was nodding approvingly. 'Well done! Well done! What a pity I distracted them. My fault entirely. You were doing so well.'

Beth felt pathetically cheered. 'Do you really think so? I must admit, I've been finding it better at home. They sulked horribly when I stopped letting them go upstairs, but it's definitely getting easier.'

Jenny smiled benignly. 'Progress indeed. They're actually much happier when they know what's expected of them, and who's boss. It's about time they had a firm hand.'

Beth felt herself bristle slightly. 'Well, Jacob's been far too busy over the last few years, and—'

'Oh, my dear, I know that. The rot set in long before Becca died. She had all kinds of plans to train these two herself. In fact, Jacob never really wanted them. It was all her doing, but she wouldn't let me near them, though I offered. It was just another one of her fads.' Beth felt herself freeze to the spot. It was the first time she had heard anyone make any comment at all about Becca that wasn't one of sheer adoration.

'Really?' she offered non-committally, hoping for more.

'Well, it was scarcely her thing, tramping round fields and shouting herself hoarse. I'm not sure she could cope with the unpredictability. They were more like an accessory, but she soon ran out of enthusiasm and these poor old boys have had to fend for themselves ever since. Jacob doesn't have time, you're perfectly right. But at last someone's taking things in hand. About time too. Right, shall we get on?'

Beth stored away Jenny's comments for later dissection and threw herself into the training session with renewed enthusiasm. An hour later, as they watched the dogs playing, she framed a question.

'Jenny, did you always go to the Mistletoe Meet?'

Jenny snorted. 'Of course I did, everyone did. You were only excused the Mistletoe Meet if you were dead or in prison. I gather they have resurrected it and you've got yourself landed with it.'

'Mmm. Was it always very grand?'

'Charles! Dead! Drop it! Honestly, the things that dog will pick up! What? Grand? Yes, I'm afraid it certainly was. Didn't used to be, but Becca upped the ante, as they say. I told her at the time, I said, "No one's going to want to get trussed up like turkeys on Christmas Eve." But I was wrong, they all did. So it was all black tie and best frocks and each year had to surpass the last. Lot of nonsense, really.'

Later, as they parted, Beth attached the leads, barely noticing how obediently her dogs sat waiting. She waved goodbye distractedly. Although Jenny certainly wouldn't have meant her comments about the Meet as a challenge, Beth couldn't help seeing it that way. Maybe it was time to come out of denial about this wretched party. Maybe it was time to show Milton St David, and the whole world, if necessary, that the new Mrs Layham, dog handler, wife, mass caterer, oh and university lecturer in Renaissance Art had well and truly arrived.

Beth discreetly watched Jacob later on that evening. He was engrossed in reading a pile of documents and seemed to be making heavy weather of it. He kept stopping to rub his eyes and was merely picking at the sandwiches she had placed at his elbow. She shifted uncomfortably. He had lost weight since their marriage but he was looking, she thought, better than ever. Could it be, though, that her lack of skill in the kitchen was leading to his gradual decline? Perhaps she shouldn't have wasted her limited domestic attention researching the right kind of cranberry chutney for Christmas lunch rather than rustling up gourmet meals for him? No doubt Becca would have done both. Beth scowled to herself.

He hadn't even had time to get his thick, rather unruly hair cut and he was pushing it back irritably. It gave him a Byronic air and the slight frown of concentration had brought his dark brows down to shadow his eyes. God, he was handsome. But was he finding it hard to cope, she couldn't stop herself wondering, with a wife who worked as many hours as he did, if not more? She knew Becca had devoted herself heart and soul to furthering his academic career, to raising their children and to providing a comfortable home for their family. Was she letting him down?

'Anything wrong, darling?' Beth started. Jacob was looking at her with an expression of such tenderness and concern. She realised she had been staring into space.

She stood up. 'No, love, nothing at all. Just thinking how much I love you.'

Jacob stretched his arms wide, and she went over to him at the table where he was working. He hugged her tight and she closed her eyes. 'I don't know what I'd do without you. I'm a lucky, lucky man.'

Beth smiled privately, reassured. 'Have you got anything on this weekend? I was wondering if you'd like to go and see that new French film at the Arts Centre.'

Jacob slapped his forehead. 'I knew there was something. I spoke to Holly earlier today. She said she might come down after work on Friday. We haven't seen her for ages.'

'Oh right.' Beth struggled to keep her voice light. Holly – the fly in the ointment, the snake in paradise. And so aptly named – vicious and prickly. Holly was the baggage Jacob had brought to their marriage and so different to her sweet-natured older brother Noel. 'Yes, of course, that would be great. Did she say what time she would be arriving?'

Jacob laughed ruefully. 'Oh, you know Holly. Can't pin her down to a time and a place. She said she'd call closer to the weekend when she's had a moment to firm up her plans.'

Beth stood up. 'Well, do you know if she's planning to bring anyone this time?' Even she could hear the tartness in her voice. Grow up, Beth. 'I mean, it doesn't matter of course. But it just helps if I know how many I'll be feeding and when.' She was still stinging from the last time, when Holly had arrived at half past ten on Friday night with two girlfriends instead of Saturday morning with one, as she had arranged.

Jacob put his glasses back on and picked up his pen again. 'I'll call her tomorrow and try to find out. She's such a little flibbertigibbet. It's rather fun, you know – she's always calling me at work now. Her office seems very relaxed about that sort of thing. She says they don't mind at all.'

Beth forced a smile and walked out of the room.

*

Tim stood in the doorway beside Miss Jeffries, looking out at the playground and scanning the faces of the mums standing chatting to each other, waiting for their children to come out of class. His head came up to Miss Jeffries' waistline and he could hear the swish of her skirt as she moved. Her sweet perfume filled his nostrils and he could hear the ting of her bracelets as she lifted her arm to adjust Zuwena's hairband. It was always skew-whiff.

He knew every bit of Miss Jeffries, because he loved to watch her in class. He knew how she swayed when she wiped the white board clean, and how she flicked her hair over her shoulder as she bent down over his desk. He liked it when she crouched down to help him with a difficult sum and talked quietly to him, and he especially liked it now, in wintertime, when she wore her soft cardigans and she gave him a hug at the end of the day. They weren't as soft as Mummy's cardigans, of course, but he liked them anyway.

'Right there, Timmo? Can you see Granny? Oh there she is, on time as ever. I can just see her pink coat.' Tim could too. He wasn't sure the coat looked quite right on Granny – her cheeks were a bit too rosy red and it had looked far better on Mummy, but for some reason she'd given it to Granny last year because she'd said she liked it.

'Yoo-hoo!' Tim cringed slightly as Granny waved frantically at him, and he felt Miss Jeffries' hand on his back gently encouraging him out of the door.

'Bye, Timmo, see you tomorrow and keep up that great reading.' Tim pushed his way gently through the waiting mothers to be enveloped in Granny's arms. She smelt of cake. Perhaps there would be some waiting at home for tea.

'Now how was your day today, little fella?' Granny refolded the scarf tightly around his neck against the wind, though Tim didn't feel especially cold. Funny how grown-ups always seemed to get cold. 'Let's get home quick. I'm fair perishing out here.' The two of them set off along the road, hands held and heads down, Granny tugging at his arm occasionally when a car drove too close to a puddle in the road. She hated getting splashed. On the odd occasions Mummy collected him and it was raining, she'd usually bring his wellies with her and they'd both wade straight through puddles. It hadn't happened often but she was always in a good mood on those days.

Sitting at the table a bit later, Tim watched Granny bustle about, clearing up his plate – though not before he'd picked up the last of the cake crumbs by pressing his finger down hard on them so they stuck to his fingertip. She always bustled, chatting away, and Tim felt a bit guilty that sometimes he carried on watching the telly while she talked. Most of the time she didn't seem to need an answer though.

Later, over cottage pie, Tim told Granny his good news. 'Guess what? I'm a giftgiver in our One World celebrations.'

'Your One what?'

'You know, Granny, One World. Miss Jeffries says it's when we celebrate the divorcity of our cultures.'

Strangely, Granny threw back her head and laughed. 'Sure and the world's gone stark staring mad. And here was me thinking it was about Our Blessed Lord's birth. Silly me!'

'Gerpal is the hostel keeper. He gets to say a few words.'

Granny poured him some more milk. 'And what does this hostel keeper do then? Give a room to Mohammed?'

'No, Granny. Mohammed's playing in the steel band. He's got to offer the stable to all the little animals.' Granny made a strange snorting noise with her nose.

'And why's that then?' she asked, and she seemed to be trying not to laugh.

'Well, doh? *Obviously* because they can't find anywhere to sleep because the rain forest has been cut down. Miss Jeffries said I'd be better for the giftgiver part though cos I look important when I stand up very straight.' Granny threw up her arms in delight and, putting her hands on his cheeks, kissed him on the forehead.

'Well, if that's not the most important person in the whole story! We'll have to make sure we have the best seats in the house and remember to tell Mum so she can cancel any meetings that day.' Tim suddenly felt very proud and could feel his cheeks getting warm. It wasn't a big part really. He'd wanted Joseph but Greg had got that. Tim was pretty sure that was because he had a loud voice and he was the best at maths – clever people always seemed to get the best jobs to do. Tim wasn't sure yet what lines he'd have to say – Miss Jeffries had said she'd tell them all by half term – but he was going to be the best giftgiver ever. He had butterflies in his tummy at the thought of it.

'And what about Gerard? Who's he going to be?' Granny liked his best friend and sometimes she'd take them both to the park.

'He's got a special part in an extra bit of the play about Divali.' He wobbled his front tooth. It was definitely getting looser now. 'Granny, did Jesus go to India?'

'Sure Jesus is everywhere, darling, and I expect he went there too. Now see what I got us.' She lifted up a big, thick book from the side and plonked it down in front of him. 'I thought maybe we could have a wee peek in there and do a special letter to Father Christmas – that's if he still gets a look-in these days.' The Argos catalogue. Oh heaven. Tim grabbed it eagerly and leafed his way swiftly past the boring stuff – lawn mowers, silly suitcases, phones (though he wouldn't mind one of those) – until he came to the bit he wanted. Pages and pages of toys to pore over. Not the girly stuff obviously, though he did pause slightly over some of the trendy dolls, but it was on the Lego, spy gadgets and Batman cars he feasted his eyes.

As he scanned the pages greedily, he wobbled his loose tooth with his tongue. It had to come out soon, and maybe he could add the money from under his pillow to his pocket money. Then on Saturday he could get some Top Trumps like Jamie's in his class. He could taste the blood in his mouth. It was like the rust on a screw he'd once licked. Funny how Jamie got two pounds for his teeth and he only got one. How did that work then?

'What ya seen that you liked?' Granny came over to him, drying her hands on a tea towel, then she fished out a piece of headed paper from the cupboard, putting it in front of him with a pencil.

'Won't Mum mind if we use her posh paper?'

Granny looked stern. 'Well, and how's Father Christmas supposed to know where you live if you don't have the address at the top?'

Much later, after Granny had kissed him and said Mum would be back before the Sandman came, he lay on his back and looked at the shadows on the ceiling of his room, thrown by the landing light. He wished she was home but she was late again as she often was these days.. He was sure he'd overheard Granny say something about her being 'married to that job,' which was an odd thing to say, when you couldn't really marry a job.

Perhaps, he mused, making a crocodile head out of the shadows, perhaps she'd come home earlier if there was a grown-up to talk to and keep her company. A boyfriend. Tim could feel his eyes getting heavy, but knew he had to put one more thing on his Christmas list on the bedside table and, propping himself up, added it just under where he'd written '3D space projector'.

*

By Friday, it was still apparently impossible to pin Holly down to a day, a time or even a hint of whether she would be bringing just herself or a whole football team. Beth's only consolation was that her cleaner, Mrs Havers, was in a filthy temper too. Mind you, Mrs Havers was always in a filthy temper. Beth had inherited this sturdy little sixty-year-old along with everything else – Becca's legacy. Having run the house alongside Becca for so many years, Mrs Havers was stubbornly resistant to any suggestion of change.

After several pointless run-ins, Beth and Mrs Havers had settled into an uneasy truce, although she seemed uncharacteristically indulgent over Holly's constantly changing plans. 'Poor mite,' she grunted, as she mopped the floor, aiming quite deliberately, it seemed, to splash Beth's best suede ankle boots with bleachy suds. 'She needs her home to come back to so she can be with her father.'

It occurred to Beth that Mrs Havers had never actually

referred to her by name, but would simply address her directly when she needed an answer to something. Jacob, of course, called Mrs Havers 'Ivy' and, naturally, she adored him, clucking over him, as protective as a mother grizzly bear of her cub. Beth was careful never to position herself between them, for fear of a mauling.

By the evening, Beth thought she'd covered every eventuality. The fridge and freezer were full to bursting, the spare rooms had all been made up, and there was always the possibility of the French art film that, surely, even Holly couldn't dismiss with a roll of her over-made-up eyes. Beth felt quietly confident. When Jacob arrived home especially early he looked so pleased and excited that Beth felt quite guilty for her uncharitable thoughts.

'She's not sure what time she'll be getting the train. It all depends on her work, but she said she'd call on her mobile.' Jacob busied himself uncorking a bottle of Bordeaux so it could breathe. 'It sounds as if she's doing very well at this magazine of hers. I'm sure she'll go far. Apparently no one else there has much of an idea. It's odd, though. I can never find her name in it. She did say it was called *Style*, didn't she?'

Beth stirred the casserole, specially chosen to be as tasty if served at ten to midnight as at half past seven. She checked her watch … again. Still no call and Jacob was beginning to look twitchy.

'I hope she's all right,' he fussed. 'Those trains are so unreliable. Perhaps hers has been cancelled. Or perhaps she was too tired to come tonight at all. Well, I'd rather she didn't push herself. Maybe I'll try to call her again. Where's her new number?'

'Another new number? She changes her phone like other people change their socks.' Beth was too late to bite back the words, and Jacob's look of mild reproof only irritated her further.

'She needed one of those hand-held things, you know, to check her emails wherever she is, so we went to have a look last time I was …. Ah! Look she's trying to call us now! What a relief. Where are my car keys?' And he bounded for the door, phone to his ear, leaving Beth silently counting up to ten.

Chapter 4

Mid-October

Only 63 shopping days to go

When you are doing your Christmas shopping, start at the top of a department store and work your way down. That way you won't be carrying heavy parcels up the stairs.

Holly pulled the quilt up over her head to block out the insistent buzz of the alarm clock. Joe stirred sleepily beside her and sat up, shaking his head the way he always did. She felt awful – achy all over. Maybe it was tonsillitis or the start of food poisoning after the weekend at home, more likely. 'I don't think I'll go into work today. I feel shitty. Will you call in for me?'

'No way!' Joe tugged at the covers. 'There's nothing much wrong with you that going self-employed wouldn't cure. God, if I stayed in bed every time I felt like it, I'd make no money at all, and then where would we be? Come on! I'll make you a cup of tea but that's my best offer.'

She groaned and buried herself more deeply in the warm folds. 'Oh I hate being a grown-up,' she moaned. 'It's so much easier when you're a kid. All you need is a note from your mum. Can't you write me one? "Please excuse Holly from work today because she feels a little poorly." Just think – we could stay in bed all day.'

Joe laughed and reached under the covers to pull her close,

running his hand down over her hips. 'I bet you were like that all the time at school.' He pitched his voice to a whiny, lisping falsetto. "Mu-um, don't wanna do swimming. Mu-um, don't wanna do games." Bet you were a right spoilt brat.'

Holly stiffened and felt her throat tighten. She knew he was only mucking about, but it still knocked her sideways, even after four years, other people mentioning her mother. And when she wasn't expecting it. She pulled away and when she looked back at Joe there was a curious expression on his face. Oh crikey, he was going to respond like her previous boyfriend had – running a mile every time she showed any grief. It was so exhausting having to be brave all the time. The usual memories raised by the weekend were making her feel particularly vulnerable, and she blinked hard to stop the tears that were threatening.

But Joe leant over her and gently lifted her hair from her cheek to kiss her eyes. 'I'm sorry, babe. I didn't think.'

'It's OK.'

'Yeah maybe,' he said gently. 'But you don't have to hide it, you know?' Holly looked up at him and seeing his expression of tender concern was too much for her. If he'd been un-interested, she could have controlled it but, unbidden, the tears overflowed down her face and from somewhere wretched sobs burst from her throat. Joe sat up and pulled her into his arms while she wept against his chest, wiping her eyes periodically on the quilt cover. He murmured soothing nonsense, 'It's OK to be sad, I love you,' but she knew that this was more than raw grief that could be assuaged with a hug. There was anger too and a bubble of it filled her throat until it hurt and the words burst from her.

'It was horrible!' Joe looked at her, the venom in her voice taking him by surprise. She rushed on. 'It was like going to a stranger's house. Like a nightmare, when everything's the same but different. It's not my home any more.' She scrubbed at her eyes. 'That woman's changed everything around. And Dad just lets her do it. She's put all these horrible cheap mugs in the kitchen and coloured towels. God, Mum hated those.' She realised how ridiculous this must sound but couldn't stop herself. 'And she leaves her work stuff all over the place – as if anyone's impressed. Daddy looks miserable – like, so thin. And she's even trying to boss the boys around. She doesn't even like dogs. She's been making them stay in the kitchen the whole time, but obviously I let them sleep in my room – *my* room – and she acted really disappointed in front of Dad and said I'd put their training back weeks. It was just so obvious she was trying to get him to side with her, but he wouldn't. Who does she think she is? Fucking cow.'

Joe pushed back her hair and took her face in his hands, staring into her tense, resentful face. 'Wow! I didn't realise it was as bad as that. Do you think your dad is really unhappy?'

'How would I know? I didn't get a second on my own with him. She was around the whole time, so I couldn't even ask how he was feeling.'

'But Holly,' Joe sounded tentative, 'don't you think they might be OK? I mean happy, despite what it seems. He's not stupid, is he? He might have been lonely on his own and he was married to your mum for a long time. It takes time to adjust to people ...'

Holly was up and pacing the room now, clutching a blanket round her chest and kicking shoes out of the way. 'You don't understand. He's not like the man I know. Not like my dad. It's all changed.' And she sniffed, cross with herself for her vulnerability. 'I'd like you to meet him – them – then you'll see what I mean.' She played idly with her hairbrush on the dressing table as she thought. 'I know. I'll make sure I call him at work today. I might even go in early and call before his lectures start.' She started to rummage through her discarded backpack.

A slow smile spread across Joe's face. 'Good idea. I'll give you a lift to the bus on my way to the workshop, if you like. I've got to pick up a load of cherrywood for a cabinet. '

Hopping into her knickers, Holly glanced up at him. 'Yeah, that'd be great. Should miss the rush. Thanks, babe.'

He shook his head in mock amazement. 'Well, you've changed your tune! I thought you didn't want to go in at all today…'

Holly stopped her pacing and shot him a wry look. 'No one likes a smart-arse. Didn't you know that?'

'Not even when they make the tea?' Joe blew her a kiss and backed quickly out of the bedroom before she could retaliate.

*

De dee, de dee— Carol smacked her hand down on the alarm clock on the bedside table as fast as she could, rolled over and groaned. From the blessed Knock itself, the Ave Maria-toned gift was one with which her mother was particularly pleased. It joined a selection of well-meant offerings, including her *pièce de résistance*, a 'disco' Madonna with sparkly halo, which Carol felt obliged to display around the house for fear of offending. There had to be some compromise when her mother had sacrificed her retirement from thirty-five years as a primary school teacher to look after Tim, and being woken by this irritating tinkle was a small price to pay.

She experimented with opening her eyes, then shut them again firmly. The room was still dark, as if in deepest night, illuminated only by the shaft of light from the landing, which Tim insisted stayed on, but Carol knew the reality. Another day had well and truly begun.

Rather than risk falling back into a slumber, she shifted herself upright and sat for a moment on the edge of the bed, resting her elbows on her knees, rubbing her eyes and running her hands through her hair. Years of experience – well, about seven to be exact – and a parenting book she'd once read, had trained her to get out of her bed an hour earlier than the rest of the household, and it was a very precious sixty minutes in which she usually managed to achieve extraordinary levels of organisation, wading through a basketful of ironing, checking school bags, even writing a feature. This morning she wasn't sure she had the energy to turn on the kettle, but knew she had to pay some bills or there would be no electricity to make it boil, or any phone for that matter. As she spotted the pile of laundry neatly ironed and folded in a basket in the spare-room doorway, she smiled and sent a thank-you to her mother across the ether to her little house half a mile away.

A mere ten minutes and two cheques later, she heard a small sound behind her. 'Mum.' Carol turned to see her skinny little son standing in the doorway, his pyjamas a size too big, his fair wavy hair in a fluffy mess and in his hand a little box held open, in the bottom of which was a small front tooth.

'I think the Tooth Fairy forgot to come,' he lisped. Carol's heart gripped with remorse as he said the words and she felt panicked. 'And I even wrote her a letter asking her her name.' He held out a piece of paper on which he'd scrawled his question in his seven-year-old hand, with a funny little picture of a fairy at the bottom, her wings outstretched and her eyes crossed for no apparent reason.

Oh bloody hell. Carol could feel a lump in her throat at her own thoughtlessness. She crouched down and, gathering Tim into her arms, cast about pathetically for an excuse. 'Oh my darling, she was probably busy. You see at this time of year she sometimes has to help Father Christmas and the elves because they are rushed off their tiny feet.' She gently brushed the hair out of his eyes. 'I expect she's got a backlog of teeth to collect and she'll get to you very soon.'

'She came to Daddy's house when I was sleeping there.' Tim's eyes were wide, their lack of censure hitting Carol somewhere under the diaphragm.

'Perhaps she wasn't so busy then. Want to make some pancakes?'

Tim nodded vigorously. 'Did Granny get some eggs, do you know?' Ashamed at herself for such blatant diversionary tactics, Carol opened the fridge and surveyed the contents. Entirely her mother's domain, it was another area of enormous domestic compromise. Judging by yesterday's supermarket haul, Mary still hadn't heeded Carol's beseeching request that she buy only those *bio* yoghurts and *organic* veg.

Carol sighed as she pulled out the 'barn fresh' eggs – battery fresh more like – and got a mixing bowl out of the cupboard. Tim pulled himself up onto a stool beside her, ready to help out.

'Right, you are going to be Top Cat.' She slid the bowl in front of him.

'What?' He looked at her, bemused.

'Chief Whisker.' And she snorted with laughter and elbowed him in the ribs. He gave her that 'whatever' look, which made him look so like his father and, quite clumsily, began to whisk the eggs and flour as Carol poured in the milk. She fished out the frying pan, and began to whistle gently to herself, pleased that she was now achieving some true quality time with her son, and quashing the little voice that reminded her how much she'd planned to do during this precious hour.

'Aren't we having fun?' She smiled at his soft little face, and she poured the mixture into the pan, pulling back her hand quickly as it touched the hot handle. Tim peered over as the batter gathered in a thick clump in the middle of the pan.

'Granny says you have to move the pan quickly to spread it out.' Again he looked wide-eyed at his mother.

'Mmm.' Carol bit her lip, flicked out the squat little attempt at a pancake from the pan with the fish slice and, stamping on the pedal, tipped it smartly into the bin.

Ten minutes later and they had a growing pile of more

successful offerings, and Tim was seated at the table squeezing out his name on one with chocolate ice-cream topping, ignoring his mother's suggestion that the pancakes had plenty of sugar in already and a squeeze of lemon juice would have been enough.

Chill out, Carol, she reprimanded herself, and slid onto the bench next to him with a fresh cup of tea.

'Muum, what are you getting me for Christmas?' he asked, mouth full of pancake. 'Only Granny got us an Argos catalogue and I've marked some pages already.'

'Crikey, Timmo, it's weeks away.'

'Eight weeks and two days actually.'

Carol smiled at the determinedly certain expression on his face. 'Well, if you say so.'

'Will you look at what I've marked later when I go to bed?'

Carol's heart sank. 'Well, actually, darling, I've a meeting later that I really can't miss.'

Tim shrugged and went back to his pancake. 'Whatever.' Then, attempting and failing to suppress a look of disappointment, he leant over and switched on the TV.

'Oh God oh God.' Carol pulled out her Filofax from her bag as the train pulled out of the station an hour later. Is there ever a hope of sloughing off the guilt? Pulling her pen lid off with her teeth, and trying not to elbow the man next to her, she began another list, moving the items from the list on the page before that hadn't been attended to, and adding two fresh items: Argos, Tooth Fairy (underlined firmly). Now she wouldn't forget. Pausing to tap her teeth with the end of the pen, she looked around the carriage.

The girl opposite her was flicking through a glossy mag and Carol could see she was scouring the fashion pages. Her clothes reflected good intentions but a tight budget. Carol looked down at her own ensemble, a suit by an exciting young designer she'd got at a massive discount after London Fashion Week. She had a feeling that the stiff invitations for the new collections might not be hitting her desk next season anyway. Who'd want to invite the editor of a faltering woman's title?

Carol put her head to one side. Faltering schmaltering. She'd make it work. Think positive, girl, she chided, and turned over to a fresh sheet to start sketching out a visual idea she'd had for the contents page.

'Right, Jemima.' Carol breezed past the girl's desk and dumped her bags on the floor of her office, then shrugged off her raincoat. 'Can you chivvy up Emma and ask her how we're getting on with the sex toys feature. Also,' she picked up a letter from her in-tray, 'reply to this girl and tell her if she wants a job, could she at least find out how to spell my name and address it to the right magazine?'

Her kick-arse mood carried on all day. She tried hard not to bark at people, but her tone definitely felt sharp and determined, and she noted with satisfaction that some of her mood was rubbing off on the others in the huge open-plan office.

'Yes, vibrating knickers will be great,' she heard a features assistant say boldly down the phone, which made everyone look up from their desks, 'and we'd like a Rampant Rabbit to try out please too. Can you have them over to our office by tomorrow?'

'I fancy the sound of that one,' snorted someone else, rushing past with an armful of fashion samples.

'You'll have to fight me for it. Dildos at dawn,' guffawed Sheena.

By lunchtime, Carol allowed herself a moment to feel really quite confident. The team seemed to be pulling together and it was as though a breath of fresh air had swept through the office. Carol noted the industry going on around her as she swept to the loo then, looking in the mirror over the basin, she did some practice smiles – a technique she'd been told about by a health writer on *Style*. 'Smile at yourself and it will enhance your chi', but as she did so she realised she wasn't alone. Someone was talking on the phone in one of the cubicles.

'Well I don't know, do I?' The girl's voice was sulky and aggressive. 'It entirely depends on the trains. It's Christmas time, for goodness' sake.' There was a pause. 'Oh God, I don't know that either. There might be a party over at someone's house. Why the bloody hell do you need to know now?' Too shocked to move or turn on the tap to herald her presence, Carol stood stock still, half feeling as though she was eavesdropping, and half mesmerised by this horrible conversation.

'Well, your party's not my bloody problem, is it? You didn't have to agree to do it, did you? Why are you making such a big deal about it anyway? Dad never used to get wound up about it. Just get over yourself, can't you?' Then the voice went quiet. Unsure whether or not to make her presence obvious, Carol was hovering by the basin when the lock on the door was pulled back hard and Holly emerged from the cubicle.

The look of surprise then horror on her face wiped out Carol's own uncertainty. She'd clearly had no idea she was being overheard, least of all by her boss. Collecting herself, and putting her phone back in her jeans pocket, she smiled and shrugged.

'God, some people, hey?' And she went over to wash her hands at the basin next to Carol, who could feel her anger rising. Holly had obviously been talking to her mother, and Carol thought about Mary. Never in the world would she speak to her like that, even if she hadn't been beholden to her for keeping life and soul together at home.

'Well that "some person" must have done something terrible to get a ticking-off like that.'

Holly looked up, uncertain whether to smile or not. 'My stepmother. She's so interfering.' Carol assessed her, this girl with her wavy hair falling around her face, her pretty blue eyes and her stubborn chin, and suddenly felt mad.

'You know, it's none of my business but mothers are usually equipped to deal with their children being rude to them. It's one of those skills that sort of comes with the ability to change nappies or follow Playmobil instructions.' Holly looked quizzical and it was obvious she hadn't a clue what Carol meant. 'But stepmothers? That's a job they haven't thought up a GCSE for yet, and stepmothers need special care. It's the hardest job on the planet. Think about it, Holly.' She gave the girl's arm a gentle pat, pushed through the doors of the loo, and asked herself, where on earth did that wisdom come from?

The week went on in the same positive mood. Even Melanie got a bit skittish at times. The cover mount for the New Year issue was finalised. Georgie had managed to find a rather tasteful sparkly star decoration that would have done *Homes & Gardens* proud. The interview with the soap star had been edited (by Carol) from very boring up to interesting-if-you-are-a-fan – which was the best they could hope for – and as for the sex toys for the 'please your man' feature that came in from the PR companies, they were distributed around the office to shrieks of excitement and consternation, with instructions to have reports back after the weekend.

Carol felt in control and when the phone rang beside her she snatched it up. 'Yup?'

'Crikey, that was abrupt, Mrs Editor. Have you time to speak to someone as lowly as *moi*?' Carol smiled at the teasing from her friend Kate, relieved to hear her voice. 'Just checking that you aren't too busy to have a quick snifter with an old book editor this evening?'

Carol could feel the relief spread through her and let her shoulders drop. 'Oh how lovely to hear from you. Yup, I'll be there. Where are we rendezvous-ing?'

'What about that bar off the King's Road where we met last time?'

Carol smiled, acutely aware of how long ago it had been

since they had last met up and how many times since she'd had to cancel. Kate was one of those friends who was completely there when she was needed, Carol's rock when relationships floundered, yet never complained when work, Tim or last-minute plan changes got in the way. Carol was very aware how much advantage she took. 'Is it still in business?'

'Oh yeah, I went there the other day.' Carol could see Jemima gesticulating at the door and mouthing 'Ian, meeting five mins'.

'Look, Kate love, I've got to go. Big meeting and all.'

''Twas ever thus. Just before you go, Callum is going to meet us later – he's got a late recording session – is that OK?'

Carol was delighted and said so. She very much liked Kate's boyfriend, a rather crumpled sound technician. Then after fixing a time and a very brief exchange, she hung up, grabbed her file and headed for the sixteenth floor.

As the lift ascended she scanned her notes, which she hadn't looked at since yesterday on the tube home. It wasn't the first time a publishing director had called a meeting of the editors of the magazines under his care, and it wasn't the first meeting like it Carol had attended, but it was the first time she'd had to justify herself in front of Ian Cameron and the other three editors in the group, especially since DIY Homes had pulled their advertising. By the time she got to the meeting room, she could see the three of them were already there, sitting at the long table, all lined up down one side so she was forced to take the only available chair opposite them. She knew them all moderately well – they were on 'mwah mwah' terms, and one – the lissom Grianne (to rhyme with Onyer, as in bike) Fogerty – she'd even worked with on *Designer Homes* eight years before. They smiled warmly at her – did she detect a slight hint of sympathy in their smiles? – and adjusted the collars of their shirts or flicked fluff from their cuffs, as Carol settled herself in the seat.

'So what's this all about?' Carol looked over to Grianne, who shuffled the pile of notes in front of her. 'Bit short notice, isn't it?'

'Oh, I think he's probably got the board on his back, or he's just flexing his perfectly toned muscles.' She wrinkled her nose coquettishly. 'Frankly I could do without it. I've got a meeting with Sebastino Graccinelli later about an exclusive shoot.' Carol smiled at her colleague, biting her tongue so she didn't show the faintest hint of jealousy that this woman had managed to pin down this hotter-than-hot designer, even though his famous *décolletée* designs would have outraged the readers of *WM*.

'Anyone got Anya?' whispered Collette van Haddon, the busty private-school blonde who edited a celebrity magazine that prided itself on being several rungs further up the quality ladder than the other titles, and whose circulation matched her enormous salary.

Carol snorted as, she was relieved to hear, did the others. 'Fat chance,' Grianne moaned. 'She vants to be alone and she's not talking to anyone, though God knows we've tried her management, her agent … I've even thought of bribing her hairdresser.'

'Who, who?' Ian swept in fragrantly and slammed down his folder and a pile of titles rather too loudly at the head of the table. Grianne explained about the fêted Scouse pop legend's presence in town.

'Of course. She's staying at the Lanesborough I gather. Which one of you girls has got the interview?'

Amongst muttering of 'dream on', Ian spread out his papers. 'Shame. Right now, ladies.' Carol cringed at his superior tone. 'Sorry to ask you up here, but I think it would be constructive to have a re-cap, if you like, of all the titles – where you are heading and what you have in the pipeline. Think of it as a keep-us-all-on-our-toes exercise if you will.' Then he sat back in his chair, rested one perfectly shod foot on his knee and, steepling his fingers, prepared to listen to each one in turn.

Whether by coincidence or design Carol went last and, by the time she had listened to the plans laid out by Collette, Grianne and Naomi, whose high-fashion title sold over 350,000 a month on reputation alone, she felt that her good mood balloon had been utterly deflated. She eventually got to her feet, feeling the sweat pricking under her armpits and aware suddenly that she was fighting for the life of *WM*. She made a conscious effort to drop her shoulders as the others looked up expectantly at her, their own presentations complete and their files closed in front of them. Out of the corner of her eye she could see Ian looking at his watch.

'*WM*,' she said boldly, lifting her chin, and ignoring her notes, 'is a bit like a woman approaching the menopause.' Grianne raised her eyebrows at this unconventional start but Carol persevered. 'She knows that she can't keep up with younger woman, that she'll look ridiculous in jeans and a crop top. Even loose, floaty Missoni will show her bingo wings. She can't be bothered with the latest indie pop, and she really hasn't a clue who Wayne Rooney is, let alone who he's sleeping with. She's taken a bit of time to get used to the odd wrinkle in the mirror that doesn't disappear when she stops smiling and, like our circulation, has felt the odd ache and pain that wasn't there before. ' By this point Grianne's eyebrows were up by her hairline and Collette's weren't far behind.

'But the thing about the *WM* woman is that she couldn't care less. She has the confidence to know what she likes, to be comfortable with her life, to be interested in big and intelligent issues. She wants to read about treatments for varicose veins, sprays for rose aphids and is quite happy to admit that she sings along quite loudly to Eva Cassidy and Dolly Parton CDs in the car.' Ian shifted his position in his seat, and Carol, feeling uneasy, found herself speaking more emphatically still.

'She's not afraid of problems, and knows that floaty wedding pics in weekly celeb titles are false and unrealistic. The *WM* woman has no illusions about the death of romance, but she does want to know how to keep her husband or partner or lover happy in bed.' Naomi slid a look at Collette, which Carol read as supportive and felt encouraged. She went on to outline some of the ideas coming up – the countdown to Christmas feature, the soap star interview, the sex toys tried-and-tested, beefing each one up with a sales pitch that surprised even her. 'So that's where we are heading,' she concluded. 'To reflect the varied, wonderful interests of the *WM* woman, who's grown up and proud of it.'

There was silence. Carol looked at the faces of the three women in front of her, a broad grin on her face, and watched as Grianne put her hands together in a silent clap, her eyes twinkling. Feeling shored up now, Carol turned to Ian for approbation. But the smile froze on her face. His expression told her everything. *WM* was, as far as he was concerned, not about change of life. It was end of life.

He clapped his hands together. 'Thank you, ladies. Very interesting and in many ways very positive. I'll see you all tomorrow, and er, Carol, can you just give me a moment.'

Ten minutes later she was following the others down in the lift. Ian hadn't said 'it's over' in so many words, but he'd not left much room for misunderstanding. 'Carol, it's dire. The competition is too great. Other titles have the best writers, top designers, exclusive scoops. For all your brave talk about confident women who are happy to weed their gardens and bake cakes, we are losing circulation with every issue and I can't justify maintaining *WM* to the board.'

So why the hell, thought Carol, her face reddening with anger, had he talked her away from the lovely haven that was *Style* to help this limping invalid into its grave. 'Is that it then?' she'd said curtly.

He puts his hands in the pockets of his beautifully tailored trousers and looked down at the floor for a moment. 'Unless you can pull something quite extraordinary out of the hat, Carol, I'm afraid it is. You've got till Christmas, then we're pulling it.'

The office was empty when she walked back onto the editorial floor, except for a cleaner, picking up screwed-up paper that had been lobbed at the bin and missed. She slammed her file on her desk. Fuck you, Ian Cameron. You're not pushing us overboard yet. You want the best writers, I'll get you the best writers and I'll blow the whole measly budget to get them. And she tried Lisa Fairley's number yet again.

'Lisa? It's Carol here. How are you?' Though her by-line was in all the major papers and magazines, not least *Style* where Carol had commissioned her many times, Lisa was friendly and unpretentious and Carol liked her.

'Still tied to my keyboard of course, but just finishing a nice interview with the PM's wife for *The Times*. How's things with you?'

'Fine thanks.' They exchanged news, then, 'I wondered if you'd be interested in doing a feature for me?'

There was a pause. 'But I thought … are you still on *Style* then?'

'No *WM* – you know. All very exciting. Lots of ideas. Going to jazz it up no end. I was thinking about something on domestic violence. The middle-class taboo. Do you remember that minister's daughter who said he'd beaten her as a child?'

'Er, Carol, sorry. I really can't.'

Carol was bewildered by her abruptness. 'Oh I thought … I can give you a month to six weeks if that helps?'

'It's not the time. I just really, well, I just don't want my name in a magazine like that. No offence or anything … but it's too fuddy-duddy.' She paused than gabbled on into Carol's silence. 'I'm sure you'll lick it into shape, and do get in touch again, won't you? But just at the moment … I hope you can understand.'

They exchanged a couple of pleasantries, then Carol put down the phone. Was that really people's perception of *WM*? Fuddy-duddy? She tapped her pencil against her teeth. It would take too long to turn round opinion, especially with a title as staid and unwieldy as this. It was a cruise liner indeed, and not even a luxury one at that. And time was something she didn't have.

In the taxi to the King's Road, late now to meet Kate, she called home and tried to sound upbeat with Tim about Cubs, aware that she'd never yet managed to take him to a session herself, and listened to the woeful tale of his scabby knee. 'And, Mum,' he lisped, 'Granny says if I put my tooth under the pillow again the Tooth Fairy might come tonight.' Signing off and kissing him goodnight down the phone, she tried unsuccessfully to dislodge the knot of guilt from her chest by triple underlining 'Tooth Fairy' in her Filofax. In her heart though she felt wretched and despondent. She should have cancelled tonight's drink, but if she did it again that would probably be the end of any friendships she had left.

'Smile, it may never happen,' Kate greeted her warmly and thrust a glass of red wine into her hand as she sat at the table. The bar was busy, with lots of young couples in groups shadow boxing around each other, self-consciously nonchalant. Carol felt too dressed-for-the-office, but no one seemed to be looking towards them – another downside of getting older that no one bothers to tell you about. Kate had chosen a table in the corner away from the other punters.

'I'm so sorry I'm late.' Carol took a slug of her wine even before she had shaken off her coat. 'And now I feel horribly over-dressed. I'd forgotten the rules for these kind of places. We all have to look studied and casually casual, don't we? Oh God,' she wailed. 'Is it just me or are the young getting younger? That lot over there seem so carefree and relaxed in their designer casual. Have the mating rules changed and no one told me?'

Kate put her hand over Carol's. 'Luckily the rules never change. It doesn't matter whether your are wearing Prada or Primark, if he don't give you that buzz, then it's a non-starter.'

Carol snorted. 'Crikey, I can't remember what that buzz felt like. Will I notice it if it happens?'

'Unmissable, old love. How's life on Menopause Monthly?'

Under the gentle cajoling of her friend, Carol told her about the day, about the Tooth Fairy and Ian and the final insult, Lisa's rejection. As always Kate was frank and sensible. Even though she came from the book publishing world, she understood the way magazines worked and made the right noises to reassure Carol, between her rants, anger outbursts and despair, that her career had not hit the skids and that she did have a future, was not the worst mother in the world and would not end up sad, lonely, bitter and sexually frustrated.

'Look at you, woman, in your Giovanni St Laurent Versace number.' She peered over her D&G specs, her only concession to anything faintly trendy. With her soft, round figure and dimpled face, Kate had no interest at all in her appearance, and Carol had teased her for years about her ability to cobble together the most unlikely clothes combinations with no success whatsoever. 'You are clever, beautiful and witty. I'd give anything to look as stylish as you.'

'Liar,' Carol laughed.

'Well OK, forget the fashion, but at least your hair is straight and sleek, unlike mine, and you can wear a size eight.'

'Mmm.' Carol had another sip of her second glass of wine, and tucked her hair behind her ear. 'You don't need that when you've got a great bloke who worships you and you get to shag a lot.'

'Who's shagging?' Turning at this new voice, Carol felt a hand on her arm, then Callum leant down and kissed her, his stubble rubbing against her cheek and his skin smelling faintly grubby. He'd clearly had a very long day. 'You look as gorgeous as ever.' Then he leant over the table and kissed his girlfriend on the lips. 'You too of course.'

Carol looked warmly at this big man in his jeans and battered leather jacket, his hair all rumpled and his face creased from a lifetime of smiling.

Kate patted the chair beside her. 'We are, darling. Now, come here and tell us about your busy day twiddling knobs, then I'll get you a drink.'

'Already sorted.' Callum pulled out one of the chairs. 'Nick's getting them in. He was at the session and by the end we both needed a beer. Christ, that band are such prima donnas.' He ran his hands through his hair until it stuck out at even more bizarre angles. 'I think I spent more time picking up dummies that had been thrown out of prams than recording, and what they know about playing music would fit on the back of a mini-CD. If it hadn't been for Nick, they'd have been stuffed. Oh fantastic!' And he put out his hand to receive a pint of beer handed to him from behind Carol.

'Get stuck into that,' said a deep voice.

'Thanks. Have a seat, mate. Kate, you know Nick obviously. Nick, this is Carol, our only glamorous and successful friend.'

Carol twisted round to meet the arm that had delivered the drinks, and put out her hand in greeting. The angle was awkward and she couldn't see his face properly. He shook her hand briefly but firmly, then moved round to her other side to take the chair next to her and opposite Callum.

'You two are all right Jack. What about us?' laughed Kate, placing her empty glass ostentatiously on her head.

'OK OK, I'll get them.' Callum made a big deal of clambering to his feet from his slumped position. 'Lambrusco for both of you?' He lumbered off with Kate calling, 'Nothing less than Pinot Grigio, you cheapskate,' to his receding back.

'Lazy git,' she laughed affectionately, and turned to Nick. 'I gather today was a trial.' Nick took a sip of beer and licked off the moustache of froth from his lip, put the glass down on the table and, like Callum, ran his hands through his hair in a gesture of fatigue. Carol was aware she was staring but was held in fascination as the wavy dark brown hair fell back into place. She'd always been a bit suspicious of men with hair longer than hers – it reminded her too much of Status Quo – but on this man, with his strong face, and brown twinkly eyes that looked at her rather too directly now, it seemed to work. He too shook off his brown leather jacket, and pulled up the sleeves of a black T-shirt.

'I must be getting old. That band were practically in nappies.' Nick raised his eyes skyward. Kate leant over towards Carol to explain.

'Nick's a session musician. In fact, he's so in demand that they queue up for him, but he plays hard to get, don't you, sweetie?' Nick laughed, a sort of cynical humph from the throat, and had another sip from his pint. 'He could be playing all over the world, but your baby keeps you here, doesn't he?' Carol was rather surprised at the disappointment that she felt. After all he was bound to be married or hitched up – he looked about the right age – and they usually were.

'What do you play?' She wasn't entirely sure she knew what a session musician *was*, but thought she'd use the old journalist's technique: if you suddenly realise there's a big hole in your knowledge, ask some vague question and hope to God the interviewee fills you in with the missing information themselves.

'Lead guitar.'

'Oh.' She tried not to look blank, and he smiled at her, sympathetically.

'I'm like a guitar for hire. I get called up when bands or solo artists need back-up, or they're putting together an album or going on tour.' Carol was way out of her milieu.

'It sounds very glamorous. Have you worked with anyone famous?'

Nick shrugged. 'It's a pretty dire existence actually. Session players are treated like shit most of the time.'

'Oh come on,' Kate butted in. 'Carol, don't believe a word of it. Nick has worked with the best.' And she reeled off a list of bands and some solo artists that Carol had heard of. She even had a couple of their albums. Nick shrugged modestly.

'I don't usually work with kids like today's lot any more though, but they were paying enough so why not?'

Callum came back with two large glasses of wine. Slow down, girl, Carol warned herself. She'd had nothing to eat since lunch, and that had been only a small packet of Doritos. The chat turned back to the session, and Kate soon had both men regaling them with stories about other tricky singers, one of whom had fined her backing band for looking at her face during a recording. 'Her arse was far preferable to look at anyway,' laughed Callum, and Carol was aware Nick was looking her way as she faked consternation.

'Who's in town at the moment?' Kate asked. 'Anyone we know?' Callum frowned in thought and looked over at Nick.

'Not sure, are you, mate? Couple of indie bands doing the rounds, and the delicious Anya obviously. You'd have to have been on another planet if you hadn't noticed she's in town.'

'Oh that would explain the traffic hold-ups earlier,' said Kate. 'Her and her cavalcade. You've worked with her, haven't you? Is she really as beautiful in the flesh?'

'Yup,' Nick said emphatically, 'utterly gorgeous. Always has been. I was with her on her very first album.'

They all chatted on in a comfortable way, Nick asking her what she did, and Carol found herself playing it down, in that stupid English way, and talking more about *Style* because she knew he'd have heard of it – everyone had – than about *WM*, which she was sure he hadn't. And which, as she'd been reliably told this evening, was fuddy-duddy. He leant forward to quiz her, resting his elbows on his knees, and Carol found herself enjoying talking to him. As Callum and Kate started a domestic between themselves about the weekend, Nick carried on drawing her out about press launches and features she'd commissioned or written. She vaguely mentioned one she'd done a while back with a Shakespearian actor who'd made it big in Hollywood.

'Yeah,' he nodded enthusiastically, 'I read that one. And you wrote it? Fantastic! Was he as interesting as you made him sound?'

'Mmm,' Carol giggled tipsily, 'and utterly gorgeous!'

'What are you doing at Christmas, Carol?' Kate interrupted. 'Is Tim with you this time?' Thanks, Kate, thought Carol. Reveal me as a single mum and desperate. She explained how Paul was seeing him after the festivities and, aware Nick was listening, told Kate about her plans for a country-cottage Christmas, playing it up as though she'd lined up the most perfect festive celebrations ever. Why she wanted to sound busy and organised in front of this man she'd barely met, she wasn't quite ready to explore, especially as she hadn't even thought about Christmas since early September. Kate then spoilt it all by revealing that she and Callum were blowing everything and heading off for Antigua. Carol groaned.

'Well, if you lot will saddle yourself with offspring, what can you expect?' Carol knew that all Kate's talk was bravado. She'd have loved kids, but after two ectopic pregnancies and complications later, it wasn't to be. 'Nicko, are you tied by your little bugger too?'

'Big bugger you mean. He's nearly as tall as me. Not sure what the plans are. Kirsty will have it all under control I'm sure. She—' Whatever he was about to say was cut short by the arrival of a very effusive friend of Callum's who lunged over to their table, pulled up a chair and proceeded to dominate the conversation for the next fifteen minutes. Refusing another drink, Carol looked at her watch.

'Oh God I'd better be off,' she muttered guiltily, thinking about her mother. 'I'll be murdered,' and she began to gather up her things frantically.

'How far have you got to go?' Nick's question surprised her.

'Oh, only just south of the river. Off Battersea Park Road.' She watched as he pushed back his chair.

'Want to share a cab? I'm in Tooting.'

She sat as far against the side of the taxi as she could, suddenly shy away from the crowd in the bar and the safety of Kate and Callum. Kate's broad wink as they left hadn't helped either. The lights of the street lamps and shops they passed flashed across their faces, made even brighter as they reflected the rain on the pavements. They sat for a few moments in an excruciating silence. Carol looked resolutely out of the window.

'Makes you realise how much Kate talks, doesn't it?'

At this Carol turned to look at him. His arm was on the rest under the window, his chin resting in his hand. He was smiling at her, and she realised he was as tongue-tied as she was.

Carol smiled. 'When we were at college, she'd hold the whole pub in her thrall and some nights I realised I hadn't said a word!' There was a pause. 'Sorry. I've had a crap day too and I'm just tired.'

'What happened?' It didn't sound like an idle question, so she found herself outlining very sketchily the meeting with Ian.

'It's a bit of a tall order to turn a magazine around so quickly, and my publishing director makes Attila the Hun look like a pushover.' She didn't mean to sigh quite so deeply. 'I'm going to have to pull a bloody enormous rabbit out of the hat.' She leant forward. 'Anywhere here on the left please.' The cab driver pulled over, and Carol ripped open the door and climbed out. Nick leant out to hold it open for her.

'Night, Carol.' They both looked at each other for a moment. 'Great to meet you and good luck.'

She waved as the taxi drove away, and any feelings of anything disappeared as her mother bombarded her with news of Tim's day, the evening, his homework, even before she had dropped her bags in the hallway.

'And,' she finished, 'the phone seems to have gone dead. You did pay that red bill, didn't you?'

As she crawled into bed half an hour later, having kissed her sleeping son's forehead, she had a nagging feeling there was something else she'd forgotten. Her last thought before dropping off, however, was something Kate had said about it not mattering what you wear, so long as you feel 'that buzz'.

Her clock said three twenty-seven when she woke suddenly and, remembering, clambered out of bed to put a fiver, all she had, under Tim's sleeping head.

Chapter 5

Only 50 shopping days to go

*When making pastry for mince pies, keep a couple of
freezer bags close by to slip over your hands in case the
phone rings or the doorbell goes.*

'So that's definite then? You'll be here on the twenty-third?
That's great. Your dad will be so pleased when I tell him. Yeah,
you too ... Speak soon ... Bye ... Bye.'

Beth replaced the receiver with a sigh of pleasure. Now
that was how it should be. She searched down her long hand-
written list headed 'Things I have to do bloody sharpish' and
crossed off 'Call Noel re: Xmas'. Maybe she wasn't a terminally
crap stepmother after all, though Jacob's son made it a doddle.
She walked back into the kitchen, smiling to herself and
washed her hands again. Back to the pastry. Surely a woman
of her intelligence couldn't be beaten by a lump of flour and
butter?

She couldn't take all the credit though. Holly and her brother
couldn't be more different. Where Holly was sharp and critical,
Noel was funny and thoughtful. Where Holly was grasping
and lazy, Noel was self-sufficient and hard-working. She had
got on with him from their very first meeting. Tall, like his
father, with a gentle self-conscious sense of humour, he would
probably age to be just like Jacob: considerate of everyone
else's interests and goals. Perhaps, Beth smiled to herself, he'd
been forged by the flames of derision at school because of his,

then, soppy name. But since Oasis burst onto the scene, Noel Layham had enjoyed an increased prestige.

So she'd scored fifty per cent in the steppie stakes, at least – enough for a pass by today's lamentable exam standards. It was a better result than she'd had when she'd tentatively called Holly with a view to meeting her for coffee on her next visit to London. Barely covering up her incredulity she'd come up with an abrupt 'I've got a thing on that day' and it wasn't until afterwards Beth realised she hadn't even mentioned a date.

Now Beth thumped the dough onto the floured worktop and slapped her hand down hard on its blameless surface before setting about it with the rolling pin.

The weekend with Holly, for example, had knocked Beth for six completely. From the moment she had climbed out of Jabob's car things had been tense, what had been worse had been his pained expression, when Beth had dared to comment on Holly's late arrival.

'Never mind, here now,' he'd dismissed her blurted barb, reaching onto the back seat for the overnight bag. 'Come in out of the cold and let's get my little girl a drink.' Holly had darted Beth a smug little look as she'd passed her in the doorway, continuing the conversation they'd clearly been having in the car.

That had set the tone for the next two days. Beth had had to keep her fury to herself when Holly had managed, with glances, rolled eyes, scowls, smirks, tuts and heavy sighs to make Beth feel inadequate and interfering, demanding and negligent all at the same time. She seemed to relish the power of the familiarity she had with the house, telling her father with glee where the radiator key was when he'd asked a clueless Beth. Every possible moment she seemed to point out changes to the place with a slightly reproachful air that had Jacob rushing to placate. 'Oh, you've moved that picture Mummy loved so much,' prompted him to stumble over an explanation about decorators, when Beth knew the truth was the picture had belonged to *his* mother, and he hadn't been that keen anyway.

Picking up the ball of pastry, she slammed it down on the work surface and picked up the rolling pin again. Becca's rolling pin, as Holly had been at pains to point out. As the weekend progressed, Holly had hung on Jacob's every word, exclaiming that he was getting too thin, that he was looking tired. She'd insisted on preparing his Scotch and water for him, toyed with Beth's cooking, feeding tit bits to the dogs and leaving the rest, saying she wasn't really hungry then, straight afterwards, devouring the bread and pâté Beth had allocated for the following night's supper. Oh yes – and she'd sweet-talked Jacob out of fifty quid too. And he just sat there and indulged her. At least Holly was back in London for now, and still utterly refusing to divulge her plans for Christmas.

Damn – she'd rolled the pastry too thin. She gathered it all in again, pummelling it with her knuckles. Just for now, Beth would have to put Holly out of her thoughts. Pure self-preservation, mainly. But Beth had also noticed an entirely new, waspish tone to her own voice every time the bloody girl cropped up in conversation. To prevent that defensive look stealing over Jacob's features, she would have to avoid talking about her altogether.

Again with the rolling pin. She dipped her hand in the flour and dusted the work surface, pushing away her hair with the back of her floury wrist. Oh it was warm in the kitchen. She had no desire to get into a showdown with Holly, of course. But she wasn't at all sure Holly felt the same. And if Holly forced the issue – refused to come home while Beth was there – what would she and Jacob do? Would it come down to him having to make a choice? Holly had been his daughter for twenty-four years, after all, while Beth and he had known each other a scant two.

The bloody pastry had stuck to the rolling pin – again. Beth stared at it in disbelief for a moment, then scraped it up and hurled it at the wall, followed, in rapid succession, by the recipe book and the rolling pin.

Ten minutes later, she was sitting on the swing outside in the garden, a mug of strong coffee in hand, in a pool of low-slanting sunshine. As she allowed herself to swing slowly back and forth, her feet grazing the packed soil where the grass was still reluctant to grow, she thought about those last two years and how she had spent them with Jacob.

When they'd met on her first day teaching at the university she'd been dating Karl, a tricky commitment-phobic curator from a museum in Stuttgart. But she'd immediately admired Jacob's wit, erudition, dry humour and, gradually, she came to look forward to their conversations over coffee in the college common room. She began to admire his angular, long-legged frame, the good-humoured wrinkles round his eyes, the way he gesticulated with his spectacles to emphasise a point. Karl seemed so immature by comparison. Jacob was steady and calm, like a deep river. He had a directness that often wrong-footed her, and a wicked sense of humour, but it didn't occur to her that anything could possibly develop between them. He was so much older, after all, and everyone had told her about the death of his wife.

Certainly, he never came on to her. And yet she gradually found that she wanted him to. He filled her thoughts, waking and sleeping, but it seemed impossible and inappropriate to let him know. The rules that existed between men and women of her peer group didn't seem to apply with Jacob.

The catalyst had been telling him she'd broken up with Karl – he'd moved delicately but swiftly. They went to New York for the weekend – under the lame excuse that they both wanted to visit MoMA. And that was that. Away from their familiar surroundings anything had seemed possible, and Jacob had been so at home, so in control, Beth was ready to abandon her normal caution. The fact that he had cried the first time they made love – the first time he'd done it with any other woman since he'd married Becca – had immediately made it momentous and significant. Their relationship soon became all-consuming for them both. It was like opening the emotional floodgates. His conviction, within weeks that, of course, they would marry had felt like the most natural thing in the world. She'd left her flat in Oxford and moved in to this house with nothing except all-consuming love and the conviction everything would be fine. She'd never had to conceal her feelings from Jacob, never had to lie to him, and she'd just put his reticence about discussing Becca down to grief and the past.

But his past had now become her present. She'd been stupid and naïve. Becca wasn't going to go away just because she was dead. Holly would make sure of that.

Beth stilled the swing and stood up. She had things to do. Christmas and stepdaughter issues may be coming but the Mistletoe Meet was coming first. She walked back into the steamy kitchen, flipped open the file and reluctantly consulted her list again. She'd clipped it in the very front of the folder that had now become her torment. She kept it, along with her ever-growing Christmas stash, under the stairs. Fortunately, it was somewhere Jacob never seemed to look.

Her heart sank. She couldn't face all this right now. She glanced at her watch, relieved to see it was time for her regular meeting with Jenny. She smiled in anticipation, gathered together everything she needed and called the boys effortlessly. At least something was going right.

Down in the field, Jenny was already waiting. There was a low mist pearling the tussocks of grass and her breath hung in the still air. It was very quiet. Bundled up in layers, with a disreputable tweed hat pulled firmly on, Jenny still managed to look patrician. With posture like hers, it was probably impossible not to. She was using an ancient tennis racket to fire tatty tennis balls into the mist for the dogs to retrieve in turn.

'I'm stiff as a board today. I got thoroughly cold in the beaters' wagon waiting for the guns to finish their lunch yesterday. And afterwards they hardly shot a thing. Corporate types.' Her scorn couldn't have been more apparent. 'Still, I got a few brace for my troubles. Thought you and Jacob might like one. We often have them on Boxing Day – beats cold turkey!'

Beth sent Jig-Jag off, pointing him into the mist in what she hoped was the right direction. 'Boxing Day! I can't manage to think past Christmas Day itself.' She knew she sounded fed-up. 'It's strange – all this build-up to a single day – and then it's over.'

Jenny laughed shortly and served again. 'It's worse than ever these days. No sooner are the summer holidays over than the Christmas cards and decorations are in the supermarkets. It wasn't always like that, though. We had a bit more breathing space then. When my children were small, the build-up to Christmas started when they opened the first window on their advent calendar and not a moment before. None of your chocolate nonsense either, with cartoon characters. Ah well!' She volleyed another ball into the mist. 'Presumably you'll be doing the usual turkey routine?'

'Good boy, well done.' Beth mentally checked her lists. 'Yes, turkey on the day. I'm getting one from the supermarket in town. I've got it on order.'

Jenny raised her eyebrows sceptically.

Beth could feel herself tense up. Perhaps this was not the right thing to have done. Perhaps Becca would have done otherwise. 'What? Aren't they any good?'

'Well,' Jenny mused, 'I always get ours from a farm near Cirencester. They've got bronzes there, organically raised too. You can actually go and see the blessed things running around. Choose your own.'

Beth couldn't hide her interest and Jenny was quick to pick up on it. 'Why don't you come with me? I'll be going down soon. We could take the dogs. What do you think?'

Beth smiled broadly. 'Yes, I'd like that very much. Can I treat you to lunch on the way, perhaps?'

Jenny laughed and sent another tennis ball sailing through the air. 'Oh don't worry about that. If we start good and early, we'll be back by lunchtime. So who've you got coming for Christmas, then? Are the children coming this year? Or will it just be you and Jacob?'

'We-e-ll, Noel's coming the day before the Meet and he's bringing his girlfriend – we haven't met her yet so it'll be rather interesting. Not sure about Holly. She doesn't seem to have her diary sorted out yet.' Beth was secretly pleased with her diplomacy.

Jenny snorted. 'Oh you do surprise me!' The heavy sarcasm made Beth look up. 'She's been pulling that stunt for years – won't commit to anything until the last moment. I don't know how Jacob puts up with it. I'd have given her a good slap ages ago, if I'd been him. But she'll turn up, so you'd better cater for her.' Jenny turned to Beth and peeped over the top of her gold-rimmed spectacles, a cynical and rather mischievous half-smile on her face. 'After all, Christmas is all about presents, isn't it? Holly will be there all right. At the front of the queue.'

Jenny's comments kept Beth warm on the brisk walk home, where she changed, took out her folder again, got on with a few more phone calls and made a new list of all the lists she would have to make.

She'd bought every woman's magazine for November to crib their festive ideas (but did pass up on *Living in Spain*, which she didn't think would be helpful). She'd found a new best friend. Her name was Martha Stewart and Beth had stumbled across her on the internet and pored over her site for hours.

She might be a goddess with feet of clay but she was still the doyenne of effortless perfection. A good party theme seemed to be the message but Beth was at a loss to think of one. Every idea she came up with, Becca seemed to have done already. The budget for the 'do', revealed in Irene's notes, was astonishingly large, assuming the tickets sold. The generosity of the affluent inhabitants of Milton St David would give her a relatively free reign financially, so she'd toyed with a Moroccan tent idea, inspired by the *Sunday Times Style* section. But of course Becca had done it already, complete with kelims on the ground, meze and mint tea. She was beginning to get desperate. Was there time to sculpt an ice palace with drinks served by nymphs in fur bikinis?

Yet days were passing and bookings had to be made. So far, Beth had sorted the marquee, the portable loos, jugglers, a chocolate fountain, arranged for wine with the meal (yet to be decided), and even swallowed her pride and booked the same up-market caterers from Abingdon that Becca had used. The rather camp proprietor, who had come to see her for a planning meeting, was pleased to be invited back after the lean years since Becca's death, and had left her with reams of menu selectors, each more bewildering than the last. It was fine as far as it went, but it all seemed a bit random.

She couldn't really say she felt on top of things, especially with college issues stacking up on her desk, but if she could pull this off – and she was bloody well determined she would – she could prove that she was more than just a blue stocking, equal to Becca's graceful social skills and more than a match for Holly.

*

Waiting for Christmas, Tim had decided, was far worse than waiting for your birthday. That was bad enough, especially when everyone else in his class was going to be eight in the next few months when he had to wait until next July. But with Christmas, it all seemed to go on for ever. Like a grown-up telling you that you can have a large bar of chocolate, then saying you'll have to wait weeks and weeks before you get it.

His best friend Gerard was pretty confident that he was getting a remote-controlled car and Luke has asked for a gigantic Lego kit, but thought it might be too much for Father Christmas to bring and probably too expensive for his mum. Tim knew Luke did have a daddy but Luke didn't mention him much. Perhaps he lived far away or didn't have a good job. Perhaps he had no job at all. Tim knew there were people who didn't. Some of them lived on the streets, and they often had thin, sad-looking dogs asleep beside them. Perhaps Luke's dad lived like that and had a sad dog.

Tim turned to his mum in the driver's seat beside him. 'Does Dad help you with money? I mean would you be able to afford a Lego kit?'

His mum laughed but not in a nasty way like adults sometimes do when you say something they think is silly. 'Yes Daddy does give me some money, just so we can share the enormous cost of feeding you and getting you new clothes,' and she squeezed his leg when she said 'enormous' so he knew she was kidding, 'and yes, I could afford a Lego model, but not one like the huge things at Legoland I don't suppose. Why? What did you have in mind?'

'Oh nothing.' But he found himself telling her about what Luke had said.

'Well, I don't know him but perhaps Luke's daddy can't help out much with money. I know Daddy and I don't live together, but you are a lucky boy in that we can get you nice things, aren't you?' Tim wasn't sure what he felt about this. He could only very vaguely remember a time when his dad did live with them – he must have been only just three when he left – and they'd never been married anyway so it didn't count. Granny was no

83

help with information because she always changed the subject whenever he tried to ask, and muttered something about 'living in Sin'. But Tim didn't remember ever living there.

To Tim, Dad was the Wimbledon house and Mum was the Battersea one, which was where all his things were – though he did keep a few special things in Wimbledon too. He liked that house because it was odd and interesting. Dad did something with art and making adverts and there were always funny pictures around. Eve, Dad's girlfriend, always seemed to be working on something with pictures too because she ran a gallery and sometimes had pictures stacked up around the house that she was preparing for exhibitions.

Tim liked Eve. She wore loose skirts that almost came to the floor – completely unlike mum who had to wear neat suits to work – and had wide hazel eyes the colour of nuts – not like Mum's either, which were a greeny blue. Eve's skin was freckly. Mum only seemed to get freckles on holiday, but the rest of the year her face was soft and pink. Tim was never sure if he should compare the two of them and he didn't mean to in a bad way, but they were so different he couldn't really imagine how his dad could have lived with two such different women.

'Eve is pretty, isn't she?' he asked his mum now, though she seemed to be concentrating on squeezing the car between another car and a van that had wedged itself up on the pavement of the narrow street.

'Uh? Yes, I suppose she is.' Mum didn't seem to be listening. Tim wasn't sure either if this was the right thing to be asking his mother and decided to change the subject when she said suddenly, 'Do you like being with her, Timmo?'

Tim had a feeling he had to be careful how he answered this one. 'Mmm, it can be fun shopping with her sometimes and she likes going to the playground.' He thought this was a good bet as he knew this was something his mum did not enjoy.

'Oh. Oh right,' she said now, still looking straight ahead.

'But,' he hurried on, 'not nearly as much as I love doing things with you,' and she looked at him this time, rather dangerously ignoring the traffic, and put her hand against his cheek.

He went back to gazing out of the window at the rain, watching the people looking in shop windows or waiting to cross the road. The pavements seemed to sparkle and he could see the fuzzy reflections from the shops in them.

'Do you think it will snow at Christmas?' He hugged his knees up under his chin, and rested his head on the safety belt where it crossed his shoulder.

'It might, but I wouldn't raise your hopes. I can only remember about one white Christmas in my whole lifetime.' Mum had pulled over on a double yellow line and was reaching for her bag. 'Now listen, I'm going to fly into the cleaners before they shut. I'll put both tickers on but if a traffic warden comes, pretend you can't speak English.' With that she slammed the door behind her and rushed across the road, dodging the cars and the puddles. Tim watched her go into the cleaners, shaking the raindrops from her hair as the door shut behind her.

Tick tock tick tock. I-want-it-to-snow-at-Christmas-I-want-it-to-snow-at-Christmas. Tim set up a rhyme in his head to the rhythm of the noise from the hazard lights. He could feel a slight bubble of anxiety in his stomach at being left alone in the dark on the busy street. He knew she wouldn't be long but he kept looking out for the blur of her pink mac in the steamy glass of the cleaners' window. I-want-it-to-snow-at-Christmas. He felt sure that if he wished hard enough it might happen because sometimes things like that did.

Tim picked at the hole in the knee of his jeans. Tick tock tick tock tick tock. He tried to imagine what Christmas would be like with snow. He'd seen snow in London before but it never seemed to be thick like in the films. Just grey and slushy and then it would melt into dirty puddles. He screwed his eyes shut again and wished even harder. He'd tried wishing like this for something else too, but that hadn't worked yet.

The car door being opened broke into his thoughts, and Mum slid quickly into the seat beside him. Her mac was soaked and her hair muzzy and wet as she pushed it off her face.

'Stupid man.' She dumped something in clear plastic on the back seat. 'They've broken a button on my best jacket.'

'Granny says you shouldn't say someone is stupid. You should say they are behaving stupidly.'

'Well, Timmo,' she turned the key in the ignition and turned off the hazard lights. 'Granny is right. Except in the case of the man from the cleaners. I think he is terminally and irreparably stupid,' and she laughed.

'Mum, have you got a boyfriend?'

'Crikey, Timmo, not this again.' She looked hard at him.

He shrugged. Perhaps he shouldn't have asked. 'Just wondered.'

'Don't worry, honeybee, there's no other man in my life but you. It would be weird anyway. Some hairy chap around the place, getting in the way.'

Tim couldn't help the feeling of disappointment at the same reply; he couldn't help feeling it might be quite nice to have someone around – though perhaps not someone hairy. He tried to imagine her with a boyfriend, but it had only ever been her, or her and Granny on trips and holidays, and it felt a bit strange to imagine it any other way. She'd gone out in the evening a few times, and there had been a man called Johnny who came for supper twice but then he hadn't come any more. Tim hadn't liked him much anyway because he didn't seem interested in the cars he'd shown him. Just drank wine and laughed loudly at everything Mum said. No, what Tim wanted was someone who'd play football or cars with him.

'Mmm. It would be weird. But it might be nice I suppose. If he was nice.'

She made a humph sort of noise through her nose and pulled out into the traffic.

*

A gritty whirlwind of dust followed Beth in from the chill of Tottenham Court Road as she shouldered open the heavy glass doors of Heal's. Ahhh! She sniffed in appreciation at the ocean of scent that greeted her in the foyer and went over to look at the flowers. The white, silver and blue that predominated at one end of the display would be perfect with the theme she'd eventually decided on for the party. She had just started to ask the florist for some advice when a familiar voice projected across the chilly space.

'Hellooo, daaarling! It's brilliant to see you.'

Sally, a loosely knotted mohair scarf bundled around her neck, had made her usual dramatic entrance and only a half an hour late. Banking on this, Beth had used the time to stay on at the British Library and finish her research notes. It was probably pointless even to try bridge-building, but she had called Holly's mobile yesterday to see if she would have time for a quick cup of coffee but there hadn't been any reply. Nor one to her text message. She must be busy.

Sally hugged her warmly. 'Darling, you look as wonderfully tatty as ever. So what *gives*?' Sally asked. She had just finished a run in an American play and her speech patterns were still coloured by her New York character. She'll have to get rid of that before the panto opened, thought Beth, squeezing her friend's arm. 'I mean, why here and not our regular?'

Beth shrugged nonchalantly. 'It's a bit closer than Bertorelli's, isn't it? And anyway, I wouldn't mind a quick look round the store. See what they've got.'

'Huh! You were never into shopping before. I remember trying to drag you into those luscious boutiques on the via del Corso, and all you wanted to do was visit art galleries. Who'd have thought it! I told you you'd be getting withdrawal symptoms, stuck out in the middle of Hicksville. You see – I told you not to move out there.'

Sally made it sound like a joke, but it actually had become a source of slight friction between the two of them. Not simply her relationship with Jacob, which Sally had never really got, but the whole move to his house from her flat after they married. Her old friend had counselled against it – 'It's too creepy! Like stepping into a dead woman's shoes'. And it was still a sensitive enough topic to be tackled only through jokes and the occasional barbed aside. Beth defended herself. 'Well, I'm not totally wasting my time out in the sticks. We have to make our own entertainment, obviously, so apart from the Morris dancing, I've taught myself to cook.'

Sally's incredulous guffaw was a little galling, but Beth merely smiled. 'I'm doing proper Christmas Dinner, just like Mother used to make.'

'Not like my mother, I hope. She used to put the sprouts on to cook in November. Remember her Sunday lunches? Great training for an actor, of course, pretending it was edible.' Sally turned to look at Beth narrowly. 'This is a bit new and peculiar for you, isn't it? I wouldn't have believed you had any latent housewifely skills at all. I'm still mentally scarred from that time at guide camp with the baked potatoes. And you've never shown any interest in it since. Why the sudden change? Hope the old man hasn't been getting at you.'

Beth pretended to admire a sofa. Sally knew her a little too well sometimes. 'Certainly not! I'm just sort of aware that this will be my first time of really playing hostess with the whole family there – and I want to make it nice for everyone.'

'You mean *his* whole family, I presume,' Sally corrected. 'You used to go wherever Christmas took you. Do you remember that one in Seville? Y'know I'd pay good money to see you in your pinny dispensing bread sauce and cranberry stuffing to all and sundry. Not your style at all. Your mother would have been astounded, bless her.'

Beth put the price tag down and shook her head and smiled ruefully. 'Wouldn't she just? Remember how she used to barricade herself in the kitchen on Christmas morning? She'd reappear all red and flustered but she'd never let anyone else help. No wonder I'm so undomesticated. I still miss her even though it's been ten years, would you believe? Why didn't I pay more attention when I was growing up?'

'Because no one ever does.' Sally squeezed her friend's arm gently.

'I wish you could be there too, Sal,' Beth blurted in a sudden burst of emotion. 'In fact, I may need you! To tell you the truth, the whole thing is faintly terrifying and if I can't have you there dispensing wisdom and G&Ts every hour on the hour, I'm not sure I'll cope.'

Sally bounced on the sofa and lay back against the soft leather headrest. 'Sorry, babe. I'll have very little time off from the show and Dave and I have planned a cosy few days before he has to take his kids skiing. But I'll be with you in spirit. I can just imagine you in a party hat, organising charades before everyone ends up fighting over the remote control or gets too sozzled and stuffed with stuffing to stay awake. Speaking of which – are we having lunch? I'm starving.'

'Yes, in a minute. Can we look at the decorations first?' Beth led Sally downstairs, ignoring her look of incredulity.

But within moments even Sally was caught up in the wonderful display. 'Would you look at these! Far too good for a poxy old Christmas tree. You could wear them as earrings.' She hooped the pink feathers over her ears and went to look for a mirror, giving Beth a moment to pulled out the magazine article from her bag. There. All white. It looked fantastic. Beth hugged herself in anticipation.

Checking every item against the photo clutched in her

hand, she started to fill her basket. Half a dozen glass stars, a box of filigree snowflakes, a handful of those incredibly delicate hearts. She took another basket. Oh those lights. Did Jacob have any lights? Never mind – these were gorgeous. In they went. When Sally found her at the till, she had a mountain of carefully packed bags.

'What on earth are you doing? You've got enough decorations there to do the Norwegian tree in Trafalgar Square!'

Beth started guiltily. Perhaps she had gone over the top, just a little. Then sheepishly, she showed Sally the magazine picture. Sally took it and studied it, a frown deepening on her forehead. 'Do you want to know what I think?' she said slowly, raising her eyes to look at her friend.

'If you must.' Beth braced herself.

'I think you need lunch … or medication.'

Chapter 6

Only 45 shopping days to go

*For very special party nibbles, inject cherry tomatoes
with vodka and Worcestershire sauce and sprinkle
with celery salt and black pepper.*

When his call came, Carol was umpiring a hot dispute between Emma and Melanie over a must-haves for the spring fashion accessories page.

'But I should have that space.' Emma, for all her sweet nature, could be very feisty when riled and her voice was raised an octave as she defended her corner. 'I asked for it for the best reads page and you never said this idea was going in this month.'

'I did. I always have it and there's nothing going to change *now*.' Melanie's arms were folded across her chest and her lips were pursed, a flinty look in her narrowed eyes. 'We never miss an accessories page. Not in twelve years have we—'

'Ladies, ladies, can we just calm things a bit?' Carol found she was clapping her hands together like a teacher might to quieten a group of unruly four-year-olds.

'Well, then perhaps it's time to change.' Emma wasn't to be stopped.

Carol raised her voice. 'Yes, Emma, you may well be right. Melanie, we did talk about a spring books page and Emma has some nice ideas. Can we think about accessories next month?' If there is to be a next month, she thought despondently. 'Some lovely beach ideas perhaps – now if you'd—'

'Carol, a personal call for you. Can you take it?' Jemima put her curly head around the door. 'And Ian says he's sent an email – he'd like you to look at it as soon as possible.'

Carol could feel the anxiety rising. 'I'll take a look but put the call through. Now, you two. Let's talk later, shall we? Emma, carry on with the reviews and, Melanie, we'll talk when I get back from my meeting.'

Shooing them out, she plonked herself down in her chair again, and picked up the ringing phone, glancing at the new emails on her screen. Ian's began 'I've had the figures . . .'

'Hello?'

'Hello, Carol.' The voice was deep and warm. 'It's Nick. You may not remember but we met with—'

'Kate. Yes of course I do.' She felt a delicious feeling in her stomach. Something possibly approaching excitement. She'd filed him under 'nice but will go nowhere'. But then the little voice of self-doubt in her head reminded her he might be ringing for another reason entirely. Something utterly mundane.

'How are you?' he asked.

'Oh fine thanks. Things a bit hectic. You know.' Though God knows why he should. 'How about you?'

'I've just got back from the States actually.' Why did she feel so relieved that his being away was the reason he hadn't called? Not that she'd expected him to of course. They'd only met once after all. 'I hope you don't mind me calling – I remembered you said where you worked – but I know it's a bit of an imposition to be called at the office.'

She smiled down the phone. 'No, no that's fine. It's nice to hear from you. Makes a change from warring editors actually. Did you have a good trip?'

He laughed deeply and it sounded warm and sexy. 'It was a recording session so not much daylight. Twelve hours of each day in the studio, with time off on Sunday for good behaviour. I think I must be getting too old for a place that never sleeps.

I need one with regular naps. Like Bournemouth. It's good to be back.'

There was an awkward pause. Carol realised that, except for Kate, they had no common ground and was at a loss to think of anything to say at all. Her problems – deadlines and budget hassles – sounded so dull in comparison.

He broke the silence. 'Actually, I was just wondering if you'd like to go out for a drink with me?'

The tingle ran through her and took her by surprise – surprise at her relief he obviously wasn't attached or gay. In the brief conversation she'd had with Kate she'd discovered that he was no longer married but had ignored Kate's enthusiasm to give all the gory details. Bloody matchmaker. And, oh God, she had so much to do. The last thing she needed was a distraction. Besides she had already inveigled her mother into babysitting three times last week because of late appointments and going to press. She couldn't push her luck.

'Yes. I'd like that.'

'That's great.' He sounded genuinely pleased but then she felt that peculiar sinking feeling she got on the rare occasions a man asked her out. It would inevitably be a one-off event. Drinks with blokes always were. She had precious little time to devote to any relationship, and then there was Tim. 'Are you busy on Thursday?' he broke into her thoughts. 'A friend of mine has just opened a new bar.' He mentioned a place not far from her office and, after giving him her mobile number in case there were any changes, she agreed to meet him at seven.

'You're pushing your luck, my girl. That's three times last week and it's only Monday.' Her mother had her hands on her hips as she stood in Carol's kitchen later that evening. 'And I was hoping to go to Exposition.'

'I know, Mum, but this is quite important.' Carol was unloading a bag of Marks & Spencer food into the fridge, wedging organic pasta alongside Müller Corners and Dairylea cheese triangles.

'And our blessed Lord isn't? What is it this time? That Ian expects you to give too much. Doesn't he know you're a mum?'

'I'm not allowed to be a mum, Mum. It's a sign of weakness to let reproduction stand in the way of a double-page spread. No, this isn't Ian actually.' She pulled herself upright. Should she let on that she was going on something that sounded horribly like a date?

'I'm going on a date.'

A broad grin spread across her mother's face. Carol held her hand up firmly. 'Whoa. Now slow down. It's just a drink, and please don't mention it to Tim. He's always asking me if I've got a boyfriend and I think it might upset him if he knew I was going out. He mentioned it only the other day.'

'Mmm well, I'm not so sure. You could do with someone around the place.' Carol ignored Mary's mumbling and carried on unpacking.

But now, as she approached their rendezvous in the Thursday-evening chill, a bit out of breath in her lateness, she became more and more convinced that Nick and she had absolutely nothing in common and she'd just have a quick drink and get home. She was sure her face was flushed and her hair a riotous mess, but she'd purposely worn her black cashmere coat with the outsize buttons because it always made her feel hidden and anonymous and in control.

He was leaning against the wall next to the door of the club, one hand in his jeans pocket and one leg bent up behind him against the wall. At first he didn't see her, his head was turned the other way watching a couple of girls who were screeching with laughter as they walked down the street. He didn't turn until she was almost upon him and for a moment she studied him, his wavy hair blowing in the cold night wind and his face half in shadow. It was an even nicer face than she remembered, not that she'd thought about it a great deal of course.

'Nick.' She had to say it twice before he turned, but when he saw her he smiled broadly and pushed himself away from the wall with his foot.

'Carol.' And he leant towards her and gave her a quick kiss on the cheek. So quick in fact that she quashed a vague feeling of disappointment and got only a waft of leather jacket, something soapy and London. 'It's lovely to see you. Shall we go in?' Urging her to go first with his hand, he directed her through the double glass doors of the club and into a beautifully decorated room with a long cocktail bar down one side and bottles arrayed on lit glass shelves behind the barmen. Almost all the leather chairs were occupied and, at Nick's suggestion, she sat down at one of the remaining two, while he went to get them a drink.

It gave her a chance to look at the room, crisp and contemporary in its décor, though it was more of an excuse to look at Nick, leant up against the bar talking to a man – his friend maybe – sitting on a stool while the barman opened a bottle of white wine. Nick was taller than she remembered, and without the big leather jacket that he'd shrugged off and hung over the back of the chair next to her, he looked leaner. She had a weakness for bums, especially in Levi's – the way on some people they fold along the buttock. There were bums and there were Levi bums and Nick's fitted the bill.

He came back with beer in a tall glass for himself, and white wine for her in a large, round goblet. 'Watch it, girl,' she warned herself, remembering that she hadn't had lunch, again. Too much and she'd be boring him with her life story. She took the defensive tack just in case and asked him about himself, and it wasn't until she was on her way home afterwards that she realised that, though he'd answered her questions, he'd wormed masses out of her. In fact his powers of interrogation were so good she wondered fleetingly if he might like a job on *WM*.

At first they talked trivia – how he knew Kate and Callum, the weather, something on the news. But when she did ask him questions about his work, he talked with engaging self-deprecating humour. 'I was a lazy sod at school,' he explained, laughing and running his hand through his hair. He sat leaning towards her, his elbows resting on legs set wide apart, and looked right at her, oblivious to everything going on around them. She realised her hands were pushed firmly between her knees and she was sort of leaning towards him too. 'It wasn't because I was thick, which was what drove my dad wild. It was because all I ever wanted to do was play music. Luckily my mum sort of channelled it – to keep Dad happy I think – and made me have proper guitar lessons, but as soon as I could be wired to an amp I was there.'

'Were either of them musical?'

'Yeah, that's the funny part. Dad used to play sax a bit in a jazz band – nothing serious – but he was good, and watching him sort of inspired me. But he thought I ought to have a proper job. He worked for an engineering firm – made piping for major cabling contracts – though I think he had something bigger in mind for me. Politics or the law.' Nick laughed again at this point, his eyes creasing up at the edges.

'Did he ever see you play – you know, properly?' Carol took another sip of her drink, the cold wine making the end of her tongue tingle.

'He refused to come and experience the early gigs – mind you I don't blame him. It was all head-banging punk stuff in sweaty clubs where your feet stick to the floor, and I don't think even I could stand it now. But I did finally persuade him to come along to a big gig I did at Wembley Arena, not long before he died actually.' He looked down at his hands and absentmindedly made a steeple shape with his fingers. 'My wife – well, ex-wife now – brought him and Mum along. I was backing a big American diva and he knew a couple of her songs to hum along to.'

'Did he enjoy it?' Carol tried to imagine her own parents coping with a wave of heaving, sweating humanity and couldn't, though her mum did have a soft spot for 'that Robbie Williams'. Nick made a rather cynical shrug.

'His exact words were, "Well that was a bloody awful racket!"'

'I bet he was proud though.'

'In his way maybe, but he'd rather I'd backed Thelonius Monk I expect!'

'And ...' Carol knew it was prying to ask, 'your wife?'

'Mmmm. Being a musician is about the worst profession you could have if you have any intention of sustaining a relationship! Long periods away from home. Lots of late nights, drugs, suspicion and jealousy. Truth to tell, most nights would be spent sitting in some shitty bar in a northern town and playing pool if we weren't on stage. The rest of the time we were folded double in a tour bus – and not the flash ones with tinted glass and plasma screens either – reading endless novels. It helped ease the boredom.' His expression was suddenly sad. 'It caused awful rows in the end and began to affect Gordie, our son, so I moved out. That was eleven years ago.'

'And Gordie? How's he now?'

'He's fifteen now and a great lad, in a monosyllabic, gangly sort of way.' His face lightened. 'Actually he's showing an unhealthy interest in music. But that's why I do recording sessions now, so I can be at home more often and see him. In fact I've just bought him a drum kit for Christmas. His mother is livid and it'll have to stay at my house.'

'Mmm, Christmas – the separation nightmare.'

'Sure is.' Nick smiled in agreement. 'Season of goodwill, my arse. It's a test of who can out-do whom on the buying favours front, and Kirsty's new husband is an expert at it. Anything the boy wants, the boy gets.' He looked away, irritated. 'It pisses me off.'

'He must think his dad's well cool though?' Carol didn't think she'd ever used that expression before in her life and hoped he didn't think she was trying to be trendy.

'Well, I suppose it does afford him a certain kudos at school when he can say his old dad has backed Anya. Can I get you another drink?' Carol shook her head, and he went back to the bar to get himself one. It was when he returned that he lobbed the conversation back into her court. She had been aware for some time that with men on a first date it's best not to mention the C-word. The revelation that one had children, she knew from bitter experience, could kill a man's ardour at ten paces. On one occasion a potential suitor had actually looked at his watch and said 'Oh is that the time?' before making a swift exit. But before she knew it, she'd mentioned Tim, and worse, under Nick's gentle questioning, he wormed out of her about Paul and the-relationship-that-never-was.

'Could you not have ridden it out?' Nick didn't sound accusatory, just interested.

'It just wasn't going to happen though we faked it for a while. Paul and I were great friends, and had been since college. He and I were part of a group who hung out together and met up often in London once we all had jobs. Tim was the result of a night that should never ever have happened. Both drunk and all that crap. Paul stood by me – he was wonderful and was there at the birth – but I never felt anything close to passion with him.' She thought about the months after Tim was born when they'd pretended with friends and curious family that they were a happy little unit. 'It was like living with a brother. In the end we just had separate bedrooms and got on with separate lives. Eventually he met someone and I knew, when I felt nothing, that it was time to move out and on. The great thing is I suppose,' she ran her finger around the top of her glass, 'that Tim has parents who genuinely like each other – which is more than a lot of kids can say – but we just aren't in love. Never were.' She laughed nervously and blushed. 'Crikey. Bit too much information. I'm sorry!'

'No, not at all. It's all part of the jigsaw, isn't it? Listen, Carol, I'm starving. Would you like to eat?' and because he couched it in the need to assuage hunger – not for any other reason – she said yes and, quashing her conscience, texted her mother to say she'd be delayed. It was while they were walking down the road to a brasserie he knew, that a message came back: 'Should I go buying a new hat?'

Later, as she put on her pyjamas and cleaned her teeth, she thought about how comfortable the evening had been. They'd laughed about pretentious menus and parents and things their children had said. They even discovered they'd holidayed near to each other in Worthing as children. She given him a character profile of Ian and, heavily underplaying it, up-dated him on the dire difficulties the magazine was in.

'He's a wolf in Armani,' she found herself telling Nick. 'He's like a spoilt child with a toy and when he gets bored of it, or a more interesting one comes along, he'll just ditch the old one. And I think *WM* is the equivalent of the broken rocking horse. I've been told that unless we get circulation up, it's curtains. We go to the news-stand graveyard in the sky, and my career will be close behind!'

She blushed at herself in the mirror now as she wiped the toothpaste from around her mouth. He must think her boring – him with his glamorous life (well, it may be tour buses but all that on-stage adulation!), and her going on about advertising revenues and this season's lipstick. But as she took the lid off the jar of moisturiser she stopped and put her fingers to her lips where, as her taxi waited outside the restaurant, he had leant forward and kissed her as he said goodnight, running his tongue along her bottom lip. So brief but so exciting.

Turning off the bathroom light, she slipped into bed and picked up her book. Her whole body felt very good indeed. Oh dear, that wouldn't do at all.

*

This was the place. Still open and lit up brightly, conspicuous against the other shops that lined the street, and against the inky blackness of the sky beyond the street lamps. Inside, Holly could see PRs and shop assistants milling around the cut-outs of country garden borders, receiving their last-minute briefing, but no journos yet. She felt in her pocket for the invitation. It was supposed to start in just five minutes. She couldn't face being the first in, but there was nowhere open for coffee that she could see. She shivered inside her long black coat – another present from Daddy – and took a couple of deep breaths. She really wasn't in the mood. She had other things to do. Like an appointment with the cardboard box carefully tucked at the bottom of her bag.

To think how excited she'd been when she had gone to her first press event. Free champagne, free canapés – to a new graduate it had seemed almost too good to be true. But it hadn't taken her long to realise that there was a pecking order to these things – and that she was somewhere close to the bottom. And not just by virtue of her junior status. That she could have tolerated – at least for a while. No, it was working for *WM* that was the main problem when she should clearly be on *Style*, as she'd claimed she was to her dad. She walked towards the shop again and smoothed her hair back, glancing sideways at her reflection in a window. Holly had a plan and turning up at this sort of tedious bash, looking drop-dead gorgeous, was part of it. Maximum exposure was what she needed. It was only a matter of time before someone spotted her and gave her the kind of job she should be in – something with a bit of status, with free lunches and an expense account and loads of freebies and club-class travel and seats at London Fashion Week. It was what she'd always wanted, since she'd bought her first copy of *Bliss*. Joe would laugh at her ambitions if he knew. He never looked further than the next piece of furniture he had to make, and even the commissions came in without any effort on his part.

Meanwhile, here she was having to waste another evening looking at gardening tools and accessories for the April issue.

As she passed the store for the third time, she saw a little group of women going in together and tagged on behind, relieved to be out of the cold at last. She smiled briskly at the girl on the door with her tray of glasses. Avoiding the orange juice and fruit-filled concoctions altogether she reached past the Buck's Fizz strategically placed in the middle, and took a flute of champagne (or something bubbly anyway) from the back of the tray. That was more like it.

She took a large sip and shuddered. Yuck. It had a funny metallic taste and she ditched her glass as quickly as she could, then scanned the unseasonably decorated room for food. Anything at all. She was starving – she'd felt sick almost all day and couldn't face her sandwich. But now she'd got her appetite back and would have eaten a horse on a cocktail stick, if one had been available. There was nothing hot to eat at all. Just tiny fruit skewers, tomatoes stuffed with pesto. And this company expected a mention in the magazine?

'Would you like me to find your name badge for you?' A mildly suspicious-looking young man had sidled up. His skin was pale and his knobbly Adam's apple projected well above his collar.

Holly sighed in irritation. She'd been planning to leave soon, but she supposed she ought to get ticked off on the guest list otherwise – disaster – she might not be invited to the next event. 'Oh all right. Yes, why not. Holly Layham. *WM*.'

Mollified, the stringy bloke loped off. Honestly! How could he imagine anyone would bother blagging their way into a boring do like this? Christmas wasn't even close in the real world but here she was already thinking spring and summer. And who knew what would be happening in her life then? Holly patted her bag thoughtfully and, taking a deep breath, reached a decision. The PR boy came back with the badge and a press pack. She smiled an automatic thanks. 'Is there a Ladies I can use?'

She squeezed past the now-clustered gathering of people and made for the door he'd pointed out. The contrived décor and ambient lighting of the store gave way to something altogether more utilitarian as she headed into the bowels of the storage area. There was a weird humming from the strip lights and it felt cold. She could hear her footsteps echo on the concrete floor but at least there was no one else there. And she couldn't have stood to do it at home, where Joe might appear at any minute. He wouldn't be ready for this. This was her business. Her problem. Maybe.

She closed the cubicle behind her and pulled the box from the bottom of her bag and read the instructions through again. Quite simple. Just pee on the stick and then wait. She felt gripped by a sudden fear. Of course she hoped to God she wasn't pregnant. She couldn't be – they'd tried to be so careful. And what if she wasn't? What if these symptoms, this sickness and tiredness, meant there was actually something terribly wrong with her? Holly closed her eyes and conjured up the image of her mother, lying resting in the afternoons, exhausted and pale from those awful bouts of vomiting after the chemo. Please God don't let it be that.

Unable to wait any longer, Holly hung her coat on the peg on the back of the door, pulled down her trousers and knickers, and sat awkwardly on the loo, trying to manoeuvre the plastic wand into the stream of her pee without getting her fingers wet. When she was done, she flushed, put down the lid and sat on it, alternately staring and deliberately looking away from the little window on the tester. Could seconds pass so slowly? She closed her eyes. And opened them.

She thought she'd prepared herself for this.

This couldn't be happening. This … could … not … be … happening. She bit her knuckle hard as if the pain might jolt her back to reality. It hurt. There was no sound except the rushing in her ears and the racing thud of her heart. She looked again, her hands shaking, although she knew it wouldn't be any different to last time. There it was. A blue line in the window.

Shit, this was big stuff. Her whole life had changed in a second. What would Daddy say? What would her mother have said? And Joe? How was she going to tell him? Would he want to be involved in whatever she decided to do? For a moment, Holly felt hot and dizzy. She grabbed her stuff, unbolted the door and leant heavily against the hand basin, staring at her washed-out face in the mirror. This was not part of the plan. Not part of the plan at all.

*

'Thank you for holding. We are very busy at the moment and apologise for the delay.' Like hell you are. Sighing, Carol propped the phone under her chin again and carried on replying to her emails.

'Carol,' Jemima waved from the doorway, 'can I interrupt for a second? Only I couldn't get through on the internal phone.'

'Please do. I'm trying to get through to BT to reconnect me at home.' She made a sheepish face. 'Forgot to pay the red demand – and I've been holding on the line so long I think my neck may be stuck at this position for ever.'

'Terrible, aren't they?' Jemima put her head to one side in faux sympathy. 'I just pay by direct debit – much easier.' Mmm, I'm sure you do, thought Carol, her already intense irritation increased by the smug expression on her assistant's face and ready now to scream at the call centre staff when someone did finally reply. For a moment she had a vision of just one little man sitting in the centre of a huge room and responsible for answering every call that came in. By the time they did eventually answer, she had checked off three colour proofs, signed four letters put in front of her by Jemima and had almost forgotten why she'd called in the first place.

Since Ian's 'I've had the figures...' email, each day has been a triumph of optimism over reality. The 'figures' in question had been from the sales team and concerned the drop in advertising revenue, and the free-fall projections for the next six months. *WM* was terminally ill and, when the office was quiet sometimes, you could almost hear the death rattle.

Holly's idea for the Christmas cover mount had come to fruition – though the bauble they'd finally managed to secure to stick to the front cover was more Toys 'Я' Us than Cath Kidston. It was the girl's only triumph however. Holly's efforts at the best of times were lacklustre and often she wasn't quick enough off the mark finishing conversations that were patently to friends on the office phone when Carol walked by. Carol had even caught her asleep at her desk at one point, and she kept taking days off. If she hadn't been about to lose her job anyway along with the rest of them, Carol would have had no compunction in firing her.

Nick hadn't called for three days after their drink, though of course she was far too busy to notice really. When he did, it had been lovely to hear his warm, deep voice talking about nothing to do with sales figures, but when the inevitable question had come she'd made it plain that this was a non-starter. Work was in freefall, demanding her full attention, and then there was Tim who, from his constant questions about whether or not she was going out 'with that man again', was obviously fussed by this boyfriend issue. He'd never talked this much about it before, so it must be bothering him and that bothered her.

Which was a shame. Because for the first time since she could remember she'd met a man who made her tingle.

'I'm really sorry, Nick,' she'd sighed. 'I really enjoyed going out with you but I have to work so often in the evenings, and I can't spend any more time away from my son ...' she'd trailed off pathetically. There was silence so she had blundered on. 'Perhaps I'll see you sometime.'

'Perhaps,' he had said quietly.

So, as the November days passed, they were as dull and grey as Carol's mood. The effort of trying to appear optimistic was exhausting her, and she was aware her anxiety was rubbing off on poor Tim, whose head she'd bitten off a couple of times when he'd asked again about how Father Christmas would find them. In the end she'd ruined the surprise of the cottage by telling him exactly where they were going so he could send details to the North Pole. And she'd so wanted it to be a surprise.

As her office filled up with products for the spring photo-feature on 'bathing costumes to flatter any figure' and the smell of coconut sun cream began to pervade the open-plan area around the beauty section, her mood became more and more dismal. She tried not to look out of her window on to the twinkling Christmas lights in the street below.

Chapter 7

Only 35 shopping days to go

*Choose a turkey with a plump breast and here's a
useful tip for a professional finish: use dental floss to
truss it — but not the mint-flavoured kind!*

A bird on order is worth two in the freezer. Or something.
Even though Beth had put her name down at the supermarket
in town for a good-sized bird, the superior versions she'd seen
today would knock spots off the average bird gracing the tables
of Milton St David. Hers (and Jenny's, of course) would be the
Rolls-Royce of turkeys. And she could always put the other one
in the freezer for some other time when she felt like cooking
lunch for ten. It had been a long way to go to choose dinner,
but once she'd got over that and the slightly uneasy feeling of
meeting an animal she would, in just a few weeks, be roasting,
she'd keenly signed up for sausage meat, bacon and sausages to
be delivered all at the same time.

The turkey farm was in deepest royal countryside, and the
further from urban civilisation they got the posher and more
languid everything became. Trees were more stately, walls more
dry-stoned, pasture more rolling and the grass was definitely
greener. No wonder the celebs were settling out here in their
droves. They were probably hoping some of it would rub off
on them. Class stains.

The farm had been more than posh: a long tree-lined drive
leading to a beautiful mellow stone house nestled in the sort
of extensive, well-managed grounds that shriek old money and

privilege. Correction – they'd never do anything as vulgar as to shriek. It was more an insistent murmur in the background. Even the sheep had public school accents.

Giles, the flat-capped owner, was an old shooting pal of Jenny's and the two of them chatted animatedly on the way out to the fields where turkeys strutted round contentedly, setting up a hideous gobbling as they approached. The three of them leant against the gate surveying the birds.

'What do you think?' Jenny asked Beth. 'Fine looking flock, isn't it?'

Beth was fascinated by the strange-looking creatures strutting and pecking around the large enclosure, the excrescences on their heads making them look like extras from *Star Wars*. 'They're actually faintly repulsive.'

Jenny snorted. 'Fine country girl you are! I suppose all your meat comes from the supermarket, wrapped in clingfilm. Giles, which one do you recommend? I'm going to be feeding about fourteen, but I don't want too much left over. What about you, Beth?'

It felt rather insignificant only having six – and that was if Holly deigned to appear. 'About ten, I think.'

Giles had nodded and pointed out two enormous creatures. 'Those two look all right? I'll put you down for them and we'll be delivering from the twenty-first onwards.'

'Perfect.' Jenny had zipped up her Barbour against the cold. 'Well, that's that sorted. Come on, let's take the dogs for a run down by the lake.' They wandered down the field together for a while but it wasn't until Jenny suddenly asked 'what's up?' that Beth realised she hadn't been listening to the older woman's idle chat. She hadn't even taken in the beauty of the winter scene.

'Oh I'm sorry. I was just thinking ... do you think I should do some stuffing inside the bird? Do you do that?'

'Yes, usually.'

'Perhaps I'll put chestnuts in the other stuffing ... cos I really ought to do some separately and not everyone likes them do they?' Jenny stopped walking and put her hand on Beth's arm.

'Beth, it's a meal. A glorified Sunday roast. Don't you think you might be taking all this a bit too seriously?'

'Yes but ...' Beth could hear herself whittering.

'It's your Christmas too, dear. You need to enjoy yourself.'

'Yes I'm sure you are right.' But suddenly her head filled again with the things she had to do. 'Er Jenny, would you mind if we got back? I've got rather a lot I need to sort out. Work stuff, you know.' And she turned around to stride back to the car, checking things off on her fingers and leaving Jenny to reign in the dogs.

And now, showered and changed, Beth could get on with the seemingly interminable task of finishing the Christmas cards, an untouched cup of coffee beside her. She'd approached the tedious task with the same military precision she used when preparing a lecture and, with the help of the hateful address book, had been working on a policy of doing twenty a day for what felt like weeks. She'd reached the Ts now, the end was in view, there was plenty of time to send the overseas cards and, for once in her life, she'd be using second-class stamps on the rest. Flicking over the page in her haste to get finished, she accidentally knocked the book onto the floor.

'Damn,' she cursed and leant down to pick it up. Out of the back stuck the corner of a yellowed envelope. She pulled it out, recognising the familiar hand on the front, and held it delicately by the corners, wrestling with her conscience. Knowing she really shouldn't, she slipped the card out and opened it tentatively, holding her breath.

'To my darling husband on our first Christmas together,' it said. 'All my love always, your Becca.' Beth dropped it as though she'd been stung and put her hands over her face. The pain was somewhere in her diaphragm and she could hardly breathe. Would she never get out from this shadow – this corrosive jealousy of a past Jacob had spent with someone else? Tears filled her eyes and she wiped them away, angry at her shameful self-pity. The poor woman was dead, for God's sake. All she'd done was know Jacob first. Beth looked down at the card, at the perfect image of a country scene in the snow, and picked it up again ready to put it back in the envelope.

After a moment she violently tore it into tiny pieces.

*

Nick gently bounced the phone in his hand, looking at it as if he expected it to give him some inspiration. When it didn't he put it back on the table, and picked up his coffee cup for a refill. He'd hoped he'd get hold of her before he had to go away but she was always out of the office, and he hadn't wanted to leave a message with her rather formidable-sounding assistant.

Flicking on the kettle he looked at his watch. He had to be at the airport in three hours, and he'd yet to have a shower and pack. Shaking out the last granules of coffee into the mug, he made a mental note to get some more when he got back and lobbed the empty jar into the bin.

Why wouldn't she speak to him? All he'd wanted to tell her was that he was happy to wait until things calmed down at work. That he understood.

But suppose she was just making an excuse? Maybe he'd read it all wrong. The evening they had spent together had seemed so good. He couldn't remember the last time he'd enjoyed being with someone so much and God knows he'd thought about little else but her since. Perhaps she had just been feigning interest. Perhaps it was part of some dating game that had rules he didn't know about.

He smoothed shaving foam over his chin and wet his razor. When he'd first met Kirsty there had been no complicated rules.

She'd been so sweet and he'd been so smitten and they'd both been so young. It had been a sort of learning process about relationships which they did together and she had become part of life really, tagging along to gigs, always there at the end when everyone was on a high and it had all been glorious and natural in its way.

Until Gordie's arrival had coincided with Nick getting work with bigger and bigger names and having to be away on tour more and more.

'I'll come along,' she'd said, and he'd read that as her wanting to be supportive. Of course it was impossible. A baby and the open road were a hopeless combination but at first he'd phoned home two or three times a day wanting reports on every move his new son made. Inevitably there were constraints as to when he could call, and after a while, when he did get to a phone, the response at the other end was cooler and cooler. What he hadn't realised until later was the extent of her jealousy. He'd really played it down to Carol – was he afraid of showing how he had failed? – but in truth his lovely gentle wife, with her big baggy jumpers and hair tied up in bright coloured scarves, became bitter and spiteful with her accusations, and poisoned the atmosphere for them both. Nothing he could say would convince her that there was only ever her and only ever would be. He'd come home after weeks away desperate to hold her in his arms and she'd reject him, asking why he would want her, 'fat and post-natal, when he had so many luscious women there for the taking'. Perhaps he simply hadn't read the signs of her lack of confidence, her loss of faith in her own attractive-ness, the stress of looking after a baby on her own most of the time.

As he wiped off the foam with his towel, he ran his finger over the now faded scar on his left cheek, just above the jaw bone – a constant reminder of the night he'd come back from the States late and found her drunk.

What had started as a tense but fairly civil conversation about his trip had quickly become aggressive. 'Pick up any tarts then? Bet they were gagging for it, weren't they? How many did you have then? Did you share them with the others?' Knackered from the journey and desperate to go and look at his innocent son, asleep upstairs, all he could do was stare at the face of his once pretty wife, made contorted and ugly now with her suspicions.

'Think whatever you like, Kirsty,' he'd said with resignation after fruitless attempts to pacify and reassure her. 'Nothing I say will make you think any different, will it?' And that was when she had turned from the kitchen worktop and lunged at him with the paring knife. Somehow, amidst despair and jet-lag, he found the reflex action to block her arm, or God knows what the result would have been.

Things had limped on for a while after that. Perhaps they were both in shock from what had happened, but bitter normality soon resumed and a month later, after another altercation on his return from three weeks touring, he packed his bag and left, the pain of walking away from his little, dark-eyed son nearly ripping out his insides.

As he took down his suitcase from the hall cupboard now to go to the airport and started to assemble boxers and T-shirts, he knew it had been the right thing to do, but the next few months had been the darkest of his life. He'd tried to obliterate it all with drink – long nights nursing vodka in the shitty one-bedroomed flat he'd had to rent in Kentish Town – and dope when he could get it. Then came the anger. If Kirsty believed he was shagging, then shag he would. And whilst touring with some one-album wonder, he finally gave in to the kind of temptation that had been throwing itself at him since he'd started out in this business. He responded to the come-ons from women that he'd always thought were pathetic in their brazen desperation to be bedded by a member of a band. Yes it was tacky. Yes it was like a quick fix, but the lack of complication and their lack of demands on him made him wonder why he'd never done it before.

Then one cold February morning he had woken up in a cheap little hotel in Grimsby after a desperate gig in a sweaty venue. Beside him, lipstick smeared around her mouth and her bleached blonde hair hanging over the pillow, was a woman whose name he couldn't remember. Nick still flinched at the memory of how he'd woken her, thrown her clothes at her and kicked her out of the room.

'What the fuck …?' she'd mumbled, hopping on one leg trying to put on her knickers.

'Because,' he'd yelled in his shame, 'because … I need my son.'

And as soon as he had arrived back in London he had called his agent and put an end to touring. The recording studios hadn't always been in London. He'd been called up to record all over the place – including islands with no communications off Cornwall – but it was all over quicker. So, he thought, chucking in a last T-shirt and zipping up his case, it was a bit of bugger that he was having to go to Iona for a week right now. But at £300 a track, who was he to turn his nose up when the call came from the Northern Hemisphere's latest, weirdest and most unexpectedly successful pop hero – a Swedish bloke with wild blonde hair, black fingernails and ripped designer T-shirts whose last album had gone platinum?

He picked up his phone. Should he try to call Carol again? And what was it about her that made him keep wanting to dial her number? He thought about her sitting in that pub with Kate. Even from the back, as he'd walked towards the table to join them, he'd known there was something about her. Something he hadn't found in a woman for a long time. The way she moved her head, and put it to one side when she was listening to someone. And the scent of her. What was most appealing of all was the fact that she had no idea the impression she was making. So self-contained and independent, she seemed to have no vanity about how she appeared to other people, and wasn't that a change from the women that hung about the music business!

He shrugged on his leather jacket and texted a suitably disrespectful reply to his son's 'get her autograph you old sod, or else'. As he struggled down the narrow hallway with his bag, his mobile rang again.

'Shit.' He fumbled in his pocket. It was a London number he didn't recognise and he nearly ignored it.

'Yup?'

'Nick? Nick, it's Carol.' She sounded tentative. 'I know this is going to sound weird after what I said the other day, but I've been thinking … I mean I just wondered … say no if you like … but I just wondered if you wanted to come over for lunch with me and my son next Sunday?'

He couldn't wipe the silly grin off his face all the way to the airport.

*

Beth picked up the enormous pile of essays she'd have to finish marking for tomorrow's tutorial. It would be another dawn watch for her. The end of term was fast approaching and, although that meant some relief from frantic dissertation and MA students wanting advice and a break from her regular lecture schedule, it brought its own additional burden: the deluge of late essays from the lazier students who'd found the pub more enticing than the library, and the excruciating round of drinks parties with tutees and department heads. She wasn't sure she could stomach one more glass of mulled wine let alone a Twiglet, or how much more lost sleep she could cope with either. It was bad enough students falling asleep in her lectures, but the lecturer too?

She hoped panic and coffee would keep her awake. It may be knees-up time for the students, but she now faced two weeks of interviews with prospective students for next year's intake. Then there were the slides for next term's lectures and tutorials to think about ... She'd never been behind with work before and, until now, it would have taken a natural disaster to keep her from attending departmental meetings. She hardly thought Christmas was sufficient grounds for compassionate leave although, on second thoughts, the Mistletoe Meet might meet the criteria. Pre-Festive Stress Disorder.

Still, today's meeting with the MMPS (Mistletoe Meet Preparations Subcommittee – or Mumps, as Jacob insisted on calling them) should help her sort out a few things and, at least, she'd be able to tick off most of the items on her list and finally get back to the job she was paid to do.

She'd delegated as much of the organisation for the Meet as she could, leaving messages, dropping notes through doors and collaring any VEG members she'd seen around the village. She wasn't going to have any of the factions complaining they'd been left out!

This was the first time, she realised, that she'd invited anyone from the village apart from Jenny into the house. She and Jacob had both been enjoying each other's company so much that having anyone else around seemed like an intrusion. She looked about the room – what the MMPS would make of the mess she could only guess. Piles of books and papers, last night's newspaper still on the coffee table – the mess of two busy working people. But it was better than anal tidiness and ornaments arranged with military precision. Even the coffee tray she'd laid out carried a motley collection of old mugs.

At two thirty exactly, the doorbell rang. Beth jumped up from her marking, and went to the front door. She could see a number of well-wrapped forms outside. They'd clearly come in a flock.

'Hello! Do come in. Isn't it chilly? I thought we'd go into the sitting room ...' Beth positioned herself to herd the women through the hall. They were showing signs of scattering, staring around the hallway and peeping through open doors. 'Can I take your coats? Or perhaps you'd like to hang them on the rack there.'

At last they were settled, with a certain amount of seat swapping and shuffling around. Beth sat nearest the door and took out her folder. 'Right,' she smiled as encouragingly as she could, 'so I thought we'd go round everyone and hear how we're all doing with the arrangements for the day. Sarah, table decorations. How are you getting on?'

The yummy mummy on Beth's left rummaged in her bag and fished out a Mulberry organiser. 'Well, I called that place you told me about, but I think the number's been changed or something because it just keeps ringing.'

Beth waited. 'So what did you do?'

'Well, as I said, I couldn't get through.'

Beth swallowed hard. 'You mean you haven't sorted out the table decorations?'

Sarah bristled. 'How could I? You gave me the wrong number.'

Beth took a deep breath. 'We'll come back to the table decorations later, I think. Shall we move on? Fiona – you were organising the raffle prizes. How's that coming along because we need to start selling the tickets?'

Fiona balanced a notebook on her knee. 'I've got a voucher for ten pounds off a pair of shoes, three sacks of horse manure, coffee and muffins for four at the Teahouse, a day pass for the leisure centre and a Christmas cake.'

Pathetic. 'Tremendous. That's a great start. Do you have any other ideas? Just looking back over previous years ...' Beth flicked over the pages until she reached Becca's list. 'There was a dinner for two at The Stag, a voucher from The Beauty Box, a case of champagne, a leather briefcase ... oh lots of things. Anything else in the offing?'

Fiona blinked rapidly then opened her notebook again and scoured the pages. 'No, nothing else. It's just that I feel so awkward asking. Becca always used to ...'. She trailed off sadly.

Oh shit. Beth bent over her list and underlined the first two items. She'd have to see to them as well as everything else. 'Steph, any joy with the loos?' Please let something be sorted.

Steph sat up. 'Er what?' She'd been deep in conversation with Ellie, next to her. 'Oh yes, loos all sorted. They said they'd bring them on the twenty-second because their delivery man wants to knock off for Christmas. He's going to Turkey, apparently.'

Mrs Godfrey chimed in. 'My sister used to live there.'

'Really? How extraordinary. Did she speak the language?'

'What do you mean? They speak perfectly good English in Devon.'

'Oh, Torquay! No, I was talking about ...'

Beth raised her voice. 'Can we, er, just stay on track here? I'm sure you've all got lots to do.' She looked meaningfully at Sarah. 'I know I have. The thing is, Steph, the marquee is coming on the twenty-second so we really wanted the loos on the twenty-third so the man would know where to put them.'

'But he's going away. I thought ...' Steph trailed off lamely.

Beth underlined again. That was something else she'd have to sort out. She closed her eyes for a moment. Hadn't anyone done what she'd asked? 'How about flowers? That was you, Monica, wasn't it?'

Monica looked up blankly. 'No, I was arranging the music.'

'No, I've done that,' Ruth chimed in. 'I've got the same DJ we had for my Saffy's sixteenth. He was awfully good.'

Beth rubbed her temples. 'Ruth, I thought you were arranging to get the raffle tickets printed when we've decided on the prizes?'

'Yes, you did mention that, but I said I thought that sounded a bit dull.'

'Not to me, you didn't. And tickets may be dull but they're rather important.' Beth was no longer even trying to keep the irritation out of her voice.

'No, that was to me,' Sylvia corrected. 'Don't you remember? We met in the lane just after Beth had asked you and you said to me, "Why is Beth trying to palm me off with the boring old raffle tickets? I'd much rather do the music, like I did for Becca." Except you didn't for Becca, did you? She did it all herself. You just suggested someone, but she didn't actually use them, did she?'

'Yes,' Sarah agreed. 'Becca only asked for suggestions but she made all the calls herself.' Then she added in an undertone, 'And she would have made sure all the phone numbers were right too.'

'Anyone else ready for coffee,' Mrs Godfrey chimed in, getting unsteadily to her feet. 'I know I am. Shall I take care of that, Beth? It's all right. I know my way. Becca always used to ask me to take care of refreshments. Have you got Earl Grey? Becca loved her Earl Grey ...'

Long before the Mumps had left, the atmosphere had become decidedly strained and there had been none of the friendly chat Beth had noticed at the end of VEG meetings. Instead, the women had been exchanging furtive glances and raising their eyebrows at each other. With every new failure, they became steadily more defensive and uncooperative. By the end, Beth had a 'B' written against almost every task on her list, and on the last page she'd almost torn the paper with her furious scrawl. There wasn't a single detail she could leave without checking, because bloody Becca had done it perfectly.

She slammed the door behind them, with a most unfestive epithet, and went back to her essays.

Jacob was looking rather tired, Beth thought distractedly,

later on. Although the man from the loo company on the end of the phone sounded even worse. He had a streaming cold – surely an advantage in his line of work – and wasn't at all happy that she'd tracked him down at home. 'I'll have to check tomorrow,' he said testily. 'I don't know what time his holiday flight is, but he won't be able to deliver after midday, that I do know.'

She stuck a Post-it note with this latest detail onto her sheet and hung up. Jacob was hovering by the door. 'Tea?' he suggested hopefully. This was usually Beth's cue to jump up and make him some. It wouldn't do him any harm to make it for a change. She scanned the sheaf of papers from the meeting in front of her. 'Er, yes please. That would be nice.' She'd just get the next couple of jobs sorted and then she'd ask about his day. She sure as hell didn't feel like telling him about hers. She'd rather die in a cellar full of rats than admit what a disaster it had been. Right – flowers.

She was still on the phone when Jacob place a mug of tea in front of her and his hand on her shoulder. 'Thanks,' she mouthed, and blew him a quick kiss before she turned her attention back to the florist. 'No, they have to be white, blue and silver. No reds, no pinks. No warm colours at all. Yes, foliage is fine. What's that stuff called? Eucalyptus? Yes, perfect.'

At last she hung up the phone and drew emphatic ticks next to the relevant tasks. 'How are you, darling? Good day?' He started an account of a hideous departmental meeting. In the past his anecdotes about them – so like that scene in Malcolm Bradbury's *The History Man* – would have had her in fits, but it didn't seem quite so interesting today and she could feel herself growing restless. There was so much to do.

'How about you, my love? It was your meeting today, wasn't it? So how were the Mumps? A pain in the neck?' Jacob enquired waggishly. She was tired, she was fed up. She'd have sold her granny for a decent night's sleep. She forced a smile onto her unwilling face.

'No, absolutely fine, darling. No problem at all.'

*

'Done it!'

Tim clipped the last piece of Lego onto the model and gingerly lifted it onto the kitchen table. 'Look, Mum. What do you think?'

'Timmo, you are a genius and would give Isambard Kingdom Brunel a run for his money!'

'Who's he?'

'A very clever man but not as clever as you are.' She dropped a kiss on his head. 'What exactly is it?'

Tim couldn't believe how dense she was being. 'Well, ooobviously it's the Millennium Falcon, but with an access ramp for Yoda – or he'd be left out. Anyone can see that!'

'Oh Tim,' she smiled,' it's exhausting me, this obsession with political correctness.' Tim hadn't a clue what she was talking about. 'It'll be Postperson Pamela next or ... or Wheelchair Barbie. The world's gone mad. Now, much more importantly, shall we make the costume for your play?'

This sounded exciting. 'You're making lots of things at the moment,' he ventured. 'Like that crumble you made for lunch.'

'Well, I've been promising you apple crumble for ages, haven't I? It was quite good, wasn't it?'

Tim nodded in agreement. 'I didn't think you knew how to make it.'

'Course I did, you cheeky thing!' Her face looked bright and shiny.

'Only Granny says all the time she spent teaching you to cook was wasted cos you only ever buy ready-made stuff from supermarkets.' He looked up cautiously, not sure that was the right thing to say, but his mum just smiled and tutted.

'You spend too much time with that woman.'

She seemed to have been in a good mood these last few days and it was brilliant that she was going to make the costume. He'd been getting a bit worried because everyone else had taken theirs in – except for Luke whose mum had said they must be joking if the school thought she had the time or the money to waste sewing. Miss Jeffries had made some suggestions about what could be done with a sheet, a curtain tie-back and a tea towel, but Mum had pooh-poohed that.

'I haven't worked in magazines all my life for nothing you know. We can do better than that.' And she proceeded to pull out some odd-looking clothes and a bag of fabric from the back of her wardrobe.

It was a special moment sitting beside her as she stitched on braiding around the edge of a piece of fabric that he thought must come from work and looked like something you would cover a sofa in. He hoped it would be suitably Middle Eastern, and not too Israeli, which, Miss Jeffries said, might offend the Palestinians, but he kept quiet because he didn't want to spoil the warm feeling of sitting next to his mum. If he stayed small and concentrated on what she was doing, she might not notice that it was later than the time he usually went to bed.

'Oi, Timmo, it's later than the time you usually go to bed.' She looked at her watch. 'Have you done your teeth?'

'Not yet. That Nick who came, he said he plays the guitar for his work. How can someone do that?' Mum was concentrating hard on sewing the braid on straight.

'Well, you know these pop bands. They make lots of money and someone has to play the instruments for them. He's very good I think.'

Tim had been itching to talk about the visit of the smiley man with the messy hair who'd come for lunch on Sunday. Mum seemed to have been quite twitchy all that morning before he arrived and Tim couldn't be sure but he thought she had changed her clothes at least three times. Tim had liked the dress she'd tried on first, but in the end she'd pulled on jeans, muttering something about being overdressed, though Tim thought that just meant wearing a big jumper indoors. Which she wasn't.

*

Carol flinched as she accidentally stuck the needle into her finger. She was out of practice with sewing – frankly it had been ages since she'd had the time – but sitting here now with Tim beside her, she'd forgotten how much she enjoyed it. How it allowed her headspace to think at the same time. And she was thinking all right. In fact since Nick has come to lunch on Sunday he had completely filled her head in a way that she couldn't remember anyone having done. Except perhaps when she'd interviewed George Clooney, but that was just hero worship.

From the moment Nick had arrived – a bit late thank goodness because she'd had an uncharacteristic what-shall-I-wear crisis – it had all been so *easy*. Easy in a way that reminded her of Paul, but with a heightened awareness that she had never had with him.

'Hi Tim, I'm Nick,' he'd said to Tim, who'd gone very shy all of a sudden, but somehow, imperceptibly, they'd gravitated towards each other and, when Carol lost them both for a bit while she cooked the vegetables, she found them playing cars on his bedroom floor, Tim explaining with encyclopaedic accuracy the finer points of an Alpha Romeo. Later they'd had a walk in the park, Nick kicking a ball back to Tim without complaint while they'd chatted about nothing and everything. Nick hadn't pushed, hadn't been false or tried too hard. He just went through the day, with that relaxed stroll he had that meant she couldn't take her eyes off him.

Before he left she'd tried to find errands for Tim around

the house so they could have a few minutes together but, limpet-like, he wouldn't leave them alone for a moment. For a panicked second she'd thought Nick was just going to wave and walk away, but he'd turned at the door.

'That was lovely, Carol, thank you.' He'd ruffled the little boy's hair. 'And great to meet you, mate. Perhaps we can play again sometime.' The look he'd given Carol then had been loaded with a question and she hoped she'd given the right reply with her eyes.

*

Tim bit his lip and played with a scrap of furry fabric sticking out of the bag. He wasn't sure that this Nick was really a boyfriend because Mum hadn't seemed very lovey-dovey with him, but when he said something funny, which he did a lot, she had laughed in a way he hadn't heard before. Nick seemed to really like the new cars he had shown him and, when he'd left it had been dark outside and he'd said, 'perhaps we can play again sometime' and Tim really hoped he would. Nick had done something quite odd though. When he'd said goodbye to Mum, he'd put his hand up to the side of her face and sort of stared at her for a long time. Then he'd kissed her. Just sort of quickly but on her mouth! His mum had gone a bit pink.

Mum stirred now from her intent sewing. 'Did you like him, Timmo? Nick, I mean. Did you, you know, did you mind him coming over?'

She'd never asked anything like this before. 'Yeah, I think he's cool.' Tim screwed up his eyes now and crossed both his fingers and his legs, as an extra thing to cross, and concentrated really hard.

'Come on, you.' She nudged him gently in the ribs. 'Don't go to sleep there. Up with you cos it's school tomorrow and you have a rehearsal. Let's stick you in a bath.' And she tapped him on the bottom and threatened to tickle him.

They'd had fun making shapes with his hair with the bubbles. But that was when everything went wrong. The phone rang. Tim could feel his stomach sink. He knew that could only mean one thing. He wouldn't be getting a bedtime story again tonight.

Chapter 8

Only 25 shopping days to go

*Now that you have finished your Christmas shopping,
you will have left yourself plenty of time for those
last-minute presents you may have forgotten.*

Her mobile had rung and interrupted some serious quality time. Tim had been chatting about his letter to Father Christmas, emphasising how he'd nearly finished his list – but that he wasn't sure about which pack of trading cards he wanted – and did she know what was the latest you could send a letter to the North Pole. His face had been pink and scrubbed clean, his hair standing on end in spikes with blobs of bubbles on each one, and she'd been making a firm mental note to herself to concentrate entirely this coming week on buying his stocking presents – well, any presents at all really.

When he heard the phone go, his face had fallen slightly.

'Hold on, darling – there have been some eleventh-hour hitches printing next month's magazine. I'll sort it out quickly, then we'll curl up and have a story, shall we?'

'Hello.' The voice at the other end had sounded quiet and hesitant at first and Carol had thought it might be one of the editorial assistants. But then they wouldn't have her number.

'Yes?' Carol had wanted to sound abrupt and show her annoyance at being called at this time on a Friday night.

'Carol? It's Anya.' Tim had splashed and squealed at that moment, which had given Carol the excuse to say 'Sorry?'

because she needed the voice at the other end of the phone to repeat her name. This had to be a joke.

'Carol, it is Anya.'

'Very funny, Kate.'

'No I'm not any Kate. It might seem a little strange to you that I'm calling, and I'm sorry it's a bit late but I don't have much time. I've been given your name. You might know I'm on tour.' The Scouse accent was very convincing.

'Er yes. I'd heard.' She put her finger to her lips to quieten Tim and put a blob of bubbles on his nose as a distraction. Even though Bartok was more Kate's bag, her classically musically educated friend couldn't have missed knowing Anya was on tour. It was headline news so that was no proof of anything. Carol's antennae were on full alert.

'I'm not talking to the press at the moment, but I've been told that you are honest and discreet.'

'Well ...' If I'm being wound up here, thought Carol, then I'm going to bloody murder Kate.

The voice then mentioned one of the last interviews Carol had done for *Style* with an A-list model just out of re-hab. 'I read it on a plane to the States a while back. She's a friend of mine and when I called her about you, she said you were nice. You could be trusted.'

'Oh.' Carol didn't say a word, less sure now, but if this *was* Kate playing the fool then Carol didn't want to say anything that would make her look even more stupid.

'Yes,' the soft Liverpudlian voice continued, 'she said she'd asked you not to mention the problems she'd had with her management and that – unlike the other scum that write for the papers – you hadn't.' Now Carol had to believe this was real. Kate could never have known a detail like that.

Anya's voice was quiet, as if she didn't want to be overheard. 'I wondered. There's something I want to ... to open up about and I wondered if you'd be interested in doing the story? Only

I'm back off to the States on Sunday and I haven't got much time. Can you come over in the morning?'

Carol had done a quick mental scan of her plans – Tim had a swimming lesson but maybe his friend Kyle's mum could help out for a bit.

'Yes sure. Where are you?'

'Paris.'

Carol realised as she boarded the plane later that night from Heathrow, after a mad dash in a taxi, that the January issue of *WM* was going to be not so much eleventh hour as 'eleventh hour and fifty-fifth minute'. Kyle's mum had come up trumps. In fact, she'd come over almost as soon as Tim had got out of the bath and dried behind his ears and she'd whisked him off with her for the night without asking any questions. Tim's face was beseeching as he left. Another evening with his mother shredded but, in her frantic rush to fill an overnight bag, Carol had found a moment to sit him on her knee and explain.

'Darling I can't miss this. You don't need me to tell you how famous this woman is and it's … it's a bit like the Queen asking me and me alone to interview her. It's massive, Tim, and it's top secret. More secret even than your spy games. And I need you to promise not to mention it to anyone. But it's important I do it for lots of reasons I can't tell you about just now. I've arranged for Daddy to collect you tomorrow after swimming, and I bet he and Eve might take you to a film, and I'll be home as soon as I can, I just promise and then … and then we'll do something really special.'

He had slipped off her knee despondently and then, stopping to consider things for a moment, he'd turned to her. 'Could you get me her autograph?'

'You bet!'

Throughout the flight over, oblivious to the goings-on in the plane around her, she'd read over the singer's biography she'd printed off the internet, even though she, like everyone else, knew well the almost fairy-tale story of the beautiful young girl from the roughest part of Liverpool who'd been spotted busking at a pop festival by a record producer when she was in her early twenties. Carol gazed deeply at photographs of the leggy star. Even though she was still only thirty-three, her face was becoming even more defined and interesting as she grew older, her cheekbones almost ridiculously chiselled and her eyes almond-shaped and feline. Her face and her music were unique – so universally known as to render a surname unnecessary – but Carol had had to remind Ian of this when she'd called him as she threw knickers and a clean shirt into an overnight bag before she'd left for the airport.

'Ian, we have to hold up the presses.' She'd reached for her make-up bag and thrown in mascara and some moisturiser, gesticulating to Tim to pass her some cotton wool.

'Again? Oh Christ, not another fucking mistake.' Ian had sounded more intimidating than she'd ever heard him and she'd flinched. 'You're bloody lucky we're even producing *this* issue, Carol, this is borrowed time. We can't go on—'

'No, Ian, listen. I've landed a big interview and it's going to be worth it. Believe me—'

'Let me guess? Another *Eastenders* has-been?'

'No, this is big.' She'd reached for pyjamas, kicking the drawer closed behind her with her foot.

'It'd better be, because so far you haven't really delivered anything remarkable, to be honest.'

Carol had seen red. She'd had enough of his upper-class patronisation. What had she to lose anyway? She'd thrown her hairbrush into the red leather holdall. 'Listen, mate, you asked me – no, begged me – to come and save your ailing little magazine and I gave up bloody everything to do it. I've worked night and day to turn things around and it doesn't happen overnight. You have to give me time to make a difference.' She was on a roll now. 'I'm working with great people who've crap material to work on, and who feel undervalued. You could at least have the decency to listen and trust my judgement. If I tell you who it is, you have to keep it quiet, Ian, because if it leaks before I get there tomorrow, I'll lose the interview.'

'Go on then,' he had sighed, but then, when she'd said the singer's name there had been a gratifying silence, followed by a slightly reluctant agreement to hold up the printing of the January issue and include this last-minute addition.

He hadn't been able to resist a parting shot, though, before he hung up. 'Don't blow it, Carol, and I want the magazine off on Monday.'

She'd hopped on one leg, phone to her ear, getting changed, with Tim looking on from the bedroom doorway, as she'd contacted Brigitta and Sheena, to make sure they could come in on Sunday to lay out and check the new pages – without of course letting on why. Brigitta had been predictably annoyed – it buggered up her 'paint-ballink veekend' – but she'd been able to tell from her boss's tone that this was imperative.

The chill of the Paris night now slapped Carol in the face as she came out of Charles de Gaulle and, as she sat in the taxi looking out at the winter night, she realised she was going to get very little sleep or time to prepare before she was due at Anya's hotel at ten tomorrow. That left her eight hours to get herself sorted. Once more she felt in the bag beside her to ensure she had her tape recorder and notebook. She had adopted this mad checking ritual since the day when, as a new girl, she'd turned up at Broadcasting House to interview a sit-com star, only to find she'd left her tape recorder on her desk at the office, and had to take down the whole interview on the back of cheques in her cheque-book.

Her head had barely touched the pillow at the hotel before the alarm on her mobile went off. As she opened her eyes, she realised with horror that she really wasn't ready for this interview at all. Was there some big story that had blown recently that she'd missed? She did a quick scan of her mental radar. Surely she'd have known? Well there was only one person she knew who was up to speed with the music industry.

She hesitated for a moment, then texted Nick.

She was in the shower when his reply came back. 'THE Anya? That's a scoop. Yes new album out and quite diff from the others. But she's friendly. Let her talk. Good luck Carol.' There was something about the 'Carol' at the end that made her feel a strange tingle. She stuffed her make-up bag into her overnight case, and checked out, walking briskly from her hotel across the Place des Vosges in the bright morning sunlight, until her cheeks almost stung with the cold.

The buzz around the hotel, even this early, suggested there was someone important staying there. People were hovering, coming in and out of the doors; a big, black Mercedes limo was parked outside and a fat man in a black suit and shades was leaning up against it, arms folded, killing time. Across the street stood eight or nine paparazzi in photographers' jackets, smoking and chatting to each other and, just beyond them, fans who had clearly slept the night on the pavement and, looking bedraggled, held steaming coffee in styrofoam beakers.

Carol had been through this celebrity interview charade many times before. First there would be the stony-faced receptionist to negotiate, then the star's people and people's people to get through, before you reached the subject of your interview. And then there was the wait: sitting outside the door of a hotel suite waiting to be summoned for a brief audience, usually stage-managed by a PR girl in a black polo-neck. In one New York hotel, Carol had had to wait so long in a corridor for a particularly difficult black soul singer to finish having a massage and her hair done that she'd come up with thirty-two anagrams from the words on the instructions for the fire extinguisher on the wall opposite her. Hoping Anya wouldn't be such a diva – well, it was she who had asked for the interview, wasn't it? – Carol braced herself and stepped into the foyer, with its opulent marble floor, alabaster busts, tapestries and fabulously festive floral displays in ornate urns. Such formality seemed at odds with the iconic singer she'd come to see. She'd have been much more at home in one of the more chic boutique hotels that were popping up all over Paris, but Carol guessed only an establishment such as this, an old hand at welcoming celebrities, could cope with the entourage and security required by a star of Anya's calibre.

Anya had remembered to give her the pseudonym she used, which, she'd told her, would work like a password so the staff would know she wasn't a crazed fan. Carol took a seat in a stiff-backed formal chair, as directed, and watched the early-morning traffic passing through the reception. In one corner two men were talking intently, leaning close towards each other, looking as if they were in the Mafia. In another, a woman in a red cashmere jumper, charcoal grey wool trousers and fancy dark glasses was talking loudly in an American accent to a waiter to drive home her point.

'Is it Carol?' The girl was dark, with bright red lips and wearing the requisite black polo-neck and jeans. 'Will you come with me? She's just on the phone but she said to come up.' Grabbing her bag, Carol followed the tall girl across the lobby to the lifts. They didn't speak as they ascended, which seemed strange to Carol. Usually stars' PAs would chatter incessantly, trying to work out whether you were going to give their boss a grilling.

'Has ... er, has Anya done much press on this tour?' Carol asked tentatively.

The girl looked at her with cool, hazel eyes. 'No, very little. A few magazine shoots at the beginning of the tour. *Vogue*, and a German title. But no.' The statement was left hanging in the air: *I* don't know why she has asked you here either.

The girl swept ahead of Carol down the corridor as soon

as the lift doors were wide enough to allow her through, and let herself in through a door with a key card, holding it open for Carol. The room felt warm and smelt of a combination of tangy perfume and cigarettes.

'Yes, OK, Bruno. Right.' Carol could hear the famous Scouse accent before she came round the corner into the suite, and there, sitting in the centre of the crumpled bed in a black vest and pink jogging bottoms, was the woman herself, resembling not at all the larger-than-life rock goddess who pranced so seductively across stages all over the world. Her hair was pulled back into a tight ponytail, and her face was devoid of make-up. The dark eyebrows and unfeasible cheek bones perfectly proportioned, of course. Anya was normality in the centre of this opulent room, all pale blue silk, Louis XIV furniture and flounced pelmets.

She waved at Carol and indicated a seat as she continued talking. 'Look, darling, I have to go.' Her voice was smaller than Carol had expected. 'Someone here. I'll get back to you before the sound check. Bye. Kiss.' Then she flipped closed her phone, unfolded herself from her seated position on the bed and came over to Carol.

'Carol, thank you for coming,' She put out her hand then leant down to give her a kiss on her astonished cheek.

'Chelsea, can you leave us alone please?' Chelsea pursed her red lips, clearly unhappy with this unscheduled situation. For a moment she stood there without moving, her notepad clenched to her chest, then she looked at her watch.

'Yes,' Anya sighed, 'I know how little time I have. I will be ready. Now *please?*' Chelsea turned on her heel and flounced out of the room, pulling the door with a resounding clunk behind her.

The two of them sat in awkward silence for a moment. Carol was used to queuing up with other journalists to quiz a star in the eye of a whirlwind publicity round, desperately thinking of something original to ask and with only ten minutes to ask it. Now here she was for no apparent reason, with no beady-eyed press assistant sitting in the corner recording every word in case there was litigation, and no constructive notes on the pad in front of her except a feeble, 'What were your influences behind this album?'

'Have you—'

'Would you—' They started together then laughed.

Anya went over to the table where there was a tray of cups, a pot and a kettle, which she switched on. 'Would you like a cup of tea? Here, I'll make some for us — easier than poncy room service — but I always bring my own tea.' She leant down to a kit bag and Carol was fully expecting to be offered a sachet of something herbal and carefully chosen by a personal nutritionist. Instead Anya pulled out a packet of PG Tips. 'Live off the stuff. Not that disgusting continental rubbish with a string on like some sort of tampon dangled in your teacup!' and she threw her head back in a delighted, girlish laugh.

'Now you're talking! Have you got a packet of Hob Nobs too?' Carol teased gently, glad the ice had been broken.

'Good grief no. Can't stand them.' She pulled out a tub of milk chocolate digestives. 'Always take a case of these on tour with us. Makes me feel less homesick.' Watching her stand there in her bare feet, her toenails painted shell pink, with her strappy top and thin hips, she looked so small and vulnerable that Carol couldn't help wondering what it was about this fame thing that would make her feel in awe of this woman. Someone who was not much younger than she was and who, stripped of her entourage of screaming fans, was pretty much like she was, liking her tea plain and her digestives covered in chocolate.

'Anya, can I ask you why you wanted me to come here? It's obvious it's not a pre-tour promotion cos that's been and gone. I'm intrigued.'

Anya dropped two teabags into the pot and poured on

boiling water. She didn't say anything for a moment, her mood serious now, and she stirred the bags pensively before pouring some tea into each cup. 'Milk?'

'Yes please, and a spot of sugar.' It wasn't until Carol had taken a sip from the steaming cup that Anya spoke again.

'Like I said on the phone there's something I think I need to talk about. People say you are good – well I know you are, I've read your stuff – and I need someone who can be sensitive.' Carol could feel that tingling sensation growing in her stomach, born from years of experience, which told her she just might be on to something really hot here.

'Anya, I don't work for *Style* any more and I'm not really freelance. My magazine is called *WM*.'

Anya smiled. 'I know that, Carol. I do my research you know! I had a quick look at it.' She got up and picked up a copy of the last issue from the floor on the other side of the enormous, blue-silk-covered bed. 'I know it's not – well, perhaps what people would expect from me – but I don't care where you print what I want to say. Those shits in the press …' Her expression darkened. 'No offence, but that crowd of scum would pick up anything I have to say even if it was in *Girl Guides Gazette*.' She paused. 'Do you think there is one?'

Carol smiled. 'Bound to be, I should think.' She realised she was almost holding her breath, not wanting to do or say anything that would make Anya change her mind about revealing what it was she wanted to unburden.

There was a very long pause, then Anya spoke into the quiet of the room.

'You see, Carol, I abandoned my newborn baby.'

*

'I'm pregnant, Joe.'

Silence drew out between them. Had he heard her? Had she actually spoken?

'Oh Holly.' Joe put his pint on the table between them and looked down at his hands for a moment, then raised his head and looked at her hard. 'Are you sure?'

'Course I'm bloody sure. I did the test. I've missed two periods. And I feel sick as a dog.'

He nodded his head slowly and sighed as if with relief. 'So that's it.'

'That's what?' What was he on about?

'Well, why you've been so – I dunno – so weird, and so tired all the time. That happens, doesn't it? It's normal, isn't it?'

'I don't know.' She shrugged. 'I've never been pregnant before.'

They were in a bar near Smithfield's, a little slice of a place on a sharp corner where two streets met. Joe had been picking at a plate of fat chips placed between them. Holly couldn't eat. Her wine stood untouched in front of her. From the other side of the table, she watched him anxiously, trying to read his reaction. Couldn't he see how tense she was?

He picked up his pint again and took a long swallow. 'Wow! Well that changes everything. When did ...?'

'How the fuck do I know?' She could hear her voice rising, tight and shrill with fear. 'A hole in the condom some time? You tell me.' She could see a woman at the next table glance over, so she dropped her voice.

'No,' Joe shook his head intently and leant towards her, 'I *mean*, when did you find out? Two periods you said. Why didn't you tell me earlier?' He was frowning at her almost accusingly.

She felt suddenly sheepish. 'I don't know. I needed time to think.'

'Oh Holly! Have you been to see anyone yet?'

She stared at his concerned face, puzzled. Why was he being so calm when she was so terrified? 'What do you mean? I haven't told anyone.'

'No,' he said quietly. 'Not even me. I meant the doctor. You know, for blood tests and all that. I know my sister had to with Sammy. They have to make sure the baby's all right. You and the baby, don't they?'

Joe was staring at her, waiting for a reply, but Holly couldn't speak. The 'baby' word hung there and she felt as though the air had been punched from her lungs. So far she'd thought of it only as a blue line, an idea, a problem to be dealt with. She'd never thought of it as a life and a future. A baby. But now he'd said it.

Holly felt a sense of something changing.

'So,' Joe persisted, 'what now?'

'God, I don't know! It's not in my five-year plan, that's for sure.' She was more confused than ever now. 'I don't know what to do. I don't even know if I want this. I've got my job and everything. I just wish ... I just wish this wasn't happening. I'm only twenty-four, for goodness' sake. I wasn't going to have kids for ages – not till I was thirty, at least. I don't even—'

'What about me, Holly?' He spoke so softly, she almost didn't hear him. 'It's not just you. It's my baby too, you know.'

'What are you saying? This isn't your problem. It's not your life it's going to fuck up.'

'Yes, it is my problem.' He sounded angry now. 'Mine and yours.'

'Well, I don't care what you think. I'm not getting rid of it, y'know!' She stopped and gasped, realising that a resolve had come from within her when she hadn't even acknowledged to herself there was a decision to take.

He stared at her, then nodded slowly. 'If that's your decision ...'

Holly rose to her feet and folded her arms defensively. 'Yes, it is my decision. I'll manage. I'll carry on working. They have a crèche at work. I'll manage somehow, and you don't have to be involved at all, if you don't ...'

Joe shot to his feet, scowling. 'Sit down. What's wrong with you? Why do you have to be like this? Of course I want to be involved – if you'll let me.'

Holly sank back into her seat, glancing around self-consciously. Joe, too, sat down and went on, 'Why are you trying to shut me out? It's our baby, not just yours. Or are you saying you want to finish with me? Is that it? Is that why you've been so bloody bad-tempered? Is that why you didn't tell me?' She could see his hands trembling as he picked at a beer mat. 'If that's it, you'd better tell me now. I'll support you, of course. And I'd want to look after it. I've got rights you know. Dads have got rights.'

He looked defiant and for the first time she thought of Joe as a dad. Herself as a mother. Were they strong enough for it?

'I *want* to be involved, Holly,' he said more quietly now.

'Oh Joe.' Her eyes filled with tears. 'You've got it all wrong. I don't want to finish with you. Really, I don't. I just didn't know what to think. I've been so confused and so scared.' He reached across and took both her hands in his, a slow smile beginning to spread across his face. That did it. Her tears tumbled down her face and she whispered raggedly, 'I need you, Joe. We need you.'

He stood up again and pulled her awkwardly towards him, shuffling around the table to hold her close. 'I love you so much, Holly.'

Her head shot up and she looked at him suspiciously. 'You've never said that before,' she sniffed. 'You don't have to just because –' He gently put a finger to her lips.

'I know I don't and I've never said it before because you are so bloody independent I didn't want to scare you off with how I feel about you. Can't you see how much I love you, you silly woman?' She could see the tears in his eyes too as he smiled at her. 'I'll look after you, I'll look after both of you, I promise.' She let him hold her for a while.

'Joe, there's just one thing,' she muttered eventually into his coat. He pulled away, puzzled. 'What on earth will my dad say?'

*

So dumbstruck was Carol when Anya eventually spoke, she was unable to say anything, and even took a sip of her tea to give herself time.

'Anya, are you sure you want to go on with this?' The beautiful singer bowed her head and then slowly nodded.

'I can't keep it to myself any more. My ...' she struggled for a moment, 'my baby, my daughter will be eighteen just before Christmas, and she'd be her own woman now. An adult.' She looked down again. 'An adult, so anything that might happen to me won't affect her.'

There was a long pause as Carol turned on her tape recorder and waited for Anya to go on but, when she didn't, Carol said, 'I'm not sure, but I think it's illegal to leave a ... I mean ...'

'God! Do you think I don't know that! Nothing they can do to me would be punishment enough for the terrible thing I did. But I didn't have a choice.' And slowly, with Carol's gentle prompting, the story came out: how at fifteen and on the run from care in Toxteth, Liverpool, she had found herself pregnant. She thought the father was a student at the university – she'd smiled wryly at this: 'so there's some hope my daughter might be bright' – but then the tears started to fall. Brains or not, he'd paid to have sex with her, so desperate was she for the money. She planned to get herself to London where things were bound to be better, and what she couldn't earn, on her back or otherwise, she'd nicked or pick-pocketed from shoppers. Carol had known that Anya's start in life had been rough – it had been well documented by her publicity machine and exaggerated inevitably by the tabloids – but this was far more than had ever been revealed before.

'I got to London eventually by hitching and arrived in the August. I knew then I was pregnant and I dossed, sometimes meeting people who would let me sleep on their floor and sometimes, when it was warm enough, I slept outside in the park. As it got colder, I covered up in baggier and baggier clothes, which hid the pregnancy, and, cos I had nowhere to live, I got a job at one of the meat markets. That way I could work at night and, in the day, sleep somewhere warm like a station.' She got up and went over to the window, leaning her head against the glass. Then she turned back to Carol, as if remembering she was there. 'Do you want more tea?'

'No no, please go on.'

Anya laughed mirthlessly, and rubbed her face with her hands. Pulling the hair tie from her ponytail, she let her curly hair fall around her face and she suddenly looked terribly young and vulnerable. 'I did everything I could to lose that baby. Drank. Ate nothing, and at the market I would make sure I lugged heavy boxes on my own. I couldn't have afforded an abortion anyway – fuck no! – but it's that bloody Catholic thing, isn't it? My mam had seven of us – I was the eldest – but getting rid of one? It was just never an option. And do you know what? That baby just kept me warm.' Fresh tears came again now and she wiped her nose on the back of her hand. 'Having her in my stomach got me through that winter. Weird, huh?'

Carol nodded, not wanting to break her flow.

Anya sniffed inelegantly. 'I don't think I even thought about what I was going to do when it … she was born. In some way I thought that, if I forgot about it, she would just never be born and I'd sort of re-absorb her into my body. On the day the contractions started, I walked about trying to pretend they weren't happening. It was the twentieth of December and London was heaving. People everywhere.'

'What did you do? Where did you give birth?'

Anya put her hands over her face to cover her shame and muttered so quietly Carol had to strain to hear.

'In the toilets at Euston Station.'

'Oh Anya,' Carol whispered.

She let her hands drop. 'Incredible, isn't it? I sort of planned it in some bizarre way. I knew the station well – I'd slept there enough times – and it seemed sort of significant that it was the station for trains to Liverpool. Do you know what I mean? I nicked some blankets and sort of waited until the labour got so strong I couldn't really walk around any more. Then I just kind of bedded down in the disabled toilet. The door went right up to the top – you know, it wasn't a cubicle like – and it was bigger, and the station is so noisy anyway that I couldn't be heard.'

Carol flashed-back to the clinical, controlled, caring environment of St George's where she'd had Tim – *her* unexpected baby who by the end of the pregnancy she wanted so badly. 'You must have been terrified.'

'I was frightened but I was focused too. That's the thing about me, Carol. I am incredibly focused. I am about my music, I was about having this baby. I'd seen my mum deliver two babies, so I knew what to expect – the placenta and stuff – and sort of how to breathe. Thank God she was small and she came quite fast.' Suddenly and unexpectedly Anya came and crouched in front of Carol and took her hands. 'Oh Carol, she was beautiful. I need you to know that. I never hated her – she was perfect, and do you know what? She didn't even cry. She just looked at me, as if she knew crying would give us both away. I wrapped her up warm, and for a long time we just sat together until someone came and banged on the door.'

They kept hold of each other's hands, and neither was uncomfortable with it. It seemed important that Anya had the physical contact as she poured out her story.

'I got a place in hostels for the next few nights,' she continued falteringly. 'Having the baby with me got me in, no trouble, and I got special care, though no questions were asked, like.'

'Did you give her a name?'

'Yes.' Anya looked away. 'I tried not to because I think I knew from the beginning what I was going to do, but God it's hard not to, when you've held her and changed her nappy and fed her. I even fed her cos I couldn't afford the milk – and my boobs were like fucking balloons anyway. I dressed her properly you know.' She became more animated and shook Carol's hands to drive home her point. 'Stuff I nicked from shops. Some quite posh. Such pretty things too.'

'What was her name, Anya?' Carol asked gently.

'Natasha. I called her Natasha after my mother. Oh God.' And then the sobs came, a heaving earthquake of them, and Carol took Anya – this world-famous singer worth millions and fêted by millions – into her arms and let her cry like a child. She stroked her hair until she got control again and sobbed out the rest of the story – the story that every paper and news bulletin in the country would grab on to as soon as the interview was published. How Anya had wrapped her four-day-old baby in blankets, so she was safe against the cold, fed her for the last time and left her, with a note tucked in beside her saying her name, and with beseeching instructions to please care for her, outside Guy's Hospital on Christmas Eve night.

Chapter 9

*Buy a special decoration each year as a celebration of
that year of your lives together. Soon you will build
up a collection that really means something.*

'There – that's it. Careful. Oh, mind your head!'

Jacob backed out slowly, on his hands and knees, from
beneath the Christmas tree, newly clamped in its stand and,
more or less, vertical. Absently, he brushed pine needles from
his hair and jumper then stood back with Beth to scrutinise
their handiwork.

'Don't you think it should be a bit further over that way?'

'Oh no.' Beth said quickly. 'It looks just fine to me.' Better
not to risk shifting it yet. If it toppled over again, the bloody
thing would be bald before she'd even hung the first bauble.

To be honest, it had been a difficult afternoon. Beth had
been all excited, Jacob markedly less so. She'd seen too many
soppy American films where smiling couples, artfully wrapped
up in layers of knitwear, chose their tree with great care from
a jolly street market, then dragged it back together to their
cosy brownstone through the gently falling snow. Ahh, she'd
thought, sweet. Well, it hadn't been a bit like that. Far from
a romantic bonding experience, it had been stressful from
the word go. They'd driven to a nearby garden centre where
the whole buying experience had been briskly efficient. What
height? What type? Pay there. Jacob had, on principle, refused

to pay the price per foot for the superior bluey-green version, so they'd had the second-rate prickly type. Then a pair of surly fleece-clad assistants had trussed it up in tight plastic mesh, by passing it through a machine like a giant sausage maker, and the poor thing looked half strangled before they even got it on top of the car.

And that had been the next ordeal. Fortunately, Jacob at least had the foresight to bring some washing line with him to lash the thing to the roof but it had been a cold and nerve-racking drive home. From Jacob's attitude, she deduced he'd never had to bother with this kind of trivia before, but she couldn't bring herself to ask him how Becca had managed by herself. She probably grew her own. Or had it delivered freshly cut from Norway.

Then they had to get it inside; then they had to get it standing up. There had been a lot of terse hissing going on – not their usual style at all.

'Hold the ruddy thing straight, can't you?' Jacob had growled at one point and, pathetically, Beth could feel herself beginning to cry. She didn't think she'd ever heard him say ruddy before. By the time they'd finished, Beth was glad to see his back retreating towards his study. Good bloody riddance. She didn't even offer him a cup of tea. That would serve him right.

A couple of hours later, she had mellowed considerably. The tree looked just like the one in the Sunday supplement article. She held up the now-tattered piece of paper and compared. Not bad at all, and she even had baubles to spare. She'd stuck resolutely to white and silver – lights, baubles, fine glass snow-flakes – the lot. Every last twiggy branchlet was dangling with some delightful visual treat – the miniature white felt stock-ings and the foil-wrapped parcels look fantastic. Tinsel, white and silver and thick as a fur ruff, was coiled up the trunk and swagged from the tips of the branches, just like in Victorian story books. Perched on top was an exquisite long-legged angel with a bell-shaped dress of stiffened silver fabric and a giant halo. It looked fantastic.

'Cup of tea and a mince pie?' she called artlessly up the stairs. She flicked the tree lights on again, and waited for Jacob to join her.

'Oh! Oh I say! That really does look marvellous.'

Jacob came over and took a sip of tea, then, perhaps to make amends for his mood, put his arm round her waist and pulled her towards him as they stood, side by side, bathed in the soft silvery glow emanating from the tree and gazed at it in silence. Come on, Jacob, she thought. Gush a bit, can't you?

'Erm – did these come from the loft?'

'What? No – Heal's mostly. And some from Habitat. Oh – I see! Did you have some up there? I didn't realise.'

Jacob pulled away slightly and examined the tree from all angles. 'Yes, yes, the ones we've had for years. Don't know where we'd put them though. Not much room left on it.'

'Well, no. That's the point. I wanted it to look as though it was covered in frost. It's quite effective, don't you think?' She wondered whether to show him the magazine picture, so he could see for himself what a triumph it was. A wave of insecurity sucked at the ground beneath her feet. 'Don't you like it?'

'Of course I do, darling. It's … it's absolutely lovely. Like something from a magazine. Tell you what. It's so lovely, perhaps we could have a little tree in the hall as well. One of those newfangled ones you were looking at, that keeps hold of its needles.'

'But I haven't got enough decorations for another whole tree, and I don't want to start pulling this one apart just when it looks so perfect.'

'No, no! Of course not. I'll get down the old box from the loft and use some of those – you know, just as a little extra.

Holly and Noel will want to see them out I expect.'

Beth felt like she'd been slapped. So much for the single-colour theme. 'Yep, why not!' she said bravely. 'I'll leave it up to you, darling.' And she turned away to pick up the debris of bags and boxes, gritting her teeth.

*

Carol hadn't felt so excited since she'd held her first copy of *Jackie*, bought with precious pocket money. Well, it didn't come close to the first time she'd held Tim of course, with his scrunched-up little face making him look not unlike ET but, to her, the most perfect thing imaginable. That was a defining moment, naturally. But in its own small way, this was one too.

She looked up to ensure no one was looking through the glass panel in her door then ran her hands lovingly over the smooth cover of the January issue. She lifted it up and, closing her eyes, sniffed the paper the way she always did. Then she would know it was real. With her critical eye, she scanned the cover model's face, checking for blemishes in the reproduction. Then, slowly, she traced the words across the cover with her finger:

Anya World Exclusive: 'I can't live with my secret any longer.'

Carol still couldn't quite believe what she was seeing. She kept looking at the masthead to check there hadn't been some terrible mistake and they'd put the cover line on the wrong magazine. She had a sense of unreality. But then the last week had been unreal. Carol turned to the contents page and her eyes darted over the splash of colour. Her heart lifted. It had been worth breathing down Brigitta's neck for the last few weeks. At last the stubborn Teuton had managed to achieve something exciting, but it was Anya's face, splashed large and inserted at the last minute, that really caught the eye. Her distinctive cat-shaped eyes and dark curly hair stared right out of the page at the reader, and across the top corner of the picture again were splashed those scintillating words.

Chapter 10

Only 14 shopping days to go

Supermarkets get busier the nearer it is to Christmas.
Shop early and buy non-perishables and items with
long sell-by dates.

'Graham, I really think you should see this one.' Mobile tucked illegally and uncomfortably under the chin, Beth manoeuvred the car into the tight parking space and turned off the engine. She'd been trying to speak to the admissions tutor all morning. 'This boy really was outstanding in the interview and I'd like to offer him a place. Yes, OK, I'll email over his details but if you could possibly find a space? OK, Graham, see you at the faculty party. Yup, great.' She pressed the off button and, refocusing from impressive prospective students, pulled out her shopping list from her bag.

She hadn't been to the supermarket for a couple of weeks because of the mountain of departmental admin she'd had to deal with. Jacob, who had fewer A-level hopefuls to interview and a secretary to deal with much of his paperwork, had volunteered to do all the grocery shopping. It was a skill he had acquired during his widower years and he resisted any interference. To tell the truth, they ate rather better when Jacob was in charge than when it was up to Beth, whose ideal meal would always be a picnic, eaten with the fingers from plates balanced on knees in front of the telly or at her desk.

The car park seemed far fuller than usual and a fierce wind

sent plastic bags swirling and almost snatched the door from her grip when she opened it. As she made her way towards the entrance, grim-faced shoppers with overfilled trolleys streamed past her in the opposite direction and she shook her head in wry amusement at the siege preparations that were going on all around her. For goodness' sake – the shops would only be closed for a couple of days, tops. Why did everyone shop as though the end of the world was at hand? She only needed essentials, really. She'd be home with a cup of tea in her hand within forty minutes.

Inside the store was a seductive smell of freshly made bread. The flower stall was aflame with poinsettias and fragrant with just-opening hyacinths so she treated herself to a bowl of three. Actually, they were quite good value, so she took a couple more, laying them carefully at the front of her trolley. Turning left for the newspapers, so she could pick up a copy of the *Guardian,* Beth stopped in front of the array of magazines. The densely packed glossies, promising Christmas tips and gift guides, had been Beth's staple reading over the last few weeks but, scanning the covers, she could see they were slowly giving way to the January editions with diets, resolutions, de-cluttering. How dismal!

She stopped and scoured the shelves in case there was some fantastic nugget of Christmas lore she'd missed – something that would knock Jacob's socks off and make even Holly sit up and take notice. She laughed softly. *Woman's Monthly.* So that was still creaking on, was it? She rather furtively plucked it from the rack and studied the cover with interest. Boy, it had certainly undergone a facelift recently and from the look of the display in front of her, copies were flying off the shelves. She scanned the cover lines. 'Sex toys uncovered.' That was out of character – a bit like your granny telling a blue joke. She caught sight of another cover line. 'Anya World Exclusive,' she read. 'I can't live with my secret any longer.' Not another celebrity revelation. Her eyes moved further down the cover. But hey, what was this? She seized the copy eagerly. This was a must buy. Beth's eyes lit up with anticipation and she tucked it into the trolley, out of sight, under the hyacinths.

Beth continued on her way, vaguely aware of the sickly wash of ambient sound, syrupy Christmas carols, pervading the store, and began her shopping.

Within ten minutes, the trolley was almost full but she hadn't actually got anything she'd come for. Not good. Then, salvation arrived in the unlikely form of Irene, who was abandoning a trolley by the checkout since her husband was on hand to fetch and carry. Beth swooped.

'Did you want this?' Irene asked, pushing the trolley towards Beth and away from the teetering mounds of groceries on the conveyor belt. 'We've finished, thank goodness. I'm not coming back here until it's all over. We're even freezing milk.'

Irene had a point. If she got everything today, she could skip next week's shop. Why hadn't she thought of that? Eyeing Irene's bags and boxes of snacks and 'nibbles', a word Beth hated, she was swept with a feeling of inadequacy. Now she had a deep trolley as well, Beth was liberated. Like a push-me-pull-you, she shuffled along the aisles, a trolley fore and aft, grabbing at anything that took her fancy.

By the time Beth finally left, nearly taking the legs out from under a couple of old biddies in the fray, she'd heard 'Mistletoe and Wine' eight times. She was punch-drunk, panicked, grumpy, ravenous and several hundred quid lighter. To top it all, under the sodium lights that now illuminated the car park – it had been broad daylight when she went in – she could clearly see that someone had dinged the door of her car. But at least she had hickory-smoked and honey-roast nuts. No one would starve.

As Beth battled in through the front door with the supermarket bags she spotted a delivery card on the mat. 'Boxes left by garage' read the scrawled note. She put the bags in the kitchen and went to investigate. She found the boxes and lugged them into the kitchen. What had Jacob ordered? Wine perhaps? But the name on the delivery label was hers.

God! She'd forgotten all about this – smoked duck breast, a boned goose with apricot, lemon and thyme stuffing, organic sausage meat, vacuum-packed chestnuts, and more. Of course! She'd ordered it ages ago from a supplier in Scotland she'd found on the web. In fact, casting her mind back, she remembered ordering quite a bit of stuff that way. Where was she going to put it all? In the next package were strips of venison, pâtés and pickled walnuts, jars of jewel-like organic beef stock, oatcakes and cheeses, confit of duck crusted with salt, smoked oysters. Oh bloody bloody hell.

She had just finished re-arranging the freezer and stuffing the non-perishable stuff anywhere she could find when Jacob came home. She tried to look like the sort of woman she'd been staring at in bafflement in the magazines for the past month: calm and in control.

Jacob came into the kitchen. 'Hello, sweetheart. You look done-in. Got a headache?' He sounded tired. 'Anything to eat? I missed lunch today. Some daft girl who's stayed on during the vac having an emotional crisis. Why they can't have them between meals, I don't know. Mind you, she looked as if she didn't eat much. Another one on the road to anorexia, I fear.'

She kissed him, as much to stop him rummaging in the overflowing fridge as anything else. 'You look tired, darling. Why don't you go and sit down in the sitting room? I'll bring you a cuppa and something to keep you going until supper.'

'I'll make it. I'd rather sit down and talk to you. How's your day been? We don't seem to have had a chat for ages.' Jacob went to put the kettle on. 'I was just thinking today. This will be our first real Christmas together, won't it, my love?'

He was just thinking *today*? 'Of course,' Jacob went on, 'It won't be a huge family do, so it shouldn't be too much effort, but perhaps we could make a list closer to the time and we could share it all between us. I don't want you to take on too much.'

Beth turned away and started to unload the dishwasher, not quite trusting herself to speak. Here was Jacob, talking as if it were a day like any other, when she had been living and dreaming nothing but bloody Christmas for weeks!

'Though,' he continued oblivious, 'I know you'll take it all in your indomitable stride. Nothing fazes you, does it?'

Unable to stop herself, Beth slammed down a pile of plates a bit too hard on the sideboard. 'Yup, that's me! Nothing fazes Beth.'

Jacob's head shot up. 'Are you all right? What have I said? It's not like you to be this uptight.'

'I can't believe you, Jacob.' She slammed clean cutlery into the drawer. 'I've got easily as much work on as you – more if anything – and bloody Christmas to think about and you're talking about a *list*!'

'Hang on, darling.' He tried to put his hand on her arm but she fended him off with her outstretched hand. 'It's only the family. And you know we will all muck in—'

'Yes, exactly. The family.' Take care, Beth, she warned herself.

'Well,' he said quietly, stepping back. 'Perhaps you were foolish to take on the Meet. I did try to warn you.' Beth looked at his face, a closed expression she'd never seen before. She put down the plate she was holding and walked out of the door.

It was nearly dark and too cold without a coat but she didn't care as she marched down the road in the general direction of the church. Her arms were tightly crossed against the cold and her anger. A ball of tension had settled across her shoulders. Damn him, damn Christmas, damn the lot of them.

Through the tatty, leafless hedge she could just about make

out the Steaggles' cottage. It looked as bleak and dark as she felt. She hoped to goodness Diana had phoned that poor woman and told her it wasn't for rent. But that wasn't Beth's bloody problem, although everything else in the world seemed to be.

'Hi Beth dear.' Beth turned and looked over her shoulder. The vicar had come out of the church gate ahead of her and was disappearing down the road. He waved and called, 'All ready for the festivities?'

Beth laughed demonically. 'Never been better prepared!' she called back, and watched him hurry away.

*

Carefully Nick picked up the delicate earrings from their stand and held them up to the light. The stones, dangling on little stems of silver, caught the light and glistened with purple, green and turquoise.

'Gorgeous, aren't they?' The girl who had been behind the desk when he walked into the gallery had come up to join him, either sensing a possible sale or wanting to make sure the earrings didn't end up in his pocket. She was rake thin in pointy boots, a long black skirt and neat beige cardigan, an enormous necklace with tortoiseshell beads around her neck.

'Yes, lovely. Tell me, do they look expensive?'

'Well, you'd be sure to make an impression,' she purred.

'No, what I mean is, do they look too much? You know, a bit too extravagant?'

She folded her arms and looked at him, then smiled knowingly. 'I get it. You don't want to look too keen, is that it?'

'Something like that.'

'Nope, I think you can't go wrong with Morten Ferdinandson's pieces. Low-key and Scandinavian. She won't have heard of him. Quite inspired but little known.' The earrings seemed to be just right, and he knew how beautiful she would look in them. How they would catch the light when she threw back her head and laughed. But what if she hated them? And, worse, what if she thought they were completely over the top and was embarrassed? She might think he was desperate.

He'd rather surprised himself that he was in here at all. This morning had been set aside for the only Christmas shopping he intended to do. Kirsty used to do it and, since he'd been on his own, he'd either taken advantage of whichever enthusiastic girlfriend was on the scene at the time or treated the whole process as one might root canal work. He'd restricted himself to visiting two shops where he'd found what he wanted for Gordie – a rare Led Zepplin LP in vinyl – and a warm scarf for his mum, though he wasn't sure he hadn't got her one very similar last year. Not that she would notice. She barely even recognised him these days and the last time he'd been to visit her she'd kept calling him Derek.

So here he was in Notting Hill, frantic to get back home now he'd bought what he wanted, when he'd noticed the earrings in the shop window, lit from below in the display case. He'd pushed open the door of the gallery without really thinking but now the whole place made him feel edgy and he wanted to pay and go. The thin woman wrapped them painstakingly in several layers of burgundy tissue paper, slipped them into a special box, and then into a stiff little carrier bag and tied it carefully with a ribbon. A couple of times he wanted to shout, 'Stop, I've changed my mind. This is madness, I barely even know the woman.'

At last he bolted out of the door and, convinced the bag looked poncy, he slipped it into his jacket pocket, and braced himself to make a headlong dash towards the tube. Just as he was about to descend the stairs, he spotted a news-stand and stuck his hand into his pocket for some change for a paper – he could read about how Stoke did last night to pass the time back to Tooting – and there, propped up and front-facing, blocking out several of the other glossy titles, was *WM*, its cover model with a festive smile and its exclusive slashed across the front. Beside it was an ad board for tonight's *Standard*: 'Baby shame: will Anya face Police questioning?'

He pulled out a fiver and bought them both.

Chapter 11

Only 8 shopping days to go

It's time to think about you. Take time to relax before the festivities begin. Book yourself a day of pampering with a manicure, a good haircut and even a massage. You will look and feel marvellous for the fun ahead!

Right! Beth rolled up the sleeves of her silk-edged T-shirt. Jacob had gone out for the day, 'just shopping' he'd told her with an air of studied nonchalance. This was risky stuff, she'd thought to herself as she waved him off. He'd done well for her first birthday with him, but perhaps she should have given him some pointers for Christmas. She had no idea what he had in mind for her – she only hoped it wouldn't be underwear. The idea of unwrapping lingerie in front of Noel, Christina, Holly and Joe! Surely Jacob would have the good taste not to put her through such an ordeal.

Mind you, she hadn't been so fastidious towards Sally, whose parcel was sitting in front of her, wrapped and labelled and ready to go to the post. That heavenly négligé with feather trim was just too tempting – but Sally would probably be opening it with some of her actor buddies who'd think it was all too terribly amusing and ironic. And Sally was past embarrassing anyway. Although wait until she opened the fur-trimmed rubber gloves with the big jewelled ring attached. Beth smiled with glee. Pure kitsch and stunningly inappropriate! She'd pay good money to see the look on the face of her oldest friend, whose idea of spring cleaning was to take out the bin and kick everything else under the bed.

With everything sorted for the Mistletoe Meet, ticket sales going well according to Irene, and virtually all the wrapping done (though in the wee small hours), the groceries (except for the veg to be bought last minute of course) safely squirrelled away, Beth was feeling better today though. Since her outburst, Jacob had been treating her with extreme caution as if she might explode at any time. But interviews were done; she had even finished all her lecture planning ready to return after the holidays and was set for a day of total, guilt-free indulgence. She tidied the dining-room table and, like an addict about to plunge into their vice, took out her shameful stash of women's magazines and spread them out on the table. She lapped up the cover lines. 'Your best Christmas ever!', 'Create the ultimate Country Christmas!', 'Step by step to a truly Traditional Feast!', 'Top tips for the Big Day!', 'Deck the Halls! Top looks for your home!'

The exclamation marks positively shrieked at her from the glossy, jewel-coloured covers. It was all there – everything she would ever need to know about the art of Christmas: how to keep everyone happy and come out of it looking as if it was effortless yet, at the same time, as though you'd taken loads of trouble. She felt a glow of excitement.

Now this would be something for the History of Art department to rib her about. Beth Layhem, acknowledged Renaissance expert, armed only with her ferocious intellect and a fresh pack of highlighter pens, admitting to having annotated and catalogued every magazine feature on Christmas that had appeared since the middle of October. Suddenly she was the quintessence of Christmas wisdom.

She flicked open one of the articles she'd marked with a sticky memo label and read it greedily. 'Turn your home into a Winter Wonderland with our foolproof Christmas Garland!'

She had it all ready, stashed in one of those plastic boxes supermarkets provide for the faithful. Dry oasis, florists wire, glycerined beech leaves, tartan ribbons and a glue gun. Buying all this lot had set her back a few quid, but not nearly as much as buying a ready-made garland would have done. Plus, hers would be home-made; plus, she'd be able to make garlands every year for the foreseeable future – until she and Jacob were too little and shrivelled up to care any more. She sat back. Her and Jacob. That tiff had rocked her boat a bit. They'd never talked to each other like that before. Perhaps she was just tired, what with the end of term and all that. A perfect family Christmas was, surely, the best way of showing how much she loved him? A glossy swag of evergreens and ribbons all down the banisters couldn't fail to get her message over.

She set to work.

Within fifteen minutes, she was ready to sue the magazine for misrepresentation. Beth had covered the table in glue, accidentally stuck a bunch of pine cones to Jig-Jag's indignant head and discovered she couldn't bear the sound of florists' wire being pushed into dry oasis. After an hour and a half, with the addition of an armful of foliage from the now-denuded garden, she had, not a garland exactly – that wouldn't be the right word for something about eighteen inches long – but something that looked more like road kill – an image not helped by the slightly wonky fake robin she'd been encouraged to include. But it was her very own. She closed the reproachful article firmly, proudly tied on the last tartan ribbon, then fixed the 'something' in a corner of the hall, half-hidden by the coats. There.

She swiftly swept the detritus into the box and shoved it under the table. Out of sight. She went back to admire her efforts again. Not so bad really. If you squinted.

As a reward, Beth made herself a new pot of coffee, slipped her shoes off and took her pristine copy of *WM* into the sitting room. She smoothed the cover with her hand, ran her finger down the cover lines until she found the one she was looking for, then flicked the pages open. Past the readers' letters, past the sex toys (really!), past Anya and some 'amazing' revelation, until she found what she'd seen on the cover that day in the supermarket.

Your Countdown to the Perfect Christmas.

*

'Shit! You never said it was that soon.'

'Well, Carol, Christmas is a pretty regular event now but, if you like, I can email God and see if he can postpone it?' Jemima made her smug attempt at a joke and pushed her spectacles up her cute little nose. Her face was flushed and her bubbly mood pretty accurately reflected the mood throughout the office. Sales figures already for the January issue were nothing short of extraordinary and the news had sent all the staff into a frenzy of over-excitement. All except Holly, Carol noticed, who seemed strangely subdued. Perhaps she was too cool to enthuse. Some angle, update or 'expert' opinion on the Anya Baby Revelation featured in almost every news bulletin and they had reprinted the issue of *WM* once already. But, as far as Carol was concerned, neither was as significant as the fact that for the first time in perhaps fifteen years there were ad boards for *WM* in the reception of the building.

'But I've done nothing about shopping! Oh buggery bugger.' She frantically called up her schedule on the computer. 'Have I got any time in the next few days?'

Jemima looked at the diary on her knee. 'Weeell.' She tapped her perfect white teeth with the end of her perfectly sharpened pencil. 'You have *Women's Hour* tomorrow on the Anya thing, then lunch with the contributors ... um ...' She breathed in through her teeth. 'There's the last proofs to go off for the Feb issue, or we'll miss the presses cos they are shutting down over the holiday – and I don't think Ian's goodwill will last if we pull that trick again.' Carol bit back a comment about bacon-saving exclusive interviews and concentrated instead on trying to find some clear water between meetings, meetings and more meetings.

'You have nothing on until three today if that's any good. Then this evening it's the office party of course, and,' she looked at the delicate little watch on her wrist, 'it's only twelve thirty now?'

Carol stood up, pulled her jacket from the back of her chair and, wrapping her scarf around her neck, headed for the door. 'I'll be on my mobile. Two and half hours to do my entire Christmas shopping. Bloody hell.'

She practically threw herself in front of a taxi outside the building, shouted 'Hamleys and fast' and collapsed against the seat. The traffic was painfully slow in the cold drizzle, and cars already had their lights on despite the fact that it was only lunchtime. Lunchtime. No wonder her stomach was rumbling. She delved into her bag and pulled out a high-energy, low-flavour snack bar she must have crammed in there some time ago judging by its crumpled state, and demolished it in two mouthfuls. It would have to suffice.

The shop lights were blurred by the raindrops on the window of the cab until they were a psychedelic mass of sparkling jewels. Crikey, it's Christmas, thought Carol. What had happened to the magic she used to feel for weeks before when she was young? In the week before Christmas, she and her mum would come up to town from Catford on the train – her mother had never felt the need to learn to drive – just to see the lights, then would stay for high tea at Selfridges. They'd dress up and make an event of it. She'd wear her long white socks and party shoes and her best coat with the velvet collar and muff, and one year they had queued for an hour and a half to see Father Christmas in Harrods. Carol could still remember the excitement mixed with trepidation on entering the dark grotto and sitting on his knee – well, you could then – only to be gutted when the wonderfully wrapped gift he'd given her had turned out to be a toy dustpan and brush. Even at six her feminist instincts were evident. She had a strong suspicion the boy in the queue behind her wouldn't have been given one of those.

Had she shared the thrill of all this with Tim? Did he too associate the smell of a freshly peeled satsuma with Christmas morning? Did the opening bars of 'Oh Little Town of Bethlehem' make the hairs stand up on the back of his neck? Would he still make a wish under the tree before he went to bed on Christmas Eve like she always had? Or was she always too busy and hadn't taught him the pleasure of it all?

She looked at her watch anxiously and toyed with jumping out and walking, though she wasn't sure barging her way down Oxford Street would be any quicker. People were using full carrier bags like police riot shields and she didn't want a boxed-up DVD player from Dixons impaled in her stomach. The expressions on everyone's faces as they poured down the street, packing every second of a precious lunch hour, were grim in their determination. How strange that the pleasure of giving had become some sort of time trial. Now the cab was passing a jeweller's, busy serving men trying to make the right choice for their wives or lovers, and there was a news-stand by the tube. Carol craned her neck as they passed, a smile spreading across her face as she saw *WM* lined up across the front and a woman buying a copy.

Had she cashed in on Anya's misery? For a moment, self-doubt fell like a shadow until she reminded herself – as Ian, her new best friend, had done several times in the last few days – that it was Anya who had approached *her*.

One hour and ten minutes later, laden down with carrier bags and sweating slightly, Carol made another lunge for a taxi. Her credit card glowed red in her wallet, mainly from a last-minute and unplanned dart into Liberty's where she'd found presents for the staff and her mother a beautiful cashmere cardigan and a handbag. Very personal things she knew – and unnecessarily extravagant – but they served to salve her conscience a tad for another year of having leant very heavily on her.

But the majority of the bags were printed with the famous Hamleys logo. So decisive had she been, any onlooker might have had her down for one of those prize winners in *Supermarket Sweep*. With a clear vision brought on by sheer panic she'd done dressing up – Thunderbirds – Lego, a build-your-own robot; a set of silly plastic teeth, some pony items for a goddaughter, *Lord of the Rings* related items, and a rather adorable soft toy that had looked out at her from its lonely position on the shelf.

'Can I assist you?' One of the seasonal staff, having a break from demonstrating a blow-up flying saucer, managed to catch the chemistry set just as it fell from her arms.

'Well, there is one thing I can't find. My son just can't live without a 3D space projector.'

The boy laughed knowingly. 'Yours and every other boy on the planet. This season's hot favourite I'm afraid.' He sucked in the air. 'Don't think we'll have any more in before the big day. Soz.' Carol could feel panic rising.

'That's a disaster! Could you just check the store room for me? There might be one lurking.'

'I've checked it about ten times today already. It's a nonstarter I'm afraid. Need a hand?'

Dejected, Carol could feel something else slipping from her grip. 'Could you just escort me to the till?' Slightly freer now, she managed to pick up a novelty pencil and keyring, and a Darth Vader light sabre as she passed.

There were six or seven bags around her feet in the taxi now, and she could feel the sense of relief overwhelm her as they headed back towards the office. She'd done it – and although not entirely successfully, by the skin of her teeth she'd managed to buy some decent presents before it was too late. Once more, annual festive adrenalin and blind panic had seen her through. She pulled out her lists again and ticked off a few items, then picked out her phone to call her mum. Stupidly she realised it was still on silent from this morning's meeting and she'd missed several calls, including one from the little Irishwoman herself.

'I'm sorry, Mum,' she apologised as she called her back. 'Been Christmas shopping and forgot the phone. Can I ask you a couple of things? I forgot to get wrapping paper – I wonder could you—'

'Carol lovely, I've been trying to get hold of you. Now listen, Father Benedict called me.' Carol knew what she was going to say before she went any further. 'My friend Niamh – remember her? – has dropped out. Her leg is playing her up something awful – and there'll be a terrible lot of walking – and so there's a place come up on her Lourdes trip over Christmas.'

Carol suppressed an unfestive blasphemy and sighed. 'Oh Mum.'

'I know, marvellous news, isn't it? Now I'm out of the way you and Tim can snuggle down together in that lovely little cottage he keeps telling me about. We fly first thing on the twenty-third. Oh Carol, you know how much I've always wanted to go and it will be so magical at Christmas.'

'I know Mum, it's great news. We'll just be disappointed you aren't with us, that's all. See you later at the play.'

'If we're still allowed to call it that. Can't wait to see the little fella in all his finery – bye, darling.' Damn damn damn. Carol's heart sank. She had to confess she was relying on her mother to try and find this blasted 3D projector thing and to get in most of the provisions they'd need to take with them to the cottage. Would Carol find the time now? Was it too late to scour the internet? She looked down at her phone again, only to see she'd missed yet another call. She dialled the number.

'Hello. Radio Five Live.'

'Oh hello, yes, it's Carol, the editor of *WM* magazine. Was someone trying to call me?'

'Just bear with me, and I'll try and find out.' There was a pause and Carol was subjected to dreamy musak for a moment, until a breathy voice broke in.

'Carol? Oh at last! I've been trying to get hold of you for ages – your office said you were on your mobile but I called and called.'

'I'm so sorry. Can I help?'

'We're just about to start a discussion programme about girls being forced to abandon babies and the iniquity of the law as it stands. We would like you to contribute but we are about to go on air any second after the news and weather. Can you talk *now*?'

Carol was immediately on the back foot . Back at the office she'd been steeped in copy on Easter cookery tips and floaty skirts for spring walks in the country. She'd even just commissioned a feature on the top-ten celebrity holiday destinations for next August – confident now they'd still be publishing then. Now she re-wound her brain. 'Er ... OK.'

'Right, you'll be on air and talking to Nigel any minute. Ready?'

'Excuse me.' Carol leant forward and tapped on the glass between her and the driver. 'Can you pull over? I've got to do a radio interview.'

The cab driver glanced over his shoulder, swung onto a double yellow line, and picked up his newspaper, as if fares doing interviews on national radio stations was the sort of thing that happened every day.

'And hello.' The voice of the presenter came booming down her ear, his tone so upbeat and unnatural it was obvious he was talking on air. 'Unless you've been on the moon for the last couple of weeks, you cannot have missed the fascinating revelation from internationally successful star Anya who, aged fifteen, gave birth in the toilets at Euston Station and abandoned her baby outside Guy's Hospital here in London. This has once again raised the issue of mothers who, in desperation and often in extreme poverty, are forced to abandon their babies. With me today is Lord Henry Winterton, chairman of the select committee on child welfare, Nora Chase, writer and avid pro-choice campaigner, and the editor of *WM* to whom Anya made her shocking revelation.'

And so, surrounded by bags of toys, and with Christmas traffic streaming either side of her, Carol became embroiled in a discussion about the antiquated Offences Against the Persons Act, which had not changed since it hit the statute book in 1861 and which made it a criminal offence to abandon a child under the age of two.

'Now tell me, which is better,' trumpeted Nora Chase in her Anglicised American accent, 'to have an unwanted pregnancy terminated safely and at an early stage, or to have a baby born in sordid and squalid circumstances and then left to perish in a freezing cold phone box or on a doorstep somewhere?'

Carol, who had never been very quick in arguments – Paul used to tell her she was hopeless at confrontation – could see Nora's point of view to an extent, but didn't think she had been asked on to the programme to agree. 'Well ...'

'We cannot live in a society,' interrupted the noble lord with a boom, 'where it is condoned for a woman to give birth and simply leave her child to the mercy of strangers and the State. The law must point the way to individual responsibility. Such women should be viewed in the same category as women who deliberately harm their children by neglect or cruelty.'

Carol was suddenly back in the hotel room holding Anya as she sobbed out her grief at giving up her child. She couldn't begin to imagine what that Christmas must have been like for Anya, alone in London with no money and no baby, her breasts aching from the need to feed, still in pain from having given birth and her heart ripped out by the thought of what might be happening to her daughter in the hands of the strangers and the State to which Lord Winterton referred. And every subsequent Christmas must have raked up the memory again as every carol and Christmas light reminded her.

'I think you are so wrong,' she waded into the heated discussion. 'Abortion was not an option for Anya, as it isn't for many women, for financial or emotional reasons.' There was silence from the others. 'Abandoning your baby, naked and in a plastic bag where it could not survive for long – yes that may be neglect – but to wrap her up clean and warm, and leave her in a busy place where she would be found easily, that is done to give the child a better chance in life than its mother could hope to provide.'

'It's illegal,' replied the lord.

'It's an outdated law,' said Carol firmly, hoping he wouldn't challenge her too much. This was an area she knew little about. What she did know was the pain she had seen in Anya's eyes. 'Sometimes people have no choice but to make certain decisions because of circumstances. What she did was incredibly brave and incredibly painful, yet the reason women don't come forward to say they have left their babies is because of the stigma society places on them. It may be that the only way to make sure a baby can survive when a mother cannot care for it is to allow her to give it up anonymously and into a safe place. The only way we can do this is to take the criminal shadow out of the picture. Anya has risked everything – her reputation and her career – by standing up and admitting what she did eighteen years ago.'

Nora Chase clearly wasn't so sure. 'It's exactly because of who she is that she can say these things,' she said dogmatically. 'I suppose she thinks that because she has millions she will be above the law. That she'll be able to hide behind her star status.

You can bet it wouldn't be the same if she had nothing now and lived off the State.'

'She did once,' Carol replied. 'When she gave up that baby she had less than nothing, and gave away the only thing she did have. We should applaud her for her bravery and her success.'

The presenter broke in and the discussion turned to the likelihood of prosecution. Would, he asked with incredulity, the police dare make an example of a woman who was admired world-wide? Who was a role model for young girls with her sassy attitude and great music. The panel chewed this one over, and Carol kept very quiet, in the back of her mind the fear lurking that, by not talking Anya out of admitting so publicly what she had done eighteen years ago, Carol would be partly responsible if criminal proceedings were brought against her.

'Has there been a test case?' pressed Nora Chase.

'There is no statute of limitation,' said the lord pompously, 'so in theory a woman could be prosecuted many years after the event and for this reason no woman has come forward.'

'Until now,' the presenter interrupted. 'But we have to consider her daughter – and Anya's daughter must be out there somewhere – because presumably a daughter has to appear to prove that a baby was abandoned at all.' Carol couldn't help thinking that the emergence of a daughter would be a cruelly mixed blessing for Anya. It might bring some kind of closure to eighteen years of wondering and speculation. It could also spell the end of her career.

Chapter 12

Later the same day

*Think ahead during the year and save those off-cuts
from your curtain making. They'll be just perfect for
edging nativity play costumes for your little angel!*

Back at the office, the inevitable wind-down to the Christmas
break had begun and there was a definite sense of de-mob fever.
When Carol walked in after her unscheduled middle-of-the-
day shopping spree, her arms weighed down with shopping
bags, the staff seemed to take this as *carte blanche* to unwind
even further.

'To the beauty cupboard!' came the cry and, as one, the entire
staff lunged towards the Holy Grail, cramming themselves into
the poorly lit space that served as the depository for all the
creams, eye shadows, oils and smellies that had appeared in the
post every day throughout the year from eager PRs (all called
Sophie or Emma) hoping to have their products featured in
the beauty pages. In the last few months, keen to avoid being
associated with failure, Carol had noticed the bigger names had
knocked the magazine off their regular mailing list. But over
the last few days, with the PRs sensing success and increased
readership, even more beauty samples seemed to have poured
in than usual.

She dumped the Hamleys bags as quickly as she could in the
corner of her office and unwound her scarf, keen to join the fray
and see what goodies were being shared out. As she turned to

hang it over the back of her chair, she was faced with two of the most enormous hampers she had ever seen. Nestled in the first, and carefully protected by vibrant pink tissue and ribbons, was the entire range from Carol's very favourite brand of skincare. Fiendishly expensive and deliciously fragrant, it was the kind of product that would never lower itself to advertise in the pages of *WM*. With the hamper, tied in yet more ribbon around a bunch of shockingly out-of-season lily of the valley, was a note. 'Atta Girl,' it read. 'Fabulous scoop and you've out-sold us five to one this month! Just watch it!' It was signed from the editor of *Style*. Carol smiled, aware *Style* saw all this as a mere blip so they could afford to be magnanimous in defeat, and turned to the other hamper, a wicker basket with the famous Fortnum & Mason logo. Crammed into it was the very finest Christmas fare – port and stilton, packets of shortbread, a bottle of champagne, truffles and a mini cake, nuts and tea, and two beautiful silver and gold crackers.

When she opened the card, she let out a whoop of glee. She could barely wait to tell Ian.

'Congratulations and we look forward to a great relationship with *WM* in the future, from the Directors of DIY Homes.'

'Are you coming to join the obscene orgy of greed that is going on in the beauty cupboard?' Emma had put her head around the door. 'Oh, I see you are having an orgy of your own. Wow!' She came to look closer. 'Blimey, I've never seen anything like those. The most we ever got from them in the past was a couple of bottles of Asti and a card.'

'I think, Emma my dear,' laughed Carol taking her arm and heading towards the door, 'that this Christmas is going to be a good one.'

The scenes in the beauty cupboard were indeed depraved and made the first day of the Harrods sale look like tea in the Palm Room at the Ritz. Carol waded in there with the rest of them, and emerged ten minutes later, flushed and a bit sweaty, with some bath oil and a foot massage implement. Around her the staff had armfuls of bottle and tubes, lipsticks and blusher brushes, all of which would end up at the bottom of some unsuspecting relative's stocking.

'Crikey!' a rather skittish-looking Melanie, her hair dishevelled, nudged Carol knowingly in the ribs and indicated the foot massager. 'I fancied that too but you beat me to it! You single women!'

Carol held up the implement. 'I thought my Aunt Dolores might like it.'

'Bloody hell, Carol, how old is she?' All the staff were looking now.

'Oh, she must be knocking seventy, but she's always having trouble with her arches.'

There was silence and then someone snorted with laughter. Within seconds everyone, except Carol, was bent over with giggles.

'It's not her arches that'll fix,' gasped Sheena.

Carol looked over at Jemima – what the hell was going on? 'Sex toys feature,' she mouthed back.

'Oh God.' Carol put her hand to her mouth, her eyes dancing with mirth. 'Oh I don't know. It might make Aunt Dolores' Christmas! Does it come with instructions?'

It was later, in a meeting with Ian and the other editors, this time their faces wreathed in tight and satisfyingly envious smiles, that Carol felt her phone vibrate in her pocket. She took it out surreptitiously. It was a text and from Nick. Seeing his name on the screen gave her a warm flood of pleasure.

'Hello stranger. Heard the radio prog this pm. U sounded like the voice of reason.'

'How did you know it was on?' she replied, hiding the phone under the table.

'Didn't,' came the swift response. 'Was waiting to hear what time Stoke were kicking off tonight.'

She smiled to herself. 'Well thank you Mr.' She spelt out on the keypad. 'Wouldn't want to play second fiddle to yr beloved team!'

She expected a reply back as quickly as the last but it was quite a time before she felt the phone vibrate again.

'You don't.'

*

Holly pushed the clinking hessian bag down into the depths of her rucksack. The mounds of other stuff – the lippy, the heavenly palette of Lancôme eye shadows, the perfumes for herself, and random bath stuff she had seized from the beauty cupboard for Noel and his girlfriend – she left brazenly stacked on her desk, mute witness to her sharp elbows and steely determination. The blue bottles and jars of the Pregnancy Pamper Kit, however, which she herself had carelessly slung into the cupboard weeks ago, had now come sharply into focus. And since she'd reached her decision – since *she and Joe* had reached *their* decision – it had been beckoning her every time she went into the cupboard to stash the new freebies on the shelves. It had been a matter of honour to get her mitts on it during the clear-out, and a challenge to do so without anyone else noticing.

She glanced around the office to make sure. Everyone else was too preoccupied admiring their own spoils to notice what each other had nabbed. That would probably come later, once the euphoria had worn off a bit and they started wondering exactly who had the vibrating knickers. Holly smiled to herself. She hadn't been the only one hiding things in her bag. She turned to Emma and asked, all innocence, 'Did you get anything special, Em? Anything you'd been particularly hoping for?'

The features editor glanced quickly at Holly, then busied herself with rearranging the row of flock robins blu-tacked to the top of her computer. 'Yes, a few bits and pieces. That Chanel moisturiser, some delicious Touche Eclat. You?'

Holly gestured at the heap of boxes on her desk. 'Presents mostly.'

Emma peered vaguely. 'That eye shadow will be nice for the party.'

The rest of the afternoon was spent in a fuzz of excitement. Holly watched with disbelief the stampede for the loos at five as everybody got themselves ready, giggling over make-up and new dresses. The cloud of competing perfumes was almost overwhelming and, like everything else at the moment, made Holly want to gag. Then began the lunge for the warm Jacob's Creek, served in paper cups, and there to wash down prawn cocktail Skips balancing on a paper plate.

Holly had hoped for something a little more impressive – a decent restaurant at least – especially in view of this month's sales figures, and her disappointment at the annual jamboree being two tables pushed together in the advertising sales office made her all the more determined not to get involved. The party was strangely quiet once the initial twittering had stopped and someone turned on a tinny portable CD machine with *Now That's What I Call Music* compilations. Holly was already wondering how she could make her excuses and escape, when Carol came into the room. She had clearly come straight from a meeting and was still in her crisp suit and work face.

Carol looked at the scene in front of her, bewildered. 'Bloody hell, has someone died? I've seen more excitement at a funeral.' There was silence as everyone stood around awkwardly. She delved into her bag and, pulling out her wallet, handed her assistant a wodge of notes. 'Jemima, get your arse down to M&S. We need serious quality provisions.'

After that things improved markedly, especially on the arrival of the karaoke machine that came courtesy of the accounts department. From the lofty, clear-eyed viewpoint of someone who wasn't drinking, Holly witnessed the gradual disintegration of her colleagues' inhibitions and their perform-ances. Talk about an eye-opener! Even Carol had had a go, choosing 'I will Survive' by Gloria Gaynor and aiming quite a bit of it at Ian, in a surprisingly powerful, bluesy voice. After much cajoling, Ian did 'Sex Bomb' and even attempted a Tom Jones wiggle, shamelessly egged on by the now-caterwauling women.

Holly watched as Carol made her way around the room, handing out small Liberty gift bags to everyone, thanking them for their hard work. Holly waited until people had opened theirs and cringed when she saw the contents. Please God may hers not be something delicate, pink and sparkly too. How would she be able to fake enthusiasm?

'And this is for you, Holly,' Carol was in front of her at last. 'Thought it might just be your thing.' Holly cautiously unwrapped the tissue paper to reveal a heavy round pendant made from dark wood and mother of pearl. She gasped and looked up at Carol, who simply smiled.

Things were really swinging now, but Holly decided it was no fun being stone-cold sober on the sidelines. She wasn't the only one. Carol had on her worried face although she was trying not to show it, and kept checking her watch. Holly made a discreet exit and, as she left the building, found Carol on the pavement trying to get a cab.

'Oh hi, you on your way home too? Blast, that one didn't even try to stop, and I'm going to be late,' Carol muttered tersely.

'Do you think there'd be more round the corner? We could try there.'

Carol looked at her in surprise. 'Are you after a cab too? I thought you usually took the tube. Still it is a bit cold tonight.'

'Er, no. I was just going to help you to get one. It's miserable waiting out here on your own. I expect there are loads of Christmas parties on tonight.'

Carol seemed a bit sceptical. Well, fair enough. Holly had to admit she hadn't always been the shiniest ray of sunshine round the office. She smiled reassuringly but Carol looked positively alarmed. Perhaps she'd try small talk. 'Not long till Christmas, eh? Are you doing anything special?'

'Oh don't!' Carol looked pained. 'So little time, so much to do. And this year I've got to do it without my mum. She's taking herself off on a pilgrimage.'

For a moment Holly had a vision of her own mother at Christmas when she was a child. Completely loopy, organising that sodding party every year, with Christmas Day coming a poor second in her social calendar, while Noel, Holly and Jacob tried their best to stay out of her way. Then she thought about those few Christmases with just the three of them. Free, at last, to do just what they wanted at Christmas, yet somehow lacking the will to do it. And what about next year? Holly swallowed hard. 'Are you going away?' she asked Carol abruptly.

Carol smiled. 'Yes, actually. I've booked an idyllic-looking cottage, just for a few days. We'll hide ourselves away and recover from all this madness and it'll be sheer bliss. Wood fires, long walks. All that sort of thing.'

Holly realised she didn't really know anything about Carol's home life. 'Are you going with your partner?'

'No,' Carol laughed. 'Just me and my little boy. I'm a single mum, Holly. He's seven so still big on Father Christmas. Actually, we're going to a place I saw in the magazine. I booked it ages ago. Oh! Has he got his light on? Yes! Over here. I don't think he's seen me.' She waved frantically.

Quashing a vague feeling of disquiet – nah, it couldn't have been that one. It was probably a cottage advertised in the classifieds – Holly stuck her fingers in her mouth and let out a piercing whistle. The cab slowed and turned towards them.

Carol got in and, before she closed the door, turned back to Holly, smiling mischievously. 'Now, with a talent like that, you'll go far in publishing, Holly. See you tomorrow.'

*

The lights were already down by the time Carol crawled in at the back of the school assembly hall. Several of the parents turned around to scowl at the late-comer and it took a few moments for her to spot Paul and her mother, who had secured them such good seats she must have been hovering outside the hall door since about lunchtime. 'Yoohoo!' Mary called embarrassingly so that everyone turned to see who it was who'd put work before the primary school annual highlight. The children had already come on stage and were standing in a tableau waiting to begin, all eyes on Carol as she hissed 'sorry' every time she tripped on someone's shoes.

She caught Tim's eye, expecting disapprobation, but his face showed such relief that she had made it and such pleasure that she was there, that she couldn't have cared less what everyone else thought.

Carol had always prided herself that she got the plot of the Christmas story, but this performance was like no nativity play she'd ever witnessed. She got a strange feeling things had gone awry the moment the hostel-keeper's partner, played by little Sukvinda wearing non-sectarian dungarees, warmly welcomed in Mary and Joseph with a little speech claiming there was always room for asylum seekers. Intrigued now as to where the babe would be born – presumably by Caesarean section to ensure there was no litigation through midwife malpractice or negligence – Carol was metaphorically on the edge of her seat – though not literally as she'd been informed she was blocking the view of someone's baby brother seated behind her.

Gabriel emerged in a dressing gown shortly after to deliver the good news, but appeared to have a very small part and managed to deliver his lines without alluding at all to the Almighty, but he did urge everyone not to be afraid.

'Well, I certainly am,' whispered Mary rather too loudly.

'Ssssh,' came from those around them and Carol slid even further down in her chair.

All the children sang a little song at this point, accompanied by steel drums playing a Bollywood rap beat, along the lines of diversity of family forms, and each verse managed to celebrate everything from Diwali to Ramadan – with an astonishing passing reference to Disney World and without a mention of the Virgin Birth whatsoever. The virgin in question, Zuwena, who Carol knew was Tim's *bête noire* (a rather apt description), was playing the single mother role with such enthusiasm that Carol fully expected Joseph, played by a confused Kyle, to be apprehended by a representative from the Child Support Agency at any time.

She was beginning to wonder how long this agonising adherence to political correctness could be sustained when, with a flourish, the poor baby Jesus was placed in a cardboard box emblazoned with the words 'Fair Trade Coffee (please recycle)' because, as was pointed out by a lisping Lewis, if a baby was placed in their manger, it would deprive the lowing oxen of their straw, which would be tantamount to cruelty to animals. Up at the back of the stage, a wavering star appeared on a long broom handle – Carol caught her breath, convinced it might overbalance and come crashing down on the assembled heads – but just as the plot began to veer dangerously close to delivering a religious message, across the front of the stage bobbed six little white blobs, packed into white jumpers stuffed with cushions and pillows for the puffy effect, so thick their arms stuck out at right angles. On their hands were red gloves and on their heads were crammed bobble hats.

'Snowpersons,' hissed her mother again. 'Tim says they are intended to be a grim portent of global warming.'

'Of course. Silly me,' replied Carol, smiling at Paul who clearly was finding it hard to control himself, and she too almost had to stick her fist in her mouth to stop herself snorting with laughter.

Then came the giftbearers: first of all three wise people so diverse in their origins that Carol fully expected a gay and/or disabled representation, and then the moment she had been waiting for, Tim's grand entrance: up he came onto the stage carrying with tremendous care the hamster that had been selected in a school poll as 'the gift you think the baby Jesus would most like to receive'.

'Oh look at our boy!' crowed Mary in a loud whisper, clasping her hands together in glee. 'And doesn't he look a picture.'

Carol could feel a silly lump in her throat, half through pride at seeing his innocent little face as he knelt down with his gift by the cardboard box, and half through guilt at the Stella McCartney skirt she'd nicked from the fashion cupboard and which he now wore as a cape.

'Did you like my bit, Mum?' yawned Tim later, snuggled in the back of the car with the heating blasting out loudly. 'Dad said I was immense.'

'I thought it was the best play I've ever seen.'

'And you were the star turn, my wee one,' cooed her mother.

'What time does your plane go on Friday morning? Do you want a lift?' Carol surreptitiously crossed her fingers on the steering wheel, hoping to goodness her mother wouldn't say yes as it would only delay their departure to the cottage. She wrote herself a mental memo to call that woman again to find out where the keys would be.

'Good Lord no. Jim's kindly said he'll take me.' Jim was Mary's widowed neighbour, a great bear of a man who had dropped her round at their house a few times when she couldn't get the bus. Carol strongly suspected they were a bit fond of each other but had never dared ask. Tim had no such reservations.

'Is he your boyfriend, Granny?' he asked eagerly. 'He must like you if he's getting up so early.'

To Carol's amazement her mother looked a bit flustered. 'Now, what sort of a question's that, young man? I had a lovely happy time with your grandpa and that's enough for one lifetime thank you.'

'But Granny, he died ages ago. Wouldn't you like a boyfriend?' Carol waited with bated breath for her mother's reply to Tim's prodding.

'Oh now stop you with your questioning! Boys your age shouldn't have those sort of thoughts in their heads.' And she folded her hands in her lap with finality and looked out of the window at the night. Mmm, the lady doth protest too much, thought Carol with a secret smile.

She braked behind cars stopped at the lights and there was silence in the now-warm car. And what of her? Did she want male company? She looked out of the window at a little mini-market on the other side of the road. Couples were pushing heaving trolleys and packing carrier bags of Christmas groceries into their cars. Someone was loading a small child into a car seat, and another leant over the bonnet and gave his girlfriend a lingering kiss. Carol felt a strange pain in the back of her throat. Yes, she thought, that would be nice. And she'd like Nick to be doing it.

But would he cope? Would the novelty of having a small boy in tow behind his new girlfriend wear off as it had so often in the past? Her last 'boyfriend' experience had been when Tim was four – the dashing Johnny, a political lobbyist she'd met at a dinner party: a short-lived and ill-advised relationship. He'd barely lit her match let alone her fire, but interested men didn't pass by that often and she'd grabbed the chance. He'd been so attentive to start with, taking her out to expensive restaurants and first nights but, once she'd introduced Tim into the equation, he'd cooled, making excuses when she'd suggested visits to child-friendly places at the weekend, and she'd called it a day.

There had been a few hopeless 'dates' since then – though she wasn't sure that it was legal to call it a date once you were over thirty. They'd been nice men, and one in particular she'd been quite hopeful about, but then there was the *baggage*. Single, and they got that startled look in their eye at the prospect of trying to understand children. Divorced, and you could see them totting up the additional drain on resources having to factor in another mouth to feed on top of the maintenance they were paying for their own brood.

Then there was Nick. She said a little prayer in her head: Please God, let him be as good as he seems. Let him be the one.

Tim had fallen asleep, his mouth open and his head lolling against the seatbelt, by the time Carol had dropped off her mother and pulled up outside their little terraced house. She lifted him out and carried him upstairs to undress him and put him into his bed; he wrapped his arms around her neck and nestled into her.

Drained of energy now, she postponed the plan to wrap presents (mentally slotting it in for tomorrow night), made herself a cup of tea and began opening the day's trawl of Christmas cards. The ones earlier in the month had been from friends of her mother's and relations. The most scarily organised – and it was always people she knew only vaguely – had got it together enough to write cosy little round-ups of family news over the year. 'Bethany has passed grade twelve ballet and is our little angel, and Callum is a mean little football player when he's not doing quantum physics and t'ai chi.'

By now however, the cards were coming in dribs and drabs and from busy friends who'd bought theirs somewhere expensive and convenient. There was one from Paul and Eve to the two of them – designed by him of course with a silly cartoon involving Father Christmas and weapons of mass destruction. It made Carol smile.

Blast. Paul and Eve. She realised she'd have to wrap their present now because he was dropping round tomorrow with Tim's and she'd need to have it ready. Desperate to crawl into bed, she pulled out some paper and the Sellotape from the drawer, switched on the TV with the remote control and sat herself down on the floor to begin.

The news presenter on ITV was introducing a piece about snow in Lincolnshire that had brought the county to a standstill, though to Carol the thought of being unable to get to work sounded very appealing. As she battled with the tape, trying to make a neat job of wrapping a wicker picnic bottle carrier (Eve was always doing picnics), she looked up occasionally at the footage of children throwing snowballs at each other then traffic at a standstill on the motorway, the cars cocooned in a blanket of snow. She was tearing the tape off with her teeth, one knee holding down the paper in position, when the presenter's next words caught her ear.

'Further news, today the woman who discovered the abandoned baby on the steps of Guy's Hospital eighteen years ago has come forward.' Carol looked up, tape stuck to her bottom lip. 'The discovery of the baby, believed now to be the daughter of pop star Anya, was widely reported at the time, but no one came forward to claim her. In a recent magazine article, however, the thirty-three-year-old star admitted it had been she who, in desperation, had abandoned her four-day-old daughter.' A reporter filled out the story, explaining how a nurse, Elizabeth Drake, who had been a student at the time, had found the bundle. '"I shall never forget it,"' the reporter quoted her words, looking down at his notes, '"the baby was quiet but wrapped up warm against the cold." It is believed that the baby, who would be just eighteen this week, was eventually adopted, and in the interest of confidentiality no further information is to be released. However, speculation is increasing as to whether police will pursue any legal action against the star.'

The footage moved again to the front of Anya's hotel in New York, crawling with reporters and photographers. 'Anya has made no further statement,' he continued, 'but is believed to be talking to lawyers.' Oh Lord, thought Carol, poor Anya. What have I started?

Chapter 13

22 December

*Having people to stay? Spoil your house guests but let
them relax and enjoy themselves. Why else did you
invite them?*

A scarecrow. A scarecrow on a bad hair day. That's what Beth
saw when she looked in the mirror. The new party dress she'd
bought in haste for the Meet would just about do, but what
was she going to do about her hair? She was badly in need of
a cut, and a few low-lights wouldn't go amiss. She was starting
to look like a badger again. Maybe she could find time for a
facial or a manicure, while she was at it – something she never
did but just reward for having got so much done.

She phoned 'Cut'n'Dried'. What was it about hairdressers
that made them feel they had to have witty names for their
salons? The phone rang and rang. Surely they weren't closed?
Eventually, a breathless sing-song voice answered.

'Cut'n'driedthisisTinaspeakingcanIhelpyou?'

'Oh yes, hello there. I was wondering if you could fit me in
for a quick trim and highlights?'

'Can you bear with me? I'll just take a look.' The sound of
pages being flicked. 'When were you thinking of?'

'Well, I'm free for the rest of today and I can manage tomorrow morning until about eleven.'

Incredulous laughter. 'Oh no. Sorry. The first appointment
I've got is for the third of January. We're completely booked

up, I'm afraid. We've been solid for weeks. Would you like me to book you in for then?'

It was the same story with every hairdresser she tried. Even the ones in Oxford, the ones at hotels and the ones – she was desperate by this time – that sounded like they only catered to men. Even a short back and sides would be preferable to the way she looked at the moment. Beauticians told the same sad story – their ladies were booking up in September for the pre-Christmas rush. They couldn't even shape a single eyebrow, let alone undertake the sort of retread Beth needed.

By the time Jacob came home, she was blotchy and red, having painstakingly taken to the tweezers herself. He looked at her in consternation. Probably just as well she'd resisted trimming her own hair. She'd have to make do with a shop-bought tint and some mousse.

As they drank a glass of wine together and Beth scanned the fridge to find something for supper – foie gras perhaps? – Beth couldn't help noticing that Jacob seemed uneasy. A full ten months of marriage had taught her to save her energy and not bother asking – he'd soon choke if he wanted to. At last, he got round to it.

'With Noel and Holly both bringing their ... their friends, I don't want things to be awkward.'

'What do you mean – awkward? I'm sure they will all get on.'

'Oh,' he studied his wine intently, 'you know. The sleeping arrangements, I mean.'

Beth laughed. 'That's a very conservative concern from a man who's worked with students all his life!'

'Mmm. But it's different, darling, when it's your own children. As far as I'm concerned they will always be babies.'

This was something she hadn't even considered and she felt young and stupid. She knew Becca would have instinctively understood. She wasn't sure what tack to take. 'Have you spoken to them about it? Asked them what they'd like to do?'

'I don't know how to bring it up.' Jacob coughed uncomfortably. 'Of course, what they do when they're by themselves is up to them, but I don't want them doing it under my roof. Our roof.'

Beth smiled ruefully. Quick correction, but not quite quick enough. 'Let's not make a big issue out of it. Obviously we'll put them together because they live with their partners. This is the twenty-first century and I'm sure they'll respect the fact that it's your house.'

'Holly and Joe aren't living together. She'd have told me. But you are missing the point, Beth. Putting them in the same room implies something that I don't especially want to acknowledge.' He was growing more heated by the minute. 'And it puts pressure on them. Besides, Christina is somebody's daughter. I wouldn't like Holly to be put in a situation where she felt she had to cohabit with … Joe, or whatever his name is, just because it's more convenient for the hostess.'

Beth bit her tongue. There was nothing very convenient about having Jacob's offspring and their partners at all – but clearly she was out of her depth here. She took the diplomatic way out. 'How about this then? All three spare rooms are made up. Mrs Havers saw to that. Two with twin beds and one double. Why don't I ask Noel, discreetly, whether he'd like to share with Christina in one of the twin rooms? Otherwise he and Joe could share and each of the girls can get a room to herself.'

'Thanks. That would be the best thing.' Jacob's relief was palpable. 'Oh! I forgot to tell you, your friend Sally called. She said she'd call back. It sounded quite urgent. I took her number.'

Sally! Beth clapped her hand to her forehead in frustration. She'd only gone and forgotten to send off Sally's present – again. It would never get to her in time now. Oh how could she have been so forgetful? Especially when Sally's brown paper parcel for her and, surprisingly, Jacob, had arrived days ago. She dialled her friend's mobile number, feeling hot with embarrassment. The answerphone clicked in straight away. Of course – she'd be on stage in the panto now, striding around and slapping her thighs and failing to look behind her. She left a vague message, saying she'd call back after the show.

In fact, it was Sally who called Beth at ten forty on the dot. She could only just be wiping the grease paint from her face as they spoke. 'The whole thing's gone tits up. I'm so pissed off, I can't begin to tell you,' she ranted. 'Dave and I were going to hide out at my place during the festives, and pretend the whole bloody thing wasn't happening, but his very nearly ex-wife's gone and laid a mega guilt trip on him – you know the kind of thing. "Let's have one last Christmas together so we can make each other entirely miserable and piss off Sally while we're at it." Soooo …'

Beth held her breath. She so didn't need this, on top of everything else. Yet how could she leave Sally out in the cold? After all, a friend is for Christmas, not just for life. 'Of course, Sal!' She tried to infuse her voice with as much warmth as she could. How was she going to break it to Jacob? And what was this going to do to the fragile sleeping arrangements? 'We'd love to see you. When will you be arriving?'

*

Tim knew he shouldn't have done it. Mum had always told him that some things were private and you should respect people's property, but he'd seen a character in a cartoon say that sometimes you just have to break the rules and do what needs doing.

Which was why he'd looked at her mobile while she was in the shower and scrolled down the address book to find the number he wanted. He wasn't sure when would be the best time to make the call because he didn't want her walking in – that would be a disaster – so when she'd said she was going to wrap presents and he wasn't to peep, he'd said he was going to call Gerard in his bedroom, then he'd watch *Blue Peter*, and was that OK with her?

His fingers had shaken a bit as he punched in the number. He'd hoped he'd got it right. The number seemed to click through. What if he was cross? Tim hadn't thought he would be because he didn't seem like a cross person. He seemed quite relaxed really. It had rung for a while, and Tim had felt an ache of disappointment that perhaps he was out. He might even have people round at his house.

'Hello?' The sudden answer at the other end had given Tim a shock.

'Oh hello.' He knew he couldn't speak very loud. 'Is that Nick? It's Tim. Do you remember me?'

'Of course I remember. How are you, mate? Got any new cars for that collection of yours?'

'No, but I'm hoping Father Christmas might bring me one. I've asked him for a remote control one or Hot Wheels but I don't know which he'll bring.'

'Lucky boy. They didn't have such exciting things when I was little. I had some great Dinky cars though.'

'You should make a Christmas list like I did. Granny says you can't expect Father Christmas to know what you want unless you tell him. He'll never know about the 3D space projector unless I put that on.'

'Wise woman. Hey, Tim, does your mum know you're calling me?' Tim had paused. Nick hadn't sounded annoyed or like teachers do when you've done something wrong, but he'd still felt terrible. He ought to explain.

'Er ... not really. I just got your number from her phone. I know how to use it better than she does,' he'd rushed on. 'She always says she only needs one so she can make calls and send texts, but I've worked out how to play videos and take pictures and I showed her what to do. She's even got a picture of me making a silly face as her wallpaper.' Nick had laughed that deep, smiley laugh of his and Tim had thought this sounded encouraging.

'My mum likes going to the cinema, do you?'

Nick had sounded a bit surprised by this. 'Er, yes I do but I haven't had a chance to go recently. What sort of films does she like?'

'She watches films with me sometimes – she likes *Shrek* the best, especially the bit at the end when they sing karaoke – but I've seen her watch boring films too and they usually have people in silly long dresses in them. She cries at the end sometimes.'

'Does she?'

'Sometimes. She gets a red nose when she cries.' Nick had laughed again but not loudly this time. Just a little laugh, so it had seemed OK to ask, 'Do you think she's pretty, my mum?'

There had been a pause at the end of the phone and Tim had thought that perhaps Nick had put the phone down or gone away.

'Yes, Tim, I think your mum is very pretty. I like her smile.'

'I do too. Do you like Porsches? I've got two of them.'

Nick had laughed again. 'Actually, given a choice, I'd have a Maserati.'

'I don't know anything about them. Do you think you'll ever get one? My mum has a Peugeot. It's blue. We did the school play. It was called One World and I was a giftgiver. It was sort of the Christmas Story but a bit different. It would have been nice if you could have seen it. Dad came. Mum made my costume and I think I looked the best, or at least my best friend Gerard said I did.'

'I'm sure you did,' Nick had replied. 'My mum made my

nativity costume for me once. I was a shepherd and we used a tea towel for my headdress. How on earth does your mum find time to make costumes? She must be very busy, cos we won't be able to see each other until after Christmas.'

Tim thought this sounded good. 'Yes she is, but she always seems to find time for things. But she does get tired though cos sometimes she falls asleep on my bed after we've had a story. I like it when she does that because she smells nice. What are you going to do at Christmas? We're going to a cottage, Mum and me.'

'Where's that then?'

'She showed me on a map. I think it's somewhere near Oxford and it sounds like Milkman St David.'

'I'm not sure I know where that is, but I bet it will be fun!' In the background, Tim had been able to hear the sound of music playing.

'Is that your music in the background? Mum says you're pretty good.'

'No but it's a band called The Waterboys. That's a nice thing for her to say – but she's never heard me play so she must be guessing.'

Tim had an idea. 'Perhaps she could come to one of your concerts sometime. So where will you be at Christmas then?'

Nick made a noise as if he was getting up off a sofa or an armchair. 'I haven't got anything planned just yet. I might go and see my sister.'

He'd sounded a bit sad to Tim. 'Won't you see your son?'

'Oh I expect so, but he's quite a big boy now and he'll be with his mother.'

'Will Father Christmas bring him presents?'

'Of course he will!' Nick had sounded amazed that Tim should ask such a thing. 'He comes to everyone.'

'Not the poor in Africa.'

'No, maybe not.'

'He doesn't come to Mummy either.' Tim had stopped. He'd suddenly felt a bit sad too. 'My mummy needs someone I think. She gets sad and lonely. She's always being brave but sometimes her face is sad. Would you be her friend?'

There had been silence again at the end of the phone. 'Tim, I'd like to be her friend very much, but we'll have to see.'

This didn't sound good. Nick hadn't said yes straight out like Tim thought he would. 'She likes you,' he'd said quickly.

'How do you know that?' Tim could hear the smile.

'She laughed differently when you were here.' Nick's chuckle had now become a rumble.

'Did she now!'

Tim had hesitated for a moment, not sure if he should say this. Eeny meeny... 'Nick, I've made a special Christmas wish –' But just at the moment he had heard the door of his mum's room open. 'Timmo?' she'd called down the corridor.

'Sorry, Nick,' he'd whispered urgently, 'I've got to go now.' And loudly to be sure, 'Bye Gerard,' and he'd quickly put down the phone. He hoped he'd said everything all right.

*

The train was heaving with people taking up twice as much room as usual with their wide loads of shopping bags. Carol, squeezed to the point of breathlessness between a large woman in a wet wool overcoat and the glass partition, could just about make out which station she was at, but wasn't sure she'd ever make it to the door when they got to her destination. On the faces of the passengers was written that festive contradiction – a look of hassle and harassment when all around them was jolly music and ho, ho ho.

As people spewed out of the doors, Carol put her head down and surged towards the escalators, regretting that her office had to be in the West End. She hunched down against the bitter wind, dodging patches of ice left on the pavement despite the gritter's best efforts, and barely looked up until she was at the doors of reception, except to slow down briefly on the Tottenham Court Road on a final mental scan. Had she got everything because today was her last chance? It was already ten thirty but she'd grabbed an extra hour or so at home to frantically pack and wrap stocking presents for Tim – an exercise that she knew to be her contribution to the depletion of the rainforests, but individually wrapped bits (down to the last novelty rubber) made the whole thing so wonderfully enticing. She'd overlapped with her mother who was full of the Lourdes trip, and had briefly seen Paul who'd swung past to drop off Tim's present – roller blades, a choice that made her heart sink. She'd taken him ice skating once, a foray that had proved to be a disaster. He looked more like Bambi than Christopher Dean, so how his little stick -thin legs would cope with blades she dare not hazard a guess.

Paul had dawdled over a cup of coffee she really hadn't the time to make for him. 'We are off to Lincolnshire at lunchtime to enjoy the pleasure of Eve's mother – God bless the old bag – and of course the sister-in-law from Hell, which should prove entertaining if one of us has already seen the Christmas afternoon episode of *Only Fools and Horses* and wants to watch something on the other side.' He idly turned over the pages of the *Radio Times* on the kitchen table. 'Do you think the TV companies all get together for a meeting sometime in July and put together a schedule that will be so clashing and controversial it can only cause massive family friction? I mean, I bet they say "we'll start our movie at six and you start yours at six thirty to really piss everyone off" then on Christmas Day they sit back in their delightful homes, paper hats on their heads, peeing themselves laughing, knowing we are all about to murder each other.'

'Tim and I shall be blissfully TV free,' said Carol, sweeping past him and filling a box with parcels and supplies. Should she pack Calpol?

'So what *are* your plans? Tim has made it out to be a combination of Disneyland and Lapland.'

Carol groaned. 'Oh God, I hope it comes up to scratch. I just haven't had time to think about it what with things at work being so manic. It sounded lovely in the magazine though – all wooden-beams, log fires and cosy. But at the moment,' she pulled out a carrier bag from under the sink and stuffed in Tim's wellies and her walking boots – there were bound to be lovely footpaths to explore, 'I'm steeped in bikinis for next July's issue and making sure we have something resembling a turkey to eat on Christmas Day.'

'I like the idea of being steeped in bikinis. Well, you've certainly been in the news. I heard this morning that the tabloids are determined to seek out this daughter of Anya's and the *National Enquirer* in the States is offering a reward for anyone that finds her. In fact,' he laughed, 'on Sky News they were saying that no less than a hundred and forty-six girls had come forward announcing they were the mysterious daughter – one was twenty-seven and black!'

Carol groaned even louder. 'Oh Paul, I hope I haven't created trouble for everyone. I mean I know she came to me wanting the interview – and goodness knows it's saved me and the magazine. I think Ian wants to marry me and have my babies,' they both smiled at her tactless comment, 'but I feel desperately sorry for the shit it's stirred up for Anya and for this girl. What if she doesn't want to be found?'

Paul put his arms around her comfortingly. 'Sweetie, if she doesn't want to be found then no one will find her. Adopted children are protected incredibly well by the law. They won't get to her unless she wants it to happen. And you are right. No one made Anya tell her story. It came from her because, from what you wrote – great article by the way – she wanted to get it off her chest.'

Carol pulled away and took down anoraks from the

cupboard. 'I hope to goodness you are right and she knew what she was doing.'

Paul turned on the tap and rinsed out his cup with water, turning it upside-down on the drainer – a habit Carol had always found vaguely unhygienic. 'Oh she's not stupid that one. You don't get to be one of the highest paid pop stars in the world by being thick. You've done nothing wrong – in fact, it might be the best thing ever. Now,' he gave her another hug and a kiss on the cheek, 'look after that boy for me and have a lovely time. I'll call him on Christmas Day, and think of me coping with the Addams Family.' He was still chuckling as he left. 'Addams and Eve!'

The office was buzzing with people exchanging presents with each other. Carol's desk was piled with cards and little parcels, which she packed away to have something to open on Christmas morning. It took her until well after twelve to deal with press enquiries and requests for syndication of the Anya feature and then, bolting down the sandwich Jemima had been out to get for her, she moved on to an intense hour with Brigitta – her plaits intertwined with tinsel and novelty reindeer antlers on her head – to discuss the cover of the April issue in the midst of which she fielded a farewell call from her mother.

'You take care, Mum,' she signed off as Jemima came to hover at her office door.

'Yup?'

'The *Standard* has just come in. Look at this!' Her face shone with excitement, and she thrust the paper into Carol's hand. On the front was a picture of Anya taken through the rain-spattered window of a car, the flash lights of paparazzi cameras reflected in it. Her face looked haunted, her eyes wide and tearful as she looked out. 'Pop Star to be questioned,' shouted the headline. 'Police expected to press charges.'

'Oh my word.' Carol scanned the story. Detectives had flown to New York apparently, reporters hot on their heels, and, Carol thought cynically, no doubt as a result of the press furore. Without it the poor girl might well have been left alone but what chance was there ever of that? 'I don't know whether that's good or bad news. I'll read it later.' Carol grabbed her pad to make her way up to Ian's office. 'Listen, if I'm not down by the time you go, have a lovely Christmas and see you after the New Year. And Jemima,' the girl turned at the door, 'you've been great. You all have. Have a very relaxing time.' For once Jemima's smile seemed genuine.

Up on the sixteenth floor, Ian had the flush of a good lunch about him, and breathed fumes sweet with alcohol as he enveloped her in a warm embrace. 'I've abandoned a delightful meal at the Ivy for you, sweetie, but I thought we ought to have a little up-date on what's been going on.' Carol began to feel uneasy, as he sat down on the sofa in the corner of his office and patted the cushion beside him. The offices around him were empty, people having bunked off early for the holiday. 'Come and relax. You deserve it.'

Carol sat down on the edge tentatively and as far away from him as she could manage. 'Well, it's all been pretty exciting I suppose and the feedback from journalists who want to write for us is really encouraging. I'm having to beat them off with a stick.'

'I bet you have to do that all the time, don't you?' He moved closer and gently placed his hand on her leg. 'Projected sales figures are looking great, my darling. I think you may have saved the day. But I always knew you could.'

Like hell you did. 'Well thank you for the vote of confidence,' she replied drily and jerked her leg away. He brushed his hand through his hair to cover his embarrassment.

'I was thinking,' he went on, 'we really ought to celebrate, you know.'

'Perhaps in the New Year we could have a lunch with the section editors—'

'I meant just you and me.' He looked at her, his eyes bleary and bloodshot from too much Burgundy, then leant in towards her. 'We did it together. We turned *WM* around. I'd like to celebrate.' He moved even closer until she could smell the pear-drop-like scent of alcohol on his breath. 'You are really very lovely you know.' Bloody slimeball. Carol felt the anger rising and she stood up.

'And you, Ian, have got some nerve.' His astonished look, as he rearranged his pin-striped trousers, made her smile. Oh he'd been so sure. She leant down over him, making the most of the height advantage and his befuddlement. 'You were so ready to discredit me, to throw me to the sharks, without waiting to see what I could do.' His brow furrowed. 'You made me give up that lovely job on *Style* to read *WM* its last rites and you knew it from the very start. But now it's doing just fine and don't you dare try and take any credit for that.'

'But, darling,' he tried to stand up, 'you can go back to *Style* any time you like. I'll wangle the editorship if you like.'

Putting her finger on her lips thoughtfully, she pretended to ponder this one, enjoying every minute of his discomfort. 'D'ja know what, Ian?' she smirked, patting his cheek. 'I really don't think I'm interested in any of your offers. My staff deserve better than their editor abandoning them now, especially when their publisher has been so ready to shaft them.'

'Now wait a minute.' Ian pushed her away firmly and stood up. 'You—'

Suddenly the phone rang on his desk. He ignored it at first, until it rang again and again insistently. He turned and snatched it up irritably. 'Yup? What?' he snapped. 'Right. OK. Will do.' And he dropped it back in its cradle.

'That was your PA,' he mumbled. 'She was just about to leave and there's been a call. Your son's school apparently, they want you to ring back immediately.'

Carol didn't bother to wait for the lift, but bolted down

the stairs to the *WM* office, her heart pounding, half from the adrenalin from their confrontation and half in fear. What had happened? The office was empty now, except for Jemima who had waited, with her coat on, until Carol came down.

'They wouldn't say what has happened,' she said with concern. 'Can I do anything?' Carol rummaged for her mobile in her bag.

'No, Jemima, you get off, and thanks for waiting. I'm so glad you were still here.' She was finding the school number as she spoke. 'Hello? Mrs Frost? It's Tim's mum. What's happened?'

'Oh hello there. No need to panic but there's been a little accident. A patch of ice in the playground – I shall have to speak to the caretaker about it.' Sod the effing caretaker, thought Carol, urgently. 'I'm afraid the boys were running at playtime and Tim must have slipped. We've taken him to St George's in an ambulance – I called your mother but she can't drive I understand – and Miss Jeffries is with him, but she can't stay long. She has to catch a plane to Prague at six.'

'Yes OK,' Carol interrupted, 'but how's Tim?'

'Well, from what I can gather, they think he's broken his leg.'

Chapter 14

3 p.m., 22 December

Disaster! You've spilt wax on your table cloth. Don't panic! Pick off the excess then iron it gently through brown paper.

With urgent pleas that Miss Jeffries stay with Tim as long as she could so he wasn't on his own, and reassurances that she would get there as quickly as she could, Carol frantically gathered up her things. Most fell on the floor in her panic, and she couldn't find her glove. Damn. As she turned she knocked a pile of papers off her desk, and she simply kicked them out of the way to be sorted on her return, or binned by the cleaners. Who cared? Tim was hurt.

Outside the wind was more bitter than ever, whipping up litter on the pavement and finding its way under her coat and her scarf. She ran as much as was possible towards the tube, dodging the heaving mass of people heading both ways. She was making good ground until she reached the barrier. 'Delays on the Northern Line,' said the sign, 'due to an incident at Charing Cross.' Fuck. She turned tail and, frantic by now, headed out again onto the street to find a cab.

Ten minutes later she was still looking. The inevitable result of offices emptying out for the holiday was apparent. There was not a cab with its light on to be seen. People shoved her as they passed, trying to squeeze by on the pavement, knocking her bags against her legs. She looked at her watch. Paul would be in Lincolnshire by now. Her mother was no good and would only get in a panic. She probably was already if the school had phoned her. What should she do now? Throw herself in front of any passing car and beg them to take her to Tooting and the hospital?

With the noise of traffic and people, she only just felt the vibration of her phone in her pocket, and had to fumble quickly to get it out. 'Yup?' she shouted.

'Carol, it's Nick. I rang to wish you a happy Christmas. You're going away, aren't you?'

'Oh God, Nick.' It was such a bad time for him to call but strangely reassuring to hear his voice. 'I don't know what to do. I've just had a call to say Tim's in St George's with a broken leg and the teacher who's with him has to leave any minute, and I'm by the office and the tube's delayed and I can't get a sodding cab and I don't want him to be on his own.' She couldn't suppress the sob. The tears poured down her face. She'd failed. She couldn't be there for Tim when he needed her. What kind of a shit mother was she?

'Listen, Carol,' Nick sounded firm, 'I'm only in Stockwell and I'm in my car. I'll go to the hospital. I'll be there in about ten minutes, I expect. Can you call them and say I'm on my way so Tim knows to expect me?'

The relief that washed over her made more tears come. 'Oh Nick, can you? Are you sure? Do you know where it is?' She knew she sounded like her mother.

'I'm on my way already and the traffic's not too bad here. I'll stay with him until you get there so don't panic.'

'Oh thank God. Thank you so much.' She had a sudden thought. 'Will you be all right with Tim?' Oh dear, that made it sound as if she thought he was a paedophile or something. 'I mean, will you remember him OK?'

Nick chuckled for some reason. 'Who could forget him?'

*

The front door shuddered in its frame as Holly slammed it behind her. Two bloody hours to get home and all because some tosser had had the bright idea of throwing himself under a train at Charing Cross. How selfish could you possibly be? Joe had been back for ages, to judge from the smell of curry emanating from the kitchen. The radio was on so loudly, he hadn't even heard her dramatic entrance.

She pushed open the door. 'You're late, babe. Everything all right?' He wiped his hands on the tea cloth tucked into his trouser pocket and came to give her a hug. He'd developed this habit of rubbing her tummy possessively from time to time, although there was still nothing really to show, apart from her new and impressive cleavage.

'Look, don't do that when we're at Dad's, please. He'll know something's up.'

'What do you mean, something? You're planning on telling him, aren't you?'

Holly turned away and took off her damp coat. 'Yes. Yes, I will. But I want to pick the right moment. I want to get him on his own, for a start. Always assuming the bitch lets him out of her sight.'

'She sounds a real piece of work, your stepmother. I can't wait to meet her,' Joe said sarcastically and returned to the curry. 'Tell you what, I'll make the ultimate sacrifice and take her down the pub or something, so you can talk to him alone. She might be all right with a few drinks inside her.'

Holly snorted. 'Don't hold your breath. I'm telling you, Joe, if it wasn't for this baby thing, I wouldn't even go. It's going to be awful. We've got to get away as fast as we can after it's all over.'

'Baby thing? That's my boy you're talking about – or my girl, of course. Come on. Hurry up and sit down. The lads will be here any minute.'

'Oh what?' Holly whined. 'I didn't know you'd invited

anyone. I'm knackered – and I've got to pack and do all the wrapping. You could have told me.'

Joe handed her a glass of orange juice. 'Come on, Holls. Their leccy's been cut off cos they forgot to pay the bill. They're living by candlelight and eating at McDonald's every day – have a heart.'

She rolled her eyes. 'You're a soft touch, you are.'

'Yeah, I know. But think what a brilliant dad I'm going to make!'

*

'I spy with my little eye something beginning with D.'

Tim looked around him. 'Doctor?'

Nick knew it had been too easy, but they'd already run through T for trolley, C for curtain and P for plaster. He'd been going to do G for gas cylinder, but changed his mind. Drawing Tim's attention to the Entonox cylinder behind the bed might alarm the little boy who'd been so brave so far.

In fact, Nick reflected, looking at Tim's fair head as he cast around for something else to choose, he'd shown remarkable poise. When Nick had finally found a parking space in the packed car park and found his way to the fracture clinic, Tim had just been coming out of a treatment room in a wheelchair, looking quite pleased with himself, leg newly cast in snowy white plaster stuck out in front of him and, Nick could think of no other way to describe it, the boy's face had positively lit up when he'd seen who'd arrived, and Nick felt a surprising surge of affection for him. A tall, quite attractive woman in an overlong skirt and baggy jumper, who had turned out to be Tim's teacher Miss Jeffries, had been pushing him and she had bolted, full of apology, when Nick announced who he was and that Carol was on her way.

'I feel terrible having to abandon Tim but I'm off to Prague this evening for Christmas with my boyfriend's family. Are you

OK taking care of him?' She'd knelt down to Tim. 'Have a lovely Christmas, won't you, sweetheart, despite the leg?' And she'd delved in her rucksack and pulled out a bag of chocolate coins. 'These are for you for being such a brave boy and such a good giftgiver in the play. They were a teacher present.'

Tim's face had suddenly looked panic-stricken. 'Oh no, Mum forgot to give me yours to give you ...'

Miss Jeffries leant over and gave him a little kiss. 'Your mum has far too much to think about already, so don't you worry about that. I get too many presents anyway. There's only so much bubble bath you can use in a lifetime.' She got up, smiled winningly at Nick and swept off through the sliding doors.

Seated side by side now in the waiting area in companionable silence, Nick and Tim worked their way through the bag of coins, screwing up the foil wrappers as they munched. It was a very particular flavour of chocolate on Nick's tongue and reminded him of Christmas morning when he was younger. It was at odds with the clinical smell of the unit. Sitting here now, shooting the breeze with this uncomplicated little boy made him feel more at ease than he had for ages.

'Do you suppose Father Christmas has a huge room where he makes these coins?' he asked Tim idly, folding the last foil wrapper into a small nugget of gold. 'Only, everyone seems to get them.'

'Oh I don't know. Last year mine had Tesco written on them, so perhaps he buys some in when he's too busy.'

Nick smiled at the blissful innocence. How tragic that age and experience would one day take that all away. 'Yes he must get busy. Like mums do.' Nick didn't want to bring up the subject of The Phone Call unless Tim did. It hardly needed to be said because they both knew that Carol would arrive soon and that was what they both wanted.

Nick had forced down a cup of disgusting tea from the vending machine, they'd played a game of 'first one to guess when the number on the digital clock will change' and even had two rounds of paper, scissors, stone before Carol burst in through the automatic doors at a run, bringing the cold early-evening air with her. She was wrapped in a large and expensive-looking camel coat, her handbag clutched to her. Her fair wavy hair was in disarray, her face full of concern, and Nick thought he'd never seen anything so lovely.

'Oh sweetheart, how is it?' she fussed over Tim, asking him questions about the X-ray and the accident and how it felt now. 'And Nick, oh I'm so sorry.' Her eyes looked wide and red and he didn't think his phone call to her had seen the last of her tears. She'd obviously been in distress all the way here. 'The traffic was dire, trying to get over the river, and just nose to tail all the way. Thank you so much for waiting with him. It must have wasted loads of your time. I've asked my taxi to wait outside. I'll just see the doctor then, come on, Timmo, let's get you home.'

Nick watched as she questioned closely the young woman who'd seen to Tim, and as they looked at the X-ray her face was anxious. He had a sudden urge to take some of the responsibility off her, to make it all better, but realised that might be an interference she didn't want. He looked at his watch. He'd told Rudi he'd meet him for a drink in the Rose and Crown at six thirty, but he reckoned his loquacious friend would forgive him if he missed one of their regular sessions, even if it was Christmas. God, he'd gone on often and for long enough about how Nick should stop behaving like an ageing muso and get a life. Besides, Nick had an overwhelming sense that he didn't want these two to go.

She came back to join them. 'Can I ...? I mean, would it help if I drove you both home?' he faltered. 'It's sort of on my way.' Which it most definitely wasn't.

Both Carol and Tim turned to look at him, Carol's expression concerned, Tim was wreathed in smiles. Nick didn't need more encouragement. 'Come on,' he said, without waiting for a reply, aware he might be taking control a bit too much. 'You talk to the nurse, I'll get rid of the taxi and *I'll* drop you back.'

'Only if you are sure? I wouldn't want to—'

Nick paid off the taxi with the notes Carol had fetched out of her overstuffed bag and thrust into his hand. It had been an exorbitant fare but Nick didn't say a word. No doubt she'd have paid the earth to get to her son. He jogged across the car park, pulling up the collar of his jacket to protect his ears from the icy wind, and let himself into his car, which was cold now from being left so long. God, the state of it! He couldn't let them see this. Scrabbling around in the dark under the seat he found what he'd hoped for, a brown paper McDonald's bag he knew had been left there, and into it he stuffed the rubbish from the passenger footwell. Galaxy bar wrappers, an old apple core and the sports section of the *Sunday Times*, empty chewing-gum packets with discarded chewed gum folded inside them, and two old Minstrels (though on second thoughts they looked OK and he popped them in his mouth). At least the car smelt all right, or to his nose anyway, but he gave the seats a quick brush with his hand just to be sure there was nothing unpleasant.

The traffic was still heavy as they set off, even though they were heading north and most of the flow was out of town and away from offices and shops. In front of them was a snake of red lights going one way and white lights coming towards them. Carol was quite quiet once they'd settled Tim in the back, leg propped up and the seat belt configured so it didn't dig into him at that angle. The painkillers he'd taken had definitely kicked in and Tim kept up a steady stream of conversation, telling his mum about what had happened and about the plans for the tea party he'd missed, and she made interested and reassuring noises but seemed very tense. As they slowed in the jam in front again, Nick decided to take the risk and, after turning up the radio a bit, put his hand on her arm beside him. She looked round quickly, an unreadable expression in her eyes.

'Carol,' he said quietly, so Tim wouldn't hear, 'he was fine, honestly. He wasn't fussed for a minute and we just played games and talked. He's a great kid.' Her eyes were enormous and, as he spoke, they filled up again, tears spilling down her cheeks. Before he could stop himself, he wiped them away with his thumb. 'Don't beat yourself up. He's a credit to you. And a mean I-spy player.' At this she smiled and looked down at her hands.

'It's so stupid I know, but I just can't help it. I have a Ph.D. in Guilt. I'm a Catholic you see. ' And the smile on her face seemed to light up the car.

Nick laughed. 'Well, I did notice the odd ... er, clue at your house.'

Carol gasped. 'Oh golly, yes, the icons! I meant to move them. It's my mother – she can't resist holy bling.'

'What a relief. I was going to suggest you fire your interior designer.'

Tim had entertained them royally by the time they pulled up outside Carol's front door. The house was dark when she let them in, but she went on ahead turning on the lights, including the ones on the Christmas tree, while Nick carefully manoeuvred Tim and his cast through the door, down the narrow corridor stepping over carrier bags presumably ready for their trip to the country, and into the sitting room, to place him on the sofa. The child seemed incredibly light and frail, and there were shadows under his eyes from the pain of the break. While Carol bustled about finding something for him to rest his leg on, puffing up cushions behind him and putting on a DVD, Nick went back and locked his car, then wondered if this wasn't the moment to depart.

'Er, Carol,' he called down the corridor, 'I'd better go now. Leave you guys to it.'

'No,' she came out quickly. 'I mean, won't you have a drink, or a cup of tea at least? We can't let you just go. I've got some beer, I think, but definitely some wine.' She was shaking off her coat and underneath she was wearing a pale pink cardigan and wide-cut black trousers. Her figure looked neat and small and Nick wanted to take her in his arms and hold her.

'OK, that would be great, if you have time.'

'I'll just make Tim a sandwich and a drink. Come on into the kitchen.' And he followed her, trying not to look at her bottom. And failing.

While she prepared some food for her son, pulling out a packet of pre-cooked chicken pieces from the fridge, she chatted, more relaxed now that they were safely back. Nursing a warm lager – perhaps he should have said yes to the white wine after all – he leant against the sideboard and listened, hoping he was answering in the right places, but knowing he was staring, fascinated by how she moved and brushed her hair out of her eyes. At one point she looked at him questioningly and he realised she'd said something he hadn't heard.

'Sorry?' He felt stupid.

'Oh nothing – I was just saying I haven't managed to get Tim the 3D space projector he had set his heart on. There isn't one anywhere. I even tried to bribe the manager of Woolworth's in Newcastle to bike one down to me.' She cut the sandwich in half. 'I'll take this to Tim. I just wondered if you wanted a sandwich too? Sorry I've nothing else. We are off tomorrow and I've run down stocks.' She was holding a bag of bread poised in her hand.

'No no. Thanks all the same. I'll just finish this and be off. You must have masses to do.' He took a large swig and, balancing a glass of milk and a plate of sandwiches and fruit, Carol went through to the sitting room. He had finished the beer by the time she got back and had had time to take in once more the warm, friendly kitchen, bathed in soft light. He wanted to stay there; chat over a glass of wine. Just be there with her.

She came over to him as he shrugged on his jacket and he felt as though he towered over her. She'd taken off her shoes and seemed smaller than ever. The room was quiet.

'What you did this afternoon was really kind, Nick. It was so reassuring to know he was safe with you. Thank you so much.' Her hair was framing her face. Her skin looked smooth and her mouth looked soft and he could smell her. Before he could stop himself, he put his hand up to her cheek and touched the edge of her mouth with his thumb. He waited. Would she flinch and move away? He didn't want to blow this. She didn't move for a second, then, almost imperceptibly, she rested her cheek very gently in his hand, so he bent his head and kissed her slowly on her lips.

They felt so soft and warm, and she opened her mouth very slightly. He could smell her sweet breath and took her bottom lip between his, kissing it slowly and repeatedly, moving up to the edge of her mouth and to her top lip. Then, very slowly, he put his arms around her and pulled her closer, the kiss deepening.

After a while they pulled apart. She was blinking in surprise, but her eyes sparkled and he kissed her on the forehead.

'Oh wow,' he mumbled into her hair.

'Wow indeed,' she replied and laughed a little. 'Nick, do you—'

'Muuuum, can I have some more milk?' came the cry from the invalid. This made Carol pull away completely and he felt cold without her close to him.

'Look, Carol, I'd better go.' He felt in his pockets for his keys. 'Have a lovely Christmas, won't you?' And saying goodbye to Tim, he let himself out of the house, feeling strangely elated, and strangely bereft.

Chapter 15

Early morning, 23 December

Create family rituals and make them a positive experience. They are essential to the bonding process that makes Christmas so special for everyone.

Beth sat bolt upright in bed. D-Day! Or D-Day minus one (or two). Depending. How many D-Days was it possible to have? She knew one thing – she wouldn't have any rest until B-Day.

She mentally ticked off her list. The marquee was going up first thing, the florists were delivering later. The loos would come a bit later still – hopefully quite a bit. The helium balloons would be there by the afternoon – bit of a timing crisis, that. You couldn't have them too soon, or they started to deflate, apparently. Patio heaters would also be there in the afternoon. Dance floor ditto. Everything else would be coming tomorrow – the raffle prizes were being brought over by car by one of the committee at the last minute, for security reasons. The caterers, disco and dance band would turn up just before the whole thing started.

Beth stretched and smiled in satisfaction. She had everything covered. And the clans were gathering, just in time to witness her triumph. Sally first, mid-morning, all the way with early reprieve from panto in Bolton – her understudy bribed to do the remaining performance – to provide welcome moral support and her well-known skills at mixing cocktails and gently taking the piss. Then Noel and Christina in time for lunch.

Later – but heaven only knew when – dear, darling Holly and the much-anticipated Joe.

Meanwhile, she had tea to brew, casseroles to make and – generally – empires to build. She sprang out of bed. Half an hour later, she was washed, dressed and ready to take the dogs out. Jacob, still warm in bed, was appreciatively sipping his tea. Through the front door, Beth could make out the tall figure of the postman. Good! Everything going to plan. She flung open the door. 'Good morning!' she sang cheerily, and took the letters and last-minute cards from his gloved hands and handed him an envelope containing a card and twenty quid she'd got ready the night before. 'This is for you. Merry Christmas, and thanks for everything you've done for us all year.'

He looked suitably surprised, though he couldn't have been really. Surely everyone he'd visited so far had done the same? 'Thank you! Thank you very much. And a Merry Christmas to you. Got a houseful?'

'Oh yes. Family and friends, you know.'

The postman shivered. 'Well, I'd better be getting on. The wind's changed direction overnight. It's bitter today. Make sure you're wrapped up when you take those brutes out. Glad I'm not going to be out carol singing tonight.' He winked and trudged away.

Carol singers! They'd want warming up. What could she give them? Beth thought quickly. Yep – a quick visit to Martha Stewart's website should do it. She'd be ready and waiting before the first 'Ding-dong Merrily on High'. And wasn't that just what Sally wanted? A proper country Christmas? Well, now Beth could provide music as well. After a brisk walk down to the river, a pleasure now the dogs listened to her, she was back home, face aglow and eagerly anticipating her friend's arrival.

After making herself a cup of coffee, she gingerly removed from the fridge the bag of venison steak which Jenny had ceremoniously brought round, and started the gory task of dicing it. This was uncharted water. She had never knowingly eaten venison, let alone been faced with the raw product. The charnel house in front of her on the chopping board was enough to turn her stomach (and drive the dogs to distraction), made all the more scary by the fact that she was preparing this for other people. She'd frankly rather present a paper on Pirandello in front of three hundred academics at a conference. But the joint assurances from Jenny and the sainted Delia that venison casserole was the *only* thing to have before Christmas would have to sustain her.

She was just dealing with the pickled walnuts when the doorbell rang. Strange. Beth hadn't heard Sally's car – usually her arrivals were very audible, all screeching fanbelt and grinding gears of her M-reg Fiat Panda that should have been scrapped years ago. But it wasn't Sally. Instead of her flamboyant friend, laden down with luggage and accessories, there was a small, neat-looking woman with fair wavy hair, a pretty face and clear blue eyes. She was wearing jeans and what looked suspiciously like cashmere. Next to her was a very small, fair-haired boy on crutches. Mormons?

'Er – hello. Can I help you?'

'Hello. Mrs Layham? I have got the right place, I hope. I'm sorry, I should have phoned. I'm Carol. I think we spoke a few months ago – about Stable Cottage? Well, I found the village all right. The map on the leaflet you sent was fine and I met someone going past who thought you probably had the keys.'

Beth squinted slightly. This wasn't really making sense. The woman looked very anxious, though. A flash of recollection swept over her. That bloody Diana Steaggles hadn't got in touch to say the cottage was unavailable. Oh no! And here was this poor woman and her poor little boy, two pairs of wide blue eyes looking expectantly at her.

'Hang on a minute. Yes, I do hold the keys, but I'm afraid there may have been an awful mistake.'

Carol could feel the panic rising. Oh God these were not the words she wanted to hear. Her body ached from driving and map reading, and all that had kept her going had been the idea that she'd flop through the door of some fragrant cottage, all rose-patterned quilts and chintz curtains – perhaps even pre-Christmas decorated like a page from *Homes & Gardens* – with the log fire burning and she'd simply put the kettle on the roasting hot Aga and Bob would be your uncle.

She also wanted to be able to wallow a bit more in the strange feeling that had overcome her in the last twenty-four hours since Nick's kiss. It was not unlike the sicky feeling she used to get in the pit of her stomach on Christmas Eve when she was a little girl: a mixture of overwhelming excitement and dread that someone would pop their head up and say 'It was all a joke and I'm afraid it's not going to happen'.

Instead here she was, having got up at some ungodly hour to queue outside the butcher in Battersea *everyone* said you had to buy your turkey from, propping Tim up beside her, and had then battled with the M40, to be standing in an over-heated kitchen that reeked of wet dogs and something even more disgusting. And in front of her, a tall, striking woman in a grubby-looking apron, with hair a curious mass, or was it mess, of coloured streaks and who looked utterly appalled at her arrival as if she was the ghost of Christmas Future.

'Didn't Mrs Steaggles call you? She said she was going to.' The woman, tutting heavily now, was untying her apron and hanging it on the back of the door. It was really the only place she could have put it, so overstuffed was the kitchen, every surface used up with files and books, an inordinately large pile of magazines, Tupperware boxes of mince pies, a rather splendidly, if unconventionally, iced Christmas cake, and a pudding wrapped in muslin and ready to boil. It resembled the control room of Christmas, and any minute Santa himself would walk in, novelty braces holding up his red trousers and shrugging on his coat, pick up the keys for his sleigh, which was probably parked in the garage, reindeer chomping at the bit. Clearly this woman has Christmas taped, thought Carol, feeling even more stupid and inadequate, though she couldn't quite work out what her harassed look was all about.

Tim adjusted the weight off his good foot. 'What's that awful smell?' he asked innocently and, unable of course to kick him in the ankle, Carol had to resort to a sharp 'Tsch!'

'Horrid, isn't it?' the woman sighed, wrinkling her nose and brushing her hair off her face, which served to make it look madder than ever. 'It's venison, and I hope to goodness it improves in the cooking. Now,' she put her hands on her hips, 'before we sort this out – oh and I'm Beth by the way – let's have a cup of coffee. Won't you sit down?' She shifted some papers off a chair. 'You must be exhausted.'

Relief flooded through Carol, too shell-shocked to have worked out a solution yet to this particular little cock-up. 'I'd sell my granny for one.' As Beth bustled about with the cafetière – Carol hardly dare tell her instant would be fine so long as it was hot and wet – she asked them about the journey.

'Mass exodus,' said Carol, helping Tim into a chair. 'The whole population seems to be heading out of town, and there's still a day to go.' Seated now, she rested her elbows on the table, then lifted them off again, realising the surface was sticky with something she couldn't define. Jam perhaps? A stray soft currant suggested it might be mincemeat. 'But please don't let us hold you up. It looks as if you are catering for the five thousand. Have you got lots of family coming?'

Beth placed a plate of oddly shaped iced shortbread in front of them. Was that a star or an angel? It was hard to tell. 'Just us, and my stepdaughter, and her boyfriend, and my stepson and his girlfriend. Oh and my friend Sally who's got an early reprieve from panto in Bolton.'

'Was it for good behaviour?'

Beth looked up puzzled, then smiled a broad smile, which was a great improvement on the harassed frown they'd seen so far. 'Mmm, sounds like hell, doesn't it? But she thrives on it. Now what have you done to yourself?' She turned her smile on Tim and, picking up the plate, offered him a misshape.

'I slipped on the ice,' he said boldly, helping himself, 'and my headmistress is worried my mum might be called Sue.'

Beth and Carol looked at each other in bewilderment. Tim looked at them both. 'I heard her say so.'

It was Beth who cottoned on first. 'Ah, let me guess. You live in some trendy inner-London borough, with a school so besieged by fear of litigation from parents they've banned conkers.' She placed two cups of jet-black coffee in front of them both. 'Much better in the further education sector – then all we have to worry about is stopping them OD-ing on some illegal substance and making sure they attend at least one lecture a term.'

Carol took a tentative sip from her cup and shivered. Drink that and she'd be mainlining until Boxing Day. 'Thus speaks the voice of experience.'

'Yup, and frankly it's great to be shot of them all for the holiday. Now what shall we do about Stable Cottage? Cos stable it ain't.' She opened a drawer and rummaged around until she found a large key on a keyring in the shape of a giant safety pin. 'Here it is. I think this is the right one.' She turned back to the two of them at the table. 'Honestly, Carol, I haven't been down there for weeks and the Steaggles are away – they go to their place in Portugal every winter. In fact they go there most of the year, I think, to play golf. Does nothing for the complexion.' Carol laughed. She liked this woman; she was a breath of fresh air.

'But what I don't understand,' Beth continued, 'is why she has advertised it for rent. I'm sure she wouldn't do that –

especially without telling Jacob and me.' This sounded more like a stream of consciousness, and Carol could only assume, without any explanation, that this Jacob was her husband. Carol was intrigued to know what he must be like. The house – or the little Carol had seen of it – didn't strike her as belonging to a young couple. In fact from where she sat, Beth didn't seem to fit in at all. This woman must be the same age as her, give or take a year or two, yet the house was more like, well, her mother's generation – from the large Kenwood mixer on the side, to the battered copy of Katie Stewart on the bookshelf above the Aga.

Beth shook her head. 'Well, all I can think is that someone else has a key and has prepared it all. Yes, that's sure to be it.' She drained her cup. 'Now, I hate to be rude but I've got hordes arriving in no time and, for my sins, I've taken on the mantle of organising the annual village jamboree tomorrow night.' She laughed, abashed. 'Quite honestly I wish I'd never opened my mouth – but I'd better get on. Can I take you down there?'

Impressed by how firmly the woman told two large and slobbering dogs to 'Staaay!' in the utility room, Carol helped Tim into the back seat again, stowed the crutches on top of the luggage in the boot and cleared the map from the passenger seat so Beth could accompany them and show them the way. She folded herself into the seat, wrapped in a rather dog-haired and unflattering green tweed coat, and turned to Carol expectantly. This close, Carol could see how fresh her complexion was – must be this country air and all that dog walking – and how bright her green eyes. Oh how she'd love to get her hands on her with a decent hairdresser and a bag of make-up. Would she be offended if she suggested her for a make-over feature?

'Right, you go left out of the gate and then left again by the church,' Carol pulled out of the drive. The car had gone cold again and Carol shivered. Feeling more confident now, after Beth's assurances, she began to anticipate the thought of a hot, fragrant bath with the oil Jemima had given her. Then, once they'd settled in, perhaps they could explore the village – slowly what with Tim's leg – and perhaps find a small village shop that might have some home-made mince pies still for sale.

'That's the village hall, and behind it – there, can you see the marquee? – that's the field where we're having the party,' Beth chatted on, sounding nervous. 'Perhaps you'd both like to come along? I'm sure there's tickets and the caterers are bound to have enough food. That rather pretty house belongs to the Steaggles – your landlords – such a shame it's not used all the time, and here's the village shop.' Carol slowed to look. 'It's crap, I warn you. Sorry, Tim!' She looked behind her quickly, and dropped her voice to a whisper. 'Only to be used for essentials, when they are really essential. Even the tampons are own-label.'

Carol smiled but her heart dropped. Bang goes the home-baked-for-tea idea.

'OK, turn in here – now slow down, cos the lane gets a bit narrow.' They bumped their way down the muddy track, overhung on both sides by branches intertwined with dead wild clematis, the mud from the puddles splashing up the car doors. 'Now into this gateway – watch yourself. Totally impractical and narrow like everything round here.' And there it was: a low cottage in red brick with two dormer windows popping out of the moss-covered roof like alarmed eye brows. A gutter hung off at an angle like a painfully fractured limb. Under the canopy porch was a tub over the side of which hung something brown and died back. The windows were dark and one pane was smashed. On the doorstep, a dead bird long past identification. Carol stopped the car and turned off the ignition. They sat there in silence, save only for the intermittent ticking of the engine as it cooled down.

Beth got there before her. 'Oh fuck, ' she mouthed expansively.

Chapter 16

Later

Roll interesting-shaped fruits in beaten egg white,
then coat in a mixture of granulated and caster sugar.
Leave to dry before arranging as a table centre to
astonish your dinner guests.

Carol jingled her car keys in her hand as if weighing up the options. She didn't think she had ever been so depressed in her life.

'It's horrid. It smells like an old church.' Tim, standing beside her, had hit the proverbial nail on the head.

They'd been standing in silence in the dingy sitting room of the cottage for what seemed like ages, ever since Beth had bolted, though full of concern, telling them she had to get back because her friend was due any minute, but to call when they had made up their minds what they wanted to do. Carol knew there was a decision to be made but she really wasn't sure what it was.

The scene that had faced the three of them when they'd shouldered open the door of the cottage half an hour earlier would have put off even the most determined squatter, and the smell was the least of its faults. Through the murk, helped not at all by a bare and blown light-bulb that hung from a pendant in the middle of the room, she had just been able to make out an old sofa in green velour with wooden arms and a matching chair, a nest of side tables and a standard lamp with a shade like a fifties hat, all set around a fireplace that contained straw and debris from pigeons that had nested in the chimney above. Miserable testament to how long the room had been unused.

Beyond, through a latched cottage door, was the kitchen, and Carol had tentatively pushed it open, not unconvinced that she might find a dead body hanging in there from a butcher's hook. There was the Aga she'd dreamt about all right, an old cream coal-fired version, but as cold as the grave.

'Oh Carol, what can I say?' Beth had said from behind her. 'I feel terrible. I mean, what can Diana Steaggles have been thinking of? Let's have a look upstairs. I seem to remember there are pretty brass bedsteads.' She had strode on ahead of them, and Carol, realising that Tim would never make it up the narrow stairs, had helped him rest on the arm of the chair.

'I won't be a minute, darling, I promise. Will you be OK for a second?'

Upstairs was little better, though at least there was no bedding in evidence that could have become mildewed. The two little rooms did indeed have quaint double beds with iron bedsteads, and their low windows looked over the undulating fields beyond, dark military green now – almost black – with the darkening sky above them. In the bathroom, its wooden floor worn smooth from years of use, there was an old-fashioned cast-iron bath with feet, and a high cistern with ornate brackets over a wooden seated loo. The basin was large and square with a crackle glaze and large tarnished brass taps.

'Aren't those supposed to be fashionable again?' Beth had asked, clearly desperate to put a positive gloss on it all.

Carol had smiled. 'I was just thinking the same thing. We featured one just like it in the magazine recently. Hideously expensive, mind.'

'Are you a journalist?'

'Yes, I work on a magazine.' Carol hoped she wouldn't ask

any more questions. She didn't want to talk about her job. She wanted to think what the bloody hell to do now.

'How funny, my stepdaughter works on a magazine too. Something really glamorous I think—'

'Muuum.' They'd both started as Tim's voice came up the stairs. 'Are you coming, Mum? I'm scared.'

Before Beth had left she'd been insistent. 'Why don't you come back to our house for the night – to save you having to drive back now. Or at the very least let me make you lunch? I feel awful. I should have taken more care when you called me. My mind must have been on other things.'

'You and me both.' Then she'd strode off up the lane at a determined pace.

It was Tim who broke the silence now as they stood together in the dank sitting room. He looked anxious. 'Please, Mummy, don't let's stay here. It's horrid. Can't we go somewhere else, like that nice lady's house, or go home? Please can we go home.' Carol felt panic-stricken. She really couldn't face turning round now and heading back up the motorway and into London, but the look on her son's face was so beseeching that she realised it was the only thing she could do. She rubbed the back of her hand against his cheek, trying hard not to show her own disappointment. She'd let him down. In her haste, her mind diverted by something as stupid as work, she'd booked a place for them both for Christmas without really checking it out. She'd created a picture of the perfect Christmas in her son's mind, with sparkling lights and magic and stockings over a roaring fire.

Instead all that had materialised was a shit-heap that smelt of damp and looked worse. How on earth could it have been featured in the magazine? She couldn't remember now who's page it had appeared on, it was so long ago, but they'd be lucky to keep their job.

Christmas, the big day that had occupied Tim's mind since

Boxing Day last year, would be a disaster. She'd screwed up royally. Restless now, Tim turned to make his way out of the front door, left open behind them but which made no difference to the temperature inside. In fact, Carol would have laid ten to one on it being warmer outside than in.

'Let me help you.' She took his arm as he struggled with the crutches. His head was hanging sorrowfully low and her stomach clenched in a mixture of guilt and misery. They stood on the porch and looked at the little gate in the hedge opposite that led into the churchyard. Her mobile rang.

'Hello?'

'Hi Carol, it's Kate. Just rang to say happy Crimble before you head off.'

'We've headed off already. In fact we are here.'

'Oh brilliant! And you've escaped the madness of town,' she chatted on. 'Having Christmas Day on a Sunday should be illegal cos everyone just heads off earlier than usual. The Hammersmith roundabout is at a standstill – some idiot has lost a Christmas tree off their roof and it's taken me an hour and a half to get from Acton to the Fulham Road, then we have to battle to Heathrow. Have you been following all the stuff on the radio about Anya? Silly question, you must have – seems like things are hotting up. You were right – the press won't let it drop, will they? Did you hear the rumours about someone coming forward saying they are her daughter? Oooh, I'm so jealous of you. Is the cottage gorgeous? Have you got the tree up, the fire burning and something scrummy cooking in the Aga? Carol ... are you still there?'

'Yup I'm here.' Carol knew her voice sounded flat but somehow she just couldn't bring herself to fake enthusiasm.

'And?'

'It's not quite what we expected.' Carol turned away, aware her son was all ears. She lowered her voice. 'I think we might cut and run actually.'

'It can't be that bad.'

'It's pretty ... er, challenging.'

'What do you mean, all derelict?'

'Well not quite. But it's not exactly *World of Interiors* either.'

'Things rarely are. You of all people ought to know that.'

Carol said quietly, 'Yes but I wanted it to be just right for Timmo.' For an awful moment she thought she was going to cry. 'Just how it should be.'

'Look, Carol,' her friend's voice took on the no-nonsense tone she was famous for, 'I know you are tired. I know it might not be what you had hoped for, but you are in danger of believing all the nonsense you peddle in your magazine. Life isn't picture perfect you know. If you wanted that, you should have stayed in some vastly overpriced hotel somewhere in the Cotswolds, where you could have had log fires and shortbread biscuits and hot toddies wrapped in ribbons with brass knobs on.'

'Hey steady on, mate! You're swanning off to Antigua any minute to lie on the beach, you cow.'

'I know but at least I'm fully expecting a wait at the airport, crap on-board food and our luggage to end up in Islamabad. I'm only being realistic about life, Carol. You could do with a dose of it. And my dear woman, "just as it should be", as you call it, is not some Disney spin on Christmas. It's about you being with your little boy.'

'What's eating you then?' Carol said sniffily, thinking about the stash of presents for Tim in the car. 'Have you taken on some sort of religious conversion when I wasn't looking?'

Kate laughed. 'Sorry. Was I coming over a bit strong? I'm just suffering from Christmas-retail ennui. I realised yesterday as I was standing in a shop holding a box of rude after-dinner games in one hand and a pair of novelty socks that sing "ho ho ho" in the other that I was in danger of losing the plot completely.

You can cope, Carol,' she said earnestly. 'You are the expert at making things nice. Weave a little of your magic. *Hasta luego.* Have fun.' And she abruptly put down the phone.

Confused, but feeling a faint stirring of some sort of resolve in her mind, she opened the boot.

'Mum, what are you doing? Aren't we going?' Carol took in the Fortnum's hamper, the long queued-for turkey, and the box of ready-to-eat goodies from M&S she'd fought for at 8.30 that morning. She took in the cottage and the green fields beyond; the bold, square church tower, jet black against the grey, leaden sky. She thought about the long hours she'd spent at her desk to save the magazine, the way she'd been late so often for Tim or had to palm him off with her mother or friends. She thought about Anya and all the Christmases she'd had to spend without her daughter.

'Timmo,' she asked tentatively, 'how are you at making decorations?'

He hobbled over to her. 'Well, we did make ones with dough at school, and I can do a paper angel. Why?'

She put her arms around his thin shoulders and surveyed the contents of her boot. 'I think we should have a DIY Christmas. Now what do you think of that?'

Chapter 17

Later still

*Sprouts are as much a part of Christmas as stockings
and mistletoe. Make sure you stock up well in
advance and keep them in a cool, well-aired place
until you are ready to use them.*

By the time Beth returned, Sally was already in residence and
in full flow. Jacob threw her a grateful look and fled to his
study, leaving little room for doubt that Sally had been indul-
ging in her favourite pastime: relating, in baroque and quite
unnecessary detail, the ins and outs (literally) of her love life.
Kisses were exchanged. Then Sally stepped back, head on one
side, to contemplate her old friend.

'Well, you don't look too bad. No straw in your hair, at least.
Although,' she leant back and squinted, 'you're looking awfully
stripy. Is that the look in the country? Camouflage?'

Beth clapped her hands to her head. 'Is it really awful? I
couldn't get an appointment for love nor money so I had to
resort to DIY. I thought it would look more natural than an all-
over-tint. Do you think it'll fade a bit by tomorrow? Maybe I
could put a tint all over, just for five minutes ...'

'Calm down!' Sally took her friend's hands in her own. 'I'm
only teasing – it's what I do best, remember? Living in the
country must have softened you up. Anyway, what's so important about tomorrow? Unless I've missed a day somewhere, the
big day is the twenty-fifth. Any chance of a coffee, by the way?

I didn't dare ask Jacob for a drink, in case he offered me sherry in his study and asked me about the Hundred Years War, or whatever.' She pretended to flinch away, knowing she had gone too far with the fun-poking and was in danger of being clouted.

Beth led the way into the kitchen and started to prepare coffee, while Sally poked into cupboards and the larder, lifting lids and sniffing the contents of jars and pots. Vaguely irritated, Beth observed her progress as the phone rang. It was Carol from the cottage with her astonishing decision. Sally offered her verdict once Beth had set their mugs on the table. 'I think I can safely say you've over-catered. It looks like Fortnum and Mason in there. How many have you got coming? Just the one battalion or is it an entire regiment?'

'Do you think so?' Beth rubbed her eyes. 'I just can't tell any more. Every time I go out or read a magazine, I think of something I haven't done and something I haven't got. The only thing I haven't catered for is one of them being vegetarian. Now wouldn't that just top it all!'

Sally's face fell. 'Oh God! I didn't tell you, did I? I gave up the demon meat when I started seeing Dave. We're vegans – but I did bring some tofu with me. I've got it in my bag.'

'You have got to be joking. What on earth am I going to give you for Christmas lunch?'

Sally laughed and shrugged. 'Oh I don't mind what I eat. Well, you can't really when you're vegan. I'll have sprouts.'

'Shit!' Beth rocketed out of her seat. 'I knew there was something. I left the sprouts for last, to make sure they were really fresh. We'll have to hope they've still got some at the farm shop.'

'Yeah, don't worry. We'll manage. I'll have – oh, I dunno, rice cakes with peanut butter or something. It's really no biggie. Anyway, you're normally so laid back about these things – remember that time you added strawberry liqueur to the bolognaise sauce instead of wine? We all ate it anyway, didn't we?'

Beth shuddered at the memory. How could she have been like that – not caring at all about serving up that horrendous concoction? She remembered, with a glow of warmth, how Sally had demanded a second helping, saying how much time they were saving by having their main course and pudding at the same time. And it had been fun, now she remembered it. She went to put on her coat. If they didn't get to the farm shop before two, they would be cleaned out for sure, but Sally was taking her time over the coffee and had lit a cigarette. God how inconsiderate! Beth carefully closed the kitchen door and opened a window. But as the smoke drifted past her she longed, for the first time in years, to light one up and draw deeply on it. What had brought that on?

Beth filled her in on the depressing scene down at Stable Cottage. 'I can't believe that woman is going to stay there. She must be mad, what with the little boy in plaster too. We'll have to go round with some bedding and some towels cos Diana has left nothing. I could kill that bloody Steaggles woman. How thoughtless can one person be? Actually I'd better go upstairs to see what I can find now. Can you sort out what she'll need for the kitchen? God knows this one is over stocked – and I think there's a spare heater in Jacob's study. Can you ask him to dig out the other one?'

On the landing she pulled open the double cupboards. This was an unmined seam. She'd opened them a couple of times when she'd first moved in and had been familiarising herself with the house, but Becca's linen cupboard had been simply too intimate to address, and Beth had consciously used her own sheets on their bed. It was a pathetic way to stake her claim on Jacob. Forced, at last, to confront all these trappings of the other woman's life, Beth marvelled at the way everything had been left. Neat, tidy, organised and barely touched for at least four years. Had she, Beth wondered, stacked these sheets and blankets away one day knowing, as she did so, that she would never have the need or the ability to take them out again and shake them open the way Beth was doing now? An unexpected wave of sympathy swept over her. Maybe, leaving everything in apple-pie order had been Becca's way of saying goodbye to the family and home she knew she would soon leave. With every gesture she had been preparing for her own death.

Sally, coming up the stairs, interrupted her morbid musings. 'Come on, Beth. You said yourself you didn't have a moment to spare. Stop mooning and let's pack the rest of the stuff in the car. I've tested the heaters, as commanded. I reckon she'll have everything she needs now.'

Beth carried the towels, bed linen, blankets, eiderdowns – so wonderfully old fashioned – downstairs and looked around at the assembled emergency survival kit in the hall. Sally had done a kitchen sweep and looked out basic cleaning products, kitchen sponges, Beth's old vacuum cleaner, dusters, a coffee machine and some rip-snorting arabica – it was a start.

'Right, let's pack up and go. This is a bit like *The A-Team*, isn't it? I'll be B. A. Baracus and you can be the loopy one – what was he called?'

'Dee-dede-deee. Da-daa-da. I used to love that programme. It was Murdock,' Sally supplied helpfully. 'I always quite fancied him, not that super handsome one everyone was supposed to fall for. I bet you went for George Peppard. That explains your fascination with older men.' Sally dodged a well-aimed kick and struggled through the front door with an armful of lavender-scented blankets.

*

At the farm shop, of course, there'd been a run on the sprouts and there was not one to be had. Beth tried hard to laugh it off, as Sally was doing, but an awful sense of doom started to engulf her. Christmas dinner without sprouts? It just wasn't possible but no one in their right mind would brave a supermarket now. At least the marquee had been put up properly. Beth was looking forward to showing it to Sally, with the dance floor and flowers. But it was eerily quiet when they pulled up in the lane by the meadow. There was the marquee with the flooring all laid, there were the portable loos – but that was it. It looked more like a field hospital than a party venue.

'Oh damn. They must have been delayed. I'll go home and call them and then I'll take the stuff to Carol and her little boy once I've sorted it all out.'

Chapter 18

Lunchtime, 23 December

Don't exhaust yourself by rushing around to keep guests happy. A good guest will join in and help.

'I'm going to have to stop going out,' Beth muttered to Sally, as she went to put on the kettle again. 'Every time I come back in, someone else has appeared.'

'Oi, I take exception to that!' Sally retorted. '*I* arrived while you were out on one of your many errands of mercy.' With Noel and Christina sitting holding hands in the sitting room, Jacob hovering, offering everyone drinks at regular intervals, and Sally leaning back in her chair, watching with narrowed and amused eyes while she 'took the opportunity' to paint her nails, the house already felt too crowded for Beth. Used to having the space to herself and the dogs, Beth was – quite unjustifiably – irritated by the sudden influx of extra bodies. Of course, she was pleased to see them all. It was just that they took up so much space.

Sally followed her out to the kitchen and leant back against one of the kitchen units, right in front of the dishwasher. 'Here, let me help,' she urged. 'You've got stacks to do, by the look of things. Why don't you delegate a bit? It's not as if you're short of manpower. I'm willing and able.'

'Could you just …?' Beth took her friend by the elbows, careful not to smudge the blackish red lacquer and moved her out of the way so she could empty the clean plates and cups.

'Right, if you could put the kettle on.'

Sally obeyed, holding the kettle gingerly and spraying water over the counter tops. 'Oh sorry,' Beth muttered. 'Must get that tap fixed. I was thinking, we'll probably have carol singers round later and we really need to give them something.'

'Ooh – a poke in the eye with a sharp stick, perhaps? Or spray them with a hose? Or am I getting all mixed up with Halloween?' After dabbing her nails experimentally against her lips to check they were dry, Sally picked a walnut out of the carefully arranged dish of nuts Beth had placed on one side for later, and set about it with a nutcracker that looked like a medieval instrument of torture, then picked cautiously through the resulting mash of shell and nut, dropping little shards into the crystal glasses Beth had carefully washed.

'I know nuts are supposed to be dead good for you, and everything,' Sally went on, her mouth still full, 'but you'd have thought with all the technological advances people have made, they'd have come up with a brazil nut you could open without the need for a first-aid kit. How did cavemen manage, eh? So what are the lucky carollers in for, then?'

'Umm – mince pies, of course and maybe some egg-nog?' Beth finished emptying the dishwasher and eased her back. 'Right, I thought I'd make some vegetable soup for you. We'll have to rethink Christmas lunch. How much do you like red cabbage? I've seen a recipe for chestnut roast somewhere, too.'

'Beth, do stop stressing, for goodness' sake! You're freaking me out. It's my fault for not telling you. Tell you what, I'll make the soup while you do your lady of the manor act. Sadly, I won't be joining you in the mince pies, of course. And egg-nog, I presume contains egg? Egg and ... what? Nog? I think I can eat nogs, mind you.' She popped another walnut into her mouth and snorted. 'Egg-nog, indeed! You've gone all *It's a Wonderful Life* on me with your new-fangled American ideas.

What's wrong with good old-fashioned mulled wine? I'm allowed to drink that – by the gallon, in fact.'

'There was a recipe on the Martha Stewart website. I printed it out – loads of stuff, actually. It's in that file on the table. Look, could you have a go at making it while I call up the florist about the marquee? I wanted the flowers in before the lights but at this rate the lights will be in first.' Beth seized her Mistletoe Meet folder and pulled out a sheaf of phone numbers. As she dialled the number, she could hear Sally sifting through her Christmas file, laughing quietly. Beth clenched her fists.

'Hello, is that Evergreen? Yes, Mrs Layham here. I was expecting the flowers for the Mistletoe Meet this morning. Can you tell me what's happened and when I can expect them?'

Sally was chortling quite openly now over the website printouts. 'What the hell is a Christmas Tree Glossary? What's to know? Trunk? Branches? Prickles? Bit where the fairy goes? God! You couldn't make this stuff up, could you?'

Beth pushed her finger into her spare ear in annoyance as she struggled to listen to the faltering excuses coming down the phone. '… loaded it into the other van, you see. So by the time she got back here, it had already gone out and now they're delivering to the hospital first and—'

'When can you get them here?' Beth cut in. 'I need them by three o'clock at the latest. The electrician is arriving at half past. The lights have to go around the bay tree stems and if there are no stems, there's nowhere for the lights to go. Don't you see? Right, I'll hold you to that. And I'll be there waiting. If it's late, you'll be hearing from me again.' She replaced the receiver with a crash. 'Bloody people. They've got no idea at all.' She took a deep breath and turned back to Sally who was looking at her with an expression of mock terror.

'W-w-what planet are you from? Planet Nog? I'm right, aren't I? What have you done with the real Beth? Please, spare me and I promise I won't tell anyone that aliens have taken over my best and oldest friend.' She backed melodramatically towards the door. 'It's all falling into place now. The strange behaviour. The blank look in your eye. On your planet, Christmas trees don't exist so you have to have them explained. You enslave women by brainwashing them into making garlands for their candlesticks and wreaths for their front doors.' She held up a sheet of paper from the file, waving it in mock consternation. 'And only evil aliens could create a Cheesy Snowman. I just hope the men are safe from your evil schemes. I must warn them now ... before I ... argh. Too late!' Sally started to advance, stiff-legged and arms outstretched, towards Beth. 'Take me to your leader! Take me to this Martha Stewart!'

The doorbell rang. 'Oh for goodness' sake, Sal. Get a grip. I've got things to do,' and Beth pushed past her friend into the hall. Jacob had reached the door before her and was holding Holly in a bear hug, lifting her right off the ground – something he'd never managed to do with Beth. Behind them, Beth could see dark, watchful eyes in a pale, tired-looking face. So this was the mysterious Joe. He looked at her quickly and intensely then glanced away. A gust of icy air entered the hallway.

'Jacob,' Beth said, more gently than she was feeling. For once Holly was earlier than Beth had expected and she felt on the back foot. 'Let's get Holly and Joe inside where it's warm.' Her smile of welcome was returned cautiously. Joe was clearly on his guard. Beth turned to Holly. She'd been practising for this moment. 'Hello, Holly. Lovely to see you,' she cooed. 'I'm so glad you could both make it. It's so lovely to have the family together for Christmas. I've really been looking forward to this!'

Holly looked narrowly around the hallway. 'I'll just bet you have.'

There! Had Jacob heard that? No, of course he hadn't. He was shaking hands with Joe – overdoing it a bit, in fact, but Holly was smiling affectionately at him. 'It's all right, Daddy. You can give him his hand back now.'

Beth turned her attention to Joe. 'It's lovely to meet you, Joe. We've heard so much about you.' Damn! That didn't sound right. And it wasn't even true. 'Er, can I get you something to drink?'

Holly took Joe's hand. 'The kitchen's this way. *I'll* make you something.'

*

'So what was your excuse, you wuss?'

'Sorry, mate. I got held up.' Nick rubbed his hands against the cold. 'Come on. I'll buy two rounds just to make up for it. Any excuse to get out of this ball-numbing cold.' The warmth of the pub hit them both in the face, and Rudi made a bee-line for a table in the corner by the roaring fire. Nick, hands just about warm enough to hold the two pint glasses, joined him, and threw down a bag of pork scratchings in front of his friend by way of a peace offering.

'Bangin', and the least I deserve.' Rudi had a right to be irritated. Their grumpy old men sessions had become a sacred event that only something major, like a death in the family or free tickets to a Chelsea game, would ever be excuse enough for a cancellation. 'And you didn't even call me, you bastard. I was sat here like Johnny No Mates and all I had was Val for company.' Nick licked the foamy head from his pint off his top lip, and smiled. Val, the busty landlady, made Bet Lynch look subtle and the red tinsel and inflatable Santas festooning the pub barely competed with her glory. 'Not bloody Christmas shopping I hope?'

'Er, no I've done that – or the little I have to.'

Rudi sniffed and ripped the packet of scratchings open with his teeth. 'Load of old toss in my opinion. Purple Ronnie todger kits and foot baths – what a load of bollocks. I'm leaving mine until the last minute. Restricts the choice.'

'What are you planning to get Rachel then? Not going to repeat last year's *faux pas* I hope?'

Rudi mock-cringed. 'God, I wouldn't dare! And I thought a Rampant Rabbit was inspired. No, back to new oven gloves and the Dido album.'

'Hey don't knock her. She's got talent.'

Rudi snorted. 'Female drivel if you ask me. Dido and no dildo ... tragic.'

Nick smiled again ruefully. The amazing part was that, for all his cynicism and blokishness, Rudi was devoted to his girlfriend. Why they had never married none of their friends had dared ask, but it was clear Rachel wore *le pantalon* and Nick suspected that Rudi had asked her many times, only to be knocked back. Clever woman, keeping him on his toes.

'And what are you doing on the Dreadful Day? Is the lovely Kirsty allowing you to grace her lovely home?' Rudi had never bothered to conceal his dislike of Nick's former wife, but Nick took it as a back-handed compliment. It was a form of moral support in Rudi's clumsy and rather autistic way.

'Oh I'll see Gordie at some point but frankly he would rather listen to his MP3 player than communicate in anything more than Neanderthal grunts. The only words that manage to permeate the curtain of hair that permanently covers his face, are "McDonald's" and "cash".'

'You're not going to sit at home like a saddo, are you?' Rudi's face suddenly had a look of concern. 'I mean you are very welcome to join me and Rach, and her mum and dad of course – the indomitable Sylvia and Clive – and her rather obnoxious brother. We don't see them from one year to the next so why we have to play happy families just cos it's Christmas, God only knows.'

'Thanks, mate, but my sister has invited me over again, and frankly her kids are a nice distraction, and Harry's a laugh when he's not talking about Intel Pentium Processors.' Nick knew as he said it that, ungrateful it may be, he just couldn't face sitting round the table at his sister's chaotic house in Maidenhead, as welcome as they would all make him feel. There was really only one face he wanted to see on Christmas Day.

'Rudi,' Nick put down his pint on the table, and ran his finger around the edge of the beer mat, 'I know you've been together since time began but, when you first fell for Rach, what did it feel like?'

Rudi's eyebrows shot up to his hairline. 'Christ, mate, that's a bit heavy for a Friday lunchtime. Can't we stick to the Blues' chances of doing the double?'

Nick knew it had been a mistake to ask. 'Never mind. Forget it.'

'It was like an illness.' Rudi's voice was more serious than he'd ever heard it and he looked up at his friend. 'I'm not being funny – it was like I'd caught something. I kept thinking about her and missing what people were saying, which pissed off the punters I can tell you.' Nick tried to imagine him, spanner in hand and overalls on, away with the fairies. 'So what's up? You got the bug?'

'Yeah, feels a bit like it.'

'Anyone I know?'

'No. She's a magazine editor. Single mum with a sweet little boy of about eight.' Nick leant back in his chair and shrugged. 'God, I've only kissed her once.'

'That's all it takes, mate. What's she doing at Christmas? Are you gonna see her?'

'Well, that's just it. She's on her own in the country with the boy. He's broken his leg and I'm a bit worried about her. But she might go apeshit if I ... you know.' He picked up a beer mat and dropped in on the table again. 'Oh I don't know.'

Rudi slowly rested his elbows on the table and leant towards Nick in an alarmingly direct way. 'I may be a prize berk, but there's one thing I do know, Nick old mate. Better to regret things you've done than regret things you haven't. Know what I mean?'

Lunch for seven – instead of the five Beth had planned for – had eventually taken place rather later than intended. Sally clearly hadn't quite mastered the art of simmering and the first batch of soup had boiled away to nothing while Beth was out trying to coordinate the lights and the flowers for the marquee. The flowers that never bloody turned up. Beth was still seething about that but, as the florist had been at pains to tell her, she couldn't have anticipated the sheep in the road and the van's radiator leaking. She was terribly, terribly sorry but there was nothing they could do now, especially since they were so far away, but she'd be there with a fresh delivery first thing tomorrow. Promise.

Leaving the electrician with coils of tiny white lights and nowhere to attach them, Beth had rushed back home to find the vegetables glued to the bottom of the saucepan in a blackened mess.

For all Holly's proprietorial approach to the kitchen, she hadn't thought to take the pan off the heat when the smell of burning started to fill the house. While Beth scraped frantically at the cremated onion, she had simply drifted into the kitchen, wearing a huge and vastly unflattering jumper, to make tea for herself and Joe, wrinkled her pretty little nose in distaste at the smell, and had taken a packet of chocolate biscuits from the cupboard. When, at last, Beth had served a fresh batch along with plenty of garlic bread to bulk it out, Holly had taken a couple of mouthfuls, added loads of pepper, then left the rest. With Joe and Holly sitting in complete silence at one end of the dining room table, Noel and Christina whispering endearments at the other, and Jacob, sitting across from her, glancing anxiously around and making valiant attempts at conversation that would include everyone, it was one of the least enjoyable meals Beth had ever experienced. Only Sally, seated on her right, seemed unaffected and chattered away as though everything was quite normal. But then Sally was a very fine actress.

Beth was now holed up in the kitchen, once more, with her friend. Fortunately, the venison casserole now smelt edible, at least, although so incredibly meaty that Sally was looking slightly queasy. Noel and Christina had sloped in and offered to help, but since they seemed to be conjoined at the hand and unable to stand more than two inches apart, it made any tasks rather difficult. They were so obviously besotted with each other Beth felt like slapping them and, since their arrival, they had communicated in a secret language of murmured, half-finished sentences and meaningful glances that effectively excluded anyone else from their blissful world. Beth hit on the solution of asking them to walk the dogs, away from Holly's cynical scrutiny. Plus they could still hold hands.

Holly appeared again. 'Where's Daddy?' she demanded.

'Holly – lovely! Come and sit down for a bit. You must be exhausted! Put your feet up.'

Holly looked startled and stared at Sally for a moment, then scowled and said pointedly to Beth, 'My father – where is he?'

Beth diverted herself by stirring at the casserole. 'I'm not sure. Perhaps he's in his study. Can I help?'

'I doubt it very much. I'm looking for our decorations.'

Shit! They'd been forgotten since the afternoon she and Jacob had put up the tree and she'd hoped they'd stay that way. She looked at Holly's stubborn little face in mock puzzlement. 'Decorations? I don't understand.'

'Our Christmas decorations,' Holly repeated coldly. 'The *family* ones. The ones we always use. I want to get them out.'

'I'm sorry, Holly, I've no idea what you're talking about.' Beth refused to rise to Holly's rudeness.

Holly rolled her eyes. 'What do you think we used before *you* turned up? We have stacks and stacks of decorations in a box somewhere – things my parents collected together over the years. Things that mean something. I want to get them out.'

Sally got to her feet and stood next to Beth – a gesture of solidarity that helped Beth find her voice at last. 'Holly,' Beth said in a carefully controlled voice, 'if you want your special decorations, then you must certainly get them out. But I don't think you can expect me to find them for you. As you're so fond of telling me, this is your house as well as mine. So why don't you and Joe have a rummage in the loft and see if they're there? I'll leave it up to you. I'd just like to make this Christmas as happy as I can for your father. We've both been working very hard these last few weeks and he certainly deserves some relaxation. So let's see if we can work together on that, eh?'

Holly looked slightly shaken at the mention of Jacob. It was below the belt, Beth had to admit but she sensed it was time to take the gloves off with Holly, and nothing else seemed to get through to her. The stalemate was broken by the sound of the front door banging shut and Jacob's voice calling. 'Brrrr, it's freezing out there. Holls – come and look. I got the last one.'

Sally and Beth exchanged mystified glances and they followed Holly, who had darted into the hall. Jacob had dragged in another Christmas tree, very small and a bit spindly, but the ice crystals thawing on its needles gave it a bright, defiant look. Jacob was smiling benignly down at his daughter. He hadn't spotted Beth in the doorway. 'There – we'll put this one up in the hall, perhaps. Or in the dining room. Then you and Noel can do it the way you want – and we'll put your stockings underneath, just the way we always do.'

Beth backed into the kitchen, and went back to stirring the sodding casserole as though her life depended on it.

Sally followed her, shutting the door firmly behind her. 'Honestly, Beth, I don't know why you put up with it. If I were you, I'd have given her a slap by now!' Indignant, she pulled a bottle of Jacob's best Burgundy from the wine rack and, opening it, poured a large glassful. Beth recklessly picked up a tumbler and held it out to be filled. She took a long swallow.

'Well, I put up with it because she's Jacob's daughter, of course.' She sighed. 'Were we like that at her age, do you suppose?'

Sally lit up a cigarette, completely missing Beth's pointed cough. 'God, I can't remember. It's far too long ago. Maybe we were. Maybe she'll grow out of it.'

Beth was thoughtful. 'I think I was quite selfish before I met Jacob, actually. Maybe that's what it is – having someone else to think about sort of knocks it out of you.'

Sally stretched and yawned. 'Well I'm on my own – and will be for ever if Dave's wife has her way – and I'm certainly not selfish. Have you got an ashtray in this infernal house, darling?'

Beth handed one over and wondered whether it would be too pointed to open a window. She was just about to hunt around for some air freshener when the doorbell jangled. Sally was right. She'd have to sort this out with Holly sooner or later, but for now she really couldn't be bothered even thinking about it – provided her stepdaughter more or less behaved herself over the next few days and didn't upset Jacob.

She heaved herself out of the chair, switched on the hall light and opened the door.

A trio stood framed against the curiously livid light of the late afternoon. Their van, parked at a rakish angle behind Sally's Fiat in the driveway, was steaming gently in the rapidly cooling air. They were so bundled up against the cold in an exotic mix of multicoloured scarves and knitted hats, it was difficult to make out much detail, apart from the fact that they were all tall, young and male.

For a moment she wondered if they were carol singers. If so, they weren't making much effort on the musical front.

They just stood there, smiling rather unnervingly. Jehovah's Witnesses this time, perhaps?

'Er, hello. Can I help you?'

They exchanged glances. The one on the left spoke first, hesitantly. 'Mrs Layham? Have we found the right place? Holly gave us directions but it feels like we've been travelling for weeks. We've come all the way from East Ham. It's very kind of you to have us.'

'Hold on a moment, will you? I'll just get Holly,' and then throttle her very slowly and very painfully. Beth backed away from the door and called up the stairs in as controlled a way as she could muster. 'Holly! Holly! Could you get down here please?'

Silence. But a moment later Joe's head appeared round the top of the banisters. 'She's in the bath at the moment. Anything I can ...? Oh blimey! What are you lot doing here?'

He thundered downstairs and slipped past Beth, mumbling apologies. She strained her ears to make out a frantic whispered conversation, catching only the occasional phrase. '... but Holly said ...', '... when did she ask you ...?', '... we've got nowhere else to go ...', '... her stepmum's going to go bananas! You can't ...' The last bit was whispered urgently.

That decided it. Holly wasn't going to win this round. Beth did some rapid thinking, took a deep breath and stepped forward. 'Joe, aren't you going to ask your friends in?' she gushed. 'We can't have them standing around on the doorstep in this cold wind.'

They shuffled in past Joe, whose face was now a picture of mixed embarrassment, astonishment and gratitude. Over their well-wrapped shoulders, she saw him mouth a pained, 'Sorry! Thank you sooo much!'

Still thinking at double speed – beds? Blankets? Milk? Loo paper? – Beth turned to the new arrivals, offered up a fervent prayer that they weren't psychopaths and smiled broadly. Boy, was Holly going to pay for this!

'We're so pleased you could make it. Holly told us all about you, but I'm afraid I've forgotten all your names already. It's lovely to have a houseful at Christmas. Hope you don't mind mucking in a bit. Now, can I take those coats? Then we'll get you something warm to drink.'

Joe hovered for a moment, gobsmacked, then bolted upstairs. The layers of scarves, hats and jackets were slowly peeled off and Beth stacked them, as best she could, on the row of overburdened pegs in the hall. If only the blasted cupboard under the stairs wasn't crammed to bursting! Or perhaps, given the new arrivals, it was just as well it was.

One by one, the young men emerged. The first was stringy with severely cropped hair and a worn collarless shirt half tucked into faded jeans. He looked around. 'What a lovely house. It looks so warm and Christmassy. I'm Mel, by the way.' Beth took his icy extended hand, and felt herself warm to him at once. He gestured towards his friends, who were blinking in the light and looking around shyly. 'This is Baz.' A very tall and very black youth with little twists of hair sticking up all over his head and sleepy, elongated eyes, stuck out his hand to take Beth's. A jangle of bracelets glittered at his wrist and he wore a green velvet jacket unbuttoned at the neck to reveal a peacock-coloured silk scarf. 'Pleased to meet you, Mrs Layham. It's so kind of you to invite us. We've got some pressies for you in the car.'

The third youth carefully handed her his enormous great-coat, revealing a too large striped sweater. He had blond, slightly curling hair that fell over his eyes girlishly. 'Hello, Mrs Layham.' His slightly hesitant, posh voice was so quiet, she had to lean close to hear him and a waft of something – patchouli? dope? – caught her nostrils. 'I'm Caspar. Merry Christmas. Thank you for having us.'

Well at least they seemed like nice, well-brought-up boys

– whatever other habits they may have. But they were huge, or seemed it in the hallway, taking up almost all the available space. Where on earth was she going to put them? 'Come into the kitchen and we'll see about something to eat and drink. Are you hungry?' Silly question really. 'We won't be having supper for a while yet, but if you're vegetarian, vegan, lactose intolerant, diabetic or even on the Atkins, you've come to the right place. We've got everything covered.'

Chapter 19

6 p.m., 23 December

A pineapple sprayed with gold paint makes a stunning feature for the centre of your Christmas dinner table.

Carol stepped down gingerly from the chair. 'How does that look? Is it still cock-eyed?'

From his position perched in the chair facing the fireplace, Tim put his head to one side and considered the wreath of holly and something that looked vaguely like ivy but Carol strongly suspected wasn't. 'A bit too much to the right maybe.'

Carol tweaked his soft little cheek. 'For a boy who can't even put his wellies on the correct feet, I'm not sure how much I believe you. It will have to do, cos I'm getting vertigo and it's hot standing too close to that fire.'

She picked up another log, part of Beth's extraordinary haul that had arrived a couple of hours earlier. She had come down the lane, this time in her own car, bringing with her a boot load of goodies and an outrageously out-going friend called Sally, who had swanned into the house and pronounced it to be the most 'daaarling' place she'd ever seen, and if Carol and Tim didn't want it, she'd move in there instead. Beth had come in behind her, her arms full of crisp white linen and paisley-patterned eiderdowns, still sheepish about the cock-up, and had fussed about with heaters, and a huge batch of mince pies, which she left on the side in an old-fashioned flowery and battered biscuit tin. Then she'd muttered something about

Jacob, mending the smashed window, the Aga and bloody coal.

Jacob and the offending coal had arrived in an even filthier car shortly after the two women had left. Carol liked him immediately. Older and taller than she'd imagined, he wore a battered old coat, a rather incongruous scarf that looked suspiciously like cashmere, and a definite twinkle in his eye. It was very obvious why the younger woman had fallen for him.

'Carol I presume.' He put out his hand. 'I have come with distinct orders from the missis that you are in dire need of heat.' He rattled a box of matches.

'Well, yes we are a bit, though Beth has provided enough logs for the sitting-room fire to fuel a power station. I hope we haven't used up your stocks?'

Jacob threw back his head and roared with laugher. 'Oh no, I don't think we're in any danger of running low on anything this Christmas. Beth has prepared for a siege.'

Carol lead the way into the kitchen, her offer to help with the bag of coal chivalrously refused. 'Well, she is more organised than me. I don't know what I'd have done without her.'

She'd left Jacob to sort out the cold cooker and, with Tim, some string and a roll of red ribbon, had set to on the vast selection of evergreen branches Beth had also donated and left wrapped in an old sheet in the middle of the sitting-room floor. She'd even left a box of beautiful silver tree baubles from Heal's which looked unopened and, had Beth not refused point-blank, Carol would have handed back. Instead Tim, propped against the arm of the chair again, had been given the task of hanging them on a spectacular five-foot branch of bare wood that Carol had pulled out of the hedge that ran down the left-hand side of the cottage. Meanwhile Carol twined up mistletoe with the silver tape she had intended to use tonight to decorate the last of Tim's little packages for his stocking, but would he honestly notice?

'I think that should be hot in no time,' said Jacob, coming into the room and stepping over the debris of twigs and leaves, wiping his hands on an old rag. 'Keep an eye on the thermometer on the front, and when it gets to the line it's hot enough. Beth said she thought there was an immersion in the bathroom cupboard, oh and she said she'd be down later with a couple more things you might need. Hotties, that kind of thing I think'.

'Oh Jacob, that's so kind.' Carol carefully pulled out some entangled holly. 'You couldn't have been more welcoming, both of you, especially with the party tomorrow and things.'

'Mmm that.' Jacob stuffed the cloth absent-mindedly into his pocket. 'Christmas wouldn't be Christmas without the Sacred Meet.' Carol didn't know if she should pick up on the sarcasm.

'Isn't it fun?' she asked carefully. 'Sounds like a lovely idea to me.'

'Oh the party's usually OK. A bit over the top though for my taste. It's just the organisation seems to have a strange effect on everyone who's involved. Now I'd best be on my way. The family are descending. Do let us know if there's any problems, won't you?'

She and Tim worked on, Carol sustained by coffee made possible by Beth's donation of a kettle, some strong ground variety and a pint of milk, and Tim demolished most of the biscuits she'd left. Feeling very warm towards this new Samaritan, Carol slowly began to permit herself a modicum of positive feeling. Perhaps things might be salvageable after all.

'What's this?' From the bottom of the pile of greenery, Tim had extracted what looked like a ready-made garland. About eighteen inches long, it was an assortment of mistletoe and holly entwined, though not very expertly, around flattened wire and oasis, and held together with tartan ribbon.

'Oh look, how sweet, Mum,' Tim exclaimed. 'There's a little

bird in there. Look!' He held it up for her to see a slightly wonky feathered robin perched precariously on a thick bit of twig. 'Can we hang it on the front door?'

On the porch it was colder than before and it was difficult to bend the string around the door knocker with icy fingers. She could see her breath, and though the view of the floodlit church in the dark was a feast for the eyes, she couldn't wait to get back in front of the inferno. She was struggling with a particularly precarious knot when she heard her mobile ring inside.

'Get that, can you, Timmo?'

It took her a good few minutes to secure the heavy garland, by which time her fingers were numb. She stamped her feet as she went in and hung up her jacket on the brass pegs in the hall. The warmth of the cottage now made her cheeks flush.

'Mum,' Tim held out the phone from his perch by the makeshift tree, festooned now with paper stars, 'It was Nick but he had to go.'

Carol felt a silly surge of disappointment as she unravelled her scarf. 'Oh.'

Tim sounded vague and a bit flustered. 'Something about going out tonight and having to get ready. He said happy Christmas to us though.'

'Oh.' Her mood deflated. 'Well perhaps he's busy. Now supper for you, my lad, and nothing to cook it on till that Aga heats up. How's about we raid the hamper?'

An hour later they sat side by side on the sofa, Tim's leg propped up on one of the delicate side tables from the nest, replete from their Fortnum's feast. Carol had a glass of wine in her hand and her son's head resting on her shoulder.

'I love you, Mum,' he said sleepily.

'I love you too, little chap.' She gently pushed the hair off his forehead. 'And you need to get up to bed. You've been a star today, making this place nice, and tomorrow we'll go and explore.'

'I can't wait for Father Christmas to bring my 3D space projector!'

Carol winced. 'Er … sometimes Father Christmas runs out of things. You know, all that demand the world over. But I bet he's got you something special.'

'Will he know we are here?' For an awful moment Carol toyed with the idea of telling him Father Christmas wouldn't actually find them and they'd have to make do with what she had bought him, to get her off the hook, but she dismissed it as too cruel. 'Oh we'll have to write him a letter and put it up the chimney. We'll do that tomorrow, and perhaps if he's run out of space thingies he might be able to get you one later in the year,' when the craze has died out, she added to herself.

Tim smiled, comforted, then changed tack completely. 'Do you get lonely, Mum? I mean without Daddy and stuff?'

Same theme, but Carol didn't think he'd ever asked this particular question before. 'Well, Daddy and I didn't live together for very long, but I suppose sometimes it would be nice to have a man about. But then,' she added hastily, 'I have got you and you are the best company ever.' She squeezed his arm affectionately and then, slowly, the two of them made their way upstairs.

After bathing him in lashings of hot water in the huge bath, dead spiders dispatched down the drain, taking care not to get his plaster wet by hanging his leg over the side, she tucked him into the big brass bed in the smaller bedroom. The sheets were starched and cool and he looked tiny and frail surrounded by the pillows and thick silk quilt.

'This is comfy.' He nestled even closer into the softness and closed his eyes.

Having topped up his bathwater with some more hot, Carol poured in a generous dollop of Jemima's bath oil and revelled in twenty minutes of uninterrupted pleasure. Wrapped in some very sloppy leggings – something she wouldn't normally have been seen dead in – and her favourite baggy T-shirt and cashmere socks, she brought down the other eiderdown and curled up on the sofa with her book. She'd purloined it ages ago from the bookshelf at work of novels sent for review by enthusiastic publishers, but had barely touched it for weeks and had no idea about the plot any more.

When she heard the car in the lane a little while later, she'd managed half a chapter – some cobblers about a private detective in high heels – and was seriously contemplating adding it to the pile of fuel on the fire.

'Hellooo? I thought you might like these?' Beth had let herself in, which saved Carol having to move from her cosy spot, and was brandishing two hot water bottles. 'Oh you look quite warm enough sitting there.'

'You are a love. Thanks – who knows, we might need warm toes tomorrow night. Have you time for a glass of wine or are you back for an evening of family charades?'

'Charades?' Beth snorted. 'You've got that right! Done many family Christmases then, have you?'

Carol smiled. 'Oh dear, is it that bad?' Still wrapped in her quilt, she hobbled into the kitchen to fetch another glass and filled it with some of the delicious Burgundy from the hamper. 'How was the smelly casserole?' She quickly stuck her head back around the kitchen door. 'Sorry, no offence!'

Beth laughed and shook off her coat. 'None taken. It was a bit rank, wasn't it? But do you know, it was delicious and, with a bit of extra mashed potato, it even stretched to feeding all our unexpected visitors too. I'm glad we've got you settled so cosily here because there wouldn't have been room for you at my particular inn after all I'm afraid. My stepdaughter had rather sweetly invited three hulking youths for the festives but had omitted to tell me.'

'You're kidding!' She handed Beth her glass. 'You *are* kidding, aren't you?'

'No I'm not. I think she was hoping to sabotage my plans – she seems to take great pleasure in doing that – but luckily I played it very cool. She won't forgive me for that.'

Carol wasn't sure how far she should pry. 'Are they ...? I mean is your husband divorced?'

'No, far worse. His first wife is very much dead.'

'Ouch. You can't top that then. She's a saint, I presume, and beyond reproach?'

'Mmm and everything I'm not.' Beth took a sip of her drink.

'Oh Beth, I'm sure it's not that, but it must be a bit odd for your stepdaughter coming back home and into someone else's regime. There's a girl in my office with stepmother issues. We did an article on it once and I remember people saying how painful it was to see a cuckoo in what they felt was their nest.'

'Oh I know all that, but at twenty-four you'd have thought she'd be mature enough not to look like she's chewed a wasp all the time. It's very wearing. I know stepmother hatred is the backbone of every fairy-tale, but I think we get a very bad press.'

Carol watched as Beth rolled the glass between her hands. 'But tonight I think I might have shown her that I'm more than a match for her. Her boyfriend is lovely so she can't be all bad.'

Carol did the maths. 'Crikey, and a boyfriend there too? How many have you catered for?'

'Oh, all them and more. My stepson and his girlfriend are there too. I seem to have gone a bit mad with the provisioning – well, it *is* Jacob's and my first Christmas together – but Sally thinks I need therapy.'

'Nah.' Carol gazed into the dancing flames. 'Christmas is all about proving ourselves as wives and mothers. It's like an A level in showing we can do it all, and failure is not an option. Show me a woman who hasn't obsessed about it.'

Beth slapped her hand on her knee. 'You're so right! I spent an hour the other day pulling pissing little cranberries off their stalks to make cranberry sauce just cos some dogmatic magazine said I ought to and, do you know what, I bet no one will eat it and the rest will go in the bin.'

'Yes but would you dare *not* make it?'

Beth snorted and knocked back the last of her drink. 'That was a treat, thank you, Carol, and it's lovely to have you here.' She looked around. 'You've made it look really charming and . . .' she looked a bit sheepish, 'I'm glad you found a use for the garland on the door!'

Carol thought it best to be diplomatic. 'Tim loves it and it's been the cherry on his particular cake. Actually the cherry would be a space projector but I can't find one for love nor money, so Father Christmas has failed miserably.' She got up to see Beth out.

Beth started to pull on her coat and gloves. 'Thank God, that is the one thing I haven't had to deal with this Christmas – presents for small children. I'd be useless. My godchildren – single women of a certain age always have lots of those – are always suspiciously polite about my offerings so I just resort to money now, much safer. No,' she pushed her fingers firmly into her gloves, 'I think I've got everything else covered now for the big day and for the party tomorrow. It's in the lap of the gods.'

'I'm sure it will be fine.' Carol couldn't suppress a yawn as they went through to the hall.

'I won't keep you, and I hope you sleep well. Do pop up tomorrow and see what we've done to the marquee if you can. If my plans work, it should look quite special.' Beth put her hand on the front door knob and opened it.

*

Beth noticed immediately the change on Carol's face as she

looked past her out into the night. Her face lit up. 'Oh do look, Beth! Isn't it magical?'

Beth turned to look outside. As she watched, appalled, the first snow flakes, huge and glistening and lit by the light from the hallway, floated slowly to the ground. And stayed there.

Chapter 20

Early Christmas Eve morning

To make fake snow, add a good handful of soapflakes
to a little water and beat using an electric mixer.
Apply it to windows and garlands for a good, long-
lasting effect.

With a gasp, Beth woke and sat bolt upright, as though she were surfacing from deep water. Her first thought was that she must have overslept – from behind the heavy curtains there was a strangely bright light – yet the glowing red digits on the alarm clock were only admitting to seven twenty-five. Then she realised. That light could only mean one thing.

With a sense of dread, she pulled her dressing gown on over her pyjamas and lifted a corner of the curtain. A thick coating of dry, powdery snow had transformed her daily view of woods, river, fields and more woods into brilliant, featureless white as far as the eye could see. Nothing was moving. The sky, darker than the ground, was heavy with clouds and the promise – no, the threat – of more snow to come. As she let the curtain drop, the phone started to ring downstairs.

As quietly as she could, she rushed, instantly filled with dread, down to the kitchen, dark apart from the eerie glow of the mounds of snow outside. She answered the phone breathlessly.

'Hello?'

'Mrs Layham? Sorry to call so early, but under the circumstances ...'

Not a death in the family, at least. 'Who is this?'

'It's Laura, from Evergreen. I'm ever so sorry, Mrs Layham, but we're completely snowed in here. There's no way we're going to get to you today. I know we promised, but there are four-foot drifts in some of the lanes. We just can't risk coming out.'

As she turned off her phone and started wondering what the hell she was going to do, Beth heard a sound in the downstairs loo. Was someone else up? Rather than give them a fright in the dark hallway by going back upstairs, she sat down on a kitchen chair and tried to think what to do to decorate that vast hangar of a marquee. What on earth was that noise? Beth couldn't ignore the peculiar sounds. Someone was throwing up – and pretty violently too. Oh please, God! Don't let anyone have food poisoning from the casserole. But what else could it have been? Joe and Holly had stayed up after Noel and Christina had gone to bed, although Holly had been yawning her head off over supper. Perhaps they'd laid siege to Jacob's drinks cabinet along with Mel, Baz and Caspar, though Holly had drunk practically nothing at supper. If they'd touched the wine for the Mistletoe Meet, she'd have their goolies, but surely not? She'd hidden that away in the garage along with so much other stuff for the next few days that neither she nor Jacob could fit their cars in any more.

Whoever it was had finished now and had flushed the loo. If she opened the kitchen door just a little, she would be able to see who it was before they went off upstairs. How awful to be throwing up in a strange house. She'd have to offer dry toast or scrambled egg for breakfast and see who opted for that rather than sausage and bacon. Her musing came to an abrupt halt as the kitchen door was thrown open, only just missing her as she sat in the dark.

Holly shuffled over to the sink and poured herself a glass of water, then started violently. 'What the fuck are you doing here? You scared me half to death. Are you spying on me?'

Beth stared. Holly was the last person she'd expected to appear. 'Oh – I was just down here … I had a phone call.' Why was she explaining herself to Holly, of all people? 'Are you unwell? I heard … I couldn't help hearing you … well … are you all right?'

Holly was glaring at her. 'It must have been something I ate. Joe was feeling sick all night too. The others will probably all have it as well.'

Beth wished she could have controlled her expression better but in the cold blueish light, she knew she had given herself away. Holly's lips twisted in spiteful triumph. Beth sank back into her chair, defeated. Things couldn't get worse.

But they did. Fortunately, at breakfast time it became clear that Holly's predicted epidemic had not occurred. She seemed to be the only one affected and, if anything, the rest of their guests seemed to have larger than normal appetites. Beth looked in dismay as her supply of sausages and bacon dwindled. She'd have to defrost some if this went on. With any luck, there'd be plenty of food left over from the Meet, and she could purloin some of that too. Anything to feed this rabble. The boys – Joe, Noel and the three visitors – had bonded into a fairly amicable team and took over clearing up the kitchen after breakfast and finding shovels to clear a path from the front door, leaving Beth a chance to plunder the resources of the freezer.

Arms filled with freezer bags of chipolatas, Beth shouldered her way back through the door into the warm bacon-scented kitchen in time to hear Holly on the phone. 'Yeah. Right. Well, I'll tell her.' Beth dumped the icy armful and gesticulated wildly at Holly to pass the handset to her. Holly looked right at her then deliberately turned her back and continued. 'No, don't worry. I'm sure it'll be absolutely fine. Right. Bye. Merry Christmas.'

Joe glanced nervously between the two of them as Holly

replaced the handset and turned round. Beth forced herself to smile. 'Was that for me?'

'Yeah. Some caterer or other. They can't make it for later.' Holly smiled and raised an eyebrow. 'I said I thought that would be fine because you're obviously so organised. I hope I did right?'

The phoney solicitude in Holly's voice added to the shock of this latest news made Beth's knees weaken and she sank onto a chair, aware of the blood draining from her face. 'The caterer? But I've got two hundred people coming tonight. What am I going to feed them on?'

'Oh dear! You are in a fix, aren't you? Oh well, never mind. Joe and I thought we'd go out for a walk this morning. See you later.' And she swept from the room.

Joe hesitated, then patted Beth awkwardly on the shoulder. 'I'll be back in a minute.' And he went out to join Holly. From the hallway, Beth could hear heated muttering then Holly's raised voice. 'Do what you bloody well like then. I'm going out whether you like it or not.'

The front door slammed and, after a moment, Joe reappeared. 'Look, Beth. I'm sorry. She doesn't really mean it. It's just that – er – she's got some stuff on her mind at the moment. It's nothing to worry about but I think I should go with her, you know ... make sure she's all right.' He shrugged. 'I'm not even sure she took her coat, so I'll just—'

Beth waved him away. She had to think. 'It's all right Joe, this isn't your problem. Thanks anyway.' With a final smile of commiseration, he left the room awkwardly.

Beth was rubbing her face in disbelief, trying to sort out what her options were, when the phone rang again. This time it was the disco. Same story and he had a flat battery on his van. She replaced the phone in time for it to ring again. The chocolate fountain. Next it was the band, followed by the ice sculptures, the table centres, the jugglers, the photographer.

One by one, all Beth's carefully devised plans were tumbling, like dominoes, leaving a trail of disappointment and chaos. Noel and Christina, who had put in a brief appearance to claim the dogs for another long walk, took one look at Beth's stricken face and backed out, presumably to get Jacob, who came rushing downstairs, rubbing foam from his half-shaved face.

'Beth, darling. What on earth is wrong? Has someone been hurt?'

Beth shook her head in disbelief. 'No,' she whispered. 'Much worse. It's the Mistletoe Meet. They've all cancelled. The food, the music – everything. All my plans. Everything. It's all gone wrong.'

Jacob shifted uncomfortably from foot to foot. 'Oh well. It can't be all that bad, can it? I mean, everyone will understand, with the snow and everything.' He patted her tentatively. 'It's only a silly party, after all.'

As Beth rose to her feet, indignation and a profound sense of failure jockeying for position with her rising panic, she was only dimly aware of a ring at the front door and of shadowy figures outside in the garden. The words spilled out, matched in volume by her tears. 'Silly party? Silly party? You just don't get it, do you? It's everything. It's all I've thought of for months and it's all ruined.' She took in his bewildered face. How could he not see? 'I've tried so hard, Jacob. And it's all gone wrong. I wanted to make a perfect Christmas for you. Our first real Christmas together. Then when they asked me to do the Meet, I thought it would make you so proud of me. I didn't realise. I just didn't know how big it was going to be – and nobody's helped me, and they all said they would, but I've had to do it all by myself, and I thought—'

In full flow now, Beth sobbed helplessly as she spoke, unaware of a shocked face peering round the kitchen door and another – pale, aghast – framed in the back door against a background of whitest snow.

She took a shuddering breath and went on. 'I thought I could do it as well as Becca. I thought I could be as good as her. Have you any idea what it's like trying to live up to her all the time? Everything I touch is hers.' She knew she shouldn't be saying this but she couldn't stop herself now. 'It's like a museum, this house. I can't touch anything. This isn't my house. It's *her* house.' Beth took a handful of Jacob's jumper, trying to make him understand. 'Did you know there's a hairbrush of hers in the bathroom cupboard? It's still got strands of her hair in it, Jacob. Did you know that?' She was aware she was shaking him and she knew she mustn't mention the Christmas card she'd ripped up. 'Did you know her dressing gown is still in the linen cupboard? And the Christmas card ... the Christmas card in the address book ... It hurts me. I tore it up. I'm sorry. It hurts.' Her nose was running and she wiped it across her sleeve. 'I didn't think it would be like this. I love you so much, Jacob. I thought that would be enough. All I wanted was to make you happy. But I've failed. I even got the Christmas tree wrong. And Holly. Holly hates me. I can see it in her eyes when she looks at me. She's done everything she can to make life impossible for me and you haven't even noticed. She's not a child any more, Jacob, she's a woman.'

'Yes but, darling, it's hard for her—'

'Yes I know it's hard for her,' Beth spat the words out. She could hear her voice rising to an ugly screech but she didn't really care any more. Her world had collapsed. 'Everyone keeps telling me so. But I've done everything I can not to tread on her toes and she just gives me nothing back. She's so fucking rude.' Jacob flinched at the word she knew he hated. 'And Carol must hate me. I've messed up her Christmas too because I didn't do Diana's dirty work for her. And that's on top of all the faculty work too. And it's all gone wrong ...'

Jacob pulled Beth into his arms and held her close while she cried as she had never cried before.

Across the room, Carol stared straight into Holly's astounded eyes.

*

Carol couldn't believe what she was seeing. Of all people, what the hell was that sulky girl from the office doing in Beth's kitchen?

Then the penny dropped with such a clank that Carol was surprised no one else heard it. It all began to fall into place: the phone conversation she'd overheard Holly having in the loos at work, Beth's reference to her stepdaughter being on a magazine ('important' indeed!), even Beth's description of her attitude. And she remembered too who'd written the page in the magazine where she'd found out about the cottage. Lazy, lazy girl.

Naturally there was only one way to describe the expression on Holly's face: bang to rights. And for one satisfying moment, while Jacob was holding Beth, whispering calming words, Carol made the most of locking Holly in a stare that the younger girl was finding hard to break.

Carol realised she had a choice. She could just back out of the room, without Beth ever having known she had popped in to see if she could help her today, and go back to blissful ignorance and Tim at the cottage, who she'd left creating a snowman outside the front door, his cast wrapped in four big socks and a Tesco bag.

But something at the back of her mind – maybe something Kate had said about the meaning of all this Christmas nonsense – forced her hand.

'I think you owe Beth an apology, don't you, Holly?'

Jacob and Beth looked up, startled by the new voice in the room, and looked between Holly and Carol in total bewilderment. 'What's going on?' Beth sniffed, her eyes red and swollen. 'How do you know her name?'

'Your stepdaughter and I know each other quite well, don't we, Holly? Now, I think you owe Beth and your father an apology, don't you?'

Holly looked at her feet and scuffed her socked foot against the floor, every inch the petulant child. The humble pie was obviously sticking in her throat and Carol found herself feeling something between sympathy for the girl and anger at the trouble she had caused Beth.

'Holly?' she prompted.

'I'm sorry,' she mumbled. Behind her Carol could hear the front door opening and the five men enter, stamping the snow off their feet and laughing. They entered the kitchen but, pulling off gloves and hats, their smiles faded as they took in the atmosphere in the room.

It was obvious that Beth was beyond any kind of decision, Jacob's expression was dumbstruck, and Holly was at a loss with what to do with herself. The men hadn't a notion who this new woman in the kitchen was who seemed to be holding the others in her thrall. Carol sighed. Wasn't she supposed to be having a holiday from motivating people?

'Well,' her look embraced the room, 'we're not going to let a little snow spoil the party that Beth's worked so hard for, are we? Come on, Beth, you managed to salvage my Christmas single-handed. Between us lot, I'm sure we can weave some magic for you. Jacob, you said yourself there was enough food for a siege.' Beth looked at Jacob accusingly. 'And between you and I, Holly, I reckon we could pool some of the ideas we've used in the magazine, don't you? Come on, who's up to the challenge?'

Chapter 21

A bit later

*Planning a big bash? Put balloons in the tumble
dryer for a few minutes. That way they'll be easier to
blow up.*

Jacob banged the table in the dining room with his hand.

'Right, quiet, everyone. I call this meeting to order. Madam chair, what needs doing?'

Beth looked round at the assembled company: Carol was at the other end from her with Tim, piggy-backed by Baz from the cottage, on her lap. Next to her, Baz (Tim's new best friend), Mel and Caspar, leaning forward, elbows resting on their knees in anticipation of their instructions. Sally, booted unceremoniously from her slumbers, had been quick to commandeer the seat next to the good-looking boy, and next to her, Jenny, in a lightning response to Beth's emergency call, was still wearing her much-beloved Barbour. Noel and Christina were side by side, naturally, though concentrating on Jacob not each other for once, and Joe, pen poised over a large A4 pad, had taken the role of secretary. Beth felt huge affection for him.

Even Mrs Havers, who had made the awful mistake of ringing to try and excuse herself from the two hours she'd promised that morning, had been strong-armed by Jacob to join the crisis committee. Looking at her now, doling out coffee, a faint flush of excitement on her sallow cheeks, Beth was sure any pleadings from her would have fallen on deaf ears, but for Jacob, she'd have walked there over hot coals. She must remember to hand over her present before she left.

Conspicuous by her absence was Holly, who had been sulking alone in her bedroom. The scene in the kitchen with Carol just half an hour ago had been quite extraordinary, and Beth still wasn't quite sure what it had all been about. That was something she'd have to think about later. She'd even gently but firmly put off Jacob's request to discuss the things she'd said about Becca and Holly – he clearly had no idea of what she'd been feeling. How could he have done, when she'd been working so hard to play the role of the unfazed second wife and all round domestic goddess? That was something they needed to talk about on their own, but for the time being she had twelve expectant faces looking at her across the table. She opened one of her famous files, her heart sinking at the thought of the task ahead.

'Right. The first problem is the marquee. It needs decorating. The marquee people have left the tables and chairs, and in the garage are the tablecloths, cutlery and glasses that the party supply company dropped off on Tuesday. The dance floor is down, and the generators are in the caterers' tent along with the ovens and hot plates.'

Sally butted in. 'But no caterers presumably?'

'Er no. They called this morning while you were asleep.' Beth sighed. 'We have lights but no trees to hang them from.'

'I've got trees.'

Everyone looked at Jenny. 'Yes, I put my tree in the garden each year. I've got quite a little plantation now. It's a sort of reminder of Christmas past. We can dig them up and pot them, then pop them back when we are done. All I need is a big man with a shovel.'

'I'm your man,' Mel laughed.

Jenny smiled rather coquettishly. 'Well, drink up and let's get started.'

Mel obediently drained his cup and rose to his feet, following Jenny from the room.

Beth turned to her stepson. 'Noel, I wondered, you being an engineer and all, if you'd—'

He stood up and rubbed his hands together, so like his father. 'Yup, I'm on to it. Have you got any extension leads?'

'They are in a box in the catering tent too, but I don't know what we can fix them on to. It would be nice to have some lights outside.'

Noel rubbed his face thoughtfully. 'Dad, have you still got that timber from when we tried to make the pergola for the garden a few years ago?'

Jacob looked abashed. 'Yes, it's in the garden shed I think. Completely unused.'

'Great.' Noel turned to Holly's boyfriend. 'Joe, you're the chippie.'

'Cabinetmaker, do you mind!' Joe laughed.

'Whatever. Cleverer than me anyway. Do you think we could knock up a wooden support to go at the entrance – make it a bit of a statement?'

Joe stood up. 'Sure. Got a saw I can borrow?'

As the two men left, Baz shouted after them, 'Don't forget the mahogany inlay.'

From behind his back, Joe gave him a gesture that made everyone laugh.

Beth went back to her list. 'Table centres.'

'I can do that. Have you got any tea lights?' Christina asked hesitantly and everyone looked as if they had forgotten she was there. 'I mean they look pretty floating in water.'

'As a matter of fact, I believe I have a bag of about two hundred, as has everyone else who has ever been to IKEA!'

'Well, I'll need something to put them in. Do you have any glass bowls?'

Beth did a mental trawl of the kitchen cupboards. 'I've got

the odd one, and a couple of Pyrex mixing bowls—'

Mrs Havers cut in. 'Village hall, that's what you want. They got glass pudding dishes, they have. Pretty ones. Old-fashioned, like.'

Beth sighed. 'They'd be perfect, but I haven't got a key. I think Irene has one. I'll try and call her.'

'She's on the committee. She should be here anyway, in your time of need.' Beth looked at Mrs Havers in astonishment. Was this a show of solidarity? 'I've got a key. Always have had. Don't let them committee ladies know though – they'd have me setting up for them if they did instead of that daft Godfrey woman. I'll get it now.'

Sally jumped to her feet. 'I'll come with you, if I may. Tell me, Mrs Havers, where are you from? You have a very interesting accent.' The unlikely duo made their way to the front door.

Christina looked at Beth enquiringly. 'Do you have any secateurs I could borrow? If I could cut some foliage from your garden, perhaps I could make some little arrangements. My mum does the church flowers sometimes and I always help her when I'm at home.' Beth happily handed over the entire box of garland-making leftovers that she'd put aside in such disgust only a few days earlier. The girl's eyes lit up and she bustled from the room.

And so, gradually, the dining room had emptied as the ad hoc group broke off to take care of their appointed tasks, chattering and laughing at the prospect. Even Tim had gone with his heroes. Alone now with just Carol, Beth blinked round at the vacated chairs and shook her head in disbelief.

'I really appreciate this show of support, Carol. You've pulled us all together, but quite honestly I can't see how we can do much with such limited time and resources. I mean, I don't want to sound ungrateful, but it was always such a glittering event in the old days.' She looked at the lists in front of her and shrugged. 'At least we'll save money. The budget I've been allocated from ticket sales will barely be touched – just the marquee, the loos and the glasses and cutlery. It might be the cheapest Meet in living memory.' The trouble was, she thought grimly, it would look like it too.

'Don't lose heart, Beth. It'll be great – and that's what I do. Make magic out of nothing.'

Beth snorted wryly. 'Mmm, women's magazines. Bane of my bloody life the last few months – I'd been immune till then – just the odd copy of *Vogue* in the dentist's. But I've been completely taken in by you bloody journos with your cover-line bollocks!' She laughed and pulled out some torn-out pages, waving them dramatically. 'Have you any idea how much pressure you put women under? You should be locked away!'

Carol looked sheepish. 'Yup, I admit I'm in the illusion business but we all have to aspire. Let me make amends today and see if fifteen years on mags has taught me anything useful and maybe that employee of mine upstairs can learn a thing or two.'

Beth shook her head. 'Incredible.'

'What?'

'The coincidences. You here and Holly and stuff.'

'And all because she was too lazy to find a real chocolate box cottage for the magazine.' She got to her feet. 'Now, I'm off to the marquee and you've got stuff to sort. But, Beth?' Beth looked up from her list. 'You've got a harder job. I think there's a girl upstairs you need to talk to.' And she left the room.

Maybe, thought Beth, but the immediate problem, of course, was how she was going to feed everyone. She made her way to the kitchen to start foraging, more in hope than in expectation. What store cupboard delights could she rustle up for tonight's party? Pasta with pesto for two hundred? As she opened the kitchen door of the now empty house, she heard footsteps from upstairs. Holly still sulking, no doubt. Beth made herself a cup of tea, and gazed round the kitchen now restored to relative order since the morning's onslaught on the sausages. How many packs had she bought, in the end? With the ones from the organic farm shop, from the supermarket, from the mail order company it amounted to quite a few.

*

From her bedroom, Holly could hear the gravel crunching underfoot as people started to leave the house. She levered herself up from the bed, rubbed her puffy eyes and crept over to the window to watch. Holly shook her head in disbelief. How had Carol, of all people, ended up in that shitty cottage? Why in God's name had Beth rented the bloody place out at all? She watched as Joe and Noel walked off down the road together without even a backward glance and sighed heavily. Even they were getting on and didn't care. They must all hate her.

Turning to her bed, she picked up an old teddy – still propped up on her pillow as ever – and threw it across the room. Damn everyone. Damn them all.

But most of all, damn herself. The ranting was pointless. She knew the cottage, the magazine feature, Carol being there was no one's fault but her own. The way everyone was treating her now – even that was her fault. And who could blame them?

And worst of all she wasn't Daddy's girl any more. Someone else had taken that place.

A soft tap at the door made her spin round. She cleared her throat, sore from crying. 'Who is it?'

'It's me, Berry. Can we talk?'

She opened the door, hanging her head so Jacob wouldn't see her ruined face. Would he hate her too now? She waited.

'Oh Berry.' He sighed deeply. 'Why are you so cross all the time? Have I let you down? Haven't I given you enough attention?'

That did it. Holly felt tears spill down her cheeks again and she sank down onto her bed. She could feel Jacob watch her for a moment, then he sat down on the chair at her desk, just as he had through the years when she needed help with her homework.

'The thing is, I know it's been hard for you, these last four years since your mother died. But Holly, being angry won't bring her back, and hating Beth won't bring her back either. Your mother ...' Jacob's voice faltered and Holly looked up him. 'Your mother and I had many wonderful years together and nothing will change any of that. But I've had to be strong and to move on with my life. It's what she would have wanted. And so must you.'

'But it was so quick, Daddy.' Holly whispered the words she'd never said but had so often thought. 'So soon after she died. It was as if nothing mattered to you any more – Mummy or me or Noel. You were off in New York with Beth or Venice with Beth, and then she moved in here and just took over. First Mummy died, then it was like you didn't want me any more. I felt so alone ...' She trailed off. The look of anguish on Jacob's face said it all.

'Holly,' he sighed, 'how can you think that? You're my daughter. My only daughter. I love you as I love no one else in the world. And I'm proud of you – and your mother was proud of you. I only wish she could have seen the young woman you've become. But ...' He looked down at his hands. 'Your mother wouldn't have wanted you to deliberately try to hurt someone's feelings. It's not worthy of you. You wouldn't like it if I'd set my mind against Joe and tried to make him feel uncomfortable, would you?'

Holly stood up and tried to speak, but Jacob held up his hand. 'Let me have my say, darling. Beth makes me happy, Holly. We love each other and we want to be together, but it doesn't mean I loved your mother any the less. You must accept that. Beth has tried very hard this Christmas to make everything right. Can't you cut her some slack?'

Holly squeezed her fists so tightly she could feel her nails digging into her palms. Should she tell him about the baby now? Would he be even angrier with her?

Jacob unfolded himself from the chair. 'I'll always love you, Berry. You'll always be my little girl.' And he pulled her into a safe enveloping hug.

'Love you too, Daddy. I'm sorry.' To Holly's surprise, she really meant it, and was about to open her mouth when he ruffled her hair, as he had always done, and left her room.

*

Beth had assembled a possible menu from her stocks on the kitchen table. Not bad! She was starting to consider the feasibility of a hot dog fest, when the kitchen door opened slowly, and she turned to see a red-eyed, dishevelled Holly on the threshold.

Beth was tempted to turn away and continue with what she was doing, but something in the girl's manner prevented her and Carol's words about her needing to talk to Holly echoed in her head. Holly looked so downcast that Beth didn't have the heart to continue hostilities.

Holly was avoiding her eye. 'Where is everyone?' she asked at last in a low voice.

Beth hesitated. It was the least aggressive thing Holly had ever said to her. 'I've just made some tea. Would you like a cup? They're all scattered to the four winds, trying to improvise things ready for the Meet tonight. Your Joe is with Noel rigging up a support for the lights.'

Holly smiled wanly, her face still puffy from crying. 'Yep, that sounds like Joe. He likes a challenge.' There was a long silence as Holly sipped from the mug of tea Beth had passed her. 'Maybe that's why he likes me.'

Beth sat down and gestured for Holly to do the same. She wasn't about to pick up Holly's conversational baton and possibly cause another row, so she cast around for a neutral topic to continue with. 'Would you like something to eat, if your stomach has settled now? I could make you some toast, if you like. I don't think anyone else was affected, thank goodness. I don't think I could have handled anything else going wrong today!'

Holly looked suddenly awkward and took another quick sip of tea. 'No thanks. I might eat later, but I don't really feel like it in the mornings.' She shot a quick glance at Beth. 'Where's Daddy gone?'

Oh, here we go, thought Beth. 'He's out organising the troops, but I'm not sure where he is exactly. I think he took his mobile with him, though, if you want him.'

'No, er. No. It was you I wanted to talk to really.' Holly glanced up at Beth cautiously. 'Do you think …? Has he said anything about Joe?'

Beth shook her head slowly. 'No. No, not really. To tell you the truth, we haven't really had time to talk, what with all the guests in the house. I mean …' She hadn't meant it as a reproach, but as Holly flushed and started glancing quickly around, she cursed herself for spoiling this new line of communication before it had really started. She steeled herself for an angry retort but Holly seemed to be groping for words.

'About Baz and the others. I didn't really know for sure if they were going to come. Well, I wasn't sure. I mean … they live in a squat and it's not very … Well, I'm sorry I didn't tell you and Dad. Ask you, I mean. About them coming. I should have.'

Well, this was a first! Beth tried not to let her astonishment show too much, and nodded slowly to give herself some time to get used to this. At the back of her mind, she couldn't help wondering if she was being set up for some even worse torment later, but something in Holly's manner seemed quite different. She spoke cautiously. 'Well, it was a bit of a surprise but they seem very nice. And look at what's happened, after all. It's probably just as well we've got reinforcements. Maybe the Meet won't be such a disaster after all.' Holly sat forward in her chair and rubbed her hips. Was she going to come back with a spiteful little retort? Suddenly Beth felt tired.

'I hope you like Joe. He's ... We're ... I really like him a lot. I'm thinking we might even live together when we get back to London.' Again the cautious glance from Holly. If it weren't totally out of character, Beth would have thought she was seeking her approval.

'I thought you were together already. Seems daft not to be, really. If you're sure, I mean. Sure that he's the one. Sometimes you just know ...' Beth trailed off. It felt rather odd to be discussing love and romance with Holly, but the girl look relieved and leant back in her chair. Beth looked at her carefully. Without the scowl, she looked much younger and softer and, despite the stomach upset, she seemed to have put on weight recently. In the soft turquoise baggy jumper she had worn constantly since her arrival, she seemed more approachable. Not at all the prickly Holly that Beth had come to cordially loath. Suddenly, Beth felt a surge of remorse. Perhaps it really had been very hard for Holly, after all, to cope with the recent changes in Jacob's life.

'Holly,' she started, 'y'know, I think this is almost the first time we've had a chance to talk properly, just the two of us. I'll admit, I'm not having my best day ever but I'd like to think we can get to understand each other a bit more than we have so far.'

'What do you mean?'

'Weeell,' Beth stalled. This was going to be tricky. 'About the Carol thing. I don't just mean the cottage. I mean, I don't understand why you lied about which magazine you worked on.'

Holly blushed as Beth continued, 'You don't have to try and impress us, Holly. We may be dried-up academics, but we are so proud of what you do, and I don't like your dad trawling through the wrong women's magazine looking for your name.' She tried to smile lamely. 'I can't begin to imagine how weird and how difficult it must have been for you when I came on the scene. But it's pretty strange for me too, suddenly having stepchildren when I don't even have any children of my own. Sometimes I just don't know what I'm supposed to do. I wish I had an instruction book ...' She trailed off again, wondering if she had gone too far. Holly was staring at her with a fierce intensity.

'Beth, can I talk to you about something? Something personal?'

This was a fragile moment. Beth leant forward and laid her hand gently on Holly's arm. 'Yes, of course. Anything.'

Holly took a deep breath. And the front door bell jangled. Beth groaned. 'Sorry, Holly. Can it wait until later?' and watched in dismay as the girl slumped back in her chair, her face closed once more.

Carol was hopping from foot to foot in the doorway, her breath hanging in the chilly air and her eyes bright. 'Hi Beth. I'm really sorry but can you spare Holly? We're doing a bit of a makeover on the old marquee. Ah, there you are! I need your creative input – since you're so good at making things seem more attractive than they are.' Holly had appeared from the kitchen and, with surprising meekness, was pulling on her boots. 'And can we have a rummage through your garage while we're at it, in case inspiration strikes?'

Holly slipped past Beth and went to stand beside Carol, looking downcast and almost shamefaced once again. She really did seem to have had the stuffing knocked out of her and Beth

264

felt a wave of unexpectedly protective feeling. 'Holly, will you be warm enough? Why don't you take my scarf?'

Holly shook her head impatiently and slouched off to the garage alone, leaving Carol looking exasperatedly at Beth. 'Honestly, that girl needs a rocket sometimes.'

Beth who, only the day before, would probably have rolled her eyes in tacit agreement found herself shrugging and smiling. 'Well, y'know how it is with Holly. She's not so bad once you get past the prickles ...'

Carol laughed in surprise. 'Well, it sounds like you've had a talk. Hope I didn't break anything up but it's all go down at the Marquee de Sad. No need for you to come down yet – we'll call you when it's ready for your inspection. C'mon Holly,' she called, 'we've got lots to catch up on, haven't we?'

Holly was lurking by the garage looking pale and tired again. Beth waited in the doorway until she caught her eye. 'We'll talk later, Holly. OK?'

An almost imperceptible nod, and she turned away.

*

Carol swept into the garage with Holly in her wake.

'Right. Beth said there were some bits and pieces we could take from here,' and, spotting some boxes of fabric Christmas roses and ribbon, she began to explore. 'Oh look at this. There's lots we could do with this.' She knew she was being false, but she felt irked and wasn't going to give Holly the pleasure of wallowing in self-pity.

'Here.' she planted a bundle of decorative bits into Holly's arms. 'You can carry these for me. Now, what's in here?' As she rummaged she was aware of Holly standing silently behind her. It was a tough one, when the girl was in her home environment, but Carol didn't feel it could remain unsaid.

'Holly, I know you've had a talk with Beth and that's a good thing, but that doesn't really deal with the issue of the cottage, does it?'

Holly shifted from one foot to the other, and looked straight at Carol as she stood up from the box. 'No. No it doesn't. I'm very sorry Carol. I had no idea it would all go wrong.'

'What happened?'

'I wrote that page just before I went on holiday and I was in a hurry. I meant to call Beth to tell her that if anyone tried to book the cottage, she was to say it had been taken.' She pulled aimlessly at a bit of thread on one of the ribbons. 'But I forgot.'

'You forgot.'

Holly faced her, but the look in her eye was not her normal defiance. There was something searching and unsure.

Carol pulled out the carrier bag of fabric flowers, and several blocks of oasis. 'The thing is, Holly, what you did was selfish on two levels. For a start it was lazy journalism, and I've fired people for less than that.' Holly's expression was stricken now. 'You were lucky it was me who booked the cottage and not one of our readers. You need to take care because I don't want lazy journalists on my magazine. There are lots and lots of very keen people who'd like your job and if this kind of thing happens again, I'll have no qualms about giving it to one of them.'

Knowing that her point had been made, Carol handed her another bag to carry and moved towards the garage door. Then she turned back to the girl.

'But what annoys me more, Holly, is that you made your stepmother feel that *she* had messed up *my* Christmas. On top of everything else she's had to think about – this party, your family, keeping everyone happy – and most especially trying to make you accept her by working overtime to consider your feelings, to make this Christmas OK for *you* – you left her to shoulder the responsibility of me arriving at a damp little cottage that should never have been let to anyone.' Carol could see the tears in Holly's eyes but she felt very little remorse. The girl had to start behaving like a grown-up.

'It was a poor show, Holly. Right, now let's forget it.' Carol stooped and picked up the packages. 'Come on, we've got a marquee to decorate. Perhaps you can do a feature on it next year, hey?' And she walked out of the garage.

Chapter 22

Lunchtime on Christmas Eve

Make sure there are plenty of fairy lights. According to feng shui, they create positive energy.

This was fun, Tim decided. It wasn't quite how he'd imagined this Christmas Eve would be, but then sitting propped up on a marquee table and spraying cooking apples with gold paint was a great improvement on driving around boring villages full of old houses, which is what he suspected his mother meant yesterday when she'd said 'explore' .

Thank goodness for the snow. Wonderful, lovely snow.

Hobbling about had begun to hurt his good leg a bit, so it was quite a relief to be sitting still. He and the girl called Holly, which seemed a pretty name so it was a shame she didn't smile more, had laid out some old newspaper on one of the tables, and his mum had brought over a box of the apples that the Jenny woman had stored in her garage. Tim couldn't see the point of that really.

'I mean, why would she want to keep apples?'

Holly picked up a completed apple gingerly by the stem with her long black-painted fingernails. 'Because Jenny is that kind of person,' she explained unhelpfully. 'I've known her for years. She was a friend of my mum's and she picks her apples in the autumn and stores them in her garage. They keep that way. She always makes great apple crumble. When I was little, we used to have it with custard.'

'Yuck. I hate custard. We have it at school.' Tim fished out the next apple for Holly to spray. This one had a few holes in it, but he didn't suppose it would matter. 'Well she won't be making any crumble now, will she?'

Holly laughed and her face lit up. She looked at him. 'No, Tim, I don't suppose she will. But that's Jenny for you. She's just very good at helping people out so she's sacrificed all her apples to make tree decorations for the party.' Holly hooked her hair behind her ear like Miss Jeffries did. Tim thought Miss Jeffries was prettier, but he liked Holly and she worked with his mum.

'You work with my mum.'

Holly concentrated on spraying the next apple, shaking the can from time to time. He could hear the rattle of the little ball inside, which Holly had explained was there to keep the paint runny. 'Yes I do. She's very good at her job. Everyone likes her.' This made Tim feel very warm inside. Holly straightened up from her task. 'Do you see your dad much?'

'Oh yes, lots.' Tim swung his good leg over the side of the table, and admired the writing and drawings on his cast made by Baz, Mel and Caspar. Joe, who did great cartoons, had drawn Bart Simpson, saying 'Eat my Christmas shorts'. Granny wouldn't let him watch *The Simpsons* so he wasn't very sure what that meant, but it made him feel grown up anyway. 'We have fun, but I like being at home too. You don't have a mum, do you?'

'No I don't.' Holly seemed to be concentrating very hard on this particular apple.

'Do you miss her?'

'All the time, Tim.' And she did a strange thing. She touched his cheek with the hand that didn't have any paint on it. Or at least Tim hoped it didn't. 'But I think my stepmother just might be OK.' She bent down again to her work.

'Oh, she's nice. She doesn't seem like a stepmother at all.'

'No,' Holly scratched her nose. 'I don't think she poisons apples.' She paused. 'Does your mum have a boyfriend?'

'No, but can you keep a secret?' Tim leant closer to her.

Holly leant close too and whispered, 'Yesss.'

'There's someone she likes and I think he likes her too. He's called Nick.'

'Oh,' mouthed Holly in reply then jumped as Carol approached.

'How are you two doing? Oh they look glorious. Are any dry enough to use yet?'

Holly touched them carefully with her fingertips. 'Couple more minutes. Did Dad bring down that garden wire to hang them with?'

Carol laughed. 'He's made that many trips back and forth to your house, your poor father, and now he's muttering something like it being worse in here than *Blue Peter*. How are you doing, Timmo? Do you want to help me write some signs?'

Tim shuffled his bottom off the table and eased himself carefully down to the floor. He was sorry to leave Holly but he liked writing, and he knew this task involved a big brush and a tin of house paint, because he'd seen Noel arrive with it.

Before they moved off and as his mum was helping him with his crutches, she leant over to Holly. '*WM*, December a couple of years back.' Holly looked at her, puzzled. His mum nodded at what Holly was doing. 'The painted apples idea. You see, Holly, sometimes this nonsense we peddle is quite useful.' They both laughed, but Tim wasn't sure why.

*

Carol stretched to ease her back. She'd been bending over the little conifers for what seemed like hours and she must have tied about a thousand ribbons so she deserved a break. The marquee was a hive of activity and from her position by the door, she could see Noel up a ladder with Mel feeding him lights to wrap around the tent poles. Beneath them was Christina, who'd moved on now from the table centres and was tucking foliage into the twine Baz had wound around the poles. Sally was festooning an archway – rigged by Joe – with a length of what looked like velvet, but might have been someone's old curtains. Jenny, the lovely woman who Beth had introduced her to, and another woman she didn't recognise were laying out the buffet table, ready for the food, and Mrs Havers, the cleaner, who hadn't adjusted the rather grim expression on her face all morning – perhaps it was permanent – was laying out cutlery on the tables with alarming efficiency.

The word had obviously got out around the village and it was all hands to the proverbial pump. For the last couple of hours there had been a steady stream of people entering the tent, their arms laden with goodies. Carol half expected a group of shepherds to appear any minute with a sacrificial lamb. There was everything else besides though: Children came wrapped head to foot in warm clothing, their arms laden with foliage and holly before being allowed by their parents to go off and throw snowballs at each other. Behind them were old ladies carrying bundles of tablecloths that 'hadn't been used for years, dear, but I thought might help', and men with fairy lights. Lights, lights and more lights. Some that flashed, some that were coloured, some that pulsated. There can't have been a tree left in Milton St David that hadn't been denuded of its splendour. And when one old chap presented a wind-up gramophone, no one had the heart to turn him away.

And then came the food: tins of mince pies, ham and game pies; platters of coronation chicken and tomato salads, all thinly sliced and garnished with basil; chocolate cakes and meringues. Boxes of crackers and super-size festive chocolates for after-dinner coffee, which Tim was given the job of decanting onto small plates to put on each table – though Carol suspected there was quite a bit of 'one for the plate, one for me'.

And standing in the centre of the marquee, to accept all this bounty, was Beth, her face a picture of disbelief. Like a policeman directing traffic, she pointed people in the direction of the dance floor, the tables or the catering tent. The latter was apparently now the domain of a group Carol was sure Beth had called the Fêtes – the glamorous element of the village, Beth had explained, who measured their social status in terms of the size of their four by fours and their personal trainer's pectorals. One of them, she confided, had just come back from her annual colonic irrigation treatment at the health spa. Presumably to enable her to stuff in more Christmas lunch.

'Do you think there will be enough food though?' Beth panicked. 'It's all very well having crackers and chocolates but what about a main course? There's only one thing for it.' And within half an hour she had one turkey on the go at home and was using Carol's Aga to cook another, which she'd apparently ordered inadvertently and forgotten about – something Carol couldn't quite get her head around. 'I have something else to confess,' Beth whispered out of the corner of her mouth to Carol, when she returned from her ministrations, battling across the marquee with her arms laden with more carrier bags of food and giant packs of peanuts. 'I've made a bit of a cock-up. Promise you won't say a word? Jacob will never let me forget it.'

'My lips are sealed.'

'Well,' she looked about her conspiratorially, 'by *mistake* I ordered ten pounds of sliced ham.' She held up one of the bulging bags. 'I mean, I *meant* to order ten pounds' worth in money but the butcher misunderstood – thought it was for the party, I suppose, cos he's only from the next village and I was too embarrassed to disabuse him of the idea.' Her eyes sparkled. 'Bloody good thing too, don't you think?'

'Beth,' Carol announced, seeing the delight in the other woman's eyes, 'I think the snow was serendipity.'

As the afternoon progressed, the atmosphere was one of excitement and anticipation. The disparate little group seemed to gel as they pulled together. With his gentle teasing and shameless flirting, Caspar had Mrs Havers blushing and giggling like a schoolgirl and Noel, who was clearly a favourite of Jenny's, was charming her by asking endless questions about her dogs. Carol just kept back and observed, only stepping in to halt a game of cricket on the dance floor between Baz, Joe and Tim, much to the latter's anger, because she didn't think it was a good idea to be using his cast leg as a stump.

'Mrs Layham.' An old biddy with fat ankles had come up behind Beth, Holly and the Fêtes, who were busy ticking off things from a list of what they had and hadn't got, and coughed discreetly.

'Oh, Mrs Godfrey.' Beth turned a radiant smile on the woman. 'Is there a problem?'

'Well, it's a delicate matter really.' She leant in close. 'It's the toilets,' she mouthed. 'You know, the mobile ones. They're a bit ... er, fragrant and not in a good way.'

'Oh glory. I knew I shouldn't have opted for that supplier. I just knew there'd be a reason why they were so cheap. Come and show me.' Five minutes later she was back, her face screwed up in distaste. 'It's vile. Smells like a Bombay sewer and two hundred people have to use them. What the hell shall we do?'

'Anyone got any pot pourri?' asked one particularly luscious blonde in the group, whose pursed mouth gave away how uncomfortable she was with all this toilet talk. Perhaps she was the irrigation patient.

'I think we need something more dramatic than that I'm afraid, Tamara. Industrial-strength air freshener might just do the trick.' Beth puts her fingers to her lips, clearly racking her brains.

'I might have something,' said Holly quietly. 'Hang on a minute,' and she dashed out of the tent, only to arrive back a short while later, stamping snow off her boots, and sheepishly handing a wrapped present to Beth.

Beth, perplexed, tore off the paper to reveal three scented candles from one of *WM's* advertisers and clearly part of the beauty cupboard haul earlier in the week. Beth held them up, sniffed them and looked at Holly, with laughter in her eyes. 'Were these for me?'

Holly looked down at the floor. 'Well yes, but I thought you might like them early if they'd help.' She glanced up at her stepmother with a searching look. Beth smiled and then her smile broke into a laugh.

'Mmmm, Holly, the present that shows you really don't care. But I think for once they might be useful.' Across Holly's face flitted an expression of misunderstanding, and then, slowly, a broad smile.

'I'm sorry,' was all she replied, 'bit of a cop-out really,' and Beth seemed to understand.

By the time Jacob clapped his hands and demanded everyone stop for a tea break, it was nearly four o'clock and the marquee was unrecognisable. The stream of giftbearers had slowed to a trickle, and the core group were tying off loose ends, but it wasn't until everyone stood back and looked up from their work that they realised just what had been achieved.

There was an awed silence. Everywhere there was light and sparkle. Golden apples hung from trees and foliage, fairy lights lit up red berries and glistening baubles. In the centre of each table, Christina had used her skills with candles and greenery sprinkled with silver glitter. In the darkening afternoon, the marquee seemed to come alive with a warm magic of its own.

'Crikey,' said Beth, standing beside Carol, an extension lead in her hand. 'This is amazing. I just don't know what to say.' She turned to look at Carol who could see her eyes were brimming with tears. 'What an amazing Christmas present everyone has given me.'

'Beats socks again, doesn't it?'

Beth laughed and Jacob came and put his arm around his wife's shoulders. 'Mrs Havers?' he called, turning round to find her. 'Ivy? There you are. The chairwoman needs a cup of tea.'

Mrs Havers nodded and dipped her head back behind the flap leading into the catering tent. Carol looked questioningly at Beth and mouthed quietly, 'Ivy?'

'Yup,' whispered Beth back. 'But maybe not so poisonous after all.'

Everyone drank their tea appreciatively, with plenty of sighing after each sip.

'One thing.' Beth looked thoughtful, cupping her mug in both hands. 'The florist was going to bring a table centre as a raffle prize. Oh and the farm shop promised a Christmas cake – they'll never get that here now.' She rubbed her eyes and sighed. 'We'll just have to make do with the crocheted tea cosy and the bottle of Blue Nun someone's kindly donated already.'

'That will have them queuing for tickets!' said Sally with her usual grace. 'I can hardly wait.'

'Slug in a free annual subscription to *WM* and a make-over,' said Carol on impulse, confident now there would be another year of issues.

'Oh Carol, can we? How glamorous!' Beth looked genuinely delighted.

'Well I'm knackered,' yawned Sally. 'I shall have to go and have a long hot bath or I shall never be able to dance the night away.'

'Oh shit, the music!' Beth spluttered on her tea. 'I forgot all about it! The raffle's one thing but what about the disco? What the hell is everyone going to dance to?' There were mutterings amongst the group. This was clearly going to be a tricky one.

'I have a karaoke machine somewhere,' suggested one woman. 'I bought it for Gary a couple of years back but we only used it once at New Year cos his Uncle Jim got very pissed and kept singing 'My Way'. Would that be any good?'

'It's a possibility,' said Beth cautiously, clearly hoping someone else would come up with a better idea. 'We're going to need big noise though for that number of people. Oh God.'

Carol was just about to suggest her clock radio and CD player if things got desperate when Mel, slouched on a chair towards the back of the marquee, shifted his lanky body nervously and piped up: 'Would a band do, like?'

Beth turned to him. 'Well I don't see why not, but where on earth will we get one this late in the day – or one that could get into the village for that matter? Hang on, didn't Mrs Godfrey's husband once play the trumpet?'

'Tuba dear,' came the reply from someone. 'Hardly hip hop.'

Mel shifted again. 'Well, us three, we have a band, like. Nothing great, you understand, just the odd pub gig and stuff, but we've got our stuff in the van. Amps too and all. We can give it a go if you like?'

Beth clapped her hands in delight. 'Oh Mel, I couldn't care if you were the Nolan Sisters. Would you really? I'll pay you the balance I'd have paid the disco man – I can't give you all of it cos I've paid him a deposit and that was non-refundable. But– ' It was Baz who put his hand on her arm.

'It's cool, Beth. We'll do it for nothing. Make up for your hospitality, and besides, it'll be a gas. Come on, lads, let's unload the stuff then.' And off they strode, pursued by an overcome Beth asking if she could help.

Worried now that Tim would be getting tired and thinking that an hour's rest might be a good idea if he was going to make it through the party, Carol persuaded him to come with her back to the cottage and inveigled Noel, who looked strong enough, to piggy-back the child down there for her. Half an hour later, the cottage full of the smell of Beth's spare roasting turkey, she had him tucked up in bed with a Philip Ardagh book, and she was pulling clothes out of her suitcase hoping for inspiration for something to wear this evening, knowing full well she had packed for country walks and chilling out, not dancing and Christmas glamour. Her phone went in her pocket. It would be her mother, calling from Lourdes and in a state of grace no doubt, to see how they were.

'Hello Carol, it's Anya.' Carol started. In all the shenanigans about the cottage and the excitement of the day, she'd clean forgotten about the frenzy of press coverage about the pop star's child. It had completely passed her by. Would she be livid and blame Carol for all the furore? She felt a bit sick.

'Oh Anya, hi. How are you?' Silly question.

'Ooh Carol, I'm fine,' she replied softly, her voice strangely breathless. 'I'm sat in my car. I'm in Ipswich and I just wanted to talk to you.'

'Ipswich? What on earth are you doing in Ipswich on Christmas Eve? Have you got a gig?' It seemed unlikely. Perhaps she was the star in the East?

'No. Carol,' she sounded urgent, 'they've dropped the charges. I'm about to meet her.'

For a moment Carol was confused. 'Her?'

'My daughter.' They were both silent for a moment. 'I'm outside her grandmother's house and it's been agreed that this is where we will meet.' Carol didn't want to give away how much she had missed, but she had to know.

'What, I mean, how did it happen?'

'Oh Carol, it was weird.' Anya's voice sounded animated. 'Lots of people came forward and claimed they were 'The One.' She laughed nervously. 'Christ, I could have had about five hundred daughters at one point. Then a few days ago my agent got a call from this lady in Suffolk who said she had information. Well, to cut a long story short, they met and then I met her and she revealed that a very good friend of hers had told her she thought her adopted daughter might indeed be my daughter.' Carol could hear Anya swallow. 'Oh Carol, it was too amazing. Too much to hope for. But I talked to this woman – you know, her friend – and it all just seemed to fit together: the dates and the fact that her daughter had been a foundling. Oh that sounds so weird. That's my baby they are talking about. She had told her daughter about six years ago that she was adopted and when she saw all the news stories, it just sort of confirmed her suspicions.'

Carol moved from her kneeling position and rubbed the back of her knees to stop the pins and needles. 'How do you mean?'

'Well, and this is what's so spooky, she's always thought her daughter looked like me. In fact, people used to comment apparently when I was on TV and stuff. Then, when one of the rags covering the story published a picture of me as a baby – God knows how they got hold of that, one of my money-grabbing sisters no doubt,' she sounded bitter, 'well, she said it was unmistakable.'

'Oh Anya.' Carol could feel the excitement in her own stomach. 'Are you sure it's her? I mean you couldn't be wrong, could you?'

'No. No it can't be. We've gone through all the records of her adoption and it was that night, Carol. She knew the baby she was offered was left that night. Outside the hospital. And she's talked to her – my – daughter and she is ready to meet me.'

Carol, couldn't stop herself. 'Anya, I know you wanted to give me the interview. I know it came from you. But I hope I did the right thing for you publishing it. I hope I haven't made trouble ...'

'Carol,' Anya's voice sounded imploring. 'You mustn't think that for a minute. You are right – it was my decision and I had to do it. I had to lay this ghost to rest. It was eating me up. And as, well, as a very good friend said to me the other day, you should never regret the things you have done. Just the things you haven't.'

'Mmm, wise advice and I hope your friend is right.'

'He often is. OK,' she sighed, steeling herself, 'I'm going to go in now. I'm glad I talked to you, Carol. Have a lovely Christmas, and thank you for making this happen for me. It's amazing actually – tonight I mean. It's Christmas Eve and for once I'm on my own, away from PAs and press officers and photographers and fans. Just me, in a small street in Ipswich in the dark. That's the way it should be, isn't it? You know, for something as important as this? No fuss?'

'It's perfect. Good luck and I hope it's a happy Christmas for you.'

'And for you too, Carol. I hope it's a really special one for you. I think it might be.'

Not really knowing what Anya meant, Carol heard her open the car door. 'Anya, one last thing. Her name? What's your daughter's adopted name?'

'Holly. Pretty, isn't it?'

Chapter 23

10.30 p.m., Christmas Eve

*Dancing can make you hot and sweaty, so pop a
couple of identical tops in your bag, then nip to the
loo to change. You'll look as fresh as a daisy and no
one will know how you did it!*

Beth whirled to a finish, breathless and hot despite the fact that
they had turned off the heaters. Noel, more enthusiastic than
skilled on the dance floor, grinned, bowed comically and led
her back to her seat through the crowd. It was the first chance
she'd had for a sit-down since the party kicked off, almost three
hours ago now and she was glad of the opportunity to see how
things were going.

It was time the band had another rest really, although at the
end of each song they played – Christmas classics every one
– the round of applause from the dance floor was uproarious
and the crowd bayed for more. Caspar had a rather sheepishly pleased expression on his face, though Mel was working
hard to look cool – quite an achievement when you've just
bashed out 'Santa Claus is Coming to Town' in the style of the
Sex Pistols. Jacob had made it his job to keep them fed and
watered though, with the emphasis on the watered and, Beth
reflected, it was probably a good thing Baz was the size he was,
because not many men could down that much beer and still
remain standing, let alone be able to bash out renditions of
'Last Christmas' on a Fender Stratocaster. Maybe if she drew

the raffle, Beth thought, it would give them a chance to get something to eat. But first, she really had to slip these shoes off, just for a moment.

The queue for food was abating slightly now, so she could grab the chance to eat something herself. It had turned into a rather eclectic meal to say the least, with all the village chipping in with whatever they'd bought too much of. Beth looked around for her friend and saw Sally on the dance floor executing a pretty tidy-looking jive with Jacob, who had discarded his sweater and was looking very dishevelled, his hair sticking up, his checked shirt untucked from his cords at the back. Next to them, a pair of ten-year-old twins from the village were trying nonchalantly to copy their every move, the girl with her tongue sticking out slightly, the boy red-faced with his efforts to look as cool as Jacob. Everywhere she looked, Beth saw smiling faces: people of all ages laughing and chatting, eating and drinking.

Jenny settled heavily on a seat next to Beth. 'Phew! I haven't danced so much in years. I shall pay for this tomorrow but, frankly, I don't care. I'm having a marvellous time!'

Beth turned to her. 'I'm so glad. When the snow came down and the caterers and everyone else cancelled, I just wished the floor would swallow me up. I thought the whole thing was going to be a disaster. But everyone's been so nice and so helpful.'

Jenny nodded sympathetically. 'I can imagine. Especially when you'd put in so much hard work. But look at it this way, if it had all come off as you'd planned, everyone would have said, "What a clever girl that Layham woman is. She'd done the Meet so brilliantly this year. We can't possibly compete so I think she'd better do it for ever." But this way, everyone is thinking, What a clever girl that Layham woman is. She's made the Meet everyone's party and nobody has felt left out and it hasn't just been a chance for her to show off. See what I mean?'

Beth was mortified. 'Is that what everyone thought, that I was showing off?'

'No, no, dear, not for a moment. Although people have thought that in the past and they might have thought it about you if it had come off as you'd planned. I fear it would have been a rather grand affair, wouldn't it? Not my idea of Christmas at all. And I would've had to get all dressed up in my glad rags, I expect. No wonder the rest of your committee were frightened off.'

Beth stared at her friend as she took in the significance of what she was saying, then scanned the room. The VEG members were now out in force, although she'd barely seen them over the past few weeks, doling out mulled wine from a huge saucepan set over a gas stove, handing hot dogs to the children and plates of rice and turkey curry or baked potatoes to the adults, clearing plates, laughing and joking with everyone they spoke to. Across the room, Irene caught Beth's eye and waved enthusiastically at her, making her way between the tables to where she was sitting.

Beth turned back to Jenny. 'Do you mean to tell me the reason no one helped was because I was making the Meet too grand? But I thought that was what it was supposed to be.'

Jenny shrugged. 'It's supposed to be whatever the village makes it. But that's the key thing, isn't it – what the *village* makes it. I think we'd all had enough of it being turned into a black-tie affair, like something out of a society magazine, but no one quite had the courage to make it anything else. So the VEG committee thought that a new broom, like you, might turn it around. But then you set off like a hare along Becca's route so they all gave up. And you do have that air of efficiency that makes you seem as though you're managing perfectly well on your own.'

Irene reached them at last. 'Beth, it's been a triumph. Everyone's enjoying it – young and old. And you've had the best theme ever – Christmas! The snowman competition was inspired! It certainly kept the children amused – and some of the adults. I haven't had so much fun in years. Oh, that band have started again. I love this one. Dean Martin, wasn't it?'

And off she went to claim her husband for another dance. That was something else that had gone right. Beth gazed at the band admiringly. She hadn't dared to hope for such a success when they'd volunteered their help, and Holly had looked horror-struck when she'd heard they would be playing. But it had worked out wonderfully. And speaking of Holly. Beth scanned the marquee and saw her sitting in a relatively quiet corner with little Tim fast asleep with his head on her shoulder. Beth watched as Holly gently stroked Tim's slightly sweaty-looking hair and turned to smile at up Joe, who had just brought her a glass of orange juice. As she peeped through the dancers at the trio in the corner, Beth clearly saw Joe reach down and gently pat Holly's stomach. Beth blinked and looked again. Aha! She laughed quietly to herself. So that's what Holly had been planning to talk to her about. Well, well! She may not ever be a mother herself, she'd realised that when she fell in love with Jacob, but a step-grandmother? How on earth would she cope with that?

Beth made her excuses to Jenny, then swayed through the crowds over to where Holly was sitting with Tim alone again while Joe went foraging for food. She smiled at the girl and said quietly, 'Have you spoken to your dad about the baby?'

Holly's mouth fell open. 'How did you know? Did Joe tell you?'

'No, I worked it out for myself – although it took me a while. Is that why you've been throwing up? So it wasn't my cooking after all!'

Holly pulled a face. 'I'm sorry about that. I was being a complete cow.'

'Yep, you were.' Beth pulled up a chair. 'But I don't suppose

I was being a model stepmother either. Anyway, I reckon that impending motherhood will knock the corners off you. Or at least it may once you stop puking. Do you feel all right at the moment?'

Holly rolled her eyes dramatically. 'Starving! I can only eat after midday. It's the only time it stays down so I have to make up for lost time. Oh there's Joe. Thank goodness.'

'Hi, Beth! Great party.' Joe presented Holly with a plate. 'I couldn't get you any more of those little sausages. That friend of yours, Beth, she's wolfing them down like there's no tomorrow. I thought she was a veggie.'

Beth gasped in outrage. 'She's supposed to be. I've been stuffing mushrooms with basil and walnuts all afternoon for her. I shall have something to say about this, I can tell you! Oh, before I go, congratulations, Joe. I think you'll make wonderful parents.'

'You told her? Great! You see – I told you she'd be cool about it.'

'So?' Beth prompted. 'Does Jacob know?'

Holly shook her head sheepishly. 'No. He'll go ape about it, I just know he will. He'll say I've been irresponsible. But I need to let him know soon. I can't do my trousers up any more.'

'I think you are underestimating him, Holly. Yes, he's a different generation, but he believes in you and he wants you to be happy. You both seem to have a strong relationship and that's what makes good parents.'

Holly looked impatient. 'What do you kn—'

Beth held up her hand. 'I know he's your father, but I'm his wife, and he's more understanding than you think. Look how he rallied round for me today. And that was only a stupid party. You wait till he holds his first grandchild.' And she leant over and gave Holly a kiss on the cheek before wandering away, leaving them to talk softly over the sleeping child.

Sally started guiltily as Beth approached and quickly picked up a carrot stick. 'Go on, you old faker,' Beth laughed. 'And to think you missed out on my lovely venison casserole only to succumb to a sausage – and a chipolata at that!'

Sally grinned wickedly. 'It was the sight of them. They reminded me of Dave! Great party, by the way.'

They were both still giggling when Jacob came to claim his wife for a dance and swept her into his arms, then pulled back slightly so he could look into her eyes. 'Merry Christmas, my love. Our first of many. And I hope they're all as happy as this one is turning out to be.'

Beth kissed him on the lips. 'Now it is,' she laughed. 'But I did have a major wobbly back there, didn't I?'

'Mmm,' he agreed. 'I must admit I was a bit gobsmacked for a while. Darling, I had no idea you were so stressed and so worried you wouldn't measure up. I do wish you'd told me.'

'But that was the point. I didn't want you to know. I wanted to look effortless – like …'

'Go on, say it. You mean like Becca, don't you?'

Beth nodded shamefacedly and Jacob drew her close. 'Oh Beth, how wrong you are. I can assure you that the yearly lead-up to the Mistletoe Meet was never very easy on me or on her. Christmas tended to go by the board and every year I had to put up with weeks – no, months – of frenzy. And as for the party itself. Well, just look around you. Look – there's the vicar dancing with Mrs Godfrey. That's a sight I never thought I'd see. In years gone by, everyone was too busy trying to use the right cutlery and not getting anything on their hired suits to really enjoy themselves. I never want to go through that again – and I never want you to think you have to measure up to anyone. My darling Beth, I asked you to marry me because I wanted you, exactly the way you are. Not the way you think you ought to be.'

Jacob had steered them over to the entrance to the marquee and they stood together in silence for a moment, gazing out over the snow falling again now over the village. All was quiet and still. The only movement came from behind them, in the whirl of lights, music and laughter. Except. 'What's that?'

They both squinted out into the dark. 'It looks like … it can't be. I can't be that pissed.'

Struggling towards them through the drifts was a tall, white-haired figure dressed in what looked like a red jacket with a hood trimmed with white and with a large sack on his back. Jacob and Beth exchanged startled glances then stepped out into the darkness in time to see the figure resolve into a good-looking man about Beth's age, with longish dark hair, a lean, tired face and a faintly desperate air.

'Excuse me.' He brushed the snowflakes from his red fleece and hair as he spoke. 'I know this is a bit of a long shot. I'm looking for a friend of mine.'

Chapter 24

A moment later

If you are going to be in a hot room and you have
a tendency to become shiny, make it look deliberate
– wear lip gloss and sheen on your eye lids.

Carol came off the dance floor, panting from the exertion of jitterbugging with Joe, and peered across the marquee to see if she could spot her son.

At first she couldn't make him out through the mêlée. People were everywhere, chatting and throwing their heads back with laughter; dragging each other on to the dance floor, or holding each other close. Children were winding in between the adults' legs, making mischief, largely ignored by their parents who were far too busy having fun. Then she saw him: there he was, over by the buffet table with Holly beside him. He looked as if he's just woken up but his face was wreathed with smiles. He seemed to be looking over towards the door. Perhaps he'd seen someone. She followed his gaze and then almost choked on the water Joe had just handed to her. It couldn't be, could it?

There, in a deep red fleece and gazing round the tent, stood Nick.

Well, it looked like Nick. She must have got it wrong. Just a trick of the light, but then he turned his head and there it was: that languid stance, that tilt of the head, that messy brown hair. It was unmistakable and her heart missed a beat.

If Tim could have run, he would have. From her position

over by the bar, she watched as he scrambled to his feet, struggled with the crutches, almost pushing aside Holly's offer of help, but by the time he was ready to go, Nick had spotted him and strode over to him, gently dropping the bag he was carrying and lifted him off the floor in a huge bear hug.

'Who's that?' Joe stood beside her. 'Tim seems pleased to see him.'

'Yes ... yes he does, doesn't he?' She was aware that Joe had turned to look at her.

'Carol? If I didn't know you'd just been bopping, I'd swear you were blushing!'

Carol's hand shot up to her face. 'Never!' she cried, giggling stupidly. 'I'm just not used to dancing like that.'

'Yeah right, whatever!' he laughed. 'Dja know, I think I'll see if Mrs Havers would like a turn on the dance floor. She looks like she's hot to trot.' And he moved discreetly away.

Carol watched anxiously as Tim chatted intently to Nick then, pulling at the tall man's sleeve and peering over the heads of the adults, began to steer him across the marquee in her direction. Her stomach tightened. What would she say to him? What could she say? Everything his sudden appearance could mean rushed through her head. Perhaps he had old friends in Milton St David. Perhaps he had a girlfriend at the party but he'd just got there late. Perhaps he'd come to see how Tim's leg was doing.

Perhaps, just perhaps, he'd come to see her.

Then there they were in front of her: Tim, his face lit up with excitement. Nick, bag slung over his shoulder, just looking down at her. No one said anything.

'Hey, Tim.' Holly had come up to join them, breaking into this oasis of silence in the midst of the noise of the party. 'Think you can rock and roll with just one leg?' She took him by the elbow. 'I bet you can,' and she steered Tim away from them.

Carol couldn't be sure, but she could have sworn that Holly winked at her as she moved away.

Unsure now what to say or think, Carol looked down into her drink.

'I like the earrings. Very festive.'

Carol put her hand up to her ear. 'Oh these! Yes, well, I didn't know there would be a party and I didn't have anything to wear and Beth left some decorations for us, and they seemed far too posh just to leave on the tree.' She was aware she was gabbling. 'It's a long story. You must meet Beth, you'll like her,' she ended lamely.

'I think I did. The tall woman at the door?' There was an awkward silence again.

'Why are y—'

'I got the—'

They both laughed. 'You first.'

Nick swung the bag from his back. 'I ... well, I managed to find a 3D space projector.' He glanced at her, his face full of uncertainty. 'You haven't got one already I hope. Only you said you couldn't find one.'

'No, no,' Carol rushed to reassure him. 'How clever of you! How wonderful of you to bring it!' It sounded so feeble. Had he really battled through all this snow to bring Tim's present?

'It was the last one in the shop and, well, I know a boy who wants one more than anything. So it seemed selfish not to deliver it. When I'd found it. ' He stopped, his eyes twinkling.

'Well quite. It would be cruel to disappoint him.'

His eyes searched Carol's face. 'I haven't made a terrible misjudgement, have I, Carol?'

She took in his lovely face and his warm, dark eyes and thought how much she loved the way he looked at her. She shook her head.

'Only, something just seemed to be missing from Christmas really.'

'Oh I know just what you mean.' And she felt her face break into a ridiculous smile. He put his hand up and cupped her cheek.

'I have to say, I did get a bit of encouragement from your son.'

'How do you mean?'

'I called. Last night. I just wanted to say Happy Christmas. Well,' he looked at the floor, 'I just wanted to hear your voice actually, and Tim sort of indicated that you might like some company.'

Carol gasped in disbelief, and looked over at Tim, jiggling on one leg with Holly on the dance floor. 'The cheeky little monkey. I'll have to have words with him!'

Nick looked anxious. 'Oh no, don't, please. I think it might spoil his Christmas, and I wouldn't want to do that. He's such a special little chap.'

'Yes.' Tim looked over at them and smiled a smile so wide she could see almost all his teeth. 'Yes, he is, isn't he?'

*

This dance had gone on long enough, and as much as he liked Holly, Tim thought that his mum and Nick must have talked enough by now and it would be all right to interrupt.

As Holly swung round to laugh at something someone said behind her, he made his escape, hobbling as fast as he could manage over to the bar where they were standing. When he got closer he realised they weren't saying that much to each other, which was a worrying sign. He had been sure they'd have been chatting madly, just like the other people were around the marquee. In fact, it was all very noisy and it was making him tired, but he wasn't going to admit that or he'd be sent to bed, and that would be a disaster. Instead his mum was standing looking up at Nick and he was looking down at her and they were silent. This wouldn't do at all.

'Hey Nick,' he panted up to them. 'Come and meet the band. Baz is my favourite – he's so cool – but the others are nice too.' He was aware he was tapping Nick's foot with his crutch but he couldn't think how else to get him to come over with him. Luckily the band were taking a break, and he'd miss the chance to introduce them if he didn't do it now. 'Come on, come on.'

Nick laughed. 'OK, mate. Slow down. You're supposed to be an invalid. You coming too, to look after me?' He addressed this to Carol, though he didn't seem to need looking after.

'Baz. Baz,' Tim called to the big man, who was leaning his guitar up against the amplifier and was heading towards the bar. 'Baz, meet my friend Nick. He plays the guitar too.' Baz turned to them, his eyes crinkled and his large face split into a big grin showing bright white teeth.

'Pleased to meet you, Nick.' He shook the taller man's hand. 'Perhaps you'd like to take over for a while then! This gig is the hardest I've ever done – the crowd won't let us stop.' And he wiped his brow.

What a great idea! 'Yes, yes you could, Nick.' Tim turned, desperate to make Nick agree. He turned back to Baz. 'He's really good.'

Nick ruffled his hair. 'Hey, mister. For one, you've never heard me play and secondly, I haven't brought my guitar. I've left it in the car.'

It seemed blatantly obvious to Tim. 'Borrow Baz's.'

'Sure thing.' Baz picked up the instrument and handed it to Nick, who slowly put down his bag again and took it reluctantly.

'Tim, I can't I—'

'Please?' Tim whined his whiniest whine.

Nick put the strap over his head. 'OK, just this once. Just one number while those boys take a break. But that's your lot, or you'll have to call my agent.' He laughed and Tim had no idea what he meant but who cared? Nick was going to play.

*

Lit by one of the lights Noel had rigged up earlier, Nick stood alone now on the impromptu stage gently plucking at the strings, familiarising himself with the new instrument. Caspar and Mel had bolted for the bar even before Baz.

Realising the band were taking their break, and not having noticed this new person on the stage, people began to leave the dance floor and chat again, fanning their faces after the frantic pace of the last couple of numbers, and keen to get themselves refreshment. The murmur of voices and laughter rose; people jostled good-naturedly with each other and promised themselves another dance once they had their breath back. Standing with her arm around Tim as his rested his head against her, Carol wondered what Nick was going to do now. She couldn't see his features properly as his hair had fallen over his face, but there was something incredibly erotic about the angle of his head as he bent over the guitar.

'What's he doing, Mum?' Tim craned his head to look up at her. 'Why isn't he playing?'

'I don't know. Perhaps he's trying to think of something to do. He might even be waiting for the others. Come on, let's find you a drink. You must be hot after your dancing.' And she turned away reluctantly to fight through the crowds queuing for a drink.

But suddenly, from behind her, in a vast wave of sound, the marquee was filled with the opening bars of 'Silent Night'. Everyone stopped in their tracks and turned to the stage, mesmerised by the incongruous mixture of electric guitar and melody that was almost haunting in its intensity. Voices fell silent; movement stopped and Carol could feel the hairs stand up on the back of her neck.

Nick, his body almost leaning backwards and his hips pushed

forwards as he plucked at the strings, eeked out every moment, his left hand bending the notes. Watching him concentrating so intensely on what he was playing, though the tune itself was so simple, Carol couldn't believe he was here. Here in the marquee playing to all these people; people she'd spent the day with. And he'd come to see her. How utterly, utterly amazing.

'He's good.' Carol could feel Baz's bulk beside her without even turning around. He had a pint in his hand, but like everyone else, he seemed suspended, listening to the music.

'Yes, he's pretty great, isn't he?' she whispered loudly back.

'Makes me look like a right amateur. I feel like a right pillock suggesting he fill in for us! Do you know him? Well. Obviously you do. Is he a professional?'

'Well, I know him a bit but not really. He's a session musician. You know, backs solo artists when's he's asked to.' She felt immensely proud. 'His name's Nick. Nick Blythe.'

'You mean *the* Nick Blythe?'

'Well I don't know if he's *the* Nick anything.'

'It is, isn't it? He's immense. Backed loads of the greats. Some wouldn't tour without him.,' Baz's face was lit up with excitement. 'Wait till I tell the others.' Baz shook his head in wonder and peered round eagerly to see if he could see the boys through the crowd, now standing silent, drinks halfway to their mouths, as the melody rang out.

'I know he's backed some people, you know like Anya and—'

'Oh yeah, he's done loads of stuff with her,' Baz gushed. 'He was there right at the beginning I think. They were very close. I read in an interview with her once that she trusted him with her life, that he was like a best mate. Nothing emotional, like, just like brother and sister. He must be quite involved with that adoption thing I should think. Helping her out, like.' And it was then that something went 'ping' quite loudly in Carol's head.

It all began to fall into place. Her talking to Nick about the state of the magazine. The phone call to her mobile that night when Tim was in the bath. Anya knowing about stuff she had written and trusting her. Anya saying that thing about Christmas being special for Carol. Suddenly she felt angry. Angry with herself for believing Anya had chosen her on her merits to do the interview and angry – no, disappointed – that Nick had manipulated the situation. She didn't need help. She could have saved that magazine on her own.

'Come on, Tim.' She tugged at the boy's arm and the tone in her voice made Tim and Baz turn to look suddenly at her. 'It's time you were in bed. It's late.'

'But Mum, Nick's come all this way and he's still play—'

'I know.' No she didn't want to spoil it for him, but she felt foolish. She'd been made to look an idiot because she'd been blind. She felt a huge lump in her throat that made it ache.

'Can't we just wait until the end? Till he's finished?' Tim's big eyes, swimming with tears, were looking up at hers beseechingly.

'OK. I'll meet you by the door.' And she stalked off, even madder at herself for taking out her anger on Tim.

From her position, half hidden behind one of Jenny's decorated trees by the door, she could see the small, makeshift stage. As Nick finished playing, the marquee erupted with people whistling and cheering. He pushed the hair off his face and smiled broadly, as if taking as much pleasure in this adulation as he might at a big gig – though, Carol thought, forgetting her ire for a moment, he probably didn't get to play solos very often.

'Thanks, thank you very much,' Nick said into the mike. 'It's great to be here and what a lovely party.' He squinted into the crowd to try and spot the others. 'You boys sounded great and you deserved a good break. How about a round of applause for

... er, what's the band called by the way?' There was a vague mumbling from the front row. 'Sorry?' Nick asked again.

'Um ...' Caspar's voice now, and he muttered something to Nick.

'Great!' Nick's face broke into a huge smile. 'Ladies and gentlemen, a big hand please for the excellent and festively entitled,' he paused for effect, 'Urban Vomit!'

The crowd roared with laughter and the applause was deafening. 'Now,' Nick continued, 'if you boys have had your well-deserved refreshment, perhaps you'd like to join me?' Baz, Caspar and Mel were back up there like a shot and there was a moment's confusion on stage about who should have Baz's guitar, him or Nick. Nick's back was turned, and then he bent down slightly, but Carol, though she stood on tiptoe, couldn't see what he was doing because of the crowd. Next, there was Baz's voice, saying how 'awesome' it had been to have Nick with them, and he gave everyone a potted résumé of Nick's career to lots of ooohs and aahs from the crowd. Even Mrs Godfrey seemed impressed, though Carol hadn't had her down as a big rock fan. Carol couldn't stop herself listening – it was a much more impressive CV than she'd thought – but she gave up trying to see what was going on, over everyone's heads, and pulled her cardigan further around her shoulders against the chill wind coming in through the tent door.

As the applause died away, the vicar bustled up in front of the band, a party hat askew on his head. 'I've just noticed the time. It's eleven thirty and I'm supposed to be running the midnight service in the church. I've had such a wonderful evening that I've completely lost track of time, but I know everyone's here anyway. I'll be going down to the church now and if any of you could come and help me get set up, we'll probably be able to start in about half an hour. Bit late I know, but I couldn't drag myself away from the fun. I'll just go and fetch my surplice.' And he trotted off, followed by a few of his more stalwart helpers, brushing past Carol through the door and out into the night.

'Carol.' Nick's voice was soft beside her, but still Carol started. She'd been watching the progress of the cleric and not noticed what was happening on stage. She glanced quickly as if to discover how he had got to be beside her and saw that just the three boys were playing, softly now, a popular Christmas love song.

'What's wrong?' His dark eyes searched her face. 'Tim said you suddenly seemed very upset. Has something happened?' He took her shoulders, turning her to face him.

*

Her eyes look wide and confused, and for the life of him Nick couldn't work out why she'd scuttled off and hidden here. It had been some old dear serving coffee who'd pointed her out to him. Perhaps she'd hated him playing, or he'd talked on the mike too long. He felt stupid. It would have been a much better idea not to interfere and play, but at the time he'd thought it would be fun. He'd blown it.

'Nick, tell me,' she looked down, 'did you manufacture that interview with Anya?' Oh God, it had all backfired on him and now she was mad. He could feel her shoulder tensing under his hands and the softness of her cardigan.

'No, Carol. No I didn't.'

'Don't lie to me, Nick. I don't need your pity. I don't need you to help me to save my magazine. I could have done it on my own, you know.' Her eyes, looking right at him now, were strong and determined, and he knew that if he took his hands from her, he'd lose her.

'I know you can, Carol, because you are a very clever woman, but Anya is a good friend of mine. A really good friend – we've know each other since before her fame and all that shit. I knew about the baby because she told me all about it ages ago, but

296

no one else did, and over the last few years I've been aware that she needed to get some sort of closure on it. The guilt was terrible for her.' Carol's head was slightly to one side and he hoped to God the look on her face represented the beginning of some sort of acceptance of the truth. She had to understand. He couldn't take his eyes off her soft mouth.

'Anyway, we talked, oh I don't know, in the summer some-time, and I suggested she say something about it in an interview or a book. You know the sort of thing. But Carol, she loathes the press and you can understand why. They shred celebrities and she's not immune. She said she'd think about it. Then in November – when she got to Paris – she called and she asked if I knew anyone who might handle it well. I immediately thought of you. Not cos of the state of *WM*,' he shook her gently to make her see, 'though, OK, I knew it wouldn't do you any harm. But you have to see, the impetus came from her – and she's not stupid, Carol. She'd have checked you out. Read your stuff. She wouldn't trust information like that to just anyone.' He stopped. Had she believed him?

'So,' she shuffled her foot against the hessian floor, 'is that why you came here? You weren't ... you weren't just using your connections just so you'd ... so you'd get the girl?' Her expression was questioning and he adored her face as she looked at him. Get the girl. He hoped to goodness he'd got the girl and slowly, hardly daring to hope she wouldn't pull away, he put his forehead against hers and spoke very quietly so as not to break the moment.

'I came here because I couldn't stop myself. I wanted to see you so much, Carol, and a certain little boy told me you were going to be in Milkman St David.' He could feel her shoulders move as she chuckled. 'So I looked at the map and made an educated guess.' He moved his mouth slowly to her cheek and her ear and felt her respond, almost imperceptibly at first, under his touch. 'I didn't mean to interfere. I just hope that in some way it has helped everyone though. Wouldn't that be great? Is it OK, Carol, because I really really wish it would be?' He felt her murmur and he moved his mouth slowly onto hers and took her in his arms.

Chapter 25

Ten minutes later

Enjoy it all in the spirit in which it's meant, and may your baubles sparkle and all your Christmases be white.

Beth handed Carol the glass of champagne. 'Here you are. I had to wrest one off the vicar before he left or he'll never manage midnight mass. He's pretty wobbly with the chalice at the best of times.'

'Yummy, thank you.' Carol pulled Nick's fleece closer around her. It smelt of him and she inhaled deeply. 'It's good to get a bit of fresh air, isn't it? The heat that's been generated in there tonight could run the National Grid.'

'It's been fun though, hasn't it?'

'A blast. Really, Beth, it has. Everyone has had fun. I think you've really cemented something here tonight. They are already talking about next year.'

Beth groaned. 'Oooh no, never again. I'm handing on the baton. I've been soundly out of my depth with this party planning thing. I'll stick to Botticelli from now on. But tell me, where's that dishy man that battled to you through the snow?' Her eyes twinkled. 'How romantic!'

'I think,' Carol peered behind her into the tent, 'he's doing one last number with the boys and his new, slightly diminutive and invalided, front man, before everyone packs up.' She took a sip of her drink. 'Bit gorgeous, isn't he?' And she giggled.

'Mmm, I'd hold on to that one if I were you. You don't get one of those in your stocking every year. Lucky girl.'

There was silence between them for a moment as they looked at the clearing sky and watched the vicar making his way hurriedly down the road towards the dark church to prepare for the service, his surplice over his arm and his black robes flapping behind him, unaware that his paper hat was still on his head.

'Looks like it'll be a twelve-fifteen mass tonight then,' Carol chuckled. 'And everyone will be slow off the mark tomorrow getting the turkey in.'

Beth clapped her hand to her mouth and gasped. 'Oh goodness, I'd forgotten all about Christmas!' Her eyes were wide with horror. 'I think we've just eaten our lunch! I've been cleaned out. Not so much as a mince pie left and a house full to feed. I'm a disaster!'

Carol put a reassuring hand on her arm. 'Oh no, Beth I don't think anyone could accuse you of that. And anyway I have the Rolls-Royce of turkeys. Every organically reared, pampered and nurtured pound of it, plus all the trimmings. Why don't we share it?'

'But can you spare it?'

'Well, there's only two, well three of us, for goodness' sake, and Tim hates turkey.'

Beth smiled broadly. 'Oh three now, is it? Are we to assume Mr Gorgeous in there will be joining you?'

'Well, I can't send him off in this weather, can I? That would be just rude. Not when he's battled the elements to get here.' Carol looked as though brandy butter wouldn't melt in her mouth.

'Oh absolutely not.'

From across the field, lit now to a deep navy blue by the moon that had finally escaped from behind a snow cloud, came the first peals of the church bells. From inside the marquee behind them came the shout of 'Happy Christmas'. Carol turned and clinked her champagne glass with Beth's. 'Here's to your best Christmas ever!'

'You know, I think it just might be.'

Epilogue

2 January
Milton St David

Dear Mrs Layham,

Thank you very much indeed for my gift. I've never had such a lovely nightie and my Reg says it reminds him of our honeymoon. I think the rubber gloves are too nice to use though, but thanks for the sentiment.

Yours,
Ivy Havers

2 January
Bolton

Dear Beth,

In haste between performances – fab Christmas and have realised the error of my ways. Just can't get enough bacon sandwiches. Dave can lump it. By the way, have you taken leave of your senses? What would I want with a pan scourer and a tin of beeswax?

Big kiss
Sal

2 January
London W1

Dear Beth,

Thank you so much for the beautiful Shirin Guild cardigan. The way it is cut will see me right though – only twenty weeks to go to splash-down! I don't need to tell you again what a wonderful Christmas you gave us all. Turkey and beans on toast is a tradition we must now stick to. And thank God there were no sprouts – I hate them and Mum always used to make me eat them. Joe and the boys think you are an angel. I think you may be too.

Call me next time you are in London and we'll meet for lunch.

Lots of love
Hol

3 January
At my desk

Dear Beth,

What can I say? Christmas was probably the most special Tim and I have ever spent. My son is entranced and now believes that this is the way all Christmases should be spent – sitting on your sitting-room floor, surrounded by dogs and unexpected guests, eating posh cheese straws and Jelly Babies for pudding, followed by the biggest snowball fight in history. What the orthopaedic consultant will say about the state of his cast when we go back to the hospital next week I shudder to think!

Baz and Caspar have been over to see us and check his progress, and Mel has started an email friendship with him, which is sweet. My mother has been regaled by her grandson about all the excitement of the festivities in minute detail (including finding Nick in my bed on Christmas morning – ooops!), which has fortunately distracted her from regaling *us* with the excitement of the torchlight procession through Lourdes ... however her gifts have more than compensated and I plan to use my papal pillow case any time soon.

And as for my unexpected Christmas present ... well, every day has been like Christmas since then, and it began with the most beautiful pair of earrings. I hardly dare enjoy him as much as I want to, but he is very persuasive and I am loving every minute of it. In fact, I am beginning to realise that the world of magazines and deadlines won't crumble just because I take a night off. By the way, waiting for me on my email when I got back was a rather juicy job offer from my old magazine but, do you know? I'm going to stay right where I am. In any case, your stepdaughter needs a guiding hand. That's if she comes back to work after the baby is born ... yes she came and told me this morning. At the moment she says it won't make any difference. I disagree. I think she will grow up overnight, don't you, step-Granny?

Must dash – there's a rather dishy lead guitarist waiting to take me out for dinner. Strangely Tim doesn't seem too fussed about me going out now, and seems not to mind not being the only man in my life. Perhaps I had that all wrong.

Let me drag you away from your dusty books sometime soon and show you how us 'bloody journos with our cover-line bollocks', as you so beautifully put it, spend our lunch breaks.

Much love and thank you for being our Christmas angel.
Carol x

1 new message
Carol, she's beautiful & all I hoped 4. Will gladly do follow-up feature as u suggest. Thnx so much 4 makg it happn. Anya x P.S. Isn't Nick gorge?!

Dear Farther Christmass

Thank you very mutch indeed for my 3D space projecter. I think you are so clever to find one cos my mum said there weren't any left in the hole world. Thank you too for granting my Christmas wish. Mum seems to smile all the time now and Nick's got us all tickets to go to the panto. Granny says the Lord works in Mysteron ways.

See you next year.
Love Tim

Acknowledgements

We've pooled our experiences of all the Christmases we've ever lived through from the magical ones of our childhood, through the laid-back self-indulgences of our single years to the highly stressed ones as parents. We hope somewhere along the line you've found something you can relate to. We'd like to thank the following for all their helpful advice, which has ranged from magazine editing, to the legal issues surrounding abandoned children, to the realities of life touring with a rock band. In no particular order they are Simon Harrison of B and H Management; Cal Dagul; Dr Rosalind Blakesley; Jenny Bates; Clare Jervis; Victoria Woodhall; Sarah Kilby; Shiona Buckland; Giles 'Ted' Palmer; Chris Adams, the late Jenny Walton and Kate Adie (yeah, that one!). Thanks too, as always, to all at Orion for their enthusiasm and wisdom.

Christmas 2005

What to do when it all goes pear-shaped

THE CHEAT'S CHRISTMAS
(AND HOW TO SALVAGE DISASTERS)

Customise shop-bought mince pies by prising off the lids and replacing them with star shapes cut out of royal icing or rolled-out marzipan. The wonkier the better for authenticity.

You can do the same with a hastily bought cake. Personalise a plain, un-iced shop-bought one by making holes in the top with a cocktail stick then drizzling Grand Marnier, brandy or rum over the top and allowing it to sink in. You can then decorate with rolled-out marzipan, Royal icing and as many reindeer and snowmen as you can fit on it.

Pass off bought jam and marmalade as your own by soaking off the label and sticking on a hand-drawn version. Don't forget to take the lid off and place a circle of greaseproof paper underneath before replacing.

If your Christmas tree looks moth eaten (or you picked the last one in the shop), fill in the gaps with branches of fake foliage. If you sprinkle on some pine oil and decorate lavishly, no one will notice.

. . . but if you missed the boat completely, find a dead branch and hang decorations and lights from it. Very chic and minimalist.

Avoid that needle-in-your-sock misery. Wrap a spent tree in a sheet before dragging it out of the door – to be shredded, of course.

Warm up dishes and plates by running them through the dishwasher. At the end of the cycle they stay hot for ages.

Improve on dull (or budget) crackers by carefully opening up the end and adding more exciting pressies. Diamond rings fit nicely.

Stains on your tablecloth? Arrange fresh foliage artistically over the offending patch, or sprinkle with sparkly confetti for camouflage.

If your oven packs up (doesn't it always?), you can cook turkey on a barbecue. Cut it into joints, wrap it well in foil and keep the lid down whilst it is cooking. Brown it off at the end over the coals. Now, where on earth do you buy barbecue coals in December?

To salvage a burnt turkey, discard the charred parts, chop up the dry but unburnt pieces and place in the base of a roasting pan. Pour over chicken stock enriched with butter to moisten, cover with foil and leave to stand for about 10 minutes in a warm place before serving.

Uncle Frank turned up unexpectedly? Pad out a thin turkey by slipping chicken breasts under the skin (if you stick your hand in the neck end you can carefully part the skin from the breast to make space). Make sure the meat beneath is cooked thoroughly though or there will be no Uncle Frank next year. Actually . . .

Avoid putting too much stuffing inside your turkey or it could explode, because stuffing expands when cooked.

No room in the fridge? If the weather's cold, leave food in your car (remember to lock it), or leave a cool box outside.

Avoid serving salty snacks like peanuts at a drinks party. They give your guests a raging thirst and they'll clean you out of booze!

In a power cut, open the fridge and freezer as little as possible – they stay cold for a surprisingly long time.

Trousers or skirt too tight? Tie a sturdy elastic band through the button hole and loop the free end over the button.

No sledge? You can use thick bin liners.
To minimise bruising, stuff with a doormat or a pillow.

No sticky tape or wrapping paper? Foil (unused) is the easiest alternative for present wrapping. Failing that, use newspaper with ribbon, string or wool – and pretend it's a design statement.

Suspect you've been given chocolates? Don't leave them under the tree if you have a dog. It'll gnaw its way in and scoff the lot, leaving you with a big vet bill.

*

Prove the existence of Father Christmas by sprinkling talc over the hearth. Those big boots will leave footprints.

*

Avoid the queues. Book a flight abroad.